Russell James

is a unique voice in modern crime writing. A writer's writer, he was called 'something of a cult' by *The Times* and Ian Rankin dubbed him 'the Godfather of British *noir*'.

There are no detectives in his books, and when the police do appear it is on the sidelines. James concentrates on the criminals, their victims and those caught up in events. When he started writing novels, he deliberately wrote counter to the spirit of the times – which was sex 'n' shopping and international conspiracy – and instead wrote dark, multi-layered thrillers, rich in character and locale: the kind of books more common from American authors, though Russell James' novels remain emphatically British.

Russell James was Chairman of the Crime Writers' Association 2001-2002. His previous novels include *Underground, Daylight, Payback, Slaughter Music, Count Me Out, The Annex, Oh No, Not My Baby* and *Painting in the Dark*.

Pick Any Title

by

Russell James

First Published in Great Britain in 2002 by
The Do-Not Press Limited
16 The Woodlands
London SE13 6TY
www.thedonotpress.co.uk
email: pat@thedonotpress.co.uk

B-format paperback: ISBN 1 899344 83 7
Casebound edition: ISBN 1 899 344 84 5

British Library Cataloguing in Publication Data. A catalogue
record for this book is available from the British Library.

1 3 5 7 9 10 8 6 4 2

Printed and bound in Great Britain by
The Guernsey Press Co Ltd.

For Jill – here's the one you wanted.

1

LET'S SORT OUT where everyone was when this farrago started. In London, Mickey Starr was in bed – alone – while Strachey, benefiting from an eight-hour time difference, was sunning herself in San Francisco. I hate to tell you this, especially on page one, but if she *had* been in bed Strachey would not have been alone, since she had for some three months been hitched up with what Mickey later described as 'that piece of lowlife', Lord Clive Lane. Clive had acquired the title at auction a year before for three thousand pounds sterling. You may scoff, but to Clive that was a considerable investment and one he intended to grow. For Clive Lane to lay out several thousand of his own money was an unheard-of event, one that would make most of his friends (he had several) shake their heads in disbelief. It made Clive shake his own head. Strachey wandered into the bathroom once when Clive was shaving and found him staring at his reflection as if he'd stolen it.

'Swallowed your shaving soap?' she asked.

He coughed as if trying to spit the soap out. That, coupled with the lopsided frozen grin he gave from the mirror, was enough to convince her something was wrong. And Strachey was persistent: once she set her mind to something she stayed with it like a cat on a mouse. 'Something you should tell me about?'

'Where did I leave my brown gloves?'

Clive's problem was that he could never admit to anything straight out – his first instinct was to lie. He had so many guilty secrets it was impossible for him to produce an honest answer first try. Clive felt honesty was overrated, a hangover from the Victorian era, inextricably entwined with teetotalism, hypocrisy and manly virtues. 'You only get one chance at life,' he'd say. 'Give it your best shot.'

To Strachey, this had the ring of a line he'd used before. Clive had a gold-tooled leather diary in which every page was graced with a witty quote and once, when they had been stuck in a dull but expensive Fresno hotel and Clive (for no reason he could convincingly explain) had been away the whole afternoon,

Strachey had leafed through that diary looking for coded phone numbers or concealed female names. She had also read the epigrams for each day. None suggested you should give life your best shot. There were cringe-making cracker mottoes such as 'Miracles happen to those who believe in them' and 'There are no shortcuts to any place worth going', but the nearest she could get to Clive's philosophy was 'Accept nothing but the best – you'll be surprised how often you get it'. She found, as can happen on a dull afternoon – especially in Fresno – that the 365 epigrams had a hypnotic effect. Some actually sounded profound. She found herself repeating one particularly trite motto and had to stop herself from learning it by heart. It read, 'The future comes unannounced'.

Fresno? That was where they met with another man germane to this story, a vanilla-suited farmer-turned-businessman called Lincoln Deane who had recently turned two thousand acres of semi-desert on the South Central Plain into the Lincoln's Inn Vineyard, a struggling, would-be Gallo extravagance that survived only because of an exclusive supply contract he had wormed out of the 'Happy Hacienda' chop-house chain. As he had learned during a two-year stint as a Napa Valley Wine Trail Tour Facilitator, Lincoln himself was no viticulturist – he was barely a farmer – but he was a businessman. He knew therefore that having all his bottles in the 'Happy Hacienda' wine rack made him vulnerable, and he was desperate to expand. But California was awash with decent wine and Lincoln's insipid pink Zinfandel tasted like a similarly colored mouthwash. A TV wine critic once said it had 'a flavor not unreminiscent of wholesome shampoo – bringing back childish memories one would prefer to forget'. Lincoln remembered how the critic fingered the lapel to his jacket and grinned at the camera. 'Short in the mouth but excessive in the nose.'

Summed the guy up.

Anyway, Lincoln had responded to one of Clive's advertisements because he sensed an opportunity to expand his wilting empire into the old colonialist itself – the British Isles. Lord Clive could help.

Just as Clive helped Frankie di Stefano. That afternoon, some three thousand miles from California, Lord Clive had caught a cab from JFK out to a so-called hotel on Long Island – a motel really – littered around a semi-Olympic-size swimming pool, where the cagey di Stefano had agreed to meet. Frankie at this time – to be truthful, at most times in his adult life – displayed an almighty reluctance to allow anyone admittance to his property. Meeting on his *territory* was OK, since his territory stretched in a ten-mile arc from outer Queens towards Garden City and included any number of public meeting places – quite a number of which were not controlled by his gang. These neutral venues were a safe place to meet. If, as had become increasingly the case nowadays, the visitor was from the tax office or the FBI, Frankie preferred that they poke around the furniture or computer records of an entirely innocent establishment in the mistaken belief that it belonged to Frankie's gang. He would often encourage this misapprehension by whispering to the waiters and wandering in and out of unlabeled doors.

The sun-baked poolside of the Captain Nemo provided an abundance of entrance and exit opportunities and was the kind of suspiciously innocent-looking venue you'd expect in a David Lynch movie. Several businessmen lolled around in tee-shirts and trunks. They sipped their drinks and scowled at local teenagers leaping in and out the pool, water gleaming on lithe bodies, flesh-tones golden like beer. It was easy to see why salesmen would scowl. Three other men – also bulky – sat at strategically placed tables and made no attempt to look like salesmen. One of them removed his jacket and draped it over a metal chair. The other two kept theirs on.

When he arrived, Clive Lane was in laid-back English mode. He followed the waiter across the patio, smiling as he went, right arm extended for a handshake, the striped linen of his Henley jacket setting off his shirt and Jermyn Street tie. From his left hand dangled a beautiful fawn leather briefcase. Its rightful owner, fortunately, hadn't been so vulgar as to personalise his luggage with initials, so Clive had been able to place his own subtle but unmissable baronial crest exactly where he chose (beneath the handle, a quiet spot, but high enough to catch the eye).

He sang out an unmissable 'I say, delighted to meet you,' which, although it would have been over the top in many a venue, seemed unremarkable in a glitzy motel half a mile from Queens. It was difficult to be over the top on a coral-and-apricot chequered patio where the host's bodyguards were arranged conspicuously around the pool. And Clive *was* a real-life English lord.

'You'll have a drink with me,' Frankie said.

He waved a finger at a waiter. Since he hadn't yet removed his shades he could stare at Clive, his gaze concealed by mirror lenses, while he decided whether this aristocratic faggot was the genuine muffin or a plant from the Internal Revenue office. Clive lounged in the poolside chair, one leg draped across the other like a picture in an interior decorator's catalog, showing off his only pair of Saville Row trousers. He half closed his eyes against the sun and pretended to be unaware of the various bodyguards – each of whom was staring in his direction as if daring him to go for a gun.

He would open his briefcase *slowly*.

Clive's ads ran through a box number, and when he had read the reply from Frankie di Stefano there was nothing to indicate his profession. He hadn't known how to spell 'baronial' but that didn't make the man a gangster. Clive took a dim view of the ability of most people to spell correctly but as long as a punter could write his signature on a check he didn't care. Clive was not as unworldly as his languid pose suggested. He had been around as many blocks as had a fifty-year-old mailman, and the hairs on his sensitive antennules quivered as soon as di Stefano suggested meeting at a motel someplace near Queens. It hardly seemed an appropriate spot to discuss his ennoblement and inclusion in the higher echelons of British aristocracy. The Captain Nemo Motor Lodge was no Savoy. And it was Clive's custom when arriving at any meeting to first ignore the punter and take in the room – or in this case, the poolside. Among the bathers, di Stefano's three heavies stuck out like pallbearers at a feast. They looked like busy men whose dentists were running late. Clive could guess what service they provided their boss, and the swarthy di Stefano looked to have as much noble blood in him as a warthog.

Clive wasn't fazed.

'You're not staying at this hotel?'

Frankie shook his head.

'Can't say I've come across it before.'

Frankie gave a less than friendly grin. 'They hadn't heard of you at the Claremont, neither. An' that's the best hotel in town.'

'I'm staying with friends.'

Clive checked his smile against the reflection in Frankie's mirrored sunglasses as the man persisted: 'Sellin' the family silver?'

'Not *my* silver, Mr di Stefano. Cousin – somewhat remote.'

'Short of cash, right?'

Di Stefano clearly wanted to establish his financial superiority, and as an experienced con artist Clive knew the value of letting the punter think he knew best.

'Troubled times,' he admitted.

'So the old guy wants to sell his title?'

Clive tried a teaser. 'I advised him not to. Frightfully bad show. Terrible letdown for succeeding generations of his family.'

Frankie sneered. 'Who are gonna lose the thing, right? I mean, once the title's sold, it don't come back to 'em?'

'Quite. Stays in the family of whoever buys it. Do you have a family, Mr di Stefano? I have to tell you that the very idea of buying and selling titles appals me. A title means much more than family silver.'

'Which he's sold already?'

Clive closed his eyes and nodded: the reluctant seller.

Frankie decided the Brit was kosher – or at least, wasn't a set-up from the Feds. No one was ever exactly what he said. This Clive guy was the family's number one reluctant schmuck, sent over to do the dirty deal. Sully his hands. He wouldn't like doing it, but since when did anyone like eating dirt?

'This title, then – come down the family—'

'Eleven hundred years,' Clive agreed sadly.

'An' he can sell the thing – get rid of it – just like that?'

Clive leant forward. 'Exactly. I'm so glad that you agree with me. Appalling idea. The title should stay in the family, don't you agree?'

Frankie opened his mouth as the waiter reappeared with his tray. He watched the way the man laid out the drinks as if he suspected one might have been spiked. The waiter hovered momentarily but remembered who Frankie was and disappeared.

Frankie said, 'Let me get this straight. You don't wanna sell it, but your cousin does. He don't wanna sell it neither, but he's got no choice. An' you're over here to fix the deal?'

Clive sighed and reached for his drink.

'An' if he sells it to me, it's permanent? When I die it goes to my kids?'

'One of them. There can be only one Lord di Stefano. Your eldest son.'

'Then after him, it's *his* son, right?'

'Through perpetuity.'

Frankie frowned. 'OK, the whole caboodle comes to me? Can *I* sell it?'

Clive looked surprised. 'It would be a far better investment if you *didn't* sell it. It transforms one's life – gives you status, that kind of thing. How can I put this? It's not *anyone* who can become a Lord.'

'I'm not good enough?'

In any trading situation Clive preferred to have the other person beg to buy, rather than show that *he* was anxious to sell. 'You would be joining the British aristocracy, and it's beholden upon me to ensure that the new entrant is truly fit.'

'Wanna see me do some press-ups?'

'I meant—'

'Take you on any time, buddy. Watch your step.'

Clive risked a trump, though not the ace: he took his briefcase and stood up. 'Awfully nice meeting you, Mr di Stefano. I must pop along.'

Frankie was finessed. 'Where the hell you going? Sit down.'

Clive looked at his watch and shook his head. 'Becoming a British lord is an awesome responsibility. One must be the right kind of man. Blue blood, you know?'

He was aware of a bodyguard at his shoulder. Frankie snapped, 'Be some red blood on the table, you don't sit down.'

The bodyguard prodded. Clive asked, 'Is he with you?'

'Beat it, Lennox.' Frankie removed his shades. 'So what is it, Clive – you don't wanna do business with me, or you don't wanna do business with nobody?'

Clive pursed his lips and appeared to think. 'It's nothing personal – merely that I find the idea of selling one's inheritance distasteful. But it has to be done.' He looked at his watch again. 'I'm afraid my time in New York is limited, and here on Long Island we're a long way out.'

'Goin' someplace?'

'I have to be at the Algonquin—'

'You don't have to be nowhere, buddy. You just sit down another two minutes, finish your drink – which *I* bought you, by the way – and tell me what I got to do to buy this title.'

Clive savored the moment. He had Frankie where he wanted him. The man hadn't even replaced his shades.

Strachey didn't spend the whole day sunning herself. Like anyone attached to Clive, she had become part of his schemes. So far, all she had done was act as his personal secretary – and you don't get much more personal than sharing a one-room rental in what Clive claimed was Pacific Heights but which everyone else called Western Addition. The first time Clive left her alone in San Francisco, Strachey had taken herself a long walk down through Pacific Heights, continuing through steep streets of pastel Victorian houses to reach the sea. She had drunk coffee in Union Street, taken a brief look at the Cannery and Fisherman's Wharf, glanced inside three art galleries, and had then climbed slowly up through Nob and Russian Hill. Although she could think of nowhere like it in England, the relaxed beauty of the place and the sudden long views made her wistful for home. Often in America the unfamiliar sound of her English accent would be greeted with incredulity. People would ask, 'You from Australia?' But San Francisco was populated by Americans, Italians, Chinese, Japanese, Mexicans, and the city was used to foreigners, outsiders and offsiders of many kinds. It was tolerant, easy. Cops in shorts rode on bicycles – men with big shoulders and clean hairy thighs, guns bulging on manly hips. They rode in pairs, chatting, smiling, leaning across to each other from their saddles.

Macho.

Maybe.

It had seemed that way three weeks ago, but now this beautiful city wearied her. Life wearied her. Recently she had started waking up with a headache – and she wasn't the sort of girl who suffered headaches.

Catching sight of herself in a shop window, Strachey realized that she had begun to look American. In one of his rare attempts at flattery, Mickey Starr had said her light skin was English rose, but over here her height, stride and bobbed blonde hair would persuade anyone that only a few years earlier she'd swirled batons as a majorette. Even her cool reserved look didn't seem out of place. Scandinavian, you'd say, brought up in one of those wide-open central states – Lake Woebegone country: when she left for High School she never went back. Then she would open that sexy mouth of hers, say something, and you'd know. Not American – but not Australian either, dumb cluck! Where have you been – don't you *go* to the movies?

She was striding along Geary on her way back from the Clift. This was Clive's idea: he'd told her that although there was a coin phone in their rental she should go to one of San Fran's most expensive hotels and do her phoning from there. Strachey was more at home in top hotels than he realized and she had more than enough clout to pass as a guest, but this time, rather than worm her way into the Clift's business center, she simply stopped by for English tea and phoned from the table. She was not phoning nobodies. The kind of people she called did not answer their own phone and although she might get straight through to them, she often did not. 'Have him call me,' she'd say. 'At the Clift. I shall be here until six but then, I'm afraid, I have a dinner and cannot be reached.'

'And who's that calling?'

'Lord Clive's PA.'

Many telephone con artists revel in the anonymity of a voice-only line, and to work their scams they lock themselves in a room. But Clive recommended public spaces, as upscale as possible: having people around compels one to act. Sit for hours in a room and your loneliness comes through. Certainly Strachey found it easier to sit in the Clift, surrounded by clinking coffee cups. Sometimes a waiter would be with her as the telephone rang and when she spoke into the handset and confirmed that yes, she *was* Lord Clive's PA, she could *see* a reaction as well as hear one down the line. It made her sparkle. You wouldn't get that in an empty room.

To tell the truth – somebody has to – one of those waiters hung around rather more often than was strictly necessary to keep her charged with Earl Grey tea. He had noticed that this pretty English Miss always drank tea on her own. Lord Clive's PA did not mean Lord Clive's mistress – and who the hell was Lord Clive anyway? Probably some old guy laid up with gout. The blonde English Miss never seemed to phone her boyfriend. She just sat there, cool as ice cream, and talked of titles and heritage and when would the caller like to meet? What the waiter wanted to ask was when would *she* like to meet?

It was fantasy, he knew. Million-dollar blondes at the Clift did not go with two-bit waiters who commuted daily from Oakland. But a guy could dream. A guy could hang around her table, even if she only left an English tip – because the main thing was that she left her smile. A guy could take a lot from that.

Fresno – there's a place. First is the getting to it. If you've a yen to see all the wrong parts of California just take the drive down from San Fran to dreary Fresno. You leave the city on the 101 and grind through dust and concrete sprawl, through San Jose and Gilroy, until with some relief you head inland across the flatlands that are the least scenic part of this fabulous state. The sun glowers behind a faint agricultural haze, and fields look parched. You reach the north-south 99 and make the only good move of the journey by turning south and missing Merced, a city so ugly you wonder how it ever erupted in California, when its citizens would obviously prefer to live in shacks beneath a flyover in Hermosillo. You trudge down the 99 through what's billed seductively as the San Joaquin Valley but is a desert where crop peasants grow cotton and nuts, while smarter farmers make wine.

All of which guarantees you reach Fresno with a headache.

On the outskirts (most of Fresno looks like outskirts) they had to refill the car, and Clive, temporarily free from the need to flatter and impress, made a barbed remark about Fresno to the attendant – probably assuming, Strachey thought, that the *peon* did not speak English – but the man smiled and said smugly, 'Well, at least it ain't Bakersfield, buddy,' as if that proved anything.

They drove on.

They had noticed vineyards on the way but since the town also housed the world's largest raisin-packing plant – Sun Maid – they weren't optimistic about the wine. Nevertheless, there were some big operators in the area – families that had constructed huge, sprawling haciendas to front their wine-making factories, and the sight of them helped Clive and Strachey get to the nub of their man today.

He'd want status.

Lincoln Deane greeted them himself. In the shaded courtyard of his three-year-old antique Colonial, he wore a broad-striped linen jacket and white pants. The stripes were pale pastel and the jacket looked like a deck-chair left out too long. Clive was glad he hadn't brought his Henley jacket – he and Lincoln would have looked like competing sticks of rock.

Strachey was more struck by Lincoln's head. Till now she had only spoken with him on the phone and in her mental picture Lincoln had hair. But he was spectacularly bald. As they crossed the dappled courtyard, shafts of sun bounced like laser beams off his scalp. Obviously he polished the thing – sun-factor eighteen, you bet, but also with some kind of long-lasting wax. His head gleamed. It gave a startling effect, as if the man normally wore a toupee and didn't know it had fallen off. He wore tan shoes of crocodile leather.

He led them through the main hall of the house – marble floor under natural light – and out through a large glass double door to a patio and duck pond. The pond had a clinical look, as if it had been designed as a plunge pool but had been converted. A pile of rocks created an island in the center and housed an unlikely crop of ferns. The ducks' nest halfway up was surely false. But real enough were the two black swans sailing round the outcrop as if connected to the island by underwater spokes.

Lincoln indicated a pond-side table. Marble again.

'You want a drink? Something fancy – Pina Colada, maybe, or perhaps you'd like to sample our wine? *Someone* has to!' Lincoln laughed.

'I'm sure it's beautiful,' Clive said.

Strachey asked for tea.

'You know, we had some of that. I bet there's some in the kitchen.'

Lincoln pressed a cast-iron desk bell and in the far distance they heard a four-note chime. But a haughty, dark-haired woman had followed them silently on to the patio. She looked like a flamenco dancer between breaks. She glanced at Strachey and asked, 'China or Indian?'

'China would be nice.'

Lincoln chuckled. 'Of course, the English drink tea from china cups. And what about you, my lord – some wine?'

'I can't wait to sample your wine, Lincoln, but just now I'd prefer tea.'

The maid glanced at the bowl on the marble table. 'You have tacos, burritos, chilli, artichoke hearts. I bring biscuits.'

Lincoln smiled proudly as she left. 'My housekeeper. Quite a girl. Beats a butler.' He glanced at Clive. 'I guess I'll be led by you on that one – I mean, you being a lord, et cetera. Think I'll need one?'

'A butler?'

'That's supposing I buy into this.'

'Forgive me, Mr Deane, but becoming a lord is not something

you buy into. It's an institution. The financial arrangement is incidental.'

'It still costs something, right?'

'Surprisingly little,' Clive purred.

Lincoln shrugged and looked aside. 'How much is surprisingly little?'

'We can't say exactly. There will be an auction, as you know.'

'How many will be bidding at this auction? Fill in the details.'

Clive glanced at Strachey. 'I thought Jane had explained?'

Lincoln grinned at her. 'Jane, is it? You didn't tell me that.'

She smiled back. 'I'm a formal person.'

'Jane Strachey, right?' He turned to Clive. 'While we're on this, what do I call *you* – Lord Clive or what?'

'Lord Clive is correct, but please call me Clive. You, of course, would become Lord of the Manor of Hexcombe.'

'I wouldn't be Lord Deane?'

'My Lord of Hexcombe has more of a ring about it, wouldn't you say?'

Lincoln sat back in his chair. 'I want Lord Deane.'

Lord Clive smiled wistfully. 'I'm offering my cousin's title. He has... fallen upon hard times, and has decided to relinquish his heritage. I can't say I think him right, but I'm here to help him out.'

'You didn't think of helping him out with cash?'

Clive sighed. 'I did think of it. But I'm not a rich man myself, and I'd never have got my money back. Lord Hexcombe has not always been wise where finance is concerned.'

'Lord Hexcombe, eh? What d'you think it'll cost me?'

Clive turned to Strachey. 'What have we heard on the rival bids?'

She pursed her lips. 'Difficult. Everyone is keeping their cards close to their chests.'

Clive nodded. 'Well, a number of titles have been sold in recent years – some as low as a few thousand, ten to twenty, that kind of thing. But the Manor of Hexcombe... I'd say fifty plus.'

'Dollars?'

'Pounds.'

'Fifty thousand pounds?'

'At least.'

'You know, I might pay a *hundred* thousand for plain 'Lord Deane'. It sounds smarter. Think about it, Clive: if I get to become Lord Deane you could pull in a hundred grand. Worth considering.'

Clive smiled. 'I have a single title to offer and I'll confess I'm loathe to sell it – which is why I must ensure that the title falls into the right hands. Any *parvenu* could buy it.' Clive looked around him. 'But I'm reassured.'

They paused while the maid laid out gold-rimmed tea cups and a pot of tea, with a silver jug of coffee on the side. She replaced the Mexican appetisers with sugared biscuits. Although Strachey's headache lingered she managed, 'Lovely tea.'

Lincoln grinned. 'Let's cut to the chase then, Clive. I want to be called Lord Deane, not Lord Hexcombe. You can fix it?'

'Sadly not.'

'Sounds to me like you get a hundred thousand one way, a cup of tea the other – and you've drunk the tea. You should make an effort, Clive. Could be a long trip back.'

Clive nodded sadly. 'It *has* been a long trip. And if you don't mind, Mr Deane, we'd better start that journey back.' He smiled. 'Shame, of course. I could just see you as the Lord of Hexcombe. Never mind. How's the wine business?'

Lincoln waved a hand. 'It flows.'

Strachey appeared to have been struck by a sudden thought. 'I hope you hadn't thought of putting the baronial crest on your wine labels – to increase sales or give the product a special *cachet*? Not that it matters now, of course.'

'Can't I do that?'

She glanced inquiringly at Clive, who pulled a face. 'We couldn't stop you profiting from the lordship, of course – if you *had* bought it. You'd have a number of rights and privileges. Anyway—' He downed the remainder of his tea. 'Good to meet you, Mr Deane. We must get on.'

Lincoln watched them rise, then stood up himself. 'You'd just walk out on me – walk out on a hundred thousand dollars? You must be genuine.'

Lord Clive shrugged modestly. Lincoln scratched his shining head and grinned. 'Don't be insulted, Clive, but we're talking big money here. I thought I'd see how you responded to temptation.'

'Temptation?'

'Let you into a secret. I've been reading up on this lordship business because I do not go into any deal I know nothing about. You're offering this English lordship and I don't even if know if the damn thing can be sold. So I check up and I find you can't buy any old lordship – you've got to buy one that's on the market. Like your cousin's. Like you say.'

Clive made his lip tremble. 'I'm not used to having my word doubted.'

Lincoln chuckled. 'Well, no, you being a lord, et cetera. But I'll tell you this: I checked up whether the Lord Hexcombe title exists.'

Clive raised an eyebrow. He *appeared* untroubled but didn't trust himself to speak.

Lincoln continued: 'My attorney checked something called the Manorial Documents Register and it shows this title of yours going back to the fifteenth century.' He smiled. 'Which is reassuring. But are you entitled to sell it, Clive?'

Clive stiffened and looked English, but Strachey touched his arm. 'Make allowances, my lord. America's a long way from home.'

Clive said, 'A gentleman's word is his bond.'

'Well, like she says, Clive honey, America's a long way from home. So if you sell me this thing, you have to produce the documents – what d'you call them – the deeds? Anyway, my attorney can deal with that. My guy tells me you're on a percentage – is that right?'

Clive lowered his eyelids. 'It is customary.'

Lincoln grinned. 'Ten per cent, right?'

Clive said, 'You certainly know your stuff.'

'Too right, Clive. If I get the documents, you get the cash.'

'I dare say your attorney also mentioned the deposit?'

Lincoln's eyes narrowed, but he still looked good-humoured. He felt himself in charge now – which is how a mark should feel. 'I thought he just meant his fee. Look, Clive honey, come back and sit yourself down. We'll talk about it.'

Clive held his ground. But he smiled too. 'We wouldn't be wasting each other's time?'

'Oh, sit down, for Christ's sake. We're talking details, aren't we?'

Which is where Clive and Strachey were two days later, with a tall mark in Carmel. This one had his attorney with him. It didn't worry Clive: paying an attorney meant the mark was set to do business.

'The first step,' the lawyer said, 'will be for me to write a contract with Lord Clive's attorney, specifying exactly what is being sold and for how much.'

Clive murmured: 'The sale is by auction.'

'I don't like that.'

Clive nodded sympathetically. The attorney wore a suit of pale blue, made of a material so lightweight it was a miracle it remained opaque. Though he looked desk-bound his skin was tanned. He turned to his client: 'You must realise, sir, that there will be restrictions on what rights the lordship confers. You may not even have the right to pass on the title.'

'He will,' Clive cut in soothingly. 'Mr Delarme will be able to pass the title directly to his children – natural children, that is.'

He added this to tease Delarme – because he had already learnt that the man was a fervid bible reader. He was a huge man, hopefully possessed of Christian restraint. He must have been six foot six and he sported a black beard so daunting it could have stood for president on its own. And won. The deep voice buried within it declared: 'All God's children are natural. I can assure you that mine were born inside wedlock.'

'Naturally,' said Clive.

The voice rolled again: 'And the title will be Lord of Hexcombe? My son would be called what?'

'He'll keep his present name. He'll refer to you as 'My father, Lord of Hexcombe', but for him there can be no title till he inherits.' Clive smiled. 'Does that worry you, sir?'

Delarme's eyes were black as unlit coal. The attorney cut in: 'You said something about lands and property?'

Clive shook his head. 'Just the title, and some rights to verges and unclaimed land stemming from the original 'copyhold' lands of the manor. There are some mineral rights also, I believe,' he added nonchalantly.

The attorney and Delarme responded in unison: 'Mineral rights?'

'Oh, don't worry – "copyhold" lands can be explored only with *your* permission. You don't want people digging for gold all over the parish, do you?'

Clive chuckled at the absurdity of the idea, well aware that it sounded far from absurd to the mark and his attorney. While their minds raced Clive continued: 'Have no fear: your prerogatives are clearly documented and once the sale has gone through, these documents – which incidentally are rather charming things on ancient vellum – pass over to you with the title. You don't pay, in fact, till you have those documents in your hand.'

Delarme's eyes gleamed.

Strachey threw in her two-penn'orth: 'D'you know, vellum documents can often be worth money? Apparently there have been cases of people selling them for quite considerable sums. Ridiculous, isn't it?'

'Vulgar,' snapped Clive. 'Putting money before heritage.'

Strachey added, 'You may unearth other amusing benefits such as the right to fly your banner from the church tower on your birthday. I believe you're a God-fearing man, sir?'

Delarme's voice resonated. 'I certainly am.' He stared back at them. 'I trust you have both found the Lord?'

Clive said, 'We have only one to sell—'

Delarme cut across him: 'My thoughts are not your thoughts, neither are my ways your ways, saith the Lord!'

Clive and Strachey said, 'Amen.'

Tell me, have you ever been to Carmel? Strachey had checked in everything from Frommers to California On Twenty Dollars A Day and discovered that in that part of California – and on Clive's budget – they couldn't afford a night in a tent. So it meant another slog up Route 101 to San Francisco. When they got there – tired and dark-eyed – their resemblance to British aristocracy had waned. Clive parked the hired auto San Francisco style – on a twenty per cent hill, engine in gear, wheels forty-five degrees to the curb – and they trudged up the stairs to their rental. Which smelled stale. As she trudged up the stairs, Strachey realized that despite her persistent headache she relished the tawdriness. As Mickey used to say, she enjoyed slumming.

Inside the room, Clive aired a thought that had been worrying him: 'The trouble is we have to wait so long for our money. We don't get so much as a deposit until auction day.'

'So it's the diner tonight?'

'Oh, Strachey, I can afford a meal. But this room... '

'Is no place for a lord?'

He smiled wearily. 'Nor his lady.'

He threw his tan briefcase on the bed where it raised a small cloud of dust.

She poked a finger in his side. 'Don't come the aristo.'

'I paid good money to become one.'

'Three thousand. And how much was Hexcombe?'

He clucked her gently beneath the chin. 'Five and a half. You see, *my* title was a *folie de grandeur*. I'm Lord Clive of Lower Marsh, and that's it – no attachments. But Hexcombe is the real McCoy.'

'It'll *have* to be if you're going to get a hundred thousand for it.'

'It's a rural hereditament, nice part of the country, some scraps of property rights.'

'But a hundred thousand – seriously?'

'It's all down to presentation. When they sold the Barony of Clanmaurice, as you know, it went for £27,500 – in *Britain*, not America, though at the same auction other titles went for laughably small amounts. Renacres in Lancashire cost a mere £4,250, and even Amberley in Sussex fetched less than thirteen grand. Peasemore, a gem in Berkshire – imagine it: the Lordship of Peasemore – went for a derisory £6,000.'

'You'll have your work cut out on Hexcombe.'

'Trust uncle Clive.'

He took her out that evening to a modest restaurant in Haight Ashbury, and while they were eating (and long before they ran out on the bill) he expounded on the delights of Hexcombe – the wild Devon countryside, the thatched cottages, the high-banked lanes – and in what seemed a natural consequence he gave her a single air ticket and told her what she had to do.

2

FOR SOMEONE WHO looked as if he emerged from a coffin at night, Frankie di Stefano was a hot shot in the mornings. He would be up, bouncing around his empire at seven when others in his line of business had just crawled into bed. Truth was, he was a hard-eyed man who needed little sleep. Maybe he suffered from bad dreams. Maybe Satan had a conscience.

He was strutting across an empty bar-room floor, unaware of the stale smell of burnt tobacco and long-spilt ale, when Drew Peynoll, who ran the place, materialised at the yellow louvered door. Drew lingered on the far side of it. Frankie might be up, but Drew hadn't got to bed yet. Eight in the morning was late to Drew. He normally slept from dawn to lunch but because he knew Frankie was due today he'd thought it politic to wait.

'Everything OK then, Frankie?'

'Place is dirtier each time I see it.'

'Customers like it that way. They can relax.'

Frankie showed no sign of coming out of the bar room, and Drew wasn't coming in. He elaborated on how a bar should be run: 'Other places, they shine the tables, spray air freshener, put cola in your drinks and call 'em cocktails, that kind of shit. If you wanna smoke, they stick you outside in an annex. Who needs that? Guys who come here look on this place as their den.'

'Thanks for sharing that with me, Drew.'

'Anything you need, Frankie?'

'Just passing by.'

'Like you do every Tuesday.' Drew shifted his frame against the doorjamb. 'Gary Stitz was here last night.'

Frankie was about to run his finger across a table, but when he saw the grime he changed his mind. 'So?'

'Shooting off his mouth.'

Frankie stared at him. Drew said, 'He reckoned you was trespassing on his territory – the Captain Nemo?'

'His territory?'

'You turned up there with a bunch of guys?'

'So?'

'Terrified the manager. Thought you was gonna put the squeeze on him.'

'And did I?'

Drew shrugged. 'Gary protects him. Supposed to.'

'Gary Stitz? Who the hell is he?'

'You know Gary – Gary Stitz.'

'But who *is* he?'

'Like, who does he *think* he is?'

'Jesus Christ.'

'No, Gary Stitz.'

Frankie thought aloud: 'Gary comes in here, gives all that shit. He talks to you alone, or he lets the whole bar listen?'

Drew grunted. 'Well, he didn't hide it.'

'So.' Frankie stared at the wall. 'It's a message.'

If a seed is dropped on fertile ground it should germinate and flower. When Strachey casually suggested that Lincoln Deane could boost wine sales by printing a genuine baronial pedigree on the label, she dropped a seed that sprouted into life like mustard seed on flannel.

Lincoln had a wife. But being a man who liked to get a deal set up before he talked about it, he had not yet broached the scheme to her. He had also not mentioned that their Fresno mansion was about to get a social call from a genuine English lord. Instead, he had sent Gloria to Fresno to enjoy a shopping trip.

She came back with a single carrier bag. He peered at it. 'Having the rest delivered?'

Gloria pouted fetchingly beside the car. 'Come on, darlin'. Sometimes you talk as if all I ever do is spend money.'

She dropped the bag, jutted out her hip, and waited for him to make the move to *her*. It was barely a year since Lincoln had plucked Gloria from a promising career in movies – less of a disruption than it sounds, since promises were all she'd had in her career. But Gloria was the kind of girl men made promises to. She had enough blonde hair to stuff a pillow and she drove men's thoughts in exactly that direction. Even in California, she made days sunnier.

Lincoln shook his gleaming bald head and came across to her with a kiss. 'D'ya have a good day?'

'Uh-huh – an' I didn't buy a thing.' He *made* himself not

glance at the bag. 'Except this cute wooden puppet. Look darlin', it's Mr Punch. That's English. Antique.'

'English?' he mumbled.

'Well, not really antique, I guess.' She pulled it from its bag. 'They had this puppet show? All the way from England. An' you know I *love* anything English.'

Lincoln felt a need to change the subject. 'Just leave the car here. I'll shift it later.'

When he tried to lead her inside, Gloria waggled the painted wooden doll before his face. '*That's* the way to do it,' she squeaked in a puppet's voice. 'Isn't he wonderful?'

Lincoln pulled her towards the steps, nodding enthusiastically. 'Great stuff, kid.'

'They had this striped tent, really small, just one little man inside. Well, not so little really.'

She didn't tell him that the man who had unfolded himself from the tent was tall and young, and had buttoned on to Gloria straight away. 'He just *had* to sell me this Mr Punch.'

Lincoln got her to the top of the steps. 'Guy sold you his most important puppet?'

'He had a load of 'em. You know, he sells 'em as souvenirs?'

Gloria was inside the hall now, her heels clattering on the marble floor. '*That's* the way to do it! – Look at his nose.'

'Sure is some hooter.'

'Phallic – that's what Quentin said.'

'The hell is Quentin?'

'You know, the puppet man? I told you. An *English* man.'

'Phallic, huh – what's he talking to you like that for?'

She opened her eyes. '*I* don't know.'

'Where *was* this?'

'The puppet show, I *told* you. In Storyland.'

'That's a *kid's* place.'

'I love Storyland.' She lifted Mr Punch's hand to stroke Lincoln under the chin. 'An' it's an *awful* lot cheaper than going shopping. Isn't that right? Come on, darlin', give your girl a smile.'

Lincoln gave a cursory glimpse of his teeth.

'*That's* the way to do it!' She kept the puppet voice: 'Give us a kiss.'

He hesitated. 'I ain't kissing that.'

'Well, that's what Monica Lewinsky said the first time.'

Gloria burst into a peal of laughter and Lincoln had to smile.

Storyland was in Roeding Park, the vast 157-acre urban playground with lakes and flower gardens, dance pavilions, champion tennis courts and Fresno Zoo. Most girls might have headed for the dance pavilions or, depending on how muscular the young men were that day, to the tennis court but Gloria preferred the kiddie's playland with its Mother Goose's Fountain, its Owl Tree, its Crooked Mile, and where the nearest to anything phallic was Jack's Beanstalk. There were worse places she could go.

She kicked her high heels off and watched them slide across the marble floor.

'So darlin', what have *you* been doin' today?'

On the afternoon of Strachey's flight the tall, bearded, Edgar Delarme looked particularly patriarchal in a purple-black gown he was having edged with ermine. He had arranged an afternoon session with his tailor so they could select and attach regal trimmings. Delarme was better read than either di Stefano or Deane (which is not a great boast) and had conducted some research into what becoming an English lord might mean. He knew, for instance, that he was not buying the right to sit in the House of Lords – which he couldn't anyway, since it had been struck down by socialists – he knew that he would become Lord of Hexcombe (the 'of' was crucial) and that in the eyes of some people such lordships were worth little more than the vellum they were written on. But he had also satisfied himself that these minor lordships, though practically defunct, were genuine titles dating back several hundred years and that in many cases they carried genuine privileges and rights.

He would be Lord of the Manor, and his research suggested that this meant he had the right to hold something called a Manor Court. From what he could tell, these meetings were not an everyday part of British life – but neither was *religion* in many parts of that benighted land. Delarme believed that Britain had lapsed into heathenism. The plight of true religion was bad enough in America but in those far-off fog-laden British Isles, churches were deconsecrated and turned into cottages, gambling halls and worse. In Britain, people told him, deconsecrated chapels had been turned into Centres for Martial Arts, furniture storage depots, and even Hindu Community Centres. Clearly, there was an urgent need there for vigorous missionary work.

'This is your cap of maintenance,' his tailor purred. The

tailor – John Crampole – was what might be tactfully called a lean man, with a torso like a clothes peg and a fondness for black gabardine. He was an expert on ecclesiastical cloth but, like Delarme, was out of his depth when it came to the 'tinctures' and 'furring' of a cap of maintenance. In his hands he held a kind of Normandy beret trimmed with scarlet fur.

'Red fur?' Delarme queried.

'Technically it's *Gules*,' Crampole corrected him. 'Which is red in heraldry. As a British lord your ermine can be either *Gules* or *Azure*: *Gules* means you're still in possession of the barony while *Azure* means you're not.'

Delarme nodded. 'Blue wouldn't look right.'

'Though it could be worn by your heirs, till they inherit.'

Delarme tried the cap. In scarlet and black he looked daunting – as if he'd been on the winning side at the Spanish Inquisition.

Crampole whispered, 'It looks good on you.'

'I am concerned only with what the vestment signifies, not how it looks,' declared Delarme, tilting his head before the mirror to catch the light.

The Lordship of Hexcombe was not an essential part of his missionary plan but – at a few thousand dollars – it ought to help. It worried him that at their recent meeting Lord Clive had talked in terms of a few *tens* of thousands of dollars, but that had probably been a weak English attempt to talk up the bidding. Delarme knew that the market price for these lordships started around five thousand English pounds (for mere titles with no realistic rights) and only rose to the kind of money Lord Clive was talking about for the plums. The Shakespearean sounding 'Lordship of Henley in Arden' had fetched way over a hundred thousand pounds, and another, with a feudal earldom, a castle and about 1,000 acres of land, had once sold for approaching four hundred thousand pounds. The land alone was worth twice that now.

What did Hexcombe have?

Certainly the Manor of Hexcombe should be more exclusive than baronial lordships sold at open auction. And more expensive – it was, after all, a private sale direct from the family of Lord Clive Lane. Nevertheless, there *would* be an auction and Delarme didn't kid himself the sale would be run by amateurs.

Crampole coughed discreetly. 'Over your robe you'll wear a mantle.' He opened a box.

Delarme peeped inside. 'Let all things be done decently and in order.'

Crampole produced a garment wrapped in tissue paper. '*Gules* should be paired with *silk Argent* – that's silver – while the fur collar has to be ermine or *miniver*, which is white as you know – and the whole piece is fastened on the right shoulder by five spherical gold buttons.'

Delarme frowned. 'Gold, silver and ermine? I'm a modest man.'

'Even a bishop wears silk and gold.'

'I am not a bishop. This smacks of vanity.'

'You have to stand out in ceremonies.'

As Lord of the Manor, Delarme would have the right to preside over periodic meetings of his tenantry, should they exist. According to what he had read, a manorial court could administer the agriculture of the manor and the tenants' rights, duties, and disputes. If Hexcombe court was a *Court Leet*, it could also rule on the election of constables, ale-testers and other officials. It might even have a role in police matters, such as maintenance of the lockup and judgements on disturbances of the peace. Lord Clive had been most instructive on these matters.

Crampole stood with the mantle across his arms. It was an expensive garment and he didn't want to press Delarme too hard. In his line of business the tailor was well used to selling vestments to men whose professions meant they were supposed to show no outward signs of vanity or extravagance. Crampole would wait till Delarme had slipped the mantle on.

With apparent reluctance, Delarme took it.

3

NO ONE WHO takes the eleven-hour flight from San Francisco to London Heathrow steps off the plane eyes sparkling and light of foot. The flight across is one endless night: staff thump up and down, passengers get restless, a baby starts to cry. You detach yourself: this is a time you must get through. It is, after all, an extraordinary experience – you are flying thirty-thousand feet above the planet, travelling several hundred miles per hour, crossing a vast distance in the time it used to take people to get from a village into the next county. Somehow this does not seem as impressive as it should.

For Strachey it was the first time she had been alone with herself – truly alone, isolated – in about three months. Occasionally during their time together Clive had disappeared for a couple of days, but in America there were always other distractions, so her mind never slowed as it could now, each compartment of her brain emptying until the only things left were the unwanted, unconsidered scraps of trash. Among the scraps were questions: *why* was she here, *what* was she doing, *how* had she got involved in this? Strachey had gone to America with an introduction to an art auction house and the virtual certainty of a decent job. She had started it, impressed her new employers, but within three weeks had hooked up with Clive. Even at the time she could tell the signs: here we go again, she thought – why do I fall for unworthy men? Do I lack a centre to my life? Was Mickey right when he told me I'd had things too comfortable too long?

Two hours from Heathrow, as the plane stirred into life and an unpalatable breakfast hoved into view, Strachey left her seat and locked herself in the washroom to freshen up. Beside the tiny basin were two courtesy bottles of cologne, but they smelt of someone else, like a cloying scent on the jacket of an unfaithful lover. She didn't use them. Her face had aged five years. When she loosened her hair her features softened – but then she scraped the hair back into a severe bun. She repaired her make-up. Her clothes were of a modern crease-resistant

fabric and when she left the washroom Strachey looked crease-
resistant too.

Breakfast had been served in her absence and the plastic tray
sat on her seat. Her first thought was to ignore it but she had a
long day ahead. From here on she would be travelling economy.

And Clive? Well, at that moment, he was tucked up in bed (eight-
hour time difference) but as the day wore on he decided that
economy was not his style and he strolled along Geary to the Clift
for morning coffee. He placed some phone calls and while he
waited for replies he sat reading the property sections of upscale
English newspapers, supplied by the hotel for the convenience of
its patrons. He made notes with an old marbled Waterman.

It has to be admitted that Lord Clive got less attentive service
from the staff than had the untitled Miss Strachey. But to be left
undisturbed was how Clive liked it. His latest discreet
advertisement was pulling well and although he would have
preferred the first contact with potential customers to be with his
secretary, he liked the slight shock of silence on the line when he
announced his name. There was no doubt about it, he thought –
buying a lordship was a shrewd investment.

Edgar Delarme had shifted into that most vulnerable of buying
modes: he'd assumed the title to be his. Any doubts were
assuaged by the ministrations of his tailor. Crampole – who had
never met Lord Clive or any other English lord – was no mean
salesman. Determined to wrap up the sale before competitors got
the scent, he introduced the basic robe at a 'realistic' price
(realistic being his word for a hundred per cent profit) and once
Delarme had swallowed that, he added a succession of tasty
nibbles – tinctures and furring to the robe, a flat cap of justice, a
pack of ceremonial buttons and an irrelevant set of badges and
pendants he thought suitable for an English lord. In these
detailed areas Crampole's ecclesiastical catalogs were little help,
but he had a sizeable library of movie photographs to suggest
ideas. Delarme had been wary at first – like an old pike in the
river, too cautious and experienced for obvious bait, but
increasingly lulled and cajoled to Crampole's hook. After he had
quibbled over the price of the basic robe he fell to nodding
dumbly – he hoped wisely – at the succession of impressive
trinkets and accessories added on.

By this time Delarme was out of depth. His own researches were no match for Crampole's lifetime of specialist humbug – nor was his wariness guard against the more practised eye of his adversary. He was sold scraps of trimming which owed more to Hollywood than to heraldry and he was now ripe for Crampole's final three thousand per cent *coup de grace*.

'When you preside over your Manorial Court, my Lord,' murmured Crampole with due deference, 'you'll require a white Ell-wand – that's a Wand of Peace – one ell in length, and, if I may advise you, you should accompany that with a medieval horn. I have them here.'

As Clive sipped coffee at the Clift he was startled to receive an incoming call from a name on an earlier list.

'Hey, Clive – I mean *Lord* Clive, forgive me – it's Lincoln Deane.'

Lincoln had rung the Clift in the belief that it was where Lord Clive and his secretary stayed. They'd have a suite or something, Lincoln assumed, though he hadn't quite made Strachey out. Was she *with* Lord Clive or did she just work for him?

'The thing is, Clive, I'm in the doghouse here. Gloria – that's my wife – is mightily upset with me. Oops!'

Lincoln was making the call with Gloria leaning against his shoulder – her ear pressed against the other side of the handset so she could hear for herself what an English lord might sound like. She had just thumped her husband. He said, 'All *right*! Hey, look Clive, Gloria says – no, we *both* say – we'd like to invite you down to dinner, you know, maybe Friday night? What d'you say?'

'Friday?' hedged Clive. It was a one-hundred-and-fifty mile journey. Each way. 'For dinner?'

He heard a whisper the other end, then Lincoln added, 'You could stay the weekend.'

Forty-eight hours with Lincoln Deane? 'I have to fly north this weekend.'

'Hell, you can fly from here.'

This seemed to confirm the rumor that more people flew *out* of Fresno than ever flew in.

'I'd love to, Lincoln—'

'That's great. I'll get Gloria to fix – what is it *now*?'

Clive spoke over Gloria's off-phone scolding. 'I'd love to but I can't, Lincoln. I'd have to leave the car with you and—'

'Gloria says to tell you – oh Jeez, Gloria, what?'

Clive could hear their voices but before he could make out what they were saying Lincoln said, 'OK, *I'm* saying – *we're* saying – hell, I don't know, but anyway our *maidservant* will fix you up.'

'Fix me up?'

'We got some great rooms here, Clive. You know, stay the weekend – I can show you the vineyard.'

'I'm terribly sorry—'

'Hold it. *What?*' Another off-phone discourse. 'OK, I *won't* show you the vineyard, Clive. Promise. I mean, you don't *have* to see it. What would you like to see – the Sierra, National Forest, the – what?' Off phone again. 'No, he *doesn't* want to go to Storyland. Hey, Clive, I mean, we're gonna be real mad at you if you don't come down, you know? We'll have a good time, right? Introduce you to some of our friends.'

'That could be tempting but—'

'We got a load of friends here who'd be real proud to meet an English lord.'

'You may soon be one yourself.'

'Hey, d'ya hear that, honey? Right, Clive – ouch – yeah, *Lord* Clive, I mean we got a bunch of folks here you should meet.'

Clive hesitated until Lincoln – without realising – played a trump card: 'I mean, my friends got loads of money but they do not have class. They're gonna be jealous as hell when they – yeah, yeah, OK Gloria – listen, Clive, will you do us a favor – what? – OK, the *honor* of coming down?'

'It's quite a drive for dinner, Lincoln—'

'Hell, *fly* down, Clive – you can fly straight here from Frisco.'

Clive didn't have to say anything because there was another bout of whispering the other end – resulting in: 'Hey, Clive, how do I put this? You're our guest, right? I mean, we don't expect you to buy your own air ticket. I'll charge it. You can pick it up at the airport.'

'That's very kind of you but—'

'You're going north after? I know a guy has his own airplane, company jet. It ain't Concorde but if you don't mind a small – what is it, sixteen seats? Huh? Gloria says *eight* seats. Should be sixteen, they took eight out, they're all so fat.'

'Company jet?'

'Yeah – runs a restaurant chain, the Happy Hacienda, you know it? *What?* For Christ's *sake*, Gloria, I'm trying to have a conversation here – he *might* have heard of it. Listen Clive, just come down, stay the weekend – stay longer, whatever you like – we'll put you up, our guest, then the Happy Hacienda will fly you up to wherever it is you want to go. How's that grab you?'

Clive thought about it: free accommodation, free flights, the company of rich and gullible friends. He said, 'You have twisted my arm.'

'I what?'

The phone blasted with Gloria's shriek: 'He's *coming*! Yes! He's coming, Linc!'

Clive waited till the noise died down. 'Shall I leave the flight details to you?'

Lincoln agreed happily and said he'd meet him at Fresno airport. He sounded almost incoherent with joy but perhaps that was because Gloria had draped her sensational body around him and was planting lipstick across his face.

Californian skies were sunny but up in New York's Long Island they were gray and ominous. Frankie di Stefano wanted Gary Stitz. He sent his home boys to look for him but they came back empty-handed. Word was out, of course, so the ball was now in Gary's court: he could lie low, provided he never wanted to come within a hundred miles of Queens again, or he could play.

Gary was grown-up, nineteen, and being ambitious had known for several years that one day he'd have his chance. He'd seen others – hey, he hadn't been *that* young when Frankie di Stefano first struck – and he knew that first you laid the ground, a process which could take several years, and then in one defining moment you leapt a league. Thinking back, he could remember a girl he'd dated once – Angela, died in a gangbang in Mount Vernon – who'd said young men were animals: stags, wolves, lions, bears, and that young men settled leadership with a fight. Survival of the fittest, he'd supposed, though Angela said the phrase meant something different and she knew 'cos she'd read books. She'd said young males spent a lot of time either ignoring females or prowling around them, protecting them and stopping other males from coming near. Every now and then one of those other males *would* come near, like they *had* to, she said, it was something in their jeans? And when the other male did come near it was a direct challenge, no way out. No matter how whacked the buck male was, when the challenge came he had to fight. Gary and Angela agreed that this gave the challenger an advantage – he chose the time, and was almost always younger. Which was why young people ruled the world.

So on the day Frankie put the word out, Gary chose his time and place. He'd meet Frankie di Stefano at the Captain Nemo. Four o'clock.

Gary arrived just after three. The way he saw it he had two options: either to get there well in advance, get settled in, have the place checked out for hidden snipers, *or* let Frankie settle first, then come in late and arrogant, the new leader of the pack. But since Gary had made the challenge, he couldn't arrive late. If he did, Frankie might turn up at four and say Gary was too scared to appear. Frankie could be named the winner before Gary had made an entrance.

Gary explained to the Nemo manager that he'd better give his staff the afternoon off. The guy protested a little until Gary demonstrated that this was not a casual suggestion. When the guy picked himself up he still seemed unaware of how to deliver customer satisfaction and they had to lock him in the steel room behind the bar. Gary's boys then scurried through the guest corridors checking that no one was in the rooms. Being mid-afternoon only one room was occupied and she shouldn't have been with the guy anyway so they both left quietly. It was now half-past three and Gary said he'd have a swim.

You may know that the pool at the Captain Nemo falls a long way short of Olympic standard. Since Gary was a pretty good swimmer he swum up and down the moderate-sized pool like a German shepherd dog pacing a back yard. He took a rest around four, drank some orange juice, and at a few minutes past the hour plunged back in the water and swam up and down. He reckoned correctly that Frankie would turn up a quarter after.

Which he did.

Frankie's first thought was that Gary's brain was waterlogged. This was the sort of game they played in the backwoods: you floated apples in a barrel of water and stood off and shot at them. Or if it wasn't apple season you went to a trout farm and shot fish. There wasn't a lot else to do in Nebraska.

But when the boy climbed, dripping, from the pool Frankie saw the point the kid was making: Gary was six foot three, dark hair, water streaming from his young body. He stood with a towel, flicking water off his shoulders, acting as if he was Tarzan meeting runt-sized hunters. He'd brought a bunch of friends and ne'er-do-wells to enjoy the show.

Gary said, 'You're standing on my territory.'

Frankie guessed he was supposed to respond with something bright like 'Oh yeah?' but he didn't say anything.

Gary said, 'You don't come here without I say so.'

Frankie studied him.

Gary said, 'Do what you like in Queens, but from here to Garden City is mine. Is that understood?'

Frankie said, 'Dry yourself and listen. Once a year a kid like you speaks up an' I put him down. This year it's your turn. I know you brought your friends along but that's too bad. Say you're sorry and I let you go.'

Gary laughed. 'You'll let *me* go!' He looked scornfully at the three men Frankie had brought with him. 'Get out of here in one piece and you'll be lucky, man.'

Gary held the towel behind his back and dried himself with a vigorous movement. He needed to get warm. Frankie stood fully dressed, wearing a lightweight coat, six inches shorter than the younger man. He asked quietly, 'You take advice?'

'What are you, my father?'

Gary knew this was his defining moment. Everyone around the pool was watching. It didn't matter who was on which side: they would reserve judgement till the fight was done. 'Get it straight, di Stefano. You're on my territory.'

Frankie looked at him.

Gary said, 'You're a has-been. I'm the new kid on the block.'

Frankie looked disappointed.

Gary continued. 'I'm taking your territory – like this was *ever* yours – and you can stuff that where the gaolbird stuffs his toke. You may be the old champion, but you're finished – an old stag with a pack of deer. You see these people? They're like roe deer or whatever they call 'em, the females in the pack. Well, Frankie, listen to me – I'm the new buck here, I'm taking the herd. You know what stag deer do? They lock antlers an' fight. You wanna settle it that way? You wanna strip your jacket off, Frankie, you wanna step over here and lock antlers by the pool, just say the word. I'm ready for you. What d'you say?'

Frankie said, 'You talk too much. You always did.'

'I'm waitin' for you.'

Frankie asked, 'Didn't a bunch of Cuban kids fuck your sweetheart to death?' He opened his coat and pulled out a handgun. 'Angela, wasn't it? And you did nothin'.'

Frankie fired twice, though the second wasn't necessary. Gary fell backwards to the floor, tilting a poolside table so it crashed beside him. In his naked chest two small craters filled with red.

Frankie turned to Gary's ex-companions. 'Anyone have a problem with that?'

Nobody spoke.

'Anyone see what happened here?'

They looked away.

He tried a third time: 'Were any of you guys here this afternoon?'

No one caught his eye. The only noise came from traffic outside, unceasing, undisturbed by the sound of gunshots at the pool.

Frankie turned to two men quivering at the nearest table. 'Don't we know each other?' They didn't answer. 'Well, it's good to make your acquaintance and here's what you're to do. As soon as I leave here you will pick up that pile of shit and take it in your car and dump it well away from this motel. Let's say Woodbury – nothing happens there. Is that all right with you?'

They nodded obediently.

'Everyone else goes home – since none of you was here. Right?'

No one made a croak.

'Oh, before we go,' he said, picking up a glass. 'Raise your glasses.'

They were too stunned to move.

'Get a drink!'

They sprung to life.

'A toast,' he said. 'To Angela.'

He downed his drink, but Gary's boys sipped at theirs as if each glass was filled with Lysol.

4

HEATHROW DISGORGES TRAVELLERS without ceremony. Strachey wheels her suitcase against the tide along a series of shabby corridors to find the Departure floor with its shops. She is returning home – though having lived out of a suitcase for several years, she is no longer sure where home is. She has few ties here. Even Mickey Starr belongs to the past. In the Departure Hall she finds a stationers and buys a road atlas. Clive has warned her that Hexcombe might not be in the index, but she knows roughly where it is. She sits with a coffee and marks out the area.

From Heathrow to Dartmoor looks a four-hour drive, but since Strachey wants the far western side of the moor she allows an extra hour. Her hire car is modest, and on the motorway she drives at little more than the fifty-five she got used to in the States. The rest of the traffic roars past at speeds way above the legal seventy, and it makes a pleasant change for her to be one of the few people inside the law. Curious, thinks Strachey, that in tiny Britain people drive fast and in America cars traverse vast distances at less than sixty miles per hour – yet in the States it takes less time to cover two hundred miles than here.

She is thinking like a tourist, viewing Britain with American eyes. It could be useful, because she has returned as nominal chief executive of Lane Estates to prepare for any visit from a prospective Lord of Hexcombe Manor. Clive said that at this late stage the punters' lawyers would be checking the title was genuine and that Lane Estates had the right to sell it. It wouldn't look good, he said, if punters discovered he was a principal of the vendor company, so he 'sold' it to Strachey for one pound sterling. Clive now appeared independent. Three months back, when he first acquired the title, he had visited the hereditament but found nothing to gain from parading about down there, a temporary lord. No point frightening the pigeons. When the real lord came – as presumably he would – he could make his own grand entrance.

Strachey must make sure that wasn't a disappointment.

Some motorists might have been unprepared for the contrast between the main Devon road and the county's narrow high-banked lanes but Strachey was used to American dirt roads and, for her, the fact that the lanes were metalled was reassuring. Dark green hedges overhung the road and enclosed the car. Birds flew ahead along the lane, and a cow hung its head across a gate.

At the second junction all that remained of the wooden fingerpost was its pole. She stopped the car and took out her map – but it showed the lane going straight on, with a bend or two, of which this crossroad must be one. She got out of the car and listened. She peered along each lane but they curved away.

A wind stirred.

Strachey climbed back in the car and took the road straight ahead. It grew narrower. By the time she realised she had chosen wrongly, the lane was too narrow to turn round. At the brow of a hill but to her left was a gateway – narrow, muddy. Too muddy. She continued along the lane as it wound erratically down the hill until at a final bend it dropped into a river and emerged the other side. On her side was a notice with the word 'FORD'. Actually there were ten words – arranged around the frame were nine others in a small stern font: 'This Notice Is The Property Of Devon County Council'. Strachey left the car to look across at the derelict building on the other side. It was built of dark stone, much of which had fallen away, and what remained standing was overgrown with ivy and climbers.

'Hexcombe Manor,' she said with a grin.

She was joking, of course. From the look of it, the tumble-down building had been a mill, though it couldn't have worked for many years. She could see the housing for the millwheel. In other parts of the countryside, defunct mills were converted into smart dwelling places but this was too decayed and was situated in a dank, dark valley that no one with money would choose to live in. She looked in the rippling water and wondered how deep it was.

A ford, they said. She doubted it.

Unfortunately, there were only two ways to test that out – and test it she must, unless she wanted to reverse two miles back up along the steep lane. She could drive through an unknown depth of water and risk flooding the car, or she could wade through it. There was no one around to see.

She kicked off her shoes, reached up inside her skirt to pull down her tights, then tucked her skirt into her panties like a schoolgirl – no, cancel that: Strachey had not looked like a schoolgirl since she was fourteen. (Even then, her Games teacher had whispered – but no, that's another story.) Into the water she placed a long and shapely leg.

'Ouch!' She gasped at the coldness.

There were little stones in the river bed but her feet were already numb. Scraps of weed slithered by her shins. She took another breath and stepped forward. As she waded across, she got the impression that the road had been built up above the natural river floor. Perhaps there had always been a track through here with stepping stones, and the road-builders had built on that. The water never reached beyond her knees.

She looked back across to the car. Before going back for it she might as well look inside the mill. No point fetching the car and climbing out again.

The front door – perhaps the only door – stood against the road and hung half open. There was a stone step. Above the door, in the eroded lintel, two words had been carved into blackened stone: 'Hexcombe Mill'.

When she pushed the door it scraped noisily against the floor. The interior was dim but lit by gaping windows. There was no furniture. As she moved forward she placed her bare feet carefully amongst the rubble on the floor. There was a rancid smell, as if an animal occasionally used the place as a den.

'Welcome,' came a man's voice, 'to me little home.'

She spun round.

In the gloom she made out the shape of a thin, unkempt man in his twenties. He gave a grin. 'Watched you paddle across the stream. Thought I'd won the lottery.'

She listened to the silence between his words. Was he alone?

Strachey moistened her lips. 'I didn't realise anyone was here. I'll be on my way.'

'No 'urry. Come to look around the place?'

She hesitated. He didn't seem threatening, but he was between her and the door.

'Just passing.'

He chuckled. 'That's not very friendly, is it? I've been waiting for you.'

She moved her head inquiringly.

'I stood 'ere watching you. I thought, she *must* be comin' to see me. There's no one else for 'er to visit.'

'I was testing the ford. To see how deep it was.'

'You got your legs wet.' He looked down at them. 'Be my guest.'

She moved. 'I have to go.'

'It's better upstairs. I can show you somethin' you haven't seen before.'

She moved for the door.

He tried to grab her but she lashed out with the rabbit chop Mickey had taught her – straight beneath the chin, across the Adam's apple. She gave a kick to his groin. The man folded, choking. The rabbit chop stopped him but the kick missed the mark. Strachey, nevertheless, was out the door and back into the stream – when he grabbed her. She turned on him in the water, smacked up again at his throat, and he slipped, fell back – and crashed into the edge of the ford, his head cracking hard against the road. She moved closer to kick again (Mickey had told her: finish it off) but the man lay on his back, either winded or unconscious.

For a moment he didn't move. Then the current caught him and his body swung sideways into the stream and began to float away. She watched it, horrified. At the last moment she grabbed his foot. She slipped to her knees, soaking her skirt and pants. As his body pulled out into the stream Strachey clutched at his leg and heaved. His head sunk below the surface. He might be drowning. She scrambled sideways, pulling on him, hauling his heavy body to the shallow shore. His legs were out of the water now, resting on tarmac. She climbed onto the road, turned, and saw his head disappear again beneath the surface. Frantically she heaved at him, dragging him out of the water onto the road. He lay motionless. She dropped down beside him and slapped his face. Then she lifted his head and glanced underneath to see if he was bleeding from the back of his skull. He didn't seem to be. Surely he hadn't drowned? He hadn't been under the water long enough – had he? But he wasn't moving. He lay on his back in the road, eyes shut, water running from his clothes. Did he need resuscitation?

He would not get mouth to mouth.

Strachey knelt beside him, placed one knee on his stomach, grabbed his shoulders and heaved him up. He grunted like a gurgling drain. She pushed him back, then heaved him up again. He gurgled a second time – a terrible noise, half gasp, half cough. She pushed him back, heaved up, and he vomited water. She pushed him back down. He didn't move. With her knee still bedded in his stomach she pulled a fourth time. He vomited, opened his eyes and looked at her. She pushed him down.

'In for a penny,' she thought.

She pulled him up again. This time the noise he made was more sustained – a long, dry-retching sound. He looked at her again. She pushed him down.

As she leant away from him his hand clutched feebly at her skirt. He was trying to speak.

'What?' she snapped.

He slobbered again.

She bent lower. 'What did you say?'

'I knew you liked me.'

She slapped his face, stood up and marched across the stream.

When she started the car he was still lying in the roadway on the other side. She revved the engine and he rolled onto his knees. 'If he doesn't move,' she thought, 'I'll run him down.'

He was staggering to his feet. She eased the car into the stream and as she came across he lurched away to the side of the road. A wake of water came from the car wheels, and as the car made dry land the man staggered from the roadside towards her but she accelerated, bumping him a glancing blow. She peeped in her mirror and saw him lying on his side, arm raised and waving feebly. He was waving, not drowning. She couldn't tell whether he was injured or mocking her. But she continued steadily up the hill.

On the flat plateau the hedges were lower and she could see the spire of a church ahead. On her left she passed the entrance to a farmyard. There were a couple of labourer's cottages. Nothing told her where she was but she was heading for the little church. Two slow bends and she was there. Beside the gate to the overgrown churchyard stood a Welcome notice with the time of the weekly service, the vicar's name (T Gum) and a phone number. Saint Agatha's Church. Protestant.

Strachey glided the car along the narrow lane in front of the churchyard to the gate of the house next door, the only house within a hundred yards. A sign said 'The Vicarage'.

Strachey stepped out of the car and opened the white painted wooden gate. Looking along the drive she could see that this was no old original vicarage, no sixteen-bedroom Georgian manse. It was a 1950s bungalow.

Strachey drove up the drive, parked and walked towards the bungalow front door. Which opened. A woman, presumably the housekeeper, shook out a duster and smiled. She was clad in voluminous frock and apron.

Strachey said, 'I'm looking for the vicar.'

'Ye-es?'

'For the Reverend Gum.'

'My goodness,' the woman said. 'Just look at your skirt. Been in an accident?'

Strachey was uncomfortably aware of how damp she was, although not that there was blood smeared on her shin. 'I had a fall—' She was going to say at the mill but thought better of it. 'It's not as bad as it looks.'

'You didn't come through the ford?'

Strachey smiled disarmingly. 'I'm a stranger here.'

'You must be! Come in and we'll dry you off.'

As Strachey stepped inside, the woman frowned. 'That skirt would be better in the washing machine. Were you staying long?' She closed the door.

'It depends. Is the vicar in?'

'*I'm* the Reverend Gum.' She smiled, knowing it was unexpected. 'We're very modern round here.' She laughed. '*There's* the loo. Have a jolly good wash and take that skirt off. I'll find you something else to wear.' She opened another door. 'Not that you and I are the same size, but we're not expecting company, are we?'

The Reverend Gum was shorter than Strachey and the skirt she loaned fitted like a mini-skirt. But mini-skirts were created for girls like Strachey. The two women sat in the sitting room drinking hot chocolate. The Reverend Tina Gum was medium height, dark haired but freckled, in her early thirties. Strachey's face was bland: Clive had told her to seek out the vicar and Strachey had assumed the vicar would be a man. It was nice that the vicar *wasn't* a man, of course, but why had Clive not mentioned it? She eyed the Reverend Gum. A pleasant woman. No looker. So it wasn't that.

'Strachey's a curious name.'

Tina looked at her for a response.

'My given name is Jane, but everyone calls me Strachey.'

'And you prefer that?' Tina smiled. 'Surprising. Though Plain Jane you're not. Yes, we've been lucky – normally, the parish records only give part of what we need. Hexcombe ceased to exist for all practical purposes three hundred years ago.' She smiled again. 'Um, forgive me, I have to ask: are you the new um, Lady Thing?'

'Lady...?'

'You are, aren't you? Lady... Jane of Hexcombe.'

Strachey grinned. 'I'm afraid not.'

'Oh. Shame. You'd have been rather fun. That's what you've come about, though, isn't it?'

'You've met Clive?'

'*Lord* Clive? Lovely man.'

Their eyes met. Strachey smiled. 'Are people waiting to greet their new lord and lady?'

'Goodness no. Most people haven't heard of it – though there was a small piece in the local paper. I think someone wrote a letter but it's not exactly headline news. So you're not to be our lady?'

'No.'

'You're not... Lord Clive's wife?'

The Reverend studied her.

'I'm – a business acquaintance. I suppose it sounds pompous but I *represent* the new Lord of the Manor.'

Tina couldn't prevent a grin. 'Gosh. Have you brought a trumpet? – The *new* lord, you say? I thought Lord Clive... '

Strachey broke it to her gently. 'I'm afraid he has sold it.'

'But he's only just bought it!'

'I'm sorry.'

Tina looked sorry too. In a small voice – not like a Reverend at all – she said, 'He could have told me. I mean, I couldn't have stopped him or anything. Oh dear. He seemed such a nice man – he'd have been good for this little parish.'

Strachey smiled reassuringly. 'I'm sure the new lord will be even better. I wonder if I could ask you a few questions?'

Tina hooted. 'Ooh! You sound like the police. No, sorry Jane – I mean, Strachey – what do you need to know?'

'About the Manor. What it actually comprises – *where* it actually is. It isn't on the map.'

'How up to date was your map?'

'Well, I bought it at the airport—'

'Ah, that was a bit of a mistake. Road atlas, was it? Anything published after about 1650 tends to leave Hexcombe off. Even the earlier maps are rather vague.' She grinned. 'All is not lost, though. I'm a bit of a local historian, actually.'

'I know.'

'Well, it's harmless, isn't it? Better than killing butterflies and pinning their pretty little bodies onto cardboard – which was how vicars spent their evenings in Victorian times. Yes, only an amateur historian, of course, but I've always been keen. I was up to scratch on Hexcombe long before Lord Clive came down to ask about the Manor. I hold the parish records.'

Strachey nodded. 'The parish of Hexcombe?'

'Mm, though Hexcombe itself no longer exists. No, I cover several parishes – that's the way now in the country: not enough customers to warrant a vicar to every church. I have several parishes and they have me, poor things. On a Sunday, instead of holding four services in one church I hold one service in four different buildings. My busy day, of course. It must have been lovely in the old days when you lived next door to your office. You popped out, did early Communion, came in for breakfast, popped out for Matins, came in for lunch, had a little nap, popped out – you can imagine. Oh, I can dream. Now I spend all day beetling about country lanes, eating sandwiches in the car. Hard life, isn't it?'

She grinned. She was in full flow.

'My four parishes are Saint Agatha's – that's a benefice; I think it pays me four pounds a year, plus this house, more to the point – then Saint Andrew's, Saint Winifred's and Saint Bede's. Hexcombe Manor stretches nominally over bits of each: all of Saint Ag, plus Saint Bede's West and a kind of corner of Saint Winifred. It's quite big, but very rural. So, tell me about this new lord of ours. Is he rich?'

Strachey shrugged. 'American.'

'Hm. No surprise. Though that's not a *complete* description, is it?'

Strachey laughed. 'No, it's early days. I'm afraid I haven't actually met him. I was engaged on his behalf by Lord Clive.'

Tina studied her. 'Well, I look forward to getting to know this new lord of ours. He does intend to come?'

'I'm sure he does.'

'And play an active part in the life of the area?'

'Why not? I believe the title brings with it some sort of "bundle of rights"?'

'Ah yes, Lord Clive wanted to know about those rights, but I suspect a lordship is what you make of it – *duties* before rights. Yes, these new baronial lordships have become quite the thing in recent years, haven't they? Some new lords, though, play an active part in their new parish – endowing a village hall, for example, or contributing towards the repair of bells in the church. We could certainly do with some of that here.'

Tina looked at her hopefully for a response. Strachey said, 'I suppose there isn't any kind of actual Manor – a house?'

'Oh, nothing worth money. No, there's no real land, no – apart from the village.'

Strachey looked alert, but Tina said, 'Don't get excited.'

'I passed somewhere called Hexcombe Mill.'

Tina nodded. 'You were wise to pass it. Built 1814, extended 1820, went bankrupt the first time 1863. Staggered along fitfully as a business till 1931. Occasional tenants since. Though not recently, as you may have noticed.'

'Does it belong to the Manor?'

Tina pulled a sympathetic face. '*Nothing* belongs to the Manor. The *name* Hexcombe crops up here and there but it doesn't mean anything, I'm afraid.'

'You mentioned a village?'

'Oh yes. The ancient demesne of Hexcombe. You'll want to inspect it, I suppose?'

They took Strachey's car. She was relieved that they left via a different lane to the one she had arrived by – the *only* other lane – and after barely a couple of miles Tina told her to pull over. They were near the bottom of another narrow valley – a gulch, Strachey would have called it – in which a stone bridge stood across a stream and dark trees matted the valley sides.

Tina said, 'We have to walk from here.'

'There's no road to this village?'

'No.'

Tina waited beside the car while Strachey locked it. Strachey asked, 'The village does exist?'

'Since the thirteenth century and perhaps before. There's a charter description – that's the earliest record. Anyway, look, there *is* a kind of path.'

Leading from the bridge was a track into tangled trees. Strachey unlocked the car again: 'I brought some rubber boots.'

'And I thought you were a city girl.'

Tina was already clad in walking shoes. She said, 'While the car's open, can you hide that radio?'

'We're miles from anywhere.'

'Just makes it easier for the thieves. We get a lot of it round here: a car like yours – obviously a tourist. *My* car's dented and muddy – and I keep a crucifix in the window.'

Strachey was pulling on her boots. 'Holy protection?'

'So they'll know it's mine. I've nothing worth stealing, and the local lads probably think I'll put a curse on them.' She crossed her fingers in front of her face and hissed.

Strachey laughed. 'Avaunt! The curse of Dracula?'

'Much worse than that – I'm a woman priest.'

The path struggled through the trees and followed the meandering stream until it turned a bend in the hill and the trees thinned out. A second stream joined the first, and the two continued as one through a scrubby meadow. Tina paused before a rotting wooden footbridge. 'This is it,' she said.

Strachey was not surprised. 'This is the village?'

Tina nodded. 'You see the valley floor?'

The meadow was uneven, overgrown and dotted with hummocks, but the hills around formed a sheltering basin. On this summer's day the site looked pleasant enough – almost romantic – but it would hold mist and damp for perhaps eight months of the moorland year.

'There's water, you see,' Tina continued. 'So this is the kind of place you might pitch a camp.'

'Does it flood in winter?'

'It gets boggy, I wouldn't say flooded. But you're right – it's not the ideal place for a modern, bijou housing development. Did you ever read Lorna Doone? Warring families, rival gangs, smugglers? This is their country, around here.'

'Not here – the Doones lived on Exmoor.'

'Pedant. That kind of family, let's say.'

It was easy to imagine a robber gang hiding out in this

hidden valley, but it seemed an unlikely spot to make one's home.

Tina stepped onto the bridge. Despite her casual air she crossed it carefully. 'Hexcombe only seems isolated because we left the *modern* road and walked. But centuries ago the road came along this valley. The modern road may not have existed then, even as a path. We're standing on the old road now.'

Strachey had followed Tina across the bridge, and she looked doubtfully about her at the rough damp meadow. 'This path?'

'This is where the old thoroughfare would have been. There were no cars. People only needed a track. Britain had practically no roads you'd *call* roads before 1800, and Hexcombe existed at least four hundred years ago. It was a tiny village, and any *town* from that long ago is unrecognisable now. If you look about, you'll see signs of excavation.'

'Archaeologists?'

'Treasure seekers, more likely. Freaks with metal detectors. No one ever found anything – they wouldn't. Anyone who lived here would have been poorer than a rural vicar is today.' Tina bowed. 'The village failed because it was an unhealthy place – plague and pneumonia. Over the years local farmers took away useful bits of stone or building material – though the original cottages were probably made of cob, and that'll have melted back into the earth hundreds of years ago. Still, under these bumps you might find remains of ancient dwellings. Medieval.'

'This is all that remains of the Manor of Hexcombe?'

'No, no, this is just the village. It *was* the village. The Manor covers a much wider area – as I told you.'

'Does it include your churches?'

'Saint Ag's, Saint Winifred's? Yes, in a sense – but no, he doesn't own them. They belong to the Church Commissioners. Your Lord of the Manor might have the odd ancient right – in fact, I know he does. For instance, he can order a special peal of bells at Saint Winifred's on his birthday.'

Strachey pulled a wry face and Tina asked, 'But how much is *that* worth on the open market?'

5

STRACHEY HAD TAKEN a room at a local pub and was downstairs in the bar having her first hot meal of the day when Clive's call came through on her cell phone – no, she thought: back in England now, it's a mobile phone.

'Remember Lincoln Deane? I'm a guest at his house.'

'Good Lord.'

'He hopes to be. He hasn't bought the title yet but he's coming across.'

'With how much?'

'Coming to England, with a friend—'

'And *her* name?'

'A male friend – and having met *Mrs* Deane I'd say there's no chance Lincoln's gay. His friend – Maxwell Homeforth – claims to be coming for the ride. But *I* think Maxwell wants to sniff around the Manor himself.'

'As a detective or potential customer?'

'A buyer, I think – but he can't admit it because that would make him Lincoln's rival.'

'And *my* role while they're here?'

'Puff up the lordship. Find any way to make it seem grand. What d'you think of Hexcombe?'

'It doesn't exist, does it?'

'I wouldn't say that.'

'You must have realised when you bought it.'

'I was carried away. I'd read that the Lordship of Wimbledon went for a quarter of a million dollars so this one seemed a snip.'

'It isn't Wimbledon. No tennis courts.'

'No strawberries?'

'Not a pip. There's a ghost village – some wasteland beside a stream in the middle of nowhere – but nothing tangible. What did you expect for five-and-a-half thousand pounds?'

'Oh, not a lot. I was buying what they call an *incorporeal hereditament*, not the actual lands of the manor. But I'd rather we didn't emphasise that to Lincoln and his friend.'

Jeremy Barrington Downey had predicted an uneventful day. Most additions to the housing market arrived on Mondays, the owners having decided over the weekend to put their houses up for sale. Buyers emerged on Saturdays – a succession of straggling couples, harassed husbands, hopeful fiancées, weekend retreaters, the recently bereaved. Midweek was dull.

The blonde woman who strode in at nine-thirty was not dull. And with those looks, whether she was buying or selling she was guaranteed to get Jeremy's undivided attention. Pray God she hadn't come for a free map.

'I'm looking for property,' she said.

Yes!

He was already on his feet, his fingers gripping the edge of his desk to anchor him to reality. 'You've come to the right place.'

She waited. He asked, 'What kind of thing had you in mind?'

He knew what *he* had in mind.

She said, 'Something upscale.'

'Up*scale*?'

'Upmarket, sorry.'

'No, no, *my* fault. Of course. Upscale. Yes, in*deedy*.' He coughed. 'Something upscale.'

He made as if to move from behind his wooden desk but decided to hang onto it a little longer. 'Had you a price in mind?'

She shrugged. 'Depends on the place.'

'Yes, yes, of course.'

He sensed his face was fixed in a grin, so he glanced at the New Property file on his desk.

'Bedrooms?' he asked faintly.

'Preferably.'

He looked up. She smiled. 'Of course,' he mumbled – then, gaining confidence: 'Better begin at the beginning, eh?' He had to clear his throat again. 'What was the name?'

'Strachey.'

'Str – a – chey.' He was writing it down. '*Mrs* Strachey?'

'Miss.'

Sunlight glowed in the office. He managed: 'First name?'

'Just call me Strachey.' Their eyes met.

He nodded. 'Miss. Just 'Miss Strachey'. No first name?'

'Not even a 'Miss'. Just Strachey. After all, we're not on first-name terms yet.' She smiled. 'We haven't been formally introduced.'

He gulped. 'You must call me Jeremy.'

'Not Mr Downey? I saw the sign outside.'

'That's me.'

'I always like to deal with the man in charge.' It was a description that sent a small charge of electricity through his loins. 'Let's talk about your... upscale properties.'

It felt strange to receive calls from Clive late afternoon – his day just beginning, his demeanour that of a man just out of bed – when her day was closing after a solid eight hours viewing properties, inspecting sites, learning the lie of the local landscape. It emphasised the difference in the contribution they each made – Strachey working hard in the English countryside, Clive in Californian sun.

'Things are moving,' he said. 'As soon as I announced an auction date it shocked the punters into action. Three more have booked tickets for England.'

'Three more! They're not arriving together?'

'Within a day or two of each other. It won't be a problem, darling.'

Strachey frowned. Clive didn't normally call her Darling. He said, 'Let 'em stumble over each other. At this stage the more competition the better.'

'Who else is coming?'

'A Mr Cantabulet, a Mr and Mrs Nibbet, and Mr Delarme. There may be more eventually. Where are you staying?'

'In a pub – unless we can afford better?'

'*Is* there better?'

'Not really. It's quite a quaint pub – the Sickle and Hoe. Where will *they* stay?'

'God knows. I don't think they should know you're in a pub.'

'Give them my mobile number. I'll stay elusive.'

'They may want an address.'

'They can write me care of the Vicarage of Saint Agatha's.'

'That has a better ring. Can't you *stay* there?'

'Not unless I'm homeless and destitute. The Americans could stay at the Copthorne or the Moat House down in Plymouth.'

'That's *seaside*, darling. We must *bury* them in the country.'

'Those are the only four-stars for a hundred miles. There are a couple of decent Country House Hotels, but some way away.'

'Why is England such a dump?'

'Hotels are not our strong suit.'

'Darling, don't make things so difficult.'

'Don't call me darling.'

Lincoln Deane and his friend Maxwell Homeforth duly arrived – barely an hour and a half behind Mr and Mrs Walter Nibbet, a diminutive couple from Nantucket who Strachey vaguely remembered from the early days of her relationship with Clive. Strachey had chosen the neutral venue of Buckland Abbey, an impressive National Trust tourist site some distance from the Manor of Hexcombe – a little awkward to find but shown on all the maps. Unlike Hexcombe. Lincoln and Maxwell arrived to find the Nibbets thoroughly at home at Buckland. The charmingly dotty couple treated the whole jaunt as a glorified theme holiday and would have been perfectly happy to tour the medieval demesne with two dozen rival bidders in an air-conditioned coach. Lincoln and Maxwell seemed as guarded as a visiting baseball team.

'Any more for any more?' Walter Nibbet kept asking, while his wife took Lincoln and Maxwell Homeforth aside to assure the two men that she had no prejudice against homosexuals and thought all men and women were created equal under the Lord. She also thought baldness becoming.

Fortunately, the Nibbets had hired a huge Toyota four-wheel drive space wagon with eight adult-size seats and a refrigerator – so they were the obvious choice to act as chauffeurs for the day. Already converted to the Abbey's charms, the Nibbets urged Lincoln and Maxie (as Mrs Nibbet called him) to look around. Lincoln was willing but Maxwell muttered that he thought it was a ploy to leave them behind. It had been a long journey and he found England cold, damp and crowded.

'Supposed to be a tiny island,' he grumbled. 'Took us six goddamn hours to get here.'

Lincoln shrugged. 'My fault. Thought I'd check out Hexcombe on the way, but we didn't find it. Hey!' He turned to Strachey. 'Bet you know it like the back of your hand?'

'Mr Cantabulet should be here any moment. Why not have a coffee?'

Maxwell said he'd heard about English coffee and he'd go without.

Strachey asked, 'Have you ever been inside an English stately home?'

Mrs Nibbet jumped in: 'That's what this place is – this Buckland Abbey, you know? It's a home for British aristocracy. Walter and I went around already. You must see it, Maxie, how they live.'

'You've been *around*?' Maxwell frowned. 'You pay to get in?'

'Oh, you can afford it.'

'Of course I can afford it,' Maxwell snapped. 'But I didn't come here to drag around an aristocratic freak show.'

Lincoln was wavering. 'You mean, you got real aristocrats living here? We could meet them?'

'I did,' declared Mrs Nibbet. (God knows whom she'd met.) 'And they've got a wonderful shop.'

'A shop!' spat Maxwell.

'That's *right*,' said Walter, fumbling in a plastic bag. 'They have real antiques. I *think* they're antiques – they're clean and come in boxes – but look.' He produced a National Trust wine goblet. 'See, it's engraved. That's a family crest.'

Maxwell snorted, but Lincoln leant forward and eyed it eagerly. 'Hey, a family crest – how old is that?'

'I bought some soap,' said Mrs Nibbet.

'A family wine goblet,' breathed Lincoln Deane. 'I gotta have some of that.'

Walter said, 'And there's *English* wine! Would you credit that?'

Lincoln was astounded. 'English wine! You're putting me on. That, baby, I have got to see.'

Mr Cantabulet missed the National Trust afternoon tea – or was made to miss it. He arrived at Buckland just as the party were licking scraps of Devon cream from their fingers. (Lincoln, since he wouldn't be driving again, had sampled English wine.) Under normal circumstances, Cantabulet might have been allowed to snatch a late cup of Twinings with a date-and-walnut slice, but he had two things against him: one, he was a rival bidder and two, he'd offended the traditions of English tea by having them *paged*. A bemused National Trust volunteer, a woman thin and fifty, had edged into the restaurant to tinkle a brass handbell (National Trust Gift Shop: £19.95) and call tremulously, 'Mr and Mrs Strachey?'

Cantabulet's arrival did not help the party feel more at ease. He was a slender 42-year-old dressed in sharp young clothes – a stock trader from New York – with dark, slickened hair and hard, piercing eyes. A professional buyer. He interrogated Lincoln and Maxwell for twenty seconds, ignored the Nibbets, then spent the rest of his time watching Strachey. Lincoln tried to strike up a conversation about wine investments but got nowhere. When the party moved to the Toyota, Cantabulet went straight to the front passenger seat – Mrs Nibbet's – and sat glaring at the others as if they were late. Maxwell told him he was sitting in Strachey's seat and since she was guiding he'd have to move. It was a battle of wills that Maxwell won. And when Strachey gave up the seat to Mrs Nibbet, saying she could guide perfectly well from a window seat, Maxwell's smile grew broader. He proceeded to work a flanker with Lincoln, each of them getting into the space wagon from different sides so that Cantabulet was forced into a central seat, hemmed in between the two Californians. Maxwell's eyes were gleaming now. Strachey had the back row to herself.

The Toyota trundled along the Devon lanes, passing a rambling stone farmhouse of some age. 'Older than any building in America,' Strachey remarked.

Then she showed the party around the churches. She explained that Saint Agatha's, Saint Winifred's and Saint Bede's were parish churches within the Manor of Hexcombe, and she allowed her passengers to misinterpret that as best they may. Cantabulet noted down details of each building as if making an inventory, and at strategic moments Maxwell took the opportunity to jog his arm.

Strachey had them inspect tombstones in the graveyards, though few of the dates preceded the nineteenth century. She led them into the churches, had them soak up the atmosphere and read cyclostyled leaflets that gave the history of each building. One dated from Norman times. Pieces of stonework went back hundreds of years, and the air smelt musty enough to have been Norman. Cantabulet fingered the altar cloth and inspected the shining brass decorations. Then he turned round and complained of the cold.

Maxwell sneered. 'You feeling the effects?'

'It's chilly.'

'It's jet-lag and the six-hour drive from Heathrow.'

Cantabulet looked disdainful. 'You drove from Heathrow?'

'We surely weren't coming down by train!'

'Why Heathrow?' asked Cantabulet. 'You can fly straight into Bristol. Two hours away.'

Actually, it was nearer three, but he enjoyed the look of horror on Maxwell's face as he recalled every minute of that six-hour drive. It put a new bounce in Cantabulet's step: Californian hick.

Strachey let her guests dwell over Saint Winifred's and Saint Bede's so that by the time they reached Saint Agatha's she was able to hurry them by. If possible, she wanted to keep the party away from Tina Gum – away, indeed, from anyone who might be surprised to find that the recently transferred local lordship was up for auction. And although it might not be true that once you've seen one church you've seen them all, once you've seen two churches you tend to be cursory with the third. Strachey found it no problem to move her patrol on from Saint Agatha's without meeting the vicar from the bungalow next door. It was late afternoon and the Americans were beginning to feel the effects of their overnight flights. They needed little persuasion to locate their hotels and settle in.

No visit to England would be complete without meeting the locals – preferably a typical Englishman, and preferably one with a name like Jeremy Barrington Downey. Preferably also somewhere grand. Strachey had been unimpressed with Jeremy's office, so the following morning she had him come out to meet her party at another National Trust venue, Cotehele – out of their way but larger than Buckland. To the Nibbets, Cotehele was a palace and Mrs Nibbet was all for a two-hour tour. No one was unimpressed by Cotehele – they *couldn't* be – but they had to press on. Jeremy suggested a compromise: morning tea.

Strachey hadn't explained her relationship to this party of rich Americans but as far as Jeremy was concerned she was a gift horse – into whose mouth he might look later. *They* wanted to look at property. The Americans insisted on calling him a *real* estate agent – 'As opposed to a false one?' he asked disastrously, wasting the next five minutes re-establishing his credentials – but the key thing was that he was the *only* estate agent they had met so far. They glanced at the prospectuses of his finest houses, asked about 'facilities' and seemed keen to view. Mr Cantabulet asked why he hadn't brought a video. Mrs Nibbet asked if 'this nice Cotehele' might come up for sale – but then burst into giggles and confessed it was only a joke. She wasn't that naive. She and her husband thought it very funny.

Cantabulet had been ignoring the chat and was skimming through a Cotehele guidebook. Suddenly he smacked the table with it and cried, 'D'you see what it says here? Listen. "The number of visitors to this small and fragile house has to be limited to no more than 80 at any one time. There is *no electric light* in the rooms, so visitors should avoid dull days early and late in the season." No electric *light*?'

Strachey said, 'It's how life used to be,' and Downey overlapped with an urgent assurance that none of *his* properties were without electric light.

'No electric light?' Lincoln echoed. He found it funny.

Maxwell said, 'My grandpa served in England during the war. He could tell you tales.'

Jeremy pointed out that at this time of day there wouldn't have been any lights on anyway, so the place would look perfectly normal. He appeared calm but was beginning to see the difficulty of keeping the group in order. A well-known phrase containing the words 'barrel' and 'monkeys' rattled in his head.

Devon lunch: thick-cut chunks of good white bread, slabs of cheese, brown chutney, pickled onions, salad garnish, pint glass mugs of malty beer. Wooden tables scattered across a dappled lawn outside the pub. Five men and two women sprawling in the sun. Groups of holidaymakers at the tables. Occasional cars drawing up. Overheard scraps of conversation. Bursts of laughter. Americans peering at property brochures. Jeremy Downey wondering if they are serious. Buyers glaring at their rivals. Jane Strachey watching as the essential Englishness of the day charms itself into their bones. Mrs Nibbet asking what a chipolata is. Mr Nibbet laughing.

A distant motorist, a hundred miles into his journey, glaring fixedly at the road ahead. He has chosen to drop below the main east-west M4 motorway and cut across country on a historic route: Andover, Amesbury, the Salisbury Plain, Wincanton and Ilchester (by which point his eyes have glazed). Wisely, he pauses in this old wayside town, dirty with history, for a cheese sandwich and a glass of milk. The long flight has begun to take its toll. He stretches his legs in the steep streets of the town, then reluctantly, just as Jeremy

Downey is gathering his property prospectuses and shepherding rival purchasers back to the Toyota, Edgar Delarme climbs into his hired car and ploughs further westward, first to Ilminster, then to Honiton, where signposts point temptingly to Axminster and quaint Ottery St Mary. But he ignores distractions and continues on. He is in Devon now. Exeter he bypasses. His road sweeps along the northern fringe of Dartmoor until, near Okehampton, he turns south. The county of Devon looks small on the map, yet feels as large as many an American state. He is cutting down the western edge of Dartmoor. He is weary, but so close to his destination it would be a weakness to stop. He cannot avoid the ancient market town of Tavistock, so he grinds through but ignores its charms. He should have stopped, for the insides of his eyelids are dry as sandpaper. And now he must leave the relatively clear main roads and guide his car through those narrow Devon lanes.

It is late afternoon.

Lincoln stared at the huge, empty, inglenook fireplace. 'Could do something with that.'

Because the farmhouse had been uninhabited for several months it felt forlorn and cold. The furniture had gone – but Strachey thought that was probably a good thing: it allowed the viewers to picture their own pieces here instead of whatever lumpy monstrosities had belonged to the previous occupier. Devon sheep farmers don't have the same tastes as rich Americans.

– Who by now had had enough of their second day. They trudged behind Jeremy through the empty house, peering out of dusty windows, every one tight-lipped and wishing the others weren't along. The Nibbets would have preferred sight-seeing and Cantabulet was annoyed he couldn't get a response from his cell phone. Lincoln tried to be positive: 'That fire would take some man-size logs – and there's plenty of trees around here.'

Maxwell laughed. 'You don't seriously see yourself felling trees? Listen, if you want a mountain lodge, buy a real one back home – with a wood-burning stove and central heating. A plunge pool, games room, satellite TV, fishing, deer shooting, all you like. The only damn animals around here are cows and sheep.'

Lincoln was poking inside an empty wall cupboard. He had a smudge of dirt on his bald head. 'If you knocked this room through to the other you could make this whole space into a dance floor.'

'*Dance* floor? You don't dance.'

'You see those Merchant Ivory movies? You know, that Jane Austen, Bronte stuff? The new master moves in, he holds a ball – invites all the neighbors.'

'Oh yeah, some loveable old guy turns up with three unmarried daughters? That was the eighteenth century, Linc.'

'It's how things are done.'

'What's Gloria going to say if you start waltzing around with these unmarried daughters?'

'She could get to meet a guy in tights.'

'Get real, for Chrissake, Linc. It's a pipe dream.'

A little later, Strachey took Lincoln aside. 'I'm worried about Maxwell,' she said. 'He seems so negative. Does that seem odd to you?'

'He's always negative.'

'There might be more to it. Why did he come all this way with you just to be negative?'

'It's how he is.'

'I hope you're right, Lincoln. You obviously know him best. I just wondered – no, forget it.'

She looked embarrassed – as well she might: 'Forget it' is one of the oldest lines and never fails. 'Forget what?' he asked predictably.

'No, no, it doesn't matter. I shouldn't have told you.'

'Told me what?'

'Well... Hasn't it ever occurred to you that he might be trying to put you off?'

'He spends his whole life trying to put me off. You should've heard him when I married Gloria.'

'I mean put you off all this.'

'This house? That won't be difficult.'

'The whole idea. Only one of you can acquire the lordship. Perhaps he... '

Strachey shrugged as meaningfully as she could.

Lincoln chuckled. 'Maxwell doesn't want the lordship!'

'Is that what he told you?'

'He doesn't have to tell me. Why – did he tell you something different?'

'I shouldn't have spoken.'

She moved away.

The reverend Tina Gum was wearing trousers. She had hauled a

large and rickety wooden stepladder into the church and was
perched on it, a bale of coloured cloth across her shoulder, tacks
between her teeth, a sturdy hammer tucked in her belt, and was
attempting to fix the cloth to a batten that ran along the side of
the Lady Chapel. It was a fiddly job. As long as she kept the
weight of the cloth supported across her shoulders and on top of
the stepladder, she could arrange the hem of the cloth along the
batten, tacking as she went, hoping that the weight of the long
embroidered banner was not too much for the one-inch tacks. She
hammered each tack part way in, leaving the heads clear of the
material for when she had to take the banner down. Plenty of
tacks, that was the secret, to distribute the weight. Unfortunately,
the base material, imitation silk – was flimsy and given to
snagging on the tacks. If the material pulled, it tore around the
tack holes, and the material did pull because the various heraldic
devices appliquéd onto it were scattered unevenly on the cloth. In
places their combined weight made the banner sag.

The batten was of ancient oak – a fine piece of wood in its
own right but not best suited to this task. In places, the oak was
as hard as stone, while elsewhere it was pitted with old holes.
Apart from this, there were a number of old nails left from
centuries of use, and what with one thing and another, a simple
job like tacking material became surprisingly vexatious.

Or it was to Tina. Not the most able of handywomen – though
more adept than Mrs Hargreave, who came each day to arrange
the flowers – Tina had found that since taking the living at this
rural parish, her knowledge of basic carpentry and household
maintenance had developed greatly. She was forever making minor
repairs to her four churches. Even the vicarage, though a modern
bungalow, seemed jerry-built. Any repair she could not manage
herself, or which could not be scrounged as a favour from the
dwindling band of supporting tradespeople, was a drain on the
meagre allowance she received – and that money, in Tina's opinion,
could be spent in far better ways than on the maintenance of God's
house. Or *houses*, she corrected herself – what did He want with
four houses in this sparsely populated parish? Even at Christmas or
Harvest Festival the congregations at all four combined filled barely
half the smallest one. Everybody *drove* to church anyway, so let
them drive a bit further. If this was a business, she thought, we'd
rationalise – close down the uneconomic units and concentrate our
marketing on a smaller hub. Though if this was a business, she

continued – she was muttering to herself now – we'd close the whole thing down: sell out to a chain of rural bingo halls. Keep a few cathedrals in big towns – charge admission, let them out to film companies making costume dramas, televise the biggest services – and we'd *sell* all the rest of the property and invest the proceeds in good works. We could run the whole business more rationally on the Internet: www.easychurch.com – a hyperlink to God. Say a prayer in cyberspace.

She had finished now. She eased the material off her shoulder, the main weight still supported on the step ladder, then began pushing it forward in a great looped bale of cloth, watching the tacked hem for signs of strain, until finally the whole 144 square feet of material dangled in the air. On its laddered blue background a garishly coloured multitude of childlike cutouts had been embroidered, appliquéd, and even glued, between the words 'National Federation of Mothers' Unions. Parish of Hexcombe. Saint Agatha's. Saint Andrew's. Saint Winifred's. Saint Bede's.' A hopeful postscript along the bottom claimed, 'The Hand That Rocks The Cradle Rules The World'.

The banner had been assembled over the last three years by half a dozen dogged old ladies of the parish. Each year it gained extra emblems. In the first year, 'Saint Andrew's' had been left off because there was no old lady in that part of the parish to take the responsibility of stitching the name, and it was only after a great deal of grumbling and cajolery that it had been added in the second year. The pictorial emblems were a source of perpetual dissent and rivalry. To the one who made it, each embroidered device carried deep significance, almost as if they were family pennants or standards for the clan-like districts of the scattered parish. For Tina, and for practically anyone other than the six old ladies, the appended devices had no significance at all – perhaps because the standard of needlework meant that it was impossible to see what most of them were meant to be.

Tina patted the cloth gently to soften the folds.

A voice behind her boomed, 'As is the mother, so is her daughter.'

Tina turned too quickly, slipped, and had to clutch the handrail of her stepladder. She saw a tall, bearded man in the aisle. He added, 'Ezekial, sixteen forty-four.'

She gave a humouring smile. 'I've never been hot on quotations.'

His own smile was ingratiating. 'Motherhood is a state of holiness.'

She paused. 'Not Ezekial.'

'Not a quotation. Just my own words.'

She nodded. We have a right one here, she thought: I'll stay on the ladder.

'However,' he said. 'A man shall leave his father and his mother, and shall cleave unto his wife. They shall be one flesh.'

'Genesis,' Tina said unwisely.

The man brightened. 'You know your bible? But of course, we are in God's house.'

She smiled inanely. How long can I stay up here?

'You *are* a mother?' he asked.

'Well, no, actually.'

He looked beyond her at the banner. 'Helping *your* mother.'

'Helping six old ladies, actually. They were supposed to have finished it for Mothering Sunday.' She smiled. 'They finish later every year.'

'The old ladies work for Hexcombe Mothers' Union?'

She could hear it now: he was American. Explained a lot. She started to descend the steps. 'The old ladies *are* the Mothers' Union. Real mothers are too busy looking after the kids.' She had reached the floor. 'Still, they were mothers *once*. Some of them were. Have you come to look at the church?'

He nodded. 'All of them.' He glanced around. 'Over-decorated, of course. I don't mean your banner – that's the handiwork of the faithful – but this is an over-decorated church.'

'You think so?'

'High church?'

'Good lord, no. They don't come much lower, actually. All of what?'

'Hm?'

'You've come to look at all of *what* churches?'

'The churches of Hexcombe Manor.'

Tina eyed him differently. 'Ah. You're... ' She raised a quizzical eyebrow. 'You're not... by any chance... '

He held her gaze. 'I guess I am.'

'Oh, my goodness! The new Lord?'

'Of Hexcombe Manor? Yes.'

'Well, I didn't mean Lord of all creation!' She laughed.

Delarme tried the phrase – actually, he'd tried the phrase many times, but this was the first time aloud on English soil: 'Lord of the Manor of Hexcombe.'

It seemed appropriate to curtsey, and Tina did. She wasn't proud.

Delarme said, 'Now, tell me – where can I find the vicar of this church?'

Strachey had hoped that when she finally got rid of the squabbling visitors she could collapse at the pub for a quiet evening in front of the log fire. The pub lit its fire ten months of the year – partly to please tourists and partly because in the deep Devon valley the evenings grew cold. But she couldn't shake Jeremy. He claimed that he needed to talk business, to review the day and discuss which of 'her Americans' might become interested enough to buy some property. This justified a pint of warm beer in the Sickle And Hoe and gave him the opportunity to suggest they continue over dinner. Strachey asked where he had in mind and Jeremy blew his chance by suggesting they ate here, at the Sickle and Hoe. She agreed only to another drink.

'Good pub, this,' he said unconvincingly. 'When you suggested the Sickle I thought, here's a girl who knows a decent pub. Knows her way around.' He leered uncomfortably. 'You're not local, though?'

'Afraid not.'

'Yet your American clients rely on you as – er – the fount of all knowledge. Where *are* you from?'

'*You're* the fount of knowledge, Jeremy. You know the properties.'

He hesitated. 'If we do make a sale, I suppose your clients will pay you a fee?'

'And you're wondering how much *you'll* have to give me as a placement fee?'

He chuckled manfully. 'That's not the way we do business here in England.'

'I *am* English, Jeremy.'

'But you're not an estate agent. If you were we might split the commission, but since you're acting as agent for the buyers you are, in effect, the buyer yourself—'

'One per cent.'

'Pardon?'

'We'll take one per cent of the purchase price.'

She'd expected him to haggle but he homed in on: '*We'll* take – who exactly is *we*?'

'My company,' she said vaguely. Best not to mention Clive yet.

Jeremy said, 'We're only on one-and-a-half per cent ourselves.'

'You're sole agent?'

He nodded guardedly. She said, 'You're on more.'

'Sadly not. I suppose… if we *had* to pay a placement fee – which is most irregular – we might stretch to fifteen per cent.'

'Per cent of what?'

'Our own fee.'

'Fifteen per cent of one-and-a-half per cent? You seriously expect us to act for nought point two two five per cent – a few hundred pounds? It wouldn't pay the air fare, Jeremy.'

'You're quick at maths, aren't you? But this isn't America. Commissions on property are very low.' He chuckled again. 'I don't know how we make a living.'

'One per cent of the gross or no deal.'

He shook his head and chuckled as if humouring a child. But Strachey wasn't sure what they *would* earn from property. Clive had told her to find out what was on the market and to gauge reactions. 'See which place stands out,' he'd said. But why? She had become accustomed to following Clive's instructions. Strachey, who was normally so self-reliant, so comfortably in control, had allowed the suave con man to set the rules and make decisions. She had parked her own powers of critical analysis and had subordinated herself to him.

'You're playing games with me,' said Jeremy.

'Mhm?'

Jeremy was right. A game *was* being played. The game she knew about – selling the lordship at a hugely inflated profit – was not the only game in town. Clive had casually mentioned the property angle and Strachey, in her new unquestioning role, had assumed she was merely helping the potential lords to *see* themselves in place. If she showed them property, they could imagine themselves living there. Lords of the Manor.

Jeremy said, 'I'm rather good at games.'

'What *do* you mean?'

He wore a knowing smile. 'This 'looking at property' thing is eyewash, isn't it? You're having me on. You're playing a game, Miss Strachey, but I think it's time to deal me in.'

She downed her drink in one. 'Thanks for the drink.'

He placed a hand upon her arm. 'Not so fast. Where are you staying?'

Good, she thought – he doesn't know I'm staying here. 'With friends.'

'Anyone I know? Because I know everyone – it's my business. I bet you've got a nice little hotel room somewhere. Single, I assume?'

'Maybe I'm sleeping with Mr Cantabulet.'

He studied her. 'Maybe you're coming to dinner with me. I know some places. Or we could grab a bottle and go back to my house.'

'No, thanks.'

'You shouldn't spend the evening alone.'

'I'm tired.'

What's the matter with me, she wondered. I don't usually have trouble shaking men off. I don't usually get ensnared in this kind of irritating conversation. What has happened to me?

'Don't worry,' she said. 'One of my clients might buy one of your properties—'

He had his hand wrapped around her wrist again: 'The office is closed now,' he said. 'We're not talking property. We're discussing how we're going to spend the rest of this fine evening.'

If Mickey could see me, she thought – unable to get rid of a bar-fly. Mickey used to call me the Snow Queen, until he knew me better – until I became his Ice Princess. She said, 'I'm leaving now.'

Jeremy tightened his grip. She tensed. Aim for his throat, she thought: one chop.

They stared at each other. Then they heard a woman's voice: 'Miss Strachey – I thought I might find you here.'

They turned.

It took her a moment to recognise the dark-haired, freckled woman in her early thirties – who had already turned to Jeremy Barrington Downey: 'Well, well, Jeremy, I hope I'm not interrupting anything?'

She gave them a broad smile.

Downey nodded. 'Reverend.'

Tina raised her eyebrows. 'Reverend! That's very formal. Things all right, Miss Strachey?'

Tina's expression suggested that she suspected things might
not be.

'Absolutely fine,' said Strachey. 'If it weren't such a corny line
I'd say that Mr Downey was just leaving.'

For a brief moment they stood in tableau, then Jeremy
bowed, said goodbye and left.

Strachey muttered, 'Saved by the Fifth Cavalry.'

Tina grinned. 'Nobody clears a room faster than a vicar.
Fancy another drink?'

They had a corner table. Strachey found it amusing that she
should have been rescued by another woman – a vicar – until she
found herself subject to a second interrogation. Tina leant
forward on her wooden bar chair, her eyes bright and fixed on
Strachey, and said, 'You weren't quite open with me.'

'In what way?'

'You said you had come in advance of the new Lord of our
Manor. But he's already here.'

'Here?'

Strachey was obviously surprised, so Tina raised her pot of
beer and took a manly draught. 'Called on me this afternoon.'

Strachey frowned.

Tina continued: 'Can't say he's exactly what I'd hoped for.
Hellfire and damnation.'

Strachey stared.

'Your man is an old testament prophet. Stood ranting at me
through that great black beard of his: a woman preacher is an
abomination. You didn't tell me our lord was a fruit and nut
case.' Tina glanced around the near empty bar. 'Our temporal
lord, I mean.'

'I'm... bemused,' said Strachey. No point hiding it.

'You know what he's like. You have *met* the man?'

Strachey nodded vaguely. 'What exactly did he say?'

'The Lord's house needs no graven images – he means the
Lord *Jesus's* house, I take it. *Your* lord was wearing Gucci
shoes.'

'Gucci?'

'I may not be able to afford them, but I can read the logo.
Oh, he knows his bible. Quoted whole passages at me: fire and
brimstone, whips and scorpions. Might go down a treat on
Sundays, but he's not my type. We used to get them in

theological college but I always hoped they wouldn't escape into the outside world. They give the church a bad name.'

Strachey was beginning to realise who Tina had seen. 'Was he wearing a dog collar?'

'No – and nor was I. That didn't help matters. I was in my working clothes, hanging a banner, so he thought I was the decorator.'

Strachey smiled.

'My being a church warden or the vicar's wife would have been all right – but the vicar, no. Against the teachings of Lord Jesus Christ – and Saint Paul, when he was going through his sunstroke period. It's old ground, this – we could have kept it up for hours. The disciples, you see, were *men*. When Jesus told them to go out and spread the gospel he used words like men and father, but those were figures of speech. We are all 'mankind'. But your Mr Delarme believes in literal interpretations of the bible – dangerous ground – so to him the Lord's work is for men.'

'Delarme,' Strachey murmured.

'A woman's role in life, apparently, is to be a fruitful vine. You could have warned me, Strachey.'

'Hm.' What was best, she wondered. 'Mr Delarme is ahead of himself.' Tina tilted her head. 'He is not the lord.'

'There's a reply to that – but go on.'

'I don't quite know how to put this. Mr Delarme merely *hopes* to be Lord of Hexcombe. It's... um... it's not decided yet.'

Tina frowned. 'But the title was sold. Went for five-and-a half thousand at auction.'

'You didn't tell him that?'

'No.' Tina stared at her. 'Isn't he the man it was bought for?'

Strachey shook her head. 'How did you know it went for five and a half thousand? Does everybody know?'

'Oh, no. I only found out because I was involved originally. Hang on, Strachey, don't tell me – Mr Delarme doesn't know how much Clive bought it for... You're going to sell it at a profit.' Tina shook her head but she didn't seem appalled. 'Have you sold it to him yet?'

'No.'

Tina leant forward. 'Please find someone else. Don't lumber me with Delarme. Sell it to one of those other nice Americans.'

Strachey stared. 'Which Americans?'

'That group of tourists you've been showing round. I saw
you from the window when you were pointing out Saint
Agatha's. Mrs Hargreave saw you lead them round Saint Bede's.'
Tina narrowed her eyes. 'I may not be a Catholic, but I'll take
confession. Come on, girl, get it off your chest. You're selling the
lordship, aren't you?'

Strachey nodded.

'For a handsome profit?'

Strachey shrugged.

'Now listen, Strachey, let me tell you the rules of confession.
You have to speak to me. You can't sit there like a naughty
child, shrugging your shoulders and staring at the floor. You
have to say the words – to express and declare your sin.
Understand me? Now, repeat after me: I am selling the Lordship
of Hexcombe.'

Strachey glanced around the pub. No one was watching them
or paying any attention. It was as if the vicar's presence had
banished them to the other end of the bar. 'You're right,' she
said.

'Say the words.'

'I am selling the Lordship of Hexcombe Manor.'

'For?'

'Whatever I can get for it.'

'A lot more than five-and-a-half thousand?'

'Yes.'

Tina tutted. 'Aren't people mad? – No, really. To think that
they'll pay all this for a title and some tattered bits of
parchment. It's not a real lordship, you know? It never had a
seat in the House of Lords.'

'It *is* a real lordship – in a sense.'

Tina shook her head. 'Strachey, I'm ashamed of you. You're
peddling dreams. So come on – how much do you think you'll get?'

'I really don't know. Until after the auction.'

Tina hooted. 'Auction! Well, at least you've made confession.
Now, what should be your penance?' She leant forward. 'Should
I tell the police?'

'No,' said Strachey, smiling. 'You're bound by the sanctity of
the confessional.'

Tina spread her hands. 'But *I'm* not a Catholic. And the
Sickle and Hoe is hardly a confessional.'

'The Lord is everywhere.'

Tina threw a beer mat at her. 'Don't trade theology with me! The point is, I can't tell the police because you haven't actually broken the law. What should I do?'

Strachey waited meekly.

'I'll do a deal,' the vicar said. 'Mr Delarme is a no-no. But with the others – apart from any more religious freaks – you can go ahead and sell it to the highest bid.' She smiled. 'In fact, I might even help – just to make sure that it goes to some wonderfully rich American, someone who can be persuaded to spend lots of money on the improvement of his Manor. What d'you think of that?'

Tina's eyes twinkled.

Strachey hid her surprise. 'Do I have a choice?'

6

FRANKIE DI STEFANO turned from the window of his Garden City office and glared at the smooth man in the suit. 'What am I – some kinda hoodlum?'

'Gary Stitz was a hoodlum.'

Sunlight behind him masked Frankie's face, and the same sunlight illuminated the seated man's suit, picking out the subtle colors in the wool and glinting on the buttons, clarifying for anyone who doubted that this was a very expensive suit indeed. A man from the mayor's office had no right to be wearing such a suit. He said, 'Young man gunned down. Could've been a tragedy if he wasn't a hoodlum.'

'Kids get gunned down every day.'

'We want to stamp it out. It's on our ticket, reducing violent crime.'

Frankie snorted. 'Pick a battle you can win, that's my advice.'

'Stitz was trespassing on your territory.'

'Who told you that? The kid had hardly learned to walk.'

'Common knowledge, Frankie.'

Di Stefano narrowed his eyes. He was wondering which of the men around the Captain Nemo pool might have been so unwise as to have opened his mouth. The visitor – no, let's name him: his visit might have been covert but the man himself was not anonymous. Luther Bloch (no less) replied, 'You won't like this, Frankie. We got it from the press.'

'A journalist!' Frankie shouted. 'What's his name?'

'Three journalists. It's gone to press. Everyone knows there was a feud between you two guys.'

'A feud? Gary Stitz was a nobody, an insect. You don't have a feud with some mosquito nips your cheek.'

'You squash it, right?'

Frankie exhaled and moved in from the window.

Luther continued: 'No paper's going to say you swatted the guy—'

'I'd sue 'em.'

Luther laughed. 'One way to get you into court.'

Frankie stared at him. 'Think I wouldn't? Think I'm scared?'

'Might be wise to be.' Luther shrugged. 'I guess they'll skate around it – you know, print your name but not actually say you did for him. Maybe put an account of his death beside your photo – business rival, that sort of thing.'

'I'll sue.'

'Where'd you get this appetite for suing, Frankie? It's a mug's game. If you want to throw your money away, give it to the re-election fund!'

'I gave already.'

'And we're grateful.' Luther straightened his silk tie. 'We don't want you mixed up in a scandal.'

'*You* don't want it?'

'There could be questions.'

'I know how to handle reporters.'

'I'm thinking police.'

'Tell 'em to back off.'

Luther chuckled. 'Yeah, like I *have* that much power. You have a story ready?'

'I got an alibi.'

'That's some defense, Frankie – the cops tell you Gary Stitz is dead and you shoot back with "I got an alibi". You don't know when he was done. Hell, you don't even know *how* he was done. All you know is what you've read in the papers. No, you gotta play dumb and say you know nothing about it. Because, of course, you *don't* know anything about it. Do you?'

'I wasn't there.'

'Where?'

'At the—' Frankie caught himself. 'Don't play the DA with me, Mr Bloch.'

Luther shook his head. 'Listen Frankie, I shouldn't be here today.'

'Why not – you can't visit a friend? I ain't respectable?'

'The cops are coming.'

'They are?'

'You're in the papers, Frankie. They have to call.'

'I gotta talk to the *cops*?'

'You're respectable, aren't you? The cops are good guys, on *our* side.'

'I wish.'

'All you have to do is stay shtumm. And polite.'

'And that won't make them suspicious? I've knowed these guys all my life.'

'You're reformed.' Luther stood up. 'You're an honest citizen now – that's why we're talking, am I right? So behave like one. Frankie, this city is full of ex bad guys who turned out good. So what do we do – dig in the past and find what's buried? No. We say, "Welcome to the land of good guys." We want *everyone* to be good guys.'

'That'd be fun.'

'Get this straight. A guy climbing the ladder breaks all the rules he likes, but when he makes it to the top he *obeys* the rules. He wants everybody else to obey the rules, because the rules now protect *him*.'

'Mr Respectable.'

'Isn't that what you are now? Yes, it is. If you want to move up in the world, you got to start to act respectable. No more Frankie di Stefano – it's *Mr* Francis di Stefano now. At the top table.'

Frankie nodded. 'Top table, yeah, that's me.'

Luther touched his arm. 'This Stitz business is a one-day wonder. We bury him, who remembers? What *you* have to do, Frankie, is concentrate on the long term. Remember, you're aiming for big things; you want to be part of the in-crowd, part of the establishment. Am I not right?'

When she next assembled her scouting party Strachey sensed a subtle shift in attitude. Today they were less of a tour party, less the *group* content to be shepherded from site to site; they were competing buyers. There was only one lordship and only one of them could win it. And this was the last day of their tour.

Strachey and Cantabulet were aside from the others, beneath some trees. 'I'm underwhelmed by the properties over here – they're old and small.'

Strachey agreed. 'I'll be frank with you, Mr Cantabulet – the *property* is less important than the title and what it entails. Like when a large group buys a smaller company: the physical *assets* are of minor importance – what's being traded is the name and its intangible assets. Of course, you'd know more about that than me.'

He found 'assets' a reassuring word.

She explained things similarly to Lincoln Deane and Maxwell Homeforth: 'Between you and I,' Strachey began, 'I clarified which armorial bearings came with the title, and although some people might regard those heraldic borders, pennants and seals as mere trimming I think they're what give the title its reality. They're its tangible assets, as it were.'

Both men nodded. They liked assets too. Lincoln was particularly interested in trimmings that could be printed on a wine label, such as heraldic borders, pennants and seals.

Mr and Mrs Nibbet waylaid Strachey behind the Toyota four-wheel drive. Their casual holiday-making air had blown away and Mrs Nibbet's volley of sharply focused questions showed only too clearly why she and her husband took such an interest in the local countryside. The conveyance, Mrs Nibbet said, included a bundle of specific rights – and every potential purchaser had been presented by Lord Clive with several photocopied sheets detailing, in so far as the archaic language could detail anything, what rights there were.

Strachey said, 'You mustn't anticipate an Eldorado. There are ransom strips, common land, manorial waste and market charters. They may be worthless. When your husband is lord he'll be able to grant mineral excavation rights – but they won't necessarily lead to a great fortune. They are just assets of the estate.'

Assets went down agreeably again.

Where yesterday they had been accompanied by Jeremy Barrington Downey, today the party waited in the National Trust car park for two new members: the esteemed local archivist and historian, Tina Gum, and another bidder, Edgar Delarme. He arrived after the others but before Tina. Striding across the car park, his vast black open raincoat protecting him against whatever the British weather might hurl against him, he glared at his compatriots, dismissing them instantly as rivals. Mrs Nibbet, the lady tourist once again, asked whether he wouldn't prefer a tour of the abbey to a tramp around muddy fields.

'What kind of abbey,' he thundered, 'gives admittance through a car park?'

'This is a long walk from anywhere,' she pointed out.

'A gift shop,' he muttered. 'A restaurant. Sacrilege.'

He wrapped himself in his raincoat like a cloak.

When Tina Gum arrived he kept his mouth and cloak shut tight. He couldn't criticise Tina's country tweed skirt, waterproof jacket and warm blouse but he did recoil from the brazen white clerical collar around her throat. He sneered at her tale of the ancient village of Hexcombe, lost in the seventeenth century and apparently still haunted. 'It's a wild, mysterious place,' said Tina. 'Miles from anywhere. Who needs the loo before we go?'

In the deep Devon valley a faint mist clung to the grass. In the midday sun the hills on either side steamed like flanks of cattle. A jay scolded from the trees. Tina made the party cross the wooden bridge singly, and when they were across she raised a hand and bid them be absolutely silent so they could listen. The group stood awkwardly on the moist grass, looking around at the rocky hills, listening first to the babbling stream and then, as silence lingered, to the returning sounds of birds hidden in the trees.

Delarme broke the silence: 'We shall pray to God.'

Tina looked up, pleased – until she realised that it was Delarme himself who would utter the prayer.

'Oh, how amiable are thy dwellings, thou Lord of hosts!'

Everyone glanced at each other as he rumbled on.

'Yea, the sparrow hath found her an house,

and the swallow a nest where she may lay her young.'

A breeze stirred the leaves, but his voice resonated through the valley, quieting the birds and keeping his little congregation huddled on the valley floor. Tina knew the psalm but the others wondered how long he'd be going on. Their enforced stillness and the absence of other human sounds made the hidden valley awesome.

When he had finished, no one knew quite what to say. Though his contribution had invested the damp valley with a sacred quality, they could hardly congratulate him on his performance. Delarme strode off through the springy grass into his private Eden. The others gravitated around Tina Gum. She smiled. 'I feel better for that.'

The others muttered that they felt better too.

She said, 'This is the site of the ancient village of Hexcombe, founded at some unknown medieval date and finally abandoned in the seventeenth century – probably because of the bubonic plague.'

Mrs Nibbet shivered.

'It's no longer infectious,' Tina assured her. 'If you look around – you see those strange humps scattered across the ground? They're the remains of old village houses. Just think:

under those very mounds there once lived families. Here in this valley a tiny community eked out a hard existence – a little farming, a little thieving—'

'Thieves?' spluttered Mrs Nibbet.

'Oh, a band of robbers may have lived here once. Who knows? They may have even buried a cache of gold. Only kidding,' she laughed. But the seed was sown.

Strachey sat carefully on a relatively dry grassy mound. Tina Gum amazed her. The vicar seemed to have slipped effortlessly into the wicked craft of grifting while Strachey herself could barely remain interested enough to play her part. Tina was spinning yarns – but for the Reverend this was a solitary day of slightly tall stories, while Strachey had been at it for three months. With Clive it had seemed fun, but the longer she spent apart from him the more the game seemed shallow and mean.

She raised her face to the watery sun and listened to Tina's tale.

'The path we came along may have been an old drovers' road, cutting along the foot of the valley beside the stream and leading eventually to Yelverton. Perhaps centuries ago a family stopped here and thought it a good place for a little farm, or perhaps Hexcombe was no more than a summer settlement – somewhere to bring the sheep to graze, close to water, plenty of grass. But it is secluded, so a robbers' hideaway may not be so far from the truth.'

Strachey tried to imagine what it might have been like to have lived in this isolated dell. Quiet, yes, and lonely – yet no more so than on other scattered farmsteads. Hexcombe, she decided, looking about her, had never been more than a single farm – a family house plus one or two cottages for its workers. Some of these grassy mounds would be the remains of cattle byres. It was a medieval farm, a *failed* farm. On Devon maps today, hamlets often turned out to be no more than single buildings: Sortridge, Grimstone, Yennadon, Marchant's Cross. From Hexcombe Farm it was – what? – three miles to the nearest church, Saint Agatha's. Three miles was barely one hour's walk. Strachey's parents sometimes reminisced about their own childhood in which a three-mile walk to church, shops or school was nothing exceptional. Universal car ownership made such a walk extraordinary today. But a three-mile walk meant that, in its day, Hexcombe could have been an integral part of the parish. The Americans would understand that: to them, an isolated spot meant truly isolated. In their vast continent, many rural settlements were more than a day's hike from anywhere. Strachey remembered the plains of Nevada and Oklahoma, where the horizon lay flat and unbroken in the far distance. You could walk all day and still not reach it. England wasn't like that. In England, one was never truly alone.

Delarme had tried to follow the course of the wooded stream but after a few hundred yards had to surrender to a tangle of bramble, weed and sapling. He trudged back in a grumpy humor.

'Where does it run?' he snapped. 'To this Yelverton you mentioned?'

'Not directly,' Tina answered. 'It potters along another few miles, then disappears underground.'

'Underground?' Mrs Nibbet echoed. The very word seemed magical. 'Into a cave?'

'Streams around here pop in and out of the ground all over the place. This one struggles through the valley down past the mill and then gets lost.'

'A mill?' asked Mr Cantabulet, who had found little to interest him in the countryside. 'A working mill? Does it come with the Manor?'

Tina laughed. 'Nothing comes with the Manor of Hexcombe,' she said, glancing quickly at Strachey to check their stories didn't conflict. 'The mill doesn't work.'

'We saw it, didn't we, dear?' said Mrs Nibbet to her husband. 'Dirty place, all falling down, but with that nice mill owner.'

Strachey frowned, but it was Tina who queried: 'An *owner*, at Hexcombe Mill?'

'Oh, a charming man, a real English gentleman. Quite a character, dressed like a hobo – but I understand English gentlemen often dress that way.'

'He was the owner?'

'Yes, he explained that he would have shown us round except he was having the place converted to become an orphanage.'

Tina swallowed. 'An orphanage, at Hexcombe Mill?'

'Oh, you'd know all about it, my dear, of course. I dare say you've been helping with the fundraising.'

Tina sighed. 'He asked for a donation?'

Mrs Nibbet giggled. 'Well, I don't like to parade my charity, my dear, but yes, Walter and I did put a few notes in the nice man's tin. And to think that this is the same little stream that runs past his mill. I'm beginning to feel I really belong here.'

Which wasn't at all how Strachey felt – as she tried to explain to Clive later on the phone:

'Farms, villages, pubs that sell cream teas—'

'Perfect.'

'I'm not part of this country life. The big event around here is the annual horticultural competition in Tavistock. It'll take all day. There'll be huge marquees, hundreds of classes to be judged – fresh flowers, pot flowers, floral arrangements, vegetables, novelty gardens, home-made cakes and pies, country wines—'

'Such fun.'

'Showing a bunch of jostling buyers around is *wearing*. Anyway... I miss you. It's no fun without you here.'

Clive chuckled modestly. 'I'll be over soon.'

'I could fly across to *you*.'

'Well, that would be lovely but... I'm not sure the funds would run to it.'

'We can afford an air fare, Clive.'

'It's more than four hundred pounds.'

'*I'll* pay.'

'I didn't realise you had money?'

Strachey hadn't been entirely honest. Adore the man she might, but she knew better than to let him near her bank account. 'Keep your hand on your ha'penny,' as Mickey Starr used to say.

'Everyone's leaving this afternoon, except Delarme. He's not the social type, so he'll fly back on his own.'

'You'd better stay on to keep an eye on him.'

'What can he do? Irritate the vicar, then come home.'

'The vicar?'

'You met her – Tina Gum. She's nice – and helpful, except that Delarme wants to turn the whole Manor into some kind of weirdo religious tabernacle.'

'All the more reason to keep an eye on him.'

'He's harmless. Look Clive, we're supposed to be partners – in both senses of the word.'

'Of course we are, darling.'

'Don't call me darling. I want to fly back.'

'You've *got* to be there. Look, darling—'

'Don't call—'

'Look, *Strachey*, you've got to be there – you're Lane Estates. You *have* to be in England.'

'Why?'

'For the auction. It's the only way this will work. I remain here, the auctioneer, while you hold the fort in England. You're the owning company, and technically the Manor of Hexcombe belongs to you. When I sold the company to you I placed all my trust in you—'

'You *know* you can trust me.'

'I know, I know I can. I'm just saying. We're at a delicate stage.'

'You need me in England?'

'Absolutely.'

'But you don't *need* me in California or wherever you are? Oh, I'm being pathetic. OK, you win. I'll stay in deepest Devon.'

'You know it's best, darling.'

She inhaled, and he continued hastily: 'I mean Strachey, not darling! Strachey. Sorry. Anyway, we'll be together soon. Can't wait.' He paused. 'Love you. Really do.'

'Yeah,' she said. 'I'll see you, Clive.'

She clicked off the line button, glared at the phone, and threw it across the room.

7

CLIVE FELT THAT a little risk added an extra frisson to his love-making. He lay with Gloria in Lincoln's bed like the opening clue of a crossword (one across), knowing that at this moment Lincoln should be touching down in San Francisco while he, Clive, touched down on Gloria. Although Clive was a philanderer he didn't tire of a beautiful woman once he had bedded her. A woman as bubbly as Gloria could keep him interested for a week. And on her brief release from matrimony Gloria was like a nun on furlough. Clive was younger, better looking, had all his hair – and was a member of the English aristocracy! She grabbed his lordly buttocks for what might be the last time and steered him in. She had bitten him twice this session, not because she expected his aristocratic blood to run blue but because Gloria always made love with everything she had. She put a fresh mark on Clive's ear that looked as if he had earned it in a prize fight. But he held off from marking her because within a couple of hours Gloria had to look fresh and unsullied for her husband.

'Don't leave me,' she panted.

'I wouldn't dream of it.'

Clive knew that at moments of passion you skip the truth. Don't tell women you want sex: insist you *love* them. Shout it during sex – they won't hold you to it afterwards. At the time, yes, everything is true, the world outside does not exist – but then there are just the two of you, the world shut out. Don't ruin this moment with words of truth.

Plenty of time for that later.

Clive had not had so much exercise for months. Somewhere deep inside his pragmatic brain lay the thought that this would be – *should* be – his and Gloria's last time together, and in this performance he should wring out every drop. Afternoon it might be, but it needn't be a matinee. Their climax deserved applause but instead a sudden hush fell on the house. Clive moved to a cooler part of the sheet. Gloria followed and snuggled softly against his side. He could feel her breath against his skin as she said, 'I wish you didn't have to go.'

Show was over. 'Soon you'll be Lady Gloria – assuming Lincoln wins the auction.'

'He'll win it, darlin'. I'll make sure he does.'

Clive smiled and closed his eyes. The curtain could come down.

Two pieces of business, thought Frankie di Stefano. First, I sort out whoever blabbed about Gary Stitz, and second, I get into the in-crowd, part of the establishment. Luther Bloch says I need a respectable veneer. Which suits me. Do I want to stay a jumped-up hoodlum forever? Of course not. I deserve respect.

He called Kelly at the precinct.

Kelly said, 'Wait a minute, Frankie, you callin' on an open line?'

'Someone listens to your calls?'

'Maybe.'

'That deadbeat at the desk?'

'Who knows?'

'You guys are supposed to be stoppin' scumbags on the streets, not sittin' around listenin' to each other. Ain't you the honest guys?'

'No comment.'

'Kelly, I need to know something.'

'Hey! Hold this right there. Let's have a beer sometime – outside the office.'

'Lighten up. I'm *entitled* to know this. My name has been used, right, dragged in to some investigation about who bumped off Gary Stitz?'

'Well… '

'For Chrissake, Kelly – you think someone listens to your every word? I can talk about somethin' interestin', if you want me to. Give 'em somethin' worth listenin' *to*.'

'Gimme a break.'

'You give *me* a break, Kelly. Someone dragged me into this shit about Gary Stitz.'

'Well, I… '

'Kelly.'

'I heard your name mentioned, someone said something. I don't know.'

'You wanna talk about somethin' else?'

'No. Look, ease up. Someone said Stitz got his comeuppance in your neighborhood.'

'I thought they found the punk in Woodbury?'

'Yeah, someone drove him there. But we think he was shot at the Captain Nemo.'

'Oh, really – an' where is that?'

'The story goes you shot him.'

'Me?'

'Yeah. Because Stitz was pissin' on your territory.'

'I never knew that.'

'So you shot him by the pool.'

'Who told you this?'

'Come on, Frankie.'

Frankie paused. 'Speak to me, Kelly, no one is listenin' to this call.'

'You say. Look, Frankie, I give you the name and somethin' happens to him – how's that gonna look?'

'From his angle or from yours?'

'Maybe we ought to meet up for a beer.'

'Too late for that. Just give me the goddamn name.'

Kelly sucked his teeth, but they tasted as rotten as his dilemma. He said, 'Listen. If you don't got time to have a beer with me, maybe you oughta pay a social call on a guy called Hymie Haines.'

For a man who'd spent the last fourteen hours in airports and airplanes, Lincoln Deane seemed in remarkably good cheer. Even when his wife held him off, claiming it was the wrong time of the month, he strode happily around the patio, rubbing his hands together, saying, 'Well, at least you're not pregnant. And I am not too full of beans myself. Hey, what a flight! Maxwell spends the whole time bending my ear about what a bad idea it is. You know what? I think he's gonna make a bid himself. That's what Strachey says, and I reckon she's right.'

Gloria frowned. 'Strachey?'

'Lord Lane's secretary.'

'She's in England? Wasn't she here?'

'Yeah, she came down to see us that day you were out. Nice girl. You and she would have got along.'

'I bet.'

'Know something? She and that Lord Lane – well,' Lincoln placed a finger beside his nose. 'I would not be surprised.'

'Oh, really?'

'I can sense these things. So what have *you* been doing while I've been away?'

'You know me, darlin'.'

'Spending money, I bet?'

'Lying around.'

Lincoln wandered beside the pond, trailing his fingers in the water and keeping a watchful eye on the black swans. 'Did Clive leave any messages?'

Gloria shrugged. 'I think he enjoyed his stay. How'd you like Hexcombe?'

'Great place.' Lincoln's eyes lit up. 'Middle of nowhere. Little hills and valleys, and green, so goddamn green. England, Christ, you'd love it.'

'Good shops?'

Lincoln laughed. 'It's the backwoods, right? But pretty – great place for a quiet few days.'

'Like this place?'

'No. Round here is flat. Over there it's like someone took a map of the countryside and scrunched it up. When you're not going up a hill you're going down one.'

'So you're gonna buy us some of that?'

'Well, Strachey says we're not actually buying the surrounding countryside.'

'You saw a lot of Strachey?'

'An honest girl.'

'And pretty?'

'We're just buying a title, Strachey said. Most of the land belongs to other people – except for some wasteland and bits of stuff.'

'What kind of stuff?'

'But I was thinking: there's nothing to stop us buying a piece of real estate if something does come up. She took us around, showed us some places up for sale.'

'Oh, *she* took you around?'

'Yeah, a whole bunch of us – and she had some kinda English faggot come along. He had some decent properties.'

'A castle?'

Lincoln laughed. 'You'd like that, wouldn't you?'

Gloria shrugged. 'Lady Gloria sounds good enough to me.'

The jury is out on which kind of auction encourages the highest bids. A majority verdict finds for a conventional auction, where the rival bidders sit in the same room in direct competition, pride on the line and judgement warped by the urge to win. A sizeable minority favors the Dutch auction, where bidding starts at a higher price than any fool might reasonably pay and gradually comes down till the first braveheart leaps in with a high bid to snatch the prize. It's a chicken game: how long dare you stand aside? Because if you don't leap fast, the prize is gone. A few vendors prefer sealed bids, where they all write their maximum offer in advance and the highest wins. This is a dull game and buyers hate it – and when you're milking buyers, you do not set up a game they'll hate.

Clive considered these alternatives.

Each required the bidders to be present in the same room, and Clive had reasons for avoiding that. What he really wanted was a telephone auction, all bidders on the phone, Clive in control, no bidders who could see each other. But that sounded dodgy, and a dodgy auction puts buyers off. He toyed with a Web auction, where bidders log in to a private site and bid on the Internet – and he liked the way that this game could dawdle, the bids creeping up over several days. But over several days, he thought, some of the excitement might ebb away – and maybe the bidders would phone each other between bids. Too many opportunities for buyers to rig the game.

He decided: keep it simple.

From San Francisco he got on the phone. The first call was to the *Examiner* to check returns to a box number he was running, but all the rest of his calls were to his friends. (Clive's customers were all his friends. No one does business with their enemies.) First the preliminaries, and then: 'The auction's still on Thursday but... I'm afraid the auctioneers have changed the venue.'

Sympathetic clucking as they protested. Then:

'I know. What can you expect from an English auction house? Though I guess they do have a point. Most of the interested bidders are based in England, and it's hardly logical to sell an English lordship in the United States. Can you get across to London by Thursday?'

Clive was confident no one would want to.

'Here's the good news – good for *you*, I mean. Since most of the buyers are English they won't be able to match your price. You can sit here in the States and wipe them out. You won't even have to get up from your armchair.'

He explained how a telephone auction worked, how simple it

was, and he gave everyone the phone number. A piece of cake with most of them. Except Delarme: the man wasn't there. Someone with an outrageously plummy Boston accent (even Clive winced, and he was used to plummy accents) announced that Mr Edgar Delarme had been detained on business in the United Kingdom. Clive explained that he was calling about that very same business, though not from the yo-naighted ken-dom, don't you know, and that Mr Edgar Delarme would be incensed if he didn't get his message.

The Boston Plum gave him a London number – which worried Clive. What was Delarme chasing up?

At that moment, as it happened, Delarme was chewing his supper in an unspeakable Paddington hotel – and if he was flattered to be paged at dinner, the hotel staff must have been astounded: no other guest had *ever* been paged at that hotel. Most wouldn't admit they'd *been* there.

Clive's story changed for Delarme: 'Sorry about the change, Edgar. This means you won't be back in the States in time for the auction. But don't worry – you can phone your bid from England.'

'I must attend.'

'Well, naturally you'd want to. I'll give you a number you can phone.'

'I'm flying home.'

'To San Francisco – when?'

'Tomorrow.'

'That's cutting it fine. The auction is in New York, you see, three thousand miles away. Better if you phone.'

'Then I'll fly to New York.'

Clive grimaced. 'Fine.'

Wrong-footed, he put down the phone. All the others had toppled easily, agreeing to phone in to the number he had supplied. But Delarme had thrown him by being in London, where he might have dropped in on the Manorial Society or the Historical Records Agency or who knows where? Clive would have felt less anxious if he had known that Delarme had been to Tufton Street in Westminster, enquiring after church furnishings and supplies.

Being a lord is not something one should do full time. In certain areas of business a title is a handicap: no one expects to buy cheap from you. There are things a lord cannot sell. So for a couple of hours Clive dropped his genuine, if cheaply bought, title and reverted to his long-held alternative name of Julian Klein.

It was Klein who had placed the small ad in the *Examiner*:
> One-room condo with facilities off Pacific Heights.
> Six-month low rent. Suit couple. No restrictions.
> Landlord off-site. Box 2246.

It was Klein – charming, unworldly, off for a sabbatical in the UK – who showed couples around the cramped condo, apologizing for the disarray, uncertain what price to ask, anxious to let to someone sympathetic, preferring to let to any *nice* people who could put up three months' cash today to get it sealed. He – Klein – wouldn't be here to collect the second three months but he *knew* that he could trust them, he could just tell.

And since the rent he was asking was way too low, he managed to rent out the place four times over. They could move in Saturday. All four couples.

When the last viewers left he packed his trunk.

Edgar Delarme was unreasonable. Coming through to Clive Lane on his cell phone he insisted on knowing *now* exactly where the auction would be held. He had changed his ticket for a stopover in New York and, although tired, would be fresh enough by tomorrow to be at the auction, whatever time. Clive was going to tell him the venue had changed but thought better of it. It sounded like a dodge routine. So he gave an address. Told him the time.

Cutting across New York on the subway Clive leafed through a discarded newspaper whose headline had caught his eye: HOODLUM BUTCHERED AT THE CAPTAIN NEMO. The name struck a chord but it was only when Clive got into the article that he remembered that the Nemo was the hotel where he had met one of his less salubrious clients, Frankie di Stefano – who seemed a bit of a hoodlum himself, Clive thought with a smile. Apparently, the body of some local no-good, name of Hymie Haines, had been found beside the pool – or in fact, as the paper lip-smackingly pointed out, his *head* had been found there. The rest of his body had not been traced. Police were onto the case – no suspects – though there was a possibility that the gruesome killing had been an execution, some kind of warning to Hymie's friends. More than a possibility, Clive thought. He wondered if Mr di Stefano would use that hotel again – he wouldn't want to *eat* there, that's for sure. The hotel itself might appreciate the notoriety: played properly, there shouldn't be a free table there for a week.

America, he thought. Nobody respects the law.

Clive's knowledge of Long Island was scanty to say the least, but he had a good working knowledge of Manhattan and New York City, dating back to his days on the fringe of the auction trade. It was at Sotheby's he had met Strachey. She had been acting for an English family whose Americanised son had died of AIDS. They didn't want his possessions shipped back home, either because they were afraid his things were contagious or because they belonged to a life he had lived elsewhere. She had valued his possessions and arranged their sale. (Most didn't warrant Sotheby's.) Clive often hung around the auction sales and he noticed the novice who behaved honorably to distant clients. He admired conspicuous honesty: it was an effect he strived for himself. A crook you could spot was a poor crook.

Strachey wasn't a crook and her conspicuous honesty was not a front. She was straight. Clive liked them straight. With a straight, he knew where he was. And Strachey was a straight with a sense of fun – not to mention that she was the best-looking woman he'd seen that month. Not to mention either that she had a sadness in her eyes – the kind of sadness he thought that he could shift.

He smiled at the memory. Then he realised he was thinking of her in the past tense.

Today, the day of the auction, Clive was back on familiar ground. He was also back in the familiar position of having barely enough cash to last the day. The Julian Klein money was in the bank but hadn't been in long enough to be drawn as cash. For the room that Clive was hiring he could pay by check. He could pay for the telephones the same way. But the six accomplices would want cash.

He had hired a room for the day in what was described as Greenwich Village but which was actually a side street off Delancey, and he had arranged the re-routing of phone calls via London back to New York with one of the few telecommunication companies he had not yet rooked. He had lined up accomplices two weeks ago – just in case – but until Delarme had insisted on attending the auction in person Clive had hoped to get away without actually having to stage the show. Delarme's little whim would cost twelve hundred dollars.

Now twenty more. The janitor at the hall had lined the room with two dozen chairs and, more importantly, had removed all banners and signs from the previous day's Redemption Meeting. He even helped Clive hang the Auction Rules and fake Parker Bennett sign. When he saw Clive distribute three additional phones along one side of the hall the janitor pointed out that there were no jacks there, but Clive assured him the jack at the desk would do fine. The others, he said, were cell phones. He distracted the man by presenting him with a crisp twenty-dollar bill as his advance and – had the man known it – his only payment.

'We won't have many visitors,' warned Clive.

There were twenty-three. Clive had lightly fly-posted the area with a photocopied notice stressing the quirkiness and unique nature of the happening in the hope of attracting a few casual spectators drawn by the quaintness of the occasion, and the bills had brought in eighteen souls with nothing better to do. The show was free, after all. You didn't have to queue for it, like for Oprah – and you might get to see an English lord. Among these eighteen spectators, five of Clive's six accomplices mingled – acquaintances from earlier auction days, selected from his circle of knockers, runners and ringers for their ability to look halfway respectable and not to ask questions. Each knew the value of two hundred dollars.

By 10am the auction hall had filled with spectators and rival bidders for the Lordship of Hexcombe Manor. These bidders would comprise Edgar Delarme and two men he wouldn't recognize. Clive explained that more bids would come by phone. 'But of course,' he announced, 'those of you on the floor will have the advantage. You can see and hear what's going on.'

Delarme glared at the rival bidders and they glared back at him.

Clive fiddled with the phones. He tested the mike.

'The auction will commence,' he said, 'in seven minutes.'

'Today's special and unique auction concerns the disposal of the Lordship of the Manor of Hexcombe, England. The purchase of this lordship, in addition to potential manorial rights, will give the new owner the unfettled right to style himself Lord of the Manor of Hexcombe.'

Clive glanced up gravely.

'I must emphasise that becoming an English lord of the manor does *not* give you the right to a seat in the historic House of Lords. However—' Clive smiled. 'After taking up your lordship and doing research you may unearth such benefits as flying your manorial banner from the church or other prominent place on special days. You will find that the Hexcombe title also confers rights to 'wasteland' – sundry roadside verges and parcels of common land – and includes certain mineral rights which can only be exercised with your permission. You may consider this a valuable right.'

Clive had undertaken this research and had discovered the rights were worthless. But they sounded good.

'We are today embarking on a solemn – nay, historic – transaction: the transfer from an ancient British family of a noble lordship and all it entails. A sad occasion for the noble family but perhaps a joyful one for today's successful bidder and his descendants. You will note that I say 'his', not 'his or her'. We are selling a lordship. Every potential buyer must be male. Are the telephones in order?'

This was addressed to three of his colleagues along the wall. To brighten the atmosphere Clive had arranged that two of these should be off-duty hookers. He explained their presence now:

'Telephone bids for this historic sale are coming in from Britain and Japan – and I believe, in one case, from Australia?'

He glanced out into the room. One of the girls raised a phone. Two girls and a thin man crouched over a pair of handsets each. Clive's two other stooges sat on stacking chairs close to the brooding Edgar Delarme.

Clive glanced again at his watch.

'Let the auction commence,' he said. 'Today's auction, as you know, comprises only one lot – the entire sale and transfer of the Lordship of the Manor of Hexcombe, England and all that it entails. Today's sale will be final. At close of bidding the successful bidder will be asked to deposit twenty per cent of the agreed purchase price and to commit to paying the residue within a week. Payment may be by check or banker's draft but, I repeat, must be made today. Upon payment of the remaining portion the Lordship will be formally transferred. The relevant documents—' Clive held up a large manila envelope, '—will be issued on vellum and passed with the title at that time.'

He replaced the envelope carefully on the desk beside him and checked with his porters: 'Are the international lines open?'

They concurred.

'Good morning, ladies and gentlemen – or good afternoon, as it is with some of our international callers – and welcome to this special sale of the Lordship of the Manor of Hexcombe. As you know, no lands or property are to accompany this title, and the purchaser will be ultimately responsible for all legal fees. We stress that the only rights being sold today are the use of said title and the ability to pass it on to all natural children.'

When closing a dodgy deal Clive was at his most grave.

'Upon completion of the contract and receipt of payment we will prepare a certificate granting title. The coat of arms will be included in same. From that point the successful bidder will become absolute lord.'

He paused to let the enormity sink in. One of the spectators said, 'Gosh.'

Clive said, 'You will know that in Britain, feudalism was introduced by William the Conqueror after the Battle of Hastings in 1066. Following his conquest, all the land was owned by him alone, and he parcelled huge chunks of it out to earls, barons and suchlike in return for their military support. The person holding feudal land was known as a tenant-in-chief.'

A couple of spectators stirred. They hadn't come for a history lesson.

But Clive continued: 'Over a large part of England the typical manor contained a village with a church and agricultural land in which the freeholding franklins – i.e. the farmers – held scattered strips. The Lord of the Manor was all-powerful. He presided over the manor court which governed tenants' rights and duties, changes of occupancy, and disputes. The origins of manorial courts are lost in antiquity, though documents on them survive from the thirteenth century. Around the sixteenth century they began to surrender their power to royal courts – and in the nineteenth century manor courts came to an end. They formally ended with the *Law of Property Acts*, 1922 and 1924.'

This was impressive stuff – boring but impressive. And true, in case any local academic had wandered in. Clive believed that the essence of an effective scam was to surround it with facts – and to base the scam on greed.

'Today is a rare opportunity for someone here in this room or participating on the telephone, to take possession of an English title. A number of you have visited the demesne and inspected the fair property which snuggles in the beautiful English county of Devon. We make no estimate of what those properties and property rights are worth today, though some of you, I know, will have formed your own judgement.'

One of his phone porters raised her hand. 'Line's beginning to crack up from Japan – I think we're losing the satellite – we've maybe got five minutes.'

Lord Clive took the hint. 'Lot one – the only one,' he chuckled. 'The Lordship of the Manor of Hexcombe. Who'll start me at twenty thousand dollars?'

Two or three people sniggered. But there was an immediate flurry of activity from the phone porters. The bidding shot up rapidly to thirty-five thousand. Then a floor bid made thirty-six. There was a pause. Had he known it, Edgar Delarme was the object of scrutiny. He had been marked out by Clive when he came in, and the various accomplices were now watching Delarme to see how he would react. They mustn't freeze him out before he started. Experienced bidders themselves, they knew that novices could get so nervous they became unable to raise their hand. But once they started...

Delarme caught Lord Clive's eye. He nodded.

'Thirty-seven,' Clive snapped, his gaze swivelling round the room. 'Eight, nine, forty. Who'll pop us over to forty-one?'

He didn't even glance at Delarme – who was wondering if that thirty-seven had been *his* bid. The bids were rising so fast it was hard to see who was calling what. And in any case, they were now awaiting forty-one. Delarme half raised his hand.

'Forty-one. Thank you, sir. Do I hear... Yes, forty-two.'

Delarme rubbed his black beard. He had set a ceiling at fifty and he entertained great hopes of not having to go so far.

'Forty-three.'

He jerked his hand.

'Forty-four.'

Was that him? Clive was peering at his phone porters, two of whom were in a huddle. Another pause. Delarme wasn't sure whether the forty-four had been his own bid or had come from someone else on the floor. Clive was playing with the hammer. Delarme called, 'I bid forty-five.'

Somebody sniggered and Delarme immediately flushed red. Maybe he'd upped his own bid. He was in a room full of strangers. If they thought him a fool they were wrong.

But Clive nodded at him kindly. 'Forty-five, sir, with you.'

'Forty-six,' someone called.

'Forty-seven,' snapped Delarme.

'Forty-eight.'

'Forty nine,' came Delarme.

'Fifty.'

A slight pause. The fifty barrier. Those in the ring didn't know how far he'd go but they did know the psychological markers people set themselves. They left Delarme to show his hand.

'Fifty-one.'

Clive smiled. 'Thank you – though we go in twos after fifty. That's fifty-two.'

'Fifty-four,' declared a woman on the phone.

Delarme licked his lips. Clive watched him. Delarme put his hand out, negative, palm down. If Delarme had set a fifty limit it was disappointing but Clive wasn't going to send him home empty-handed.

Another telephone porter said, 'Fifty-six.'

Clive said, 'That's fifty-six, then, on the phone.' He put his hand over the mike and spoke confidentially to the floor: 'Telephone bidders couldn't even be bothered to come. I don't know, some people! Who will bid me fifty-eight?'

He didn't even glance at Delarme but he still drew the man's: 'Fifty-eight.'

A telephone girl said, 'I have sixty.' She added, 'Japan's breaking up.'

Clive said, 'Sixty thousand from Japan.'

Delarme said, 'Sixty-two.'

He showed renewed determination. When he heard, 'Sixty-four,' he topped it with 'Sixty-six.'

The girl said, 'We've lost the satellite,' and Delarme smiled.

A porter said, 'OK Australia? I've taken your sixty-eight.'

'Seventy,' declared Delarme.

'Seventy-two.'

Clive looked squarely at Delarme. Was seventy his last bid? Clive said, 'We have seventy-two from Australia.'

Delarme chewed his lip.

Clive asked, 'Do I hear seventy-four?'

'Yes!'

But it wasn't from Delarme. It was a new voice at the back, and two of the stooges spun round in apparent surprise: a little fat guy no one had seen before. Some melon who had rolled in from the street and got caught up in the excitement.

Clive said, 'Good morning, sir. Seventy-four?'

'You got it.'

'Seventy-four.' Clive returned his attention to Delarme. 'Do I hear... '

Delarme said, 'Seventy-six.'

One of the stooges nudged the other. Delarme was getting angry. That was good.

The telephone said seventy-eight.

Delarme said eighty.

The phone: eighty-two.

Edgar Delarme: eighty-four.

The phone: eighty-six.

Perspiration on Delarme's brow. He was trying to forget he'd set a limit. He was especially trying to forget that he'd set a hopeful limit at fifty thousand. He said, 'Eighty-eight.'

'Ninety.'

'Ninety-two.'

'Four.'

'Ninety-six,' declared Delarme.

Clive licked his lips. He didn't need to signal with his palm: the whole room knew where this was heading. One of the stooges gave ninety-eight, and the rest of the pack sat on their thumbs to give Delarme the pleasure of uttering the words no buyer could resist:

'One hundred thousand dollars.'

A woman gasped and a man in a pea jacket started to clap. Clive held the pause, letting Delarme savor his moment, before one of the telephones said, 'A hundred and five.'

The stooges held back. A crucial moment. They had probably taken him to the wire. If he had gone past his limit and thought he had more than one bidder against him he'd throw in his hand.

Clive watched him. Don't give him time to think. 'Will you go the extra five?'

Second and third thoughts crowded Delarme's brain. This wouldn't be an extra five, he thought, but an extra ten: his last bid had been a hundred, it was now a hundred and ten.

'Such a shame to lose it now,' Clive said.

Delarme realised the enormity of what he'd done. A hundred thousand dollars, when he'd set a provisional limit at half that. He didn't have a hundred in the bank. The room fell silent. Most of the spectators could see they'd reached the endgame, and the accomplices knew that this was the moment to sit back and wait. It was up to Clive to tease a final bid.

He said, 'We have a hundred and five on the telephone. Who's going to give a hundred and ten?'

Delarme blushed and looked at the floor.

Clive said, 'Well, only one man can win. Gentlemen, for the sake of five thousand dollars the centuries-old title of Lord of the Manor of Hexcombe will now be irrevocably handed on. For the last time, do I hear a hundred and ten?'

He didn't stare at Delarme too hard. 'I have a hundred and five, going *once*.'

Delarme swallowed.

'We are just over the hundred thousand dollar mark. The Lordship of Hexcombe going *twice*.'

'A hundred and ten.'

But again it was not Delarme. It was the little, fat balloon-head who had blown in from the street. Delarme – and half the spectators – turned to stare at him. Was he the nut-case he appeared to be, or was there any remote chance...

'Excuse me, sir,' Lord Clive said carefully. 'But you're not known to me. You'll forgive me if—'

'You doubt my credit rating?'

Clive gave a soothing smile.

The man pulled out a Bank of Alaska checkbook and a platinum-colored card. 'The card will cover it or you can always phone through to my bank.'

A phone girl said, 'I have a hundred and ten on the telephone.'

'I bid first.'

Clive sighed. 'A bit of a quandary.'

'I bid *first*.'

'It *is* a quandary.'

'Firm bid,' the girl said. 'Unless this gentleman might care to beat it?'

'A hundred and twenty,' he said, taking out his pen.

Clive appealed to the room: 'What should I do?'

The fat man said, 'My very last bid. I'm writing this check—'

He paused to flourish his pen. 'And this is final. Damn ridiculous auction.'

Clive spoke again to the room. 'Well, it seems that the lordship is to change hands for one hundred and twenty thousand dollars. Unless, of course, anyone... ' He raised the hammer. 'Right, then. One hundred and twenty thousand dollars, going once. To this gentleman. Going twice.'

'One twenty-five,' Delarme snarled.

Clive paused.

The fat man spluttered: 'Hey, I already bought this.'

'One twenty-five,' repeated Delarme.

'One *thirty*-five,' spat the man.

Delarme protested: 'That was your final offer. You made out the check.'

'I'll make another,' said the man, tearing it up.

'No, you can't come back in. You said it was your last bid.'

'I'll bid what I like, my friend. One thirty-five.'

'One forty.'

'One fifty.'

Delarme opened his mouth, then thought better. 'Oh, take it,' he said. 'At least you'll pay one fifty, not one twenty.'

The man shrugged. 'Yes, but I'm happy and you're not, sucker. You look a big man but you ain't. 'Cos you are out.'

A man whispered in Delarme's ear: 'He's a fruit cake. He'll pay anything. You could push him higher. Anything you say the fruit will top it.'

Delarme stared at the fat guy.

The whisperer said, 'Try one eighty. I bet he'll go to two hundred.'

Delarme wasn't born yesterday. 'You think so? You try him.'

The man melted away.

Clive resumed control from the front. 'Gentlemen, can I get this quite clear? I have final bids of one hundred and forty thousand dollars from Mr Delarme versus one hundred and fifty thousand from Mr... is that right?'

The men nodded. They stared at Clive, but wouldn't look at each other.

'Well, in that case,' Clive said. 'If there are no other bids?' He paused, looking at his stooges. 'Sold then, for one hundred and fifty thousand dollars.'

He rapped once with his hammer.

The whisperer was still commiserating with Delarme when one of the telephone girls came across. 'Mr Delarme? Mr Edgar Delarme?'

'Of course,' he said irritably.

'You have a moment?' She took his arm. 'It's confidential.'

She led him out of the hall into a small office in which stood Clive Lane and the fat guy. They both looked as if they'd exhausted their conversation but when the fat guy saw Delarme he gave a yelp of despair and stamped from the room.

The girl followed him out and closed the door, leaving the two men alone.

'I don't know how to put this,' said Clive.

'Straightforwardly.'

'Quite. Can I rely on your confidence?'

Delarme recoiled as if it were an insult to be asked.

Clive took a breath. 'The gentleman was unable to pay the deposit.'

He waited for Delarme's reaction – which was: 'I see. He was kidding us?'

Clive scratched his head. 'Difficult to say. He may be genuinely confused. The checkbook was genuine but... he wasn't able to write a check for thirty thousand.'

'Thirty?'

'Twenty per cent.'

Delarme breathed. 'It *is* a large sum of money.' He had just realised *how* large. 'What happens now?'

'The normal rules of auction are that if a buyer proves unable to pay, then the option to purchase passes to the first underbidder. Which is you.'

Delarme was already on his guard. 'What if I don't want to buy?'

Clive looked genuinely concerned. 'You too, Mr Delarme? Surely you weren't wasting our time as well?'

'No, but you saw what happened. I was run up by a time-waster.'

Clive demurred. 'I don't think he realised about the deposit. He *claims* he still wants to go through with the purchase but, of course, the first step is the deposit – which at this moment he cannot pay.'

Delarme remained cool. 'You're in a spot of bother – as you British call it.'

'In what way?'

'Auction's over, potential buyers have gone home – but you're back where you started. You need a buyer.'

'Is that not you?'

'This has all been... irregular. I need time to think.'

He hadn't recognized the old 'underbidder' trick. Clive held his breath till Delarme added, 'I'm not legally *bound* to purchase.'

'Not legally, no. Believe me, Mr Delarme, I wouldn't dream of pressing you – not in any way. Whoever buys this title becomes a member of the British aristocracy, and I must be assured of their suitability. Frankly, I think the gentleman who has just left will manage to find the money eventually but, frankly again, he is not our sort.'

'Our sort?'

Clive smiled slightly. 'I ask you – does that man look like an English lord?'

Delarme licked his lips. 'He was a time-waster. Now look, Clive, when he came into the auction the bidding stood somewhere around ninety thousand dollars.'

'You bid a hundred and forty.'

'When he came in it was ninety.'

Clive shook his head. 'I hate to correct you but the first bid that man made was a hundred and twenty.'

Delarme frowned. Clive's recall was faultless: 'We had a telephone bid for a hundred and ten – a bid I'm sure would still be honoured – and then that gentleman put in his own bid of one twenty. You topped it with one two five.'

'So you're asking me to pay one twenty-five.'

'To have *automatic* purchase as the underbidder – with nobody else allowed to bid against you – you would have to honor your last bid, which was a hundred and forty thousand. We need a deposit of twenty-eight thousand – if that isn't too much?'

'Twenty-eight?'

Delarme paled. His limit had been fifty thousand – for which a twenty per cent deposit would have been ten grand. Fifty thousand might have been a tad low, he thought, but a hundred and forty – with a deposit of twenty-eight? He wasn't sure he had twenty-eight on call. He stalled: 'I bid one twenty-five. Now, let's see... twenty per cent of that is... twenty-five.'

'That would make you happier?'

Delarme wanted to appear decisive. 'Yes, twenty-five on a banker's draft – against my hundred and twenty-five.'

'One forty, actually. But I'll concede on the deposit, if that might help.'

Clive was prepared to concede further, but wanted to draw Delarme into bargaining mode. He watched Delarme deliberate. Eventually he muttered, 'The bid of a hundred and forty was extracted from me unfairly.' He didn't know how right he was. 'In fact, one *twenty-five* was extracted—'

'The phone bid for one twenty—'

'My one two five topped that.'

Clive leant forward confidentially. 'Look, to bring this to a close, I'm prepared to trim the one forty to one three five.'

Delarme shook his head. 'My last *legitimate* bid—'

'You give me no choice.' Clive inhaled through his aristocratic nose. 'If you can't raise your bid I shall have to open the bidding to all the other bidders again.'

'I'm not paying one three five.'

Clive glanced across his shoulder as if to check the door was shut. 'I've offered one three five. You've said one *two* five... '

'We split the difference?'

Clive shrugged.

'All right, Mr Lane. A hundred and thirty. That's my last word.'

'*Lord* Lane, please.' Clive smiled. 'You'll find we lords insist on it – you will too. Lord Delarme sounds rather good.'

Delarme's face didn't crack. He was suffering a mixture of emotions: here he was about to become Lord Delarme – yet was more bothered about whether he had beaten Clive down or been talked up. Maybe they had both won.

8

WHEN STRACHEY TOOK the call she was lying up to her neck in bath water in her tiny en suite at the Sickle and Hoe. The phone was in the soap rack and Strachey hardly had to stir. She raised one languorous arm, lifting – had there been anyone there to glimpse it – a perfect glistening breast above warm, scented, frothy water, the nipple pink as a raspberry at midday, the surrounding flesh soft and apricot... But why am I telling you this? She was alone. Clive was three thousand miles away.

He said, 'Wonderful to hear your voice, my love. I've missed you.'

His sincerity dripped like bath water from Strachey's hand. He added, 'We'll be together soon.'

'When?'

'A week or two. Some loose strings. Can you talk – are you alone?'

'Alone, lonely and in the bath.'

'Miss me?'

'Miss you.'

'That's my girl.' He hoped so. 'Still down in deepest Devon?'

'Where else? Who won the auction?'

'He won't necessarily come over yet. I imagine the first thing he'll do is go to work on a family crest – have it printed on his letter headings, embroidered on his handkerchiefs. Maybe emblazoned on a dinner service.'

'Who won it, Clive?'

'It's not absolutely settled—'

'Delarme?'

'He did put in a good bid – a very good bid – but I think he over-committed himself. He may not be able to pay.'

Strachey changed hands in the bath. 'And if he can't?'

'We'll see. Anyway, you're happy to stay on?'

'I'm bored. I'm living over a pub and if I have to stay much longer I shall *look* like a glass of beer.'

Clive laughed sympathetically. 'Lots of healthy walks, that's the ticket. We should know where we are in a couple of days.'

'Two days?'

'A week at the outside.'

'Another *week*?'

Strachey sat up with a splash – and if Clive could have seen the water stream from her chest he might have thought twice about staying in America. But he was a man of purpose. He said, 'The Americans were full of you. Just play the same game again – a tour around the manor, giving a general feel of the place without letting him get too close to the locals – then safely back on the plane.'

'I can't face it.'

'Our lord – and his lady, perhaps – will hang on your every word. Go to the finest restaurants – he'll pay.'

'There aren't any fine restaurants. Why can't *you* come over?'

'I can't greet his lordship, can I?'

'Why on earth not?'

'I'm the auctioneer.'

'Big deal.'

'We've been through this. I'm the salesman and auctioneer while you represent the vendor. You *are* the vendor – it's your company, after all. At the end of the day, he can moan from here till doomsday but he's bought it, even if he did pay more than he needed.'

'How much?'

'We'll be rich, don't worry.'

'How much?'

'I can't be sure till the final deal's complete. Ring you in a couple of days, darling.'

'Why have you started calling me darling? You've never used to call me that.'

'Well, I should have – because I love you. Must go, my love. Kiss, kiss.'

He cut off, and Strachey glared at the phone as if the bath water had turned cold.

She spent the next day dutifully driving her hire car from one tourist venue to the next, putting together a schedule of visits that would avoid the tacky and commonplace but concentrate instead on the historic; the kind of places that might impress the dismal Delarme. She knew he'd won the prize. Clive's evasiveness hadn't washed. She would have to escort that dreadful man as he sniffed disapprovingly at every ancient building from here to Tavistock: Buckland Abbey, the

Monachorum and Bickham House. Perhaps she could tempt him further to the historic tin and arsenic mines or Morwellham Quay. What was the point? Before realising Delarme had won the prize Strachey had imagined guiding an appreciative lord round pretty Dartmoor villages with mouth-watering names like Peter Tavy and Mary Tavy, Lydford Castle, Lydford Gorge. She could have taken him for a stirring trip on Dartmoor to wander the dark and lonely fell. She had hoped it might be Walter Nibbet but now, despite Clive's evasions, she knew that the winner of the worthless lordship could only be Delarme.

As she drove the lanes planning her itinerary she kept well away from Saint Agatha's and Tina Gum.

Clive and his wretched antics. When she had been with him in America she had been bewitched – bedazzled by his charm, hypnotised by his voice and beautiful skin. But reduced to a disembodied voice on the telephone, Clive's artifice became transparent. She could imagine him in their room – no, of course, it wasn't *their* room: he wasn't in San Francisco now – she could imagine him nevertheless, his large hand cradling the phone, his generous mouth framing a smile, his beautiful body relaxed as he left the next message on her phone:

'Oh, aren't you there? I hate these answerphones. Look darling, I'm afraid Lord Hexcombe is *determined* to visit his fiefdom. Bit of a bore, I know, but I've given your cell phone number – I know you won't mind – and when he arrives he'll probably call and ask you to show him around. Um... I'm afraid I'd forgotten the time difference. I thought you were behind us, not ahead. Silly me. Look, I'll call you later, is that all right? Afraid *my* phone's on the blink, but I'll give you my new number next time I call. Bye, bye. Sleep tight.'

Forgotten the time difference! He'd called deliberately, late evening stateside, knowing she would be asleep. Knowing also – as Clive did, perfectly well – that she never kept the phone on through the night.

Why had he done it? The answer was all too clear. By leaving a message on the answerphone he didn't have to name the new 'Lord Hexcombe'. As if she couldn't guess.

Strachey lay in bed, frowzy in the morning, the little phone impotent in her hand. Edgar Delarme. Could she bear a second bout of his company? She yawned and stretched. When I say

Strachey stretched, you may think I mean the kind of stretch anyone does half awake in the morning, but Strachey's was enormous, a cat's stretch, a full arching of the back, an extension of her limbs until the mattress seemed too short and her ankles bounced against its seam. Alone in bed, Strachey revelled in a body stretch, ankle flex, wriggling of her toes; the hip raise, shoulder roll, isotonic drills; then a final double body roll as she kicked off the covers and stepped to the floor.

A jungle cat needs one stretch, and then is ready to hunt. But although Strachey's drill took longer, by the time her feet hit the floor she was as awake and vibrant as a cat. Fresh blood coursed through her veins. Like the cat, Strachey slept naked, and she strode around the small bedroom grabbing wisps of clothing, as natural in her movements as any feline. As strokable, Clive once believed. She slipped into her panties and then her bra. Clad like a starlet she stood at the basin and splashed cold water against her face. In the Sickle and Hoe the hot water took its time. While it trundled from the farthest reaches of the building, Strachey continued to dash cold on face and torso. Her skin tingled with the shock. As the temperature became tepid she began an upper body wash.

Damn him. Damn every last follicle of his hide. Why should she wait for a crabbed American zealot? Why should she help Clive play out this farce?

She grabbed a toothbrush. And squeezed the tube too hard.

Perhaps she should phone Mickey – he'd know what to do. He'd have ideas, certainly. Though come to think of it, Mickey usually left decision-making to her. They had met while running errands for the art fence Gottfleisch – she was his investigator, sniffing out fakes, while Mickey was the muscle, settling scores. Mickey should have been ideal for her, a crim with attitude, hard as nails. But he wasn't a *dedicated* crim; Mickey had been trapped into the job by Gottfleisch and had used his earnings to break away. Up till then, he said, he'd spent his life at other people's beck and call – do what your father says, do what the warden says, do what Gottfleisch says. He'd even listened to Strachey for a while.

He surfaced later, running a drinking bar in Deptford. But fond as Strachey was of Mickey, she couldn't waste her life behind a bar. Especially not in Deptford. Whether it was Deptford, the South of France or Greenwich Village, Strachey didn't stick around any place for long.

Hell. She flicked water from her toothbrush. She hadn't

spoken to Mickey Starr for three long months. She missed his voice but... life goes on.

A strand of toothpaste hung obscenely from her brush. She flicked off the end and saw it drop to the porcelain inner of the basin. She ran the water but it stuck doggedly. The water ran against it, divided and flowed away.

She cleaned her teeth.

Lane Estates had barely five thousand pounds in its bank account and no office of any kind. Did she, as owner, have to stick around and complete the sale? Did she have to hand something over, as it were? Not really. She had no title documents. Clive had those. She was there for courtesy's sake.

But if she didn't play her part Clive might feel released from any obligation to share the proceeds with her. Not that he'd split fifty-fifty, but to get anything she must play along. Since she had been playing along with Clive for the past three months it would be pretty stupid for her to give up now.

There was a quiet spot on the river Tamar, deep in a valley thick with trees, where Strachey waded in the water, shoes strung round her neck, far from twentieth-century sounds. Because the Tamar marks the border between Devon and Cornwall, the surrounding area is ignored by tourists; they rush across on the main trunk road, determined to reach their destination before too late. These pockets of border country remain unchanged. Strachey had been to the isolated piece of river twice before and each time had been alone.

It was only when she was back in the car and heading out of the gorge that the ever-present mobile phone bleeped on the seat beside her. One bleep – a message. Someone had called while she was out of range. She pulled into a gateway to an overgrown field. Two thirty. Clive should be out of bed.

But it wasn't him. It was the new Lord of Hexcombe. But most unexpected of all, the voice on the answerphone was not that of Edgar Delarme.

'Strachey? Lord Hexcombe here!' Strachey stared through the windscreen. 'I flew to Bristol this time – none of that long drag from Heathrow. I'm driving down. You can't call *me* but maybe we could meet at that abbey place? If you get to hear this, I'll be there half after three, maybe four o'clock. I'll wait for you. Right. Isn't this a lark, as you English say? I'll see you.'

She had to replay it to convince herself the voice really belonged to Lincoln Deane. Lord *Lincoln*! She clenched her fist and punched the dashboard. 'Yes!' she said, as she leapt out of the car.

Strachey gazed across the tangled meadow. Never had grass looked so green. Never had blue sky looked so fresh. Lincoln Deane was such a sweetie. She remembered his oiled, bald head, his strutting gait, his striped linen jacket and crocodile leather shoes. A national treasure – in her view, the perfect Lord of Hexcombe. In the azure sky above, small white clouds scudded merrily across the sun, causing waves of pale shadow to ripple across the fields.

To make Lincoln an English lord was the most delicious joke – and with any luck a joke that he would share. Provided he didn't try too hard to mingle with English aristocracy, Lincoln should have a delightful time. Locals would be amused and friendly, because a wealthy, good-natured American was always welcome, and by Devon standards Lincoln *was* wealthy. He could enjoy the benefits – designing a coat of arms, flying a flag from the local steeple, presiding at dinners, opening fetes, making an annual speech at the local school. And he could print the Hexcombe crest on his wine labels. *And* he was a farmer, like many of his new neighbours. Strachey clapped her hands. There could be no better lord than Lincoln Deane.

Before meeting him at Buckland Abbey she dropped by the vicarage to break the news.

'You're lucky to catch me,' Tina said. She had her head inside the engine of her ancient Mini, and from the look of the oil smudges on her cheek she was in touch with whatever problem the car had. 'Distributor,' she said mysteriously. (It was mysterious to Strachey.) 'Buy British, I say.'

She straightened up. 'That's sorted that. I was going out, but I could put it off for a pot of tea?'

'I can't stop.' Strachey smiled at her. 'Hexcombe Manor has a new lord.'

'Oh, my goodness, I'd forgotten that.' Tina brandished her spanner like an incense burner. 'Will he be visiting us?'

'Almost immediately.'

Tina grimaced and shuffled her feet. 'Go on, tell me. I can take it.'

'Lincoln Deane.'

'Hooray!' Tina threw the spanner in the air. 'You know what I was dreading?'

Strachey ducked as Tina caught it. 'You and me both.'

'That's marvellous.' Tina's smile stretched from ear to oil-smudged ear. 'You can't stay for tea?'

Strachey glanced at her watch. 'I'm on my way to meet him. Better not.'

Tina was still grinning. 'Well now, will you curtsey to him?'

'I'll let him buy me tea.'

'*Tea*? Champagne, my dear – no less. Oh, my goodness, the Lord of Hexcombe – Lord of the *Manor* of Hexcombe – one must be correct! Is he rich, this Lincoln Deane? I couldn't tell.'

'I hope so.'

Tina looked at her filthy hands. 'I'm going to clean up.' Her eyes twinkled. 'Isn't everyone?'

She laughed aloud.

Strachey was waiting in her car at Buckland Abbey when the mobile rang again. She smiled as she picked it up.

'Edgar Delarme here.'

She couldn't reply.

He said, 'We need to meet, of course.'

The sun disappeared.

'Where are you?'

'Bristol airport. This is a call box, as you can hear.'

Delarme, she thought – two hours away, or three in traffic. Oh, Clive, you bastard. 'You're driving down?'

'Can you find me a hotel?'

Her mind raced as she replied mechanically: 'Same place as last time?'

'Somewhere more appropriate. Now I'm a lord... '

'We're rather short on castles.'

'The best hotel in town.'

'Town?' This was deepest Devon. The only town nearby was Tavistock.

But he closed the call imperiously: 'I shall phone again upon the hour.'

She clicked off the call and stared across the half-empty car park. A mud-splattered, drop-head roadster glided in. Afternoon sun glinted on the driver's shining head. He turned to her, waved, and brought the sports car to her side.

Like a young man he leapt out without opening the door.

'Well, hello!' said Lincoln. 'Isn't this a fantastic day?'

Looking very Californian in a pale blue Oxford shirt and fresh cream chinos, free of the restricting presence of Maxwell Homeforth, Lincoln was like a kid who'd escaped his parents. For a man in his late thirties he appeared surprisingly lithe and youthful. He had spent ten hours inside a jumbo jet, had had little sleep, had spent a whole day travelling, yet seemed fresh and snappy as a chief executive. Maybe it was the car. Maybe it was being without Homeforth.

Maybe it was Strachey. Certainly he buzzed around her like a bee on honeysuckle. He strode the grounds of Buckland Abbey, throwing out his arms, gesticulating, talking loudly and freely as if at home. Of course, she thought, he feels at home. He is living like a lord. At other tourists he threw cheerful glances as if they were his tenants. For a moment Strachey wondered if he thought the abbey came with his title and he was already stamping out the land but, as he prattled on, she realised he was just happy. He was a lord. The happier he was, the sadder she. Strachey knew that somebody would have to break the news that the lordship was in dispute. Edgar Delarme thought *he* had bought it. Lincoln, Edgar...

Her mobile rang.

'Excuse me.'

She tried to draw away, but Lincoln was so exuberant he stayed, chatting cheerfully as she raised the phone. 'Hello?' She covered the mouthpiece. 'It's personal.'

'I don't mind.'

She made a scything gesture.

'Oh, right.' Lincoln grinned and walked away.

She watched him bounce across the lawn. She removed her hand. 'This is Strachey.'

'Lady Jane?'

'Pardon?'

'Lady Jane Strachey?'

'Jane Strachey.'

'You remember us,' the woman said. 'The Nibbets? We met a week ago. My husband and I...'

Strachey's heart sank. 'Yes?'

'I simply had to call and thank you. So gracious. And now to think... '

'Where are you calling from, Mrs Nibbet?'

'Oh, we're all in London – you know, London, England? Standing outside Parliament?'

Strachey closed her eyes.

'Well, naturally, now we're part of it. We think it's the cutest place. We're going inside. Of course, they don't know us yet but we don't mind. We're queuing with ordinary people. That's why I'm calling.'

'Your husband's with you?'

'Of *course*! And Myrtle – that's my sister, and her husband Conrad – and Julie, who – you'll never believe this – she's actually managed to drag old Hunter with her – and we're all over here for seven days.'

'Lovely.'

'What I wanted to ask you, Lady Jane – well, I was saying to Lord Walter just a minute ago, I said, Walter, Lady Jane is sure to know.'

'I wouldn't count on it.'

'Oh, you can't fool *me*! Lord Clive told us all about you. Now tell me – you being a lady and all of that – when we get to the front of this queue, what's... what's the right procedure? I mean, this is the House of Parliament and us being lords as well—'

'I don't think you should announce yourself.'

'Oh, *no*! They won't recognise us – not yet – we've just arrived. I mean, that man, the usher at the front of the queue – do we tip him? What's the rule?'

'Just pretend to be a tourist.'

'You're sure?'

'You don't want to embarrass him. Keep a low profile. Tell me, Mrs Nibbet—'

'*Lady* Nibbet!' She shrieked with laughter. 'Oh, Lady Jane!'

Strachey dropped her voice. 'Lady Nibbet. Tell me, Lady Nibbet—'

'Oh look, fancy! You've made everyone turn to look at me! Bet they didn't know they had a real-life lord and lady in the queue.' This last was in a louder tone.

'Tell me, *Lady* Nibbet, you're coming down?'

'Of *course*! We've got to find a manor house.'

Again the tone was louder. Strachey imagined the entire queue listening to her. Mrs Nibbet said, 'Now we're neighbors, Lady Jane... ' She paused dramatically. What *had* Clive told her? 'We must arrange a ball. But more of that later, dear Lady Jane—' Mrs Nibbet seemed to be speaking solely for the crowd's benefit. 'Oh, the busy social round!'

'When are you coming down?'

Strachey saw Lincoln growing impatient. She had to end this call.

Mrs Nibbet was in no hurry: 'We're staying at the Ritz, of course.'

Strachey sighed.

'And we *do* want to fit in some shopping at Harrods and – where is it, Walter? – Fortnum and Maceys.'

'When are you coming down?'

Lincoln was within earshot. Mrs Nibbet condescended: 'Oh my dear *Lady Jane*—' She bellowed out the name. 'Most *awfully* kind of you. Perhaps we could meet up tomorrow – if that's not too soon?'

'Tomorrow will be fine.'

As Mrs Nibbet's voice rose an octave higher, Strachey cut the call.

Lincoln asked, 'Boyfriend?'

'Hm?'

'You said 'tomorrow's fine'. Was that your boyfriend – or are you and Clive an item? I never worked that out.'

She was no longer sure herself. 'We have a professional relationship.'

Lincoln laughed. 'Don't ever say that in the States! So... ' His eyes were sparkling. 'You and Clive are... *not* an item?'

Strachey was fishing. 'Did Clive say we were?'

Lincoln was fishing too: 'I'm asking *you*, Strachey.'

He smiled at her – that young man smile, that young man in a white soft-top roadster smile.

She asked, 'Where's *Mrs* Deane?'

'What are you – Jewish?' She frowned. He said, 'You answer every question with a question. No, since you ask, Mrs Deane is spending a couple of days at home. Emphasis on spending – probably buying herself a tiara! Hell, I don't know. Several weeks now she's been nagging at me to get this goddamn lordship and now she loses interest. What d'you make of that?'

Since Strachey hadn't met the fabulous Gloria she made nothing of it.

Lincoln came in closer. 'Anyway, I'm all alone, a lonely lord in a foreign land, and the only gal I know is you. But I tell you what—' He reached out to touch her cheek but had the sense to think better of it. 'I couldn't ask for better company.'

It was only when she was back in her room at the Sickle and Hoe that Strachey bothered to try Clive's American number. To her surprise he answered immediately. Expecting the answerphone she could only say, 'I thought you said this phone was dead?'

'Did I? A temporary fault.'

'Are you playing with me, Clive?'

'Playing?'

'Why haven't you come over? As if I didn't know.'

'Strachey, you don't seem in the best of sorts.'

'You didn't tell me you'd sold the lordship several times.'

'Ah. Yes, I was coming to that. Wonderful news, isn't it?'

'Wonderful? I've got three people here in England who all think they're the Lord of Hexcombe.'

'Three? My goodness! All together?'

'Of course. You didn't think they'd hang your certificate on the wall and stay in America?'

'I didn't expect them to fly across immediately. Gosh, how embarrassing.'

'How many people have you sold it to?'

'Um. Twelve actually.'

'*Twelve*! I'm out of here.'

'Hold on, my darling. I need you there. *We* need you there. We'll make a lot of money from this.'

'*You've* got the money, Clive – I'm holding the baby. What am I supposed to say to all these people?'

'The same to everyone. But keep them apart. Arrange your appointments for different times – preferably on different days – see one in the morning, one in the afternoon. Show them around. Settle them down in different hotels—'

'Clive, they're here *now*. They're not going to hang around at *my* convenience. They are *bound* to meet each other. They *know* each other, for God's sake: these are the same people as came on the last visit. They're the keenest – that's why they're here.'

'Three, you say?'

'Delarme, Deane and Walter Nibbet. The Nibbets have brought their relations.'

'I hadn't realised they'd be so eager. But three people, darling – surely you can keep three people apart?'

'In Hexcombe? It's not a city, Clive, it's a scattering of houses. *One* American would stand out, but three – and how many more are coming? – they'll be the biggest news since the second world war.'

'Oh, it's temporary. This is the first wave of enthusiasm—'

'And I'm drowning in it. I can't be in three different places at once. I won't be around when they find out.'

'Darling, you can't—'

'Don't keep calling me darling! Why have you started calling me that?'

'I'm simply—'

'Are you seeing someone else?'

Clive grew firm with her. 'Strachey, darl – Strachey, how would you like three hundred thousand pounds?'

'Three... ' She hesitated. As one would.

'We have twelve punters. Twelve lordships. Each paying on average fifty thousand pounds. That's six hundred thousand, isn't it? Split fifty-fifty between us.'

'Six hundred... Is that what you've got?'

'Around that,' Clive said airily. 'You wouldn't throw away three hundred thousand pounds for a few days' work? After all we've done? You have three naive Americans – all right, it'll be a tiring week. But be firm with them – make them fit to *your* schedule. Once they've seen the place and wandered off again, you might have one or two further visits from other lords, one by one, and that'll be the end of it.'

'They'll be *forever* coming. No one pays fifty thousand pounds for a property they don't visit.'

'Who said anything about forever? We only need a couple of weeks – long enough to get the money cleared and cover our tracks—'

'*Your* tracks. I'm still here.'

'Only for two more weeks. Then you can slip away. Neither of us need ever be seen again. As we agreed.'

'We were only selling one lordship then. How on earth did you sell a dozen?'

'A dozen auctions. Each punter had his own, mostly by phone. At each sale I ran them up to the maximum they would bid – it was quite fun, really. I'd had the title documents copied onto legal parchment. Bob's your uncle.'

'I don't think I can handle this.'

He could hear her hesitate. 'Of course you can. You're good, Strachey, you're my partner. I handle America, you the UK. I run

PB Auctions, you run Lane Estates. We're cruising now – on the last lap.'

Strachey could smell the flaw in this, and since there wasn't a tactful way to put it, she took a breath. 'All the money's in PB Auctions?'

'Temporarily. But we need to run it through Lane Estates – to keep everything legitimate. PBA will take a sales commission, pay the bulk to Lane Estates, then a few days later you write me a check. I can trust you, I know that. I think it's best if we pay ourselves a series of realistic amounts over several weeks – not that anyone's ever going to *audit* our accounts, but I like to keep everything above board.'

Clive was running smoothly now, diverting attention to the details. Strachey seemed to have two options: either drop out and walk away with nothing, or face the Americans and hope Clive played straight. Some choice.

Clive asked solicitously, 'You're not short of cash yet, are you?'

'I've five thousand left in Lane Estates.'

'I'll send a banker's draft. Another five thousand?'

'Wow.'

'On its way. You'll be OK for these next few days?'

'I suppose so.'

'Where's my tough little Strachey? You've never been a 'suppose so' girl. Strachey, my dar – Strachey, you can survive two more weeks to pick up three hundred thousand pounds.'

'Well… '

'Don't you dare say you *suppose* so! Are you ready now?'

She said, 'Yes.'

It was later that evening as Strachey sat in her small room sketching out her schedule that she got another call on her mobile.

'Is that Strachey?'

'Yes?'

American accent. She couldn't place him.

'Good to meet ya. This is the new Lord Hexcombe.'

'Fine.' She sighed. 'Welcome to Britain.'

'Right. So you heard I got the title?'

'Oh, certainly. Are you in London now?'

'Heathrow. But I guess I'll stay up here the night. I got to talk to someone in town. You free tomorrow?'

'That'll be difficult—'

'Because I'm comin' down. Where can we meet?'

Somewhere far away from everyone else, she thought. 'Your hotel?'

'OK, I'll ring you.'

'Will you be registered as Lord Hexcombe or do you have another name?'

'You can call me Frankie. Frankie di Stefano.'

9

A HABIT LINCOLN Deane had never got into was staying in bed. Certainly not when he was alone – and not, according to Gloria, at any time. In fact, among the indiscreet titbits she dropped to Clive during the many hours she and he had stayed in bed, was that Lincoln was not a bed person. Not that she was complaining, you understand.

But the impression Lincoln made on Strachey was of a stallion on the rut. He practically clung to her the first day and the only way she got rid of him that evening was to point out that after a ten-hour flight he really did need to get some sleep. At around 6pm he was fading anyway and, thinking that his performance might not be all-American, Lincoln snuck off to bed.

The following morning he was up at seven – unremarkable, you might think, till you remember that on his body clock this was somewhere around midnight. But he felt refreshed, ready to party. He washed briskly, shampooed his bald head, and not even an English breakfast slowed him. He jumped in his hired white roadster and charged across to the Sickle and Hoe. He barged in through the dark oak door and instantly spotted Strachey at a corner table, working on a cup of coffee and a notebook, looking for all the world like a Scandinavian school mistress. Lincoln was the keenest kid in class. He shook himself like a dog fresh from the brook.

'Good morning, good morning, good morning,' he said – in case she hadn't realised the time of day.

The barman was wiping the bar. 'Afraid we're closed till ten, sir.'

'Ten? Hell, we'll be out in the sun by then. How ya doin', Strachey?'

'Fine,' she said, closing her telltale notebook. 'You?'

'Huckleberry dandy. What a great day. Hey!' He called to the barman. 'Another cup of coffee here, when you have time.'

'Closed till ten,' repeated the barman.

Lincoln grinned at Strachey. 'Bring that man before the

Manor Court,' he said. 'Clap him in the lockup, what? Hey!' He called again, in high good humour. 'Do you know who I am?'

The barman barely looked up. 'Can't you remember?'

Lincoln laughed. 'I am the new Lord of Hexcombe Manor.'

'Well, bully for you.'

'Just a coffee will do fine.' He turned to Strachey. 'Some place you have here.' He rolled his eyes like Eddy Cantor. 'You eaten yet?'

'I hope *you* have.'

'You don't recommend the local cuisine?' He leant closer. 'I hope you've kept yourself free today?'

She tilted her head inquiringly. He said, 'I was hoping you could show me round.'

Sensing a rejection he added, 'You don't *have* to look after me but the sun's shining, I got a white, drop-head roadster – and I'm just a little boy lost, nowhere to go, with a clip of English money burning a hole in my pants.'

He smiled at her. She asked, 'What had you in mind?'

'Wouldn't *that* be telling?' Lincoln laughed. 'No, I thought we could drive around, take in some sights, maybe have a nice meal someplace, you know?'

'I have a busy day.'

'Come on, step outside. The sun will make you feel a whole lot better.' He grinned. 'I got a lovely car.'

Fifteen minutes later the door crashed open like the gates of doom. The second customer of the day for the Sickle and Hoe seemed reluctant to come in. He sniffed the beery atmosphere with disdain.

'Miss Jane Strachey,' he declared.

The barman was bottling up and out of breath. 'You want her... or you've got her with you?'

'I wish to speak with her.'

'Popular,' the barman panted.

'Tell her it's the Lord of Hexcombe Manor.'

The barman seemed strangely unimpressed. 'What about him?'

'*I* am the Lord of Hexcombe. I should like to speak with her.'

The barman nodded and continued bottling. Delarme remained in the oak door frame, silhouetted against the light: 'Do you intend to fetch her?'

'If I knew where she'd gone.'

Delarme glared at him. 'When did she leave?'

'Ten or fifteen minutes ago,' the barman wheezed.

Delarme whirled round and stomped away – so he didn't hear the barman add, 'She went for a spin with the Lord of Hexcombe.'

It took practically the whole of those fifteen minutes for Lincoln to learn that in the tight Devon lanes he could not drive safely with one hand on the wheel and his arm along the back of the seat beside him. Strachey said nothing. She let unexpected bends drive the lesson home.

She didn't need her notebook to remind her that she had two Lord Hexcombes in Devon and another two, Nibbet and di Stefano, coming down from London. These were the four she knew about. From her original party, she had heard nothing of the gnomic Cantabulet, and according to Clive, another seven titles had been sold. Who else was coming? Might they have already arrived?

'I wanna see a castle,' Lincoln said.

Strachey smiled. 'Is this a dream for you?'

'What, this?' Lincoln took both hands from the wheel. 'Well, it's a funny kind of reality, that's for sure.' He quickly gripped the wheel again.

Her mobile rang. From force of habit Lincoln patted his chest, thinking it might be his, and Strachey wondered whether she had been wise to leave her phone switched on. As she answered it she leant away from him, and when she heard who it was she leant some more.

Delarme's voice: 'I went to your hotel but they said you'd left.'

'How can I help you?' She had to be careful not to use his name.

'A low-down drinking house. I must see you this morning.'

'Impossible,' she said musically.

Lincoln chipped in: 'There's no such word as impossible!'

Delarme snapped, 'Who's that?'

'A friend.'

Lincoln said, 'I heard that from here. He asked who you're with – am I right?'

She nodded, adding to Delarme: 'I'm afraid the signal's breaking up.'

'The signal's perfectly clear from here.'

'You remember Tavistock? There's a market place in the centre. How about eleven o'clock in the portals of the Town Hall?'

'I don't—'

'I'll meet you at eleven o'clock.'

She clicked off the phone and Lincoln laughed. 'Hey, hey – and who the hell was that? I don't think I got a rival there, am I right?'

'Who could rival *you*?'

Lincoln paused. 'Is that where we're going – Tavistock?'

'Mhm – but slowly. We'll take the scenic route.'

'The scenic *rout*,' he corrected.

'It might be,' Strachey laughed.

In front of the estate agent's window, Strachey and Lincoln Deane examined property details with the amused disinterest of sightseers in a nowhere town.

'These are just houses,' Lincoln grunted.

'What do you want?'

'Something different. I got a house already, and I mean, no disrespect, but English houses don't compare with Californian.'

'I have *seen* your house, Lincoln.'

'That's *right*. I mean, these don't have swimming pools. They don't got proper bathrooms. What I want is history, right?'

'We'll ask.'

Strachey doubted there would be anything to satisfy Lincoln's taste but it was one way to keep him occupied while she dealt with the other lords.

When they pushed the door a little bell tinkled, but they had already been spotted through the glass. Jeremy Barrington Downey rose from his chair and approached with hand outstretched.

'Miss Strachey – and I believe we've met, sir?'

Lincoln grinned wryly. 'Mr Real Estate. This is where you hang out?'

'It certainly is.'

Lincoln turned to Strachey. 'You're on commission here?'

Her eyes widened. Lincoln said, 'Like a tour guide always takes the party to particular joints where she gets a cut. Hey, don't worry. You turn a dollar, I got no problem with that.'

He grinned, but it wasn't such a friendly grin. Strachey smiled back briskly.

'Jeremy,' she said blithely. 'I'd like you to meet the new Lord of Hexcombe Manor.'

When you play an ace halfway through a game you're left with a nervous feeling – the all-powerful card has gone and can't be used again. Introducing Lincoln as the undisputed lord meant that Jeremy fell on him like a crow on carrion. Rich pickings indeed. Jeremy would be happy – it would be hard to stop him – conducting the new lord around the finest and most expensive properties. He would lift Lincoln from Strachey's hands. But because he'd been named now as the Lord of Hexcombe – at least to Jeremy – the remaining lords must be kept away.

The first was duly waiting outside the Town Hall. Delarme seemed taller and more forbidding than when they'd last met. His beard was bushier. Even his eyebrows seemed to have thickened. He glowered beneath the old stone portico.

'Why is Lord Lane not here to meet me?'

'Should he be?'

'I consider it discourteous.'

'Lord Lane is in America,' she said. 'Otherwise I'm sure he'd love to have been here for such an historic day.'

He grunted. Strachey smiled sweetly. She asked, 'Where's your car?'

They were barely out of Tavistock when her mobile rang. She glanced at the ominous Delarme before switching it off and saying, 'I just hate these things. Don't you?'

'Should you not answer it?'

'It's discourteous to conduct a one-sided conversation in another's company. There's an answerphone.'

'Too much gadgetry nowadays.'

Strachey relaxed as the town disappeared. 'How can I help you today?'

'I require a list of all the places of worship within my Manor, with details of each sect.'

'I know the local vicar.'

Strachey bit her lip. It wasn't fair to land Tina with her *bête noire*. It would be better to keep Tina out of this altogether.

Delarme said, 'I have met one of the local priests – a so-called priest – a woman.'

'Know one priest, know them all.'

'She may have been accepted by the fallen Church of England, but she doesn't minister to Nonconformist faith. She is not a Methodist, a Lutheran, a Unitarian. She's not a Rabbi. She doesn't speak for Brahmins, Buddhists, Mohammedans or Sikhs.'

'Not a lot of those in Hexcombe.'

'But in the surrounding neighbourhood – knocking at our door? You must realize – of course, you *wouldn't* realize – that nowadays there is fierce competition for uncommitted souls. We must be wary. We must prepare our defense.'

Strachey murmured, 'And the best defence... '

'Exactly! I want the name of every preacher in the neighborhood. But perhaps we should start with your Miss Gum.' Delarme stirred beside her. 'She must gird her loins. She must be ever vigilant. She can give me names.'

After Delarme had dropped her at the Sickle and Hoe – distasteful to him but it had to be done – Strachey stood in the pub garden and phoned Tina to warn he was coming.

Tina said, 'Tell me it's a dream.'

'Afraid not.'

'False prophet, you are. What happened to Lincoln Deane – did he pull out?'

'It's complicated.'

'It's horrible.'

Strachey rang off and stood in the pub garden, looking gloomily at the trees. Tina didn't know the half of it. To her, Delarme was the new lord while to Jeremy it was Lincoln Deane. At this moment Jeremy could be driving the new lord from prospective manor house to manor house – both men unaware that the title wasn't Lincoln's alone. Well, Strachey thought, there were no properties near Tina's vicarage, so with any luck Lincoln and Delarme wouldn't meet: yet. But Jeremy and Tina had no reason to speak to each other – Jeremy didn't look the churchy type, and Tina didn't want a new house.

Could Strachey keep the lords apart?

The display on her phone indicated a message waiting – the call she'd cut off in Delarme's car. She keyed in the number. In the trees the blackbirds tried new songs.

'You have *one* message. Message received at thirteen forty-six.'

Strachey pressed the key.

'Hey, this is Frankie di Stefano – you know, Lord of Hexcombe and all that jazz? Just to tell you I arrived at this hotel – Holiday Inn, you know it? I mean, Jesus, a Holiday *Inn*?

But you can get me somethin' better later. Anyway, come on over here. I'm gonna have a shower, get something to eat. You wanna get here say four o'clock?'

Strachey killed the call.

The android said, 'To listen to the message again, press one. To store the message, press two. To—'

Strachey pressed three. She raised her face to the afternoon sun.

When she turned for the pub the barman was leaning against the door, watching her. Whatever passed for a lunchtime rush had ended. He tilted his head and his conspiratorial grin suggested he was about to suggest how he and she could spend the afternoon together – part of the afternoon anyway. Three minutes, she thought, might be his mark. She regarded him dispassionately as she approached.

He leered at her. 'He found you then, that Lord Hexcombe?'

She looked quizzical.

The barman sniffed. 'Came looking for you earlier, just after you and the first Lord Hexcombe left. I suppose they know each other?' The barman smiled, but she didn't. He said, 'First one had a lovely car. Drop-head, drop-dead gorgeous. Next one looks like Dracula's boss. How many of these Lord Hexcombes do you know?'

She shrugged.

He said, 'Because you've got another one inside. And this one's brought his whole family. They're having ploughman's lunch and pub champagne. He's got no taste in cars though. I'd stick to the first one if I was you.'

He moved aside to let her in.

At the only occupied table sat Mr and Mrs Walter Nibbet with four other people who could only be her sister Myrtle, Myrtle's husband and their two friends. The Nibbets rose, delighted.

'Lady Jane, at last!' cried Mrs Nibbet. 'We've come to take up our estate.'

'For the moment,' her husband added, 'we're staying at the Holiday Inn.'

10

THERE WAS SOMETHING childlike about the Nibbets. They and their friends clustered around Strachey in the pub and when they followed her out into the sunshine they trailed behind like school children. Each member of the party was introduced and each forgotten within a trice. Strachey stood among them like the school marm on a trip, a polite smile glued on her face, wondering what on earth she could do with them. Like children again, they chorused suggestions where they might go, what they'd like to see, how to arrange themselves in the car. (The Nibbets had again hired the four-wheel drive.) In the pub garden they fired questions which Strachey fielded, knowing she had to meet an unknown Mr di Stefano in the Holiday Inn at four o'clock.

The barman emerged to ask if they wanted another drink. As the Nibbets confirmed that no, they were OK thank you, the barman asked innocently which might be the new Lord Hexcombe. Walter grinned from ear to ear.

'Just checking,' said the barman. 'So I recognise you next time you call. This pub has always been popular with the Lord Hexcombes.'

He grinned evilly at Strachey and went inside.

Mrs Nibbet said, 'We could go to that ancient monument by the river – you know, the mill house, falling down? Then maybe, Miss Strachey, you wouldn't mind conducting us to that sweet little enchanted glade where the old village lies beneath the grass?'

Strachey glanced at her watch. 'Lovely idea. Maybe a picnic tomorrow when we've more time?'

Walter Nibbet agreed they shouldn't rush an ancient monument.

One of the women – Julie, was her name? – asked about shopping. 'I haven't seen a single mall.'

'Tavistock,' said Strachey – hurriedly correcting herself: 'No, go to Plymouth. Much bigger. Better shops.'

Far away from other Lords of Hexcombe Manor.

'Plymouth's great,' declared Walter. 'Nautical history. Sir Francis Drake.'

'What kind of shops?' asked Julie.

'The world's your oyster,' cried Walter. 'Plymouth Ho!'

Lincoln peered along the driveway at a large grey house mouldering beneath sad trees.

'Please God,' he said. 'I can't face another one.'

'Fine Georgian manor,' declared Jeremy. 'Impressive inside.'

Lincoln scowled. 'Impressive my *back*side.'

'The interior belies exterior drabness. Wonderful mouldings. Fine wooden floors.'

'What else would a floor be made of – plastic?'

'You'd prefer another place?'

'Yeah, with a swimming pool, a couple of garages and more than one bathroom on each floor.'

'Let me see,' said Jeremy, uncertainly.

'Some famous people around here?'

'Indubitably.'

'Any of their houses on the market?'

'Not at the moment… '

'Pity. Here's a tip. A good way to spend an afternoon – you know, those times when, if your wife mentions the shingles once more, you'll come out in them?'

Jeremy missed that, but Lincoln sailed on: 'You find some famous place up for sale and go out and view the dump, you know? See inside the cupboards of the famous. Talk to the staff. Maybe if you're lucky you meet a film star or… you get the idea?'

'You're not serious about buying?'

'You act like money's no object, so they think you're a real prospect.'

Jeremy leant against the gate. 'Let me get this straight. You're not really interested in buying a place at all?'

'When?'

'Today.'

'Oh, don't worry.' Lincoln clapped him on the arm. 'Today or sometime this year.' Lincoln laughed. 'No, I'm talking about California. Great sport. Down in LA they're used to it. Down there, you don't get inside a film star's house without they've vetted you first with the CIA. But up where I live… '

Jeremy was walking back to the car. He opened it. 'Perhaps we're done today?'

'Don't get pissed at me, Jeremy. I'm a serious buyer, but not for some goddamn miserable dump from a black-and-white horror movie.' He pointed a finger and grinned. 'A *British* black-and-white movie – and they don't get more miserable than that.'

Jeremy said, 'I'll drive you back.'

Lincoln shrugged. 'You Brits are no good as salesmen. No stamina. You've got to want that sale with every sinew in your body. You should have seen the dame who sold me *my* house. Sorry, the *woman*. We're not allowed to call 'em dames in California. Not PC.'

He grinned again, and came across to join Jeremy at the car.

'Anyway, this dame – hey, you know? – I can *say* this. I can say what I goddamn like. There's freedom here.' Suddenly he bellowed along the lane: 'This *dame*! This goddamn dame. She shows me round, sees I like the place, and she tries the old "I've got another buyer – very interested" routine. But I've been round the block a few times, know what I'm saying? "Fine," I says. "Lets me off the hook. Go sell it to this other buyer." I watch her face.'

Jeremy held the door open.

'But she, of course, is not having that. She fixes another visit. And this is when I find that she has taken in what I told about myself. You listening, Jeremy? Because the next time we go – I forget when, the next day, who knows? – she has remembered that I told her I liked roses because they're kinda less showy than all that bougainvillea folks always grow in California. So what does she do? She ships in a line of rose bushes in tubs, and stands all these tubs along the driveway. I mean, that's impressive, am I right?'

'A nice welcome,' agreed Jeremy as he got in the car.

'That's *right*. We get inside the house and she has some ice-cold Californian Chablis – because you know I'm in the wine business?'

'Mhm.'

Jeremy fitted the ignition key in the lock. Lincoln stayed outside.

'Then we wander out to the pool.'

Jeremy glanced out at him and said wryly, 'I suppose every Californian home has a swimming pool?'

'Sure, when they cost a coupla million bucks.'

Jeremy hesitated. 'A couple of million?'

'Well, the asking price was two and a half but we hadn't

haggled yet, you know? Anyway, this dame and me – both of us
with these great big glasses of Chablis in our hands – we stroll
out to that swimming pool and what d'you think?'

Jeremy was thinking a couple of *million*, and muttered,
'What?'

'She has two blonde dames swimming round the pool –
because I told her I like blondes. They're naked, of course.'

'Naturally.'

'Oh, they were natural, all right.'

'Swimming in the... ?'

'Yeah. And before you know it, they're calling out, '*Hi*,
Lincoln – you coming in?' And they're – what's the word? –
frolicking.'

'And did you?'

Lincoln grinned. 'Did I what – frolic, jump in the pool with
them? I strip off with this real estate dame standing fully dressed
beside me? No, no. That wasn't the point.'

'What *was* the point – you sleep with them, then you'll buy
the house?'

'Don't you understand nothing about selling, Jeremy? She is
showing me what the place *could* be like if I buy it. Letting me
picture myself. The point is, on our first visit this sales dame gets
an understanding of my lifestyle, then on the second visit, she...
makes it like I dreamed. I mean, that is selling, Jeremy.'

Jeremy glanced away. 'So you didn't sleep with them?' he
asked casually.

'Christ, no. I *recognized* one of them. She's a novelty
swimmer from the Blue Marina Club. Nice girl. Besides, I slept
with her once before.' Lincoln got in the car. 'So what have you
got to compare with that?'

Knowing her way around the twisting lanes helped Strachey get to
the Holiday Inn before the Nibbets. Though she was half an hour
early to meet di Stefano, she had to get him out of the hotel before
they arrived. She left her hire car out front and rushed in to ask
for him to be called in his room. The desk staff – ever helpful
(Holiday Inn) – directed her to the pay phones on the wall.
Internal calls were free, they said generously. Call him yourself.

'Mr di Stefano? I'm Strachey. We haven't met.'

'What is this – my watch stopped?'

'No, it's three-thirty, but I thought we'd make an early start.'

'This whole damn day's been an early start.'

'I'm sorry, you must be tired. I can't wait to meet you,' Strachey lied.

'You wanna come up? I'm in the tub.'

Strachey closed her eyes. 'I'll wait. Will you be long?'

'About five foot ten. How long are you?'

She could imagine him stretching lazily in the bath, enjoying a conversation with the unseen woman waiting downstairs. 'I'll be waiting,' she said, and hung up the phone.

None of the tables carried magazines, but she sat and read the menu several times. In barely five minutes a large, square-shaped man appeared in front of her and asked, 'Are you Miss Strachey?'

She leapt up. 'Mr di Stefano, that was quick.'

'I'm not di Stefano—' She registered the London accent. 'I'm his driver, Ray Patterson.'

She smiled. 'How d'you do, anyway? Is he on his way?'

Ray Patterson shrugged. 'I only met the man today.'

He looked Strachey up and down – but she was used to that. 'Friend of his?' He grinned. 'Or business?'

'Business.'

Patterson shrugged.

Strachey sat down. He stood beside her. Strachey sighed. She couldn't spend the next ten minutes reading the menu again, and if she fiddled in her handbag the man would probably think he'd won a battle of wills. She said, 'You needn't wait. We'll not need a driver. I have a car.'

'Mr di Stefano don't go nowhere without me.'

'I don't go nowhere without my car.'

He shrugged. 'So we take both.'

Patterson seemed an unlikely driver for the next Lord of Hexcombe.

'Are you an agency driver?'

'I'm looking after him.'

Strachey stared into space. This time the silence got *him*. He said, 'Mr di Stefano does business with my boss.'

She nodded. 'What line of business?'

Ray grinned sourly. 'This and that.'

She let the silence hang.

'My orders are to look after him.'

Strachey shivered slightly. 'You're more than a driver,' she suggested.

'I'm more than that.'

'What else do you do?'

He studied her. 'I don't ask too many questions.'

Strachey puffed out her cheeks. This should be fun.

Eventually di Stefano arrived. Though he and Strachey had never met, there was no doubting this was him. Apart from the way Ray Patterson stiffened, there was something so purposeful in the way Frankie strode across the foyer that Strachey knew he was the man. Plenty of men were five foot ten. But he was the only one in a sharp blue American suit, cream open-neck shirt and neat gold chain. His Johnson and Murphys rapped on the floor.

He came up, shook hands, gave Strachey an appraising glance. 'Patterson looked after you?'

'He was as charming as he could be.'

'That bad, huh? OK, Patterson, you can go.'

'I got to drive you – that's my orders.'

Frankie di Stefano looked astonished. 'Will you get outa here? When I want you – *if* I want you – I'll call you. Understand?'

Ray Patterson stared at him. He was twice di Stefano's size, but after three seconds he gave up. 'You're the boss.'

'Don't you forget it,' snapped di Stefano. 'OK, Strachey. Here we go.'

Delarme caught Tina only by arriving at the vicarage early as she gulped down a hasty lunch. The second chocolate croissant was an indulgence but it would be a long afternoon, touring the whole of her spread-out parish, visiting old ladies with imagined illnesses and reading to an elderly widower who couldn't hear. Her car was playing up again. The distributor had become as faint and frail as one of those old ladies – *more* frail: old ladies ran eighty years.

Delarme came straight to the back-kitchen door, his dark shape appearing suddenly in the glass like a shock effect in a Wes Craven movie. He glared at Tina. She choked on the second croissant and rose, spluttering crumbs across the cluttered table. Damn the man! Damn the second croissant. Be sure your sins will find you out. She moved to open the door but a flake of croissant stuck to her palette and she had to turn back and swallow coffee. Red-faced, unable to speak, she signalled to Delarme to open the door. He glared at her through the glass.

Finally she let him in and staggered to the sink for a glass of water.

'I wish to speak to you,' he said unnecessarily.

She recovered enough to say, 'Oh, is *that* why you came?'

Before he could begin his address she made it clear she was going out. 'I have to go *now*. My parishioners await.'

'I want to meet them.'

She was amazed at his presumption. He waited by the kitchen door as if on a diocesan inspection, as if her stopping for lunch was a sin. Perhaps *he* thought it was. Which was hardly Christian of him.

She said, 'That's quite impossible.'

'I cannot meet my people?'

'Not while I am taking them the Lord.' This wasn't how she normally spoke, but it seemed a concept he would understand. Far from taking the Lord, she would in fact be taking Mrs Henderson her football pools, weekly groceries and three bottles of stout, and would be taking the elderly widower a couple of library books Edgar Delarme would not condone. Tina wasn't sure she condoned them either but they were what he'd ordered, and fulfilling her duty to the widower meant she could read the racy bits herself.

'I shall follow your sacred round,' he said. 'And when you have conducted the household services, perhaps you'd explain to each parishioner that their lord has come.'

'I'll put it differently.'

'I must also speak with *you*.'

Tina looked round the kitchen for an escape. 'My afternoon's tied up and this evening it's Mothers' Union.'

'I'll come to that.'

'You're not a mother.'

'Are men excluded?'

'From motherhood or the Mothers' Union? I'm afraid they hate men to intrude. You know, it's women's work – a woman's world,' she lied. The three women who attended the Mothers' Union would welcome a visit from *any* man.

Delarme looked at the ceiling. 'Then we must call a parish meeting.'

They went in two cars – both of them wary of sharing one car. At Mrs Henderson's, Tina dashed inside with the bag of groceries, stowed the stout away, then briefed Mrs Henderson on the curious gentleman who had come to see her.

'All the way from America? I had a cousin there.'

'You must tell him *all* about it. Perhaps they know each other.'

'Does he wear a hat?'

'I'm afraid he's not a cowboy. But he has a beard.'

Mrs Henderson frowned. 'I didn't think Americans *wore* beards. You know, like Japanese. They can't grow them, you know.'

'Americans?'

'Japanese. Spencer Tracy always wore a hat. Of course, he's dead now.'

'Tracy?'

'My cousin. Died in an elevator. That's what Americans call a lift.'

Tina nodded slowly. 'I'll invite him in.'

For a religious man, Delarme left nothing to chance. At each house, he insisted Tina wait outside. He would only be a minute, he said, and kept his word. Tina didn't know – dreaded to think – what he said to his subjects, but he was so quick she assumed he simply stepped in, made his declaration and stepped out. He couldn't have listened to what anyone said.

'Does he ever?' she muttered, leaning over the engine, fiddling with the distributor.

He was back before she'd blown the second spark plug. He watched her, horrified. 'If you have damaged that motor I cannot help you make it work. You should have waited till we reached a filling station.'

'I know what I'm doing.'

'But you're a woman.'

'Glad you noticed.'

Actually, she'd prefer he didn't.

Sitting in the widower's front room, reading aloud from his latest Black Lace classic, Tina was aware of Delarme lurking outside. Previously he had stayed in his car but this time, when she explained that the service she was providing for the old man might take longer (she'd kept a straight face while she said that) Delarme announced that he would stretch his legs and stroll down the lane. An odd choice: the lane comprised a drab length of concrete road in front of a terrace of equally drab houses, where the only splash of colour was the widower's garden. Many a day the widower would spend hours out there, trimming each shrub, removing yellow leaves, cutting and rolling the lawn. He worked hard, and his preferred reward was outré reading and a glass of home-made sloe gin. Tina saw no harm in it. They sat in his front room, each to an armchair, and she read from the latest.

Written to a formula, Black Lace classics cut to the chase. Freed from the constraints of serious literature, each classic gives a quick and tasty description of the first two players, wraps up the where and why, then gets down to the nub. Two paragraphs sketch the location – in this case a luxury yacht becalmed in the Sargasso Sea – while a full four paragraphs introduce the characters – the Captain (powerful, wealthy and asleep), the mistress (sexy, ambitious and bored) and the deck hand (young, keen and muscular). By the third page of this nautical narrative the hectic pace slows down. Where a single sentence can describe the calm and weed-strewn Sargasso, five paragraphs are needed to describe the intricate fastenings of her bra. An extraordinary six paragraphs are needed to explore the distortions in the deck hand's pants.

Tina normally rather enjoyed these stories. Unashamedly erotic, the classics were in their own way highly moral and clean. Naughty but not sordid. Decent, clean-limbed young people struggled with and, after two hundred pulsating pages, thwarted older degenerates. Villains were villainous – given to rape, pillage and plunder – but the rape never seemed to do lasting harm. Like a field of oilseed rape, it clashed stridently but temporarily against a pastoral background, then melted into the general scene.

Tina was reading an interesting new way of using a hammock when she glanced from the window to see Delarme push open the gate and wander onto the grass. She hesitated, and the widower opened his eyes.

'Come on, keep it up.'

He wasn't talking to himself.

She read, '"His saliva ran freely as he imagined his tongue roaming over her naked stretched body, moving from her warm erect nipples down across the tight drumskin of her belly to the soft forest floor between her thighs."'

She glanced up. Delarme must be within earshot. She said, '"He raised her legs above his shoulder –"'

'What's that? Louder – I can't hear.'

Tina glanced through the window. Delarme was inspecting a rose.

'"Brett rode the waves of her rising pleasure like a surfer above a crest –"'

'What?'

'"A deep sea diver beneath the waves –"'

'I can't hear you!'

'"His breath held out so long –"'

'Louder! I can't hear you.'

Delarme was approaching the window.

'"Satisfied, he rolled away from her –"'

'What d'you mean, satisfied? He hasn't done nothing.'

'"Satisfied, he" – Look, if you're going to keep interrupting I'll have to stop.'

'Don't tease me.'

As if she would. 'You've got a visitor.'

She slipped the books beneath a cushion.

'I don't want a visitor. Say I'm not in.'

'You're always in.'

Tina stood up and walked across the room.

'I want my book!'

Tina stepped into the hall, then out the front door. She told Delarme, 'I've been reading from the book.'

'Fine work. I'll see him now.'

'You *have* been inoculated against chickenpox?'

'Against *what*?'

'It's highly infectious and can cause scars. You don't mind?'

'Chickenpox?' Delarme pondered. He pushed his shoulders back. 'No, we must not spurn the Lord's afflicted. I shall go in.'

'That's why he smokes so much,' she added desperately. 'To stop the itch.'

'Smokes?'

'Like a chimney. In there it's not so much *passive* smoking as the full Craven A. But it's his house, so we must let him do as he likes, I suppose. You don't mind if it *reeks* of cigarette smoke?' She glanced at her watch. 'Gosh, look at the time. I must press on. I'll leave you with him, if you like, while I do my other calls.'

'No, I can tolerate chickenpox but not nicotine. I'll come with you.'

He condemned the widower to oblivion and followed Tina to the cars.

In the small country market town of Tavistock the traffic was building to what passed for a rush hour. But people going home vacated spaces, and Delarme was able to park a few spots along as Tina nipped ahead to prime Mr Anthony, the organist. A pedantic, lonely man, Mr Anthony (she had known him three years and still didn't know whether that was his first or last name) seemed a safe choice for her last call. She hadn't intended seeing the organist at all but perhaps she could leave the Lord of the Manor entrapped in a web of Mr Anthony's obsequiousness.

Her plan faltered in the front hall. No sooner had she stepped inside than Mr Anthony laid a shaky hand on her shoulder and began wittering about a Derufle mass. Whatever that was.

'There's someone you must meet—'

'So haunting. Absolutely mystical—'

'A gentleman outside—'

'Melody floating out to the churchyard—'

'We have a new Lord of Hexcombe—'

'Dreamlike harmony—'

Delarme rapped at the door. The first decent thing he'd done.

'A visitor,' Tina said. 'He'll make your day.'

Delarme recognised a time-waster when he saw one and unlike Tina, did not pander to his whims. Though she tried to leave the men together Delarme simply cut the interview and followed her out the door. They scurried to their cars, leaving Anthony on his doorstep to simper at his lord.

Tina jumped in her car and perhaps for that moment, God took time to glance on his handmaiden and take pity. Perhaps it was chance. Either way, Delarme found himself boxed in his parking space. The Lord of the Manor's only option was to shunt his hire car backwards and forwards with all the sensitivity of his medieval predecessors. By the time he had crumpled a fender and forced his car free, Tina had disappeared round the corner. He hit the gas.

However... Tina was a minister of the cloth, her car was old, she was well known in the neighbourhood – these factors inhibited her getaway. Delarme was not left behind. (By now, God must have switched his glance elsewhere.) 'Drat the man!' she said – meaning Delarme.

She accelerated. 'And drat Jane Strachey!'

Strachey had just driven by the other way! Jane Strachey,

cool as you like, driving into town with a stranger at her side. Strachey, out with a new boyfriend, blithely indifferent to the horror that she had visited on Tina. She had some explaining to do.

Tina was so keyed up she made a U-turn without thinking. One moment she was surging out of Tavistock, the next steaming back in.

Delarme braked. He stared agape at the vicar's car as it slewed round and passed. He blinked through the windscreen to where Tina's mini had just been, then heaved on the wheel and turned his own car in an arc. There was a squeal of brakes. Somebody's horn. Something thumped into his side. The jolt was hardly more than in a dodgem at a fair – not that Delarme had ever been to a fair, let alone in a dodgem – and he glared through his side window at whichever peasant had not used his brakes. Then he slammed into reverse, spun the wheel and chased after the disappearing Reverend Gum.

She was too busy keeping Strachey's car in sight to notice the confusion in her wake. She sat forward in her seat, hunched over the steering wheel, peering intently along the road at Strachey, three cars ahead. She saw a signal – Strachey turning right. Tina flicked her indicator: this should be fun. A car chase. Like an American film.

The word 'American' made her glance briefly in her mirror but she couldn't see Delarme, and as far as she was concerned, that was *swell*. Leave that mother for *dead*, the vicar thought.

Strachey was squeezing down an alley to the right – a cut-through to a small car park behind shops. Tina had to wait for two cars coming the other way but she could relax now: she had Strachey pinned.

When she drove into the car park she saw Strachey and her businessman companion climbing from the car. Tina drove straight up and jumped out.

'I want a word with you,' she said – then: 'Excuse me,' to the man. Ugly fellow – swarthy, smartly dressed.

'Tina!'

Strachey looked startled. For once she'd lost her usual calm.

'You promised me,' snapped Tina. 'How dare you?'

'Can't this wait?'

'No.' Tina raised a placatory hand to the man and said, 'I'm sorry.'

He shrugged. 'I'm in the way?'

American. One of Strachey's American friends. 'Excuse us,' said Tina.

She tried to take Strachey's arm. Strachey said, 'I'm busy,' and the man said, 'Don't mind me.'

'Can we talk alone?' asked Tina. 'Or do you want to have it out here and now.'

'Not now. I'm working.'

'I've just spent the whole afternoon with your friend Delarme.'

Strachey winced. 'Look, we're just about to have an early supper—'

'Helluva early,' drawled the swarthy American. 'So I mean, if you got some business you need to attend to—'

'No,' said Strachey. Tina: 'Yes.'

The man said, 'Why don't I go read the menu? Not that I don't like watchin' girls fight.' He grinned wickedly at Tina. 'I'm Frankie di Stefano by the way, though around here I guess I'm—'

Strachey interrupted: 'If you'd excuse us, Mr di Stefano—'

'Oh ho!' he said with a smile. 'I see. It's Yankee Go Home time.'

'I'll join you in the restaurant. I'm sorry. This won't take long.'

He raised an eyebrow at Tina. 'Is that what *you* think – it won't take long?'

'Depends on what Miss Strachey has to say.'

'Hey, it's 'Miss Strachey' now? This sounds serious.' Frankie was enjoying every moment. 'I could be sittin' all alone in that restaurant while you two are tearin' each other's eyes out in the car park. I think I oughta stay and referee. Whaddya say your name was?'

'I didn't. It's Tina Gum.'

'The *Reverend* Tina Gum,' said Strachey. 'You know – Christian forgiveness, that sort of thing?' She glared pointedly at Tina.

'You need forgiveness?' asked Frankie. 'What did you do?'

'She set me up,' said Tina. 'Set everyone up. Promised us we'd have a nice, sweet benefactor—'

'Come on, Frankie,' cried Strachey. 'Table's waiting.'

'I'm enjoying this.'

'I'm not. Talk to you later, Tina.' She tugged at Frankie's arm.

Tina spoke to him. 'A few miles from here is an ancient feudal manor. You won't have heard of it—'

'Hexcombe?'

'Why, how do you know?'

Frankie grinned. 'And it's got a new lord now, am I right?'

'An American,' she breathed.

Strachey paled. She was staring over Tina's shoulder. 'Oh, my lord.'

'Yes?' said Frankie smugly.

Strachey said, 'Here comes Delarme.'

Tina spun round. Delarme's car had eased into the car park. It had a nasty dent in one side. Tina said, 'I'm going.'

'No, please,' implored Strachey. 'Delay him. I can't see him now.'

'I've had quite enough of him. He's your property, after all. You talk to him.'

But Strachey was dragging Frankie away. 'I'll explain later,' she said. 'I'll come to the vicarage.'

Delarme called, 'Miss Gum, what's going on?'

Tina ignored him and made for her car.

He spotted Strachey. 'Excellent. Miss Strachey! I need to talk to you.'

'Later.'

Delarme stared at the two women scuttling apart. 'I must insist!'

Strachey played a cheat card. 'You might catch the vicar if you hurry.'

Delarme started after Tina as she ran for her car. Strachey whispered, 'Come on, Frankie, get me out of here.'

They slipped silently to the street. Before Strachey could think how to explain, Frankie chuckled and said, 'I'm beginnin' to feel at home.'

He felt better still in the restaurant, which was Italian, with Italian staff who brightened visibly when Frankie marched inside quipping in Italian as if he ate there every week. The owner tossed the menu disdainfully onto the next table and insisted they leave *everything* to him. Strachey realised there was little danger of Frankie announcing himself as Lord of Hexcombe since in this place he was already being treated as *Il Padronne*.

There was only one ticklish moment – when the owner wanted to seat them in the window – but Strachey said she'd prefer a more secluded seat and of *course*, said the owner, he understood *completely* and he had *just* the table tucked out of sight, where his *special* friends could be completely private, and *nothing* could be any trouble, they need only ask.

'So,' said Frankie eventually, as he tucked a napkin into his collar. 'What's between you and this Tina, or shouldn't I ask?'

She smiled. 'You shouldn't.'

'You're keepin' secrets from me – so soon in our relationship.'

'Women always have secrets.'

'I noticed.'

Frankie wanted to keep up the banter but was out of practice.

'And we don't have to read the menu,' he said proudly. He snapped a breadstick.

It was to prevent Frankie from meeting the Nibbets that Strachey had persuaded him to take her away from the Holiday Inn. The thought of the lords jousting in the hotel dining room was more than she could bear – Walter might be backed by the Nibbet clan but Frankie di Stefano looked as if they'd give him no more trouble than a breadstick. Strachey hadn't met him in America but she could see he wasn't the usual Clive Lane mug. He exuded power. In the Italian restaurant he was pleased as Punchinello – but he would be: he'd had the Caesar welcome.

The waiter brought Sicilian wine.

As she and Frankie toasted each other, Strachey heard the restaurant door. Someone was coming in. She hesitated. It shouldn't be Tina or Delarme, and the chance of the Nibbets finding the best restaurant in Tavistock was remote, so she felt she could risk a glance. She choked on the wine. It stung her palate. She couldn't hide from the beaming Lincoln Deane.

The curious thing about Lincoln's bald head was that you could tell that before he lost his hair it had been blond. His eyebrows gave it away. And for a Californian his skin was pale. Certainly no one would take him for an Italian – yet the moment he opened his mouth the restaurant owner exclaimed that he was delighted to welcome *another* American, and did this *Signore* want an *excellent* table? Of course he did.

At which, of course, Lincoln smirked into the restaurant –
and smiled straight into Strachey's face. He nudged his
companion, who smiled more suavely. Jeremy Barrington
Downey nodded in a way that suggested his relationship with
Strachey extended far back and had encompassed silken hours.

Strachey's own smile was mask-like. Don't let them come
over. Of course they did.

'Well, hi!' said Lincoln. 'I guess the food's gonna be OK?'

The owner burst into a *recitativo* of agreement. Lincoln
glanced at Frankie: 'American? So where are you from?'

'New York.'

'I'm California.'

Lincoln played the state name like a trump.

The owner asked if they might want to share the table? He
could bring extra chairs. Perhaps a *larger* table? Strachey said
theirs was a business meeting and that unfortunately –

'Moving to the area?' Jeremy asked.

'That's right,' said Frankie.

'Thinking of buying property?'

'You in real estate?'

Jeremy made a deprecatory gesture with his hand but
nevertheless produced a calling card, which he gave to Frankie.
'Drop in any time.' He turned to Lincoln. 'In fact, Mr Deane and
I were looking at some places this afternoon.'

Strachey said, 'Don't let us keep you from your meal.'

Lincoln smiled at the seated Frankie. 'You moving here too?
Well, fancy that.'

'Maybe.'

'We could be neighbours.'

Frankie was sizing him up. 'What business you in?'

'The wine trade. You?'

'I've been known to do some of that.'

Jeremy took the bottle from the table and shuddered at the
label. 'Sicilian? Well, I suppose it *is* an Italian restaurant.'

'Don't shake it,' Frankie snapped.

Jeremy replaced the bottle hurriedly. The owner asked, 'Two
more chairs?'

'No,' said Strachey.

'In fact,' said Lincoln, 'I'm over here on special business.'

'That so?'

'You might not believe it but—'

'I hate to interrupt,' said Strachey. 'But we really do have our own business to discuss.'

'Business?' queried Frankie. 'I thought this was pleasure, Strachey.'

She laid a hand on his arm. 'Oh, it is, it is. We need to be on our own.'

That remark brought an awkward pause. Lincoln said, 'Well, don't let me '

Frankie asked, 'About this special business of yours?'

Strachey said, 'Here comes the food.'

Welcome as the arrival of the Fifth Cavalry, a troop of two waiters emerged from the kitchen bearing platters of *antipasto*.

Lincoln grunted, 'Another time.'

'Right.'

Frankie's attention had switched to the gleaming platters of Italian food. There were olives and *fungi*, sun-dried tomatoes, artichoke hearts, cuttlefish, anchovies and baby sardines, *crostini* and *crespelle*, aubergines, fingers of squid and asparagus. Jeremy said, 'My goodness! Is that the starter? There's more than enough for four.'

Lincoln wouldn't outstay his welcome. 'For four it isn't. Let's find our table.'

He turned away with no further farewell.

Strachey called, 'I'm sorry, Lincoln.'

Jeremy said wryly, 'You really should be more respectful to his Lordship.'

Then he left.

Both waiters helped the owner serve *antipasto* and wine. Frankie asked, 'Respectful?'

'To *you* – your Lordship.'

Frankie frowned. 'How's he know I'm a lord?'

'It's his business to know.'

'Real estate? Yeah, I guess so – they keep their ears to the ground. What is he – a friend of yours?'

'Once was.'

Frankie nodded. 'And he'd like to be friends again? I see. Well, you don't have to tell me your life story.'

Strachey grabbed the chance: 'But you can tell me yours, Mr di Stefano.'

When they had finished, Lincoln and Jeremy were still toying with their dessert. Strachey whispered to Frankie that she had

better have a word with them and he said he'd go ahead and fetch
the car. She let him go, then approached the others apologetically.
But when they looked up they were too far gone to care.

Lincoln said, 'You've drunk Californian, Strachey. Right. So
you tell this guy – we make wine equal to any damn stuff in the
world.'

'On your *side* of the world, maybe,' agreed Jeremy. 'But not
in Europe.'

'The French aren't the only guys—'

'Even Australia runs you close.'

'Au*stralia*!'

'And New Zealand.'

'None of them,' declared Lincoln, patting the table with his
palm, 'compare with the fine stuff we churn out by the *barrel* in
the Napa Valley. In that one… place… ' He swallowed more
wine. 'In that micro-climate. Ambrosial. Riesling. Nowhere
finer.' He was groping for inspiration. 'Muscatel.'

'You make white wines for everyday.'

'Nobility – that's what they are.'

Strachey said, 'I'm sorry if I seemed rude back there.'

'Zinfandel,' explained Lincoln, 'may be ubri… may be
everywhere. But at its best, my friend, it has a pedicure second to
none.'

Jeremy chuckled. 'Well, if you *tread* the wine—'

Strachey said, 'I didn't want Mr di Stefano to know who you
were.'

'Let the world know,' said Lincoln. 'Let them all know. Who
the hell's di Stefano?'

'One of your disappointed rivals for the lordship.'

'Really?' Jeremy looked up. 'I don't remember meeting him.'

'This is his first visit,' Strachey extemporised. 'But if he'd
realised Mr Deane was *Lord* Deane of Hexcombe – well, he can
be a very angry man.'

'He looked it,' remarked Jeremy.

Lincoln stood up. 'Play the game, old boy, what, what? The
thing is… ' He fixed his audience. 'Was an honest fight. Best
man… paid the highest bid. If he *wanted* it, he should've put his
mouth where his money was.'

'All the same,' continued Strachey. 'He is not a pleasant type.
It really would be best not to rub his nose in it. If you ever meet
him again, you'd best stay shtumm.'

'*You* might say that,' boomed Lincoln. 'He's not a pleasant type. Ha! If I *do* see him again I'll take great pleasure – great pleasure – in rubbing his nose in... my lordly shit! Oh, yes I will.'

Strachey turned desperately to Jeremy: 'Keep him out of trouble. Please. Consider yourself the lord's high protector.'

Jeremy looked grave. 'This di Stefano fellow – has he been bothering you, Strachey? Because if he has, I mean, I say... ' He lumbered to his feet and stood swaying beside Lincoln. 'We'll have to deal with him. You can rely on us.'

'Exactly,' thundered Lincoln, shaking his glass. 'Protect you. Sweet girl like you.' He replaced the glass very carefully on the table. 'Call on my services any time of day or night.' He grinned blearily. 'Especially night. You can reach me *any* time at the Holiday Inn.'

When Strachey arrived back at the hotel with di Stefano she expected a tussle in the car but he tried no more than a brief 'Fancy another coffee?', then went inside. Maybe the long day was catching up with him. Maybe he was out of his depth with English girls. Or maybe he was the kind of man who didn't bother to ask twice.

She didn't hang around the car park. She didn't want Frankie's driver, Patterson, coming out to 'help her' start her car. She didn't want to be there when Lincoln Deane returned. Once she was out in the dark Devon lanes she wondered how much longer she could keep the lords apart. Delarme was in another hotel but Frankie di Stefano, Lincoln Deane and the whole of the Nibbet clan were ensconced in the Holiday Inn. Surely one of them was bound to talk to the other – over breakfast, could it be?

Maybe she could persuade them to use room service.

She found a lay-by and pulled over to use her phone. It was midnight: early evening in America.

'Strachey! Darling.'

She closed her eyes.

'Funny you should phone. I was just thinking about you. I'd have rung but – gosh, what is the time in England?'

'Midnight.'

'Mm. Are you tucked up in bed?'

'I wish. You do realise I have four different Lord Hexcombes here now?'

'Four? That's awkward.'

'Awkward!'

'I hope they haven't met each other?'

'One or two have... sort of met.'

'Gosh.' Clive sounded amused.

'So far none of them have realised.'

'Oh, well *done*.'

'It'll be impossible to keep them apart, Clive.'

'You're doing so splendidly.'

'It's going to blow up in my face.'

'You'll manage.'

'It's all very well for you—'

'Actually, I'm coming home. You've caught me at the airport. So it's goodbye, San Francisco.'

'I thought you were in New York?'

'Oh, something keeps... popping up.' He didn't explain this. 'I'll be home with you tomorrow, darling. Though with all these putative lords about, I might be better off staying here.'

'Don't you dare! You can't leave me with this mess.'

'As if I would, darling.'

11

BREAKFAST AT THE Sickle and Hoe was always generous. The kitchen was designed to cope with lunchtime trade, not single meals for the occasional resident. Floating an egg in one of their enormous frying pans was like sailing a toy yacht on a lake. Chef – otherwise known as Luke the barman at this time of day – threw in three eggs, four rashers of bacon, two large sausages, some parboiled potatoes, yesterday's mushrooms, a large tomato and a slice of bread. He lifted the pan and swilled it with both hands. Plenty of room in there.

He piled the whole lot on a plate.

Strachey munched through most of it, accompanying the food with several cups of coffee (Luke had prepared a Cona for her) but she ignored the six slices of toast and jar of marmalade. This was an English breakfast from the eighteenth century, when people ate devilled kidneys, chops and bread and washed it down with a jar of ale.

An idea she did not suggest to Luke.

He was growing fond of her and thought he'd kept his feelings hidden in his chest. Rather than watch her eat – those red lips, delicate actions, and occasional tip of bright pink tongue – Luke stood outside in the morning sunshine and gazed across the unloved garden.

Well, she thought, if she'd wanted a barman she'd have stayed with Mickey. She had taken him once to meet her mother. At first, in that scrupulously tended village, Mickey had felt out of place and had slouched about with his shoulders hunched like a bullock. But her mother took to him. She made jokes and touched his arm. Before Strachey could blink, Mother and Mickey were in the cellar sorting the wine. Before the day was out her mother had led her aside, and Strachey knew from the gentle pressure at her elbow that she was about to hear a favourable verdict on 'this nice young man'. Mother wasn't the only one, back then. People said they were a strangely well-matched couple – not so much chalk and cheese as opposing magnetic poles that had slammed together and fused.

But after a month or so that need returned and Strachey
travelled on. One day, she thought, she'd work the wanderlust
out of her system. One day, when life was done.

A white sports car had drawn up outside. Luke was watching
the driver. He sniffed. Drop-head, bald head, he thought.

'Morning, Lord Hexcombe,' he called wryly.

Lincoln beamed. 'Glad you remember me.'

'You've forgotten *my* name though, haven't you?' drawled
Luke, who had never offered it. 'I thought Americans were
strong on names.'

Lincoln walked up the path smiling: a smart aleck, he
thought. 'You know something,' he said as he came closer. 'Not
all Americans are alike.' They were face to face. 'Ours is a big
country.'

Luke smiled back – a battle of silent teeth. 'Pub's shut,' he
said. 'Doesn't open till ten.'

Lincoln inhaled. 'I can smell breakfast.'

'I enjoyed eating it.'

'I've come for Miss Strachey.'

It was a mortal wound to Luke, though he'd seen it coming –
a blow he couldn't avoid. With what grace he could muster he
stood aside to let Lincoln through.

Strachey had heard him, but since she felt Clive's con could
crumble any time and might have collapsed this very morning,
she continued breakfast. A lesson she had digested – not from
Clive but much earlier from Mickey Starr – was not to fluster. If
you were eating, Mickey said, keep eating. Don't gulp it down –
the crumbs will make you choke.

Stay cool. Hang loose. Mickey had shown her what to do.

She watched Lincoln's face as he crossed the half-lit pub. Had
he discovered yet that he was not the only lord? It didn't look
like it.

Had he a hangover? It didn't look like it.

'I ate already,' he said, looking round the pub.

Lincoln was glad to see her eating alone. Parts of last night
would remain forever vague to him but he did remember that
Strachey had been eating *tête-à-tête* with some ugly little guy in
the restaurant. Not so little, come to think of it, but ugly, sure
enough. Some girls liked them ugly.

He said, 'Guess what I learned today?'

Strachey shrugged.

'My wife – remember her?'

'I hope *you* do – but no, we never met.'

'You didn't?' Lincoln looked surprised. 'Well, there's some girls I don't introduce to Gloria. But I could've got away with you.'

'Coffee?'

Lincoln grinned. 'When did an American refuse?'

'Cups are on the bar.'

He bounced across for one and she marvelled again at how fresh he seemed.

'So,' he called out, 'about my wife.'

'You seem determined to tell me about her.'

He poured coffee. 'Different slant – you see, my wife understands me.'

'She *does*?'

'Too well. *And* she phoned me this morning to announce she'd just landed at Heathrow. So there's a surprise.'

'Would you like some toast?'

'And why is that a surprise, I hear you ask.'

Strachey sipped her coffee.

Lincoln continued: 'Because, you see, I thought she'd be staying in Fresno another week. But apparently she can't wait to see our English Manor.'

'You're wondering what to show her?'

'It isn't that. I'm wondering about you.'

'What about me, Lincoln?'

'Look, how do I put this? You and I have not gotten started yet *but* I'm afraid our relationship must be put on ice.'

Strachey put down her cup. 'Our relationship?'

Lincoln nodded. 'It's gonna be tough for both of us.'

Tina Gum dallied over a leisurely late breakfast (wholesome muesli and tea) forgetting that the least desirable visitors tend to creep around to one's back door. She was picking a flake of barley from her teeth when a shadow darkened her frosted glass.

'Sorry I'm late,' Delarme purred.

Her expression purred, 'I wish.'

He inspected the kitchen as if expecting a flask of gin. 'We'll be off when you're ready.'

'Off where?'

'On parish visits.'

'Around *my* parish?'

'Your parish is my demesne.'

Tina started a reply too fast and caught a crumb in her throat. Not again, she thought – what does this man do to me? She coughed, coughed again, and had to swallow some tea. (Tina had never been advised on eating by Mickey Starr.)

'You're not coming with me,' she said.

'Certainly.'

'I don't work with an audience.'

'God is your audience.'

'You're not God.'

He stared at her as if he hadn't heard her properly. 'I am your lord.'

'God is my Lord.' She shook her head. 'I'm beginning to sound like you.' She stood up. 'Who on earth do you think you are?'

He became severe. 'I am Lord of the Manor of Hexcombe.'

She stood hands on hips. 'Listen. You may have bought this archaic title but let me make something plain: it is just a title, it brings no rights. You have no more power over me than over the flowers in the fields.'

He cut in smugly: 'I do indeed have land rights—'

'You have no rights! You bought a redundant title, mister, a bit of fun.'

'This title, young lady, descends from the thirteenth century—'

'And died in the eighteenth—'

'Nonsense!'

'It was practically dead in the sixteenth. I know what I'm talking about.'

He shook his head. 'I'm afraid you don't—'

'I found the thing!'

He looked startled.

She said, 'I'm the local archivist, *Mr* Delarme. I hold the parish records. I was asked to furnish details of any parish titles to the Historical Manuscripts Commission. This title is one of hundreds throughout the land.'

'The Historical Manuscripts Commission,' Delarme breathed.

'They are sold for fun. For vanity.'

'*Vanity*?' he thundered. 'I am Lord of the Manor. I will redeem my people.'

Tina hooted.

He said, 'My path is the path of righteousness.'

'Tread it out my door.'

His face blackened to match his robe.

She struck again: 'I hope you didn't pay much for that title. What *did* you pay?'

'My lips are sealed.'

'I know the going prices.'

She could see she had him on the run. But she sheathed her sword. 'If you've been misled, I'm sorry. I hope... ' She shrugged helplessly. She didn't know what she hoped.

Delarme stared at the female infidel. 'You will not sway me from my path. I know the way!'

'Take it,' Tina said.

Luke made a show of cleaning the anodised brass fittings on the pub door, but really he was trying to stay within earshot of Lincoln Deane and Strachey. Lincoln was easy to make out but Strachey's voice was low. Catching less than half their conversation, Luke asked himself whether his beautiful guest might be having an affair with the new Lord of the Manor – *one* of the lords. But would a lord put his girlfriend in a pub?

Lincoln stood up. Their conversation was over, but Luke didn't know what had been resolved.

Lincoln swept straight past him, looking smug. He didn't know, surely, that he was one of three different Lord Hexcombes who'd called at the pub. How many were out there? Maybe they were holding a convention of Hexcombes. Maybe Lord was not a title but a name – like Duke Ellington, Earl Bostic or the Artist formerly known as Prince.

These guys did not look like musicians.

Lincoln vaulted into his white drop-head without bothering to open the door. Oh, very clever; very American, Luke thought. Maybe he *was* a musician, or he *had* been a decade ago. That was it, a has-been. That sounded better. Luke sneered at Lincoln in his smart car. It would have made Luke's day if the cocky American had bumped his car into the next one coming in – a huge black machine with shaded windows. He nearly did: he swung out of the park and spurted forward without looking down the empty lane. Except it wasn't empty. Lincoln swerved aside and scraped as close as he could without actually touching the thing. Then he waved cheerfully and pip-pipped his horn.

Very clever, very American.

The black car pulled into the car park and a man stepped out of the passenger side. Luke squinted but couldn't see through the tinted windows. Must be a driver still inside. The man approaching him was stocky and had hair as black as his big car. He wore a suit. Luke had never seen the man before but he looked menacing. Maybe a health inspector.

Frankie di Stefano had not seen Luke before – but he had seen Lincoln: the lush in the restaurant last night with Mr Real Estate. Strachey had suggested one of them might be her ex-boyfriend. So what the hell was he doing here at breakfast time, looking so chipper? And who was this other punk?

Luke said, 'We're shut.'

'This is a motel, right?'

Luke chuckled. 'A pub.'

'You got a Strachey stayin' here? Must have another name but I don't know it.'

Not a total surprise, Luke thought: if they're American they ask for Strachey. 'I'll see if she's in. And you are… ?'

The British got no idea of service, Frankie thought. The guy hadn't even wished him a nice day. Still, maybe *this* would work: 'Tell her it's Lord Hexcombe.'

Luke had to laugh. 'I should have guessed.'

Frankie narrowed his eyes. 'Maybe you should.'

Luke didn't heed the sign. 'You'll be – what? – the fourth Lord Hexcombe?'

Frankie studied him. 'Some kinda joke?'

'I was thinking of putting a blue plaque over the door – you know: this pub is *often* frequented by Lord Hexcombe.'

Frankie nodded slowly. 'You know what I hate? Some punk makin' a crack I'm not on the wavelength.' He prodded Luke's chest. 'You got somethin' to say?'

Luke placed his hand on Frankie's shoulder. 'Yes. We are shut.'

No one touches di Stefano. He slammed Luke in the belly. He smacked him hard on the nose. Luke found himself kneeling down in prayer. When he looked up, his eyes swimming, he saw the chunky American bobbing before him like a boxer in the ring. In the distance behind him appeared another man from the car. A big man. My lord, Luke thought.

Frankie said, 'I guess Strachey is inside?'

By now, Tina Gum had not only finished her breakfast but in a fit of nunlike zeal she had washed up – partly to help dispel her irritation with Delarme and partly because she had not washed supper the night before. Nor yesterday's lunch. Not that Tina was a slob – far from it, she told herself: but living alone meant plenty of small meals, and a basin of hot water for each single cup, plate and spoon was overdoing things. Ecologically unfriendly.

But this morning she filled her bowl to the rim. She pummelled the dishes. To have that domineering man swaggering around her parish, interfering in her work, was more than she could bear. No wonder Strachey was keeping away.

The washing-up was finished and Tina was in her outdoor clothes when the front door bell rang. Not unusual at the vicarage. Because so many visitors had troubles, Tina had replaced the original bell with a cheerful melody chime. Callers were now greeted with the first line of *Lift Up Your Hearts, Oh Ye Gates.*

She opened the door to the Nibbets.

Mr and Mrs Walter Nibbet she recognised, but her sister Myrtle, Myrtle's husband and their two friends were new.

'Reverend Gum,' said Walter Nibbet.

'Your holiness,' cried his wife.

Introductions were made.

'You'll have heard the news,' said Mrs Nibbet.

'I haven't heard the radio this morning. Has someone died?'

'No, the *local* news – our own special news!'

They looked at her expectantly. Mrs Nibbet wasn't shy. 'My Walter,' she announced, 'won the auction. He is the new lord of Hexcombe. Isn't that grand?'

'Almost incredible.'

Walter stepped forward. 'I want you to know, Reverend, that on our last visit we felt we formed a special bond – with your good self and with the whole local area. I feel sure now that we'll have many happy hours together.'

'Happy *years*,' said Myrtle. 'You're not that old.'

Tina said, 'I'm lost for words.'

Mrs Nibbet asked, 'You didn't know? Walter, we must publish an ad in the paper.'

'Right away.'

Tina invited them inside.

'That would be right kind of you,' Walter replied. 'But we

were hoping – if it's not an encroachment – that you could take us and our friends down to that little enchanted glade? You remember, you and Miss Strachey showed us the place where old Hexcombe lay buried beneath the grass?'

'The sod.' Tina saw their blank faces. 'We call old grass the sod.'

Walter smiled. 'And that's just why we'd like you to come and be our guide. That's the kind of interesting thing you know.'

Mrs Nibbet smiled cheekily. 'You're the vicar. It's your job to be our guide.'

Tina paused. She looked at Walter. 'So you're the new lord of Hexcombe.'

'Certainly am.'

She paused again. 'You must tell me all about it. *All* about it.'

By the time Jeremy arrived at the Sickle and Hoe the place was technically open, though the only customers were Strachey, Frankie and Ray Patterson, and Luke was hovering in the shadows serving nobody. He glared sullenly at Jeremy who ignored the bar and strode to the others. To his surprise, Strachey leapt to her feet and said, 'Jeremy! I'm sorry I'm late – but if you wait for me in the car I'll be with you almost immediately.'

Barrington Downey prided himself on his speed of uptake. She wanted to use him to get away from the odious Americans. (Patterson wasn't American but was big enough to be a quarterback and, since he hadn't spoken, Jeremy read his nationality wrong.) Jeremy glanced at his watch. 'Fine – but we're ten minutes behind schedule.'

'I'll be right with you.'

He left the bar in triumph, leaving Frankie glaring at his back. (Luke was glaring at everyone.) Strachey said, 'So sorry, I must fly.'

Frankie sat back. 'What is this place – your office? First the bald guy, now this faggot. Wasn't one of them used to be your boyfriend?'

Strachey laughed merrily, trying to remember what she'd said.

Patterson sneered. 'Bit like a cat-house here, out in the woods.'

Frankie spun on him. Patterson said, 'You know, she sits here – men come out.'

Frankie was reddening. Patterson continued: 'One by one.'

Frankie's hand jabbed out and grabbed Patterson by the throat. 'Shut it. Right?'

The big man's eyes bulged – not only from being throttled. Most times, he would have swatted Frankie across the room but (first) his own London boss had told him to look after him and (second) Frankie might have a gun. Patterson restrained himself. He was often bigger than the punks he served. He was used to it.

Strachey said, 'Boys, boys. I really *must* go.'

Jeremy took care to drive her deep into the countryside before revealing that his only motive in coming had been to quiz her as to whether the new Lord of Hexcombe Manor was serious in his quest for property. It took her a moment to remember which lord Jeremy meant.

'Yes,' she said. 'I think Lincoln's serious. His wife's flying out to join him.'

'He never told me that.'

'He only heard this morning.'

They were parked in a quiet lane beside a gate into a field. The sun beckoned.

Jeremy murmured, 'You've seen him this morning?'

She knew what he was thinking – he'd seen her with Lincoln late last night. Better rescue her reputation, she decided: 'I keep in touch. He's an important client.'

'So you phoned him?'

'He has a mobile. Doesn't everyone? His wife phoned from Heathrow.'

'Has she come to look at property?'

'Could be any number of things she'd like to look at.'

Jeremy nodded. 'Lord and Lady Deane.'

'Sounds good.'

'Doesn't it.'

They paused, looked at each other, then chuckled freely.

Jeremy said cautiously, 'It is a bit of a joke.' He watched her. 'How much did you sell the title for?'

Strachey hedged: 'I'm not sure of the price. My partner sold it.'

'Your partner?'

Jeremy tried to stretch the word in such a way that she might clarify its meaning.

But she didn't.

Perhaps she was no longer sure herself. Later that morning

when she had got rid of Jeremy, Clive phoned to say he was driving down from Bristol airport. Strachey was relieved he had arrived. He sounded businesslike – which she preferred. And he didn't call her darling.

'I'm sharing a hire car.'

'Sharing?'

'Funny thing – I bumped into Mrs Deane on the flight across. We've teamed up to make the journey.'

'Are you going to the Holiday Inn?'

'Yes, for my sins.'

'I'll pick you up. She can keep the hire car and we'll use mine. Save money.'

'What an efficient soul you are.'

'I assume you'll be joining me at the Sickle and Hoe? I can trade up the room.'

It was a probing question: she wasn't sure *what* to assume. Clive said, 'Don't do anything for now.'

'You *are* staying?'

'Perhaps.'

'Why else are you coming down?'

'Gloria paid for the car.'

Strachey frowned at the phone. 'I hope she didn't pay for your air ticket?'

Clive laughed. 'Well, she was buying one anyway. We should be there by two.'

'So you didn't exactly "bump into her on the flight across"?'

Clive hesitated. 'How many lords have arrived now?'

Strachey counted quickly. 'Four – that I know of. Three of them are staying at the Holiday Inn.'

'In the same hotel? Gosh, if I meet more than one at the same time... '

'I've had all four of them.'

'You *are* wonderful, Strachey.'

'Hm. Where's this "Gloria" person now?'

'Powdering her nose. I can't talk long.'

'What's your plan?'

'Lie low, I think.'

'Nothing new there, then.'

Frankie peered gloomily from the car window. The narrow lane curved between high banks, made higher by being topped with thick, green, unkempt hedges. He felt hemmed in, cut off from the sunnier world beyond. He knew now why he disliked leaving the city, and he grumbled at his driver: 'Kinda down-home here, ain't it? This the road?'

'They're like this in Devon. People come here on holiday.'

'The hell for?'

'To get away.'

'Like in the Everglades,' Frankie mused.

Patterson had stopped the car half way down a hill, at the foot of which a stream ran across the road. Beside the car a wooden notice assured them 'FORD'. Across the stream – assuming they survived the crossing – stood a dark stone derelict building, overgrown with ivy and dark green climbers. Attached to the building was a crumbling millwheel.

'People live in that?' asked Frankie.

'Not any longer. It's a mill.'

'You don't say.'

Patterson decided not to try to turn the car round so he pressed forward gingerly down the lane. Into the water. God knows how deep it was. Frankie sat very still. He had a nasty feeling they were going to sink. He stared at the floor, waiting for the first puddles to appear.

When they came out the other side the engine had developed a stutter. 'Damp in the distributor,' Patterson muttered. But cars were something Frankie knew about. 'Get out and dry the plugs.'

It was while they were standing beside the car, Patterson stooped inside the engine, that the mill door opened. A man came out – looks like a wino, Frankie thought: thin, dishevelled, stinking clothes – and he eyed the car.

'Nice motor.'

Patterson's head appeared. 'Got any WD40?'

'What?'

'To dry the plugs.'

'Some bits of cloth.'

Patterson grunted and returned to his work. The man looked at Frankie. 'Got a cigarette?'

'No. Where's this road go?'

'You're American.'

'I know that. I asked you where the road goes.'

The man sucked on his teeth. 'Where d'you want to go?'

'Where does the road go?'

The man paused again. 'Well, it's a private road.'

'So?'

'You have to pay a toll.'

Frankie looked at him. 'Don't press it.'

'It's a ford, see? Costs a fiver, one way. Tenner return.'

'I said don't press it. You live in that place?'

'Yeah.'

'Who's in there with ya?'

'No one.'

As soon as he'd said that the man saw his error. Frankie stared at him with his small black eyes. Suddenly, the day felt colder. Frankie turned to Patterson. 'You fixed that yet?'

Patterson stood up. 'Sure. It's damp, that's all.'

The thin man should have gone inside. But some inner madness made him persist: 'That's a fiver then.'

Patterson stepped towards him. Frankie said, 'Don't bother,' but the big man struck out. The thin man was still on the way down when Patterson's shoe connected with his head. The man landed like a bag of sticks.

Frankie said, 'Oh, for Christ's sake! Let's get on.'

Patterson stood over the recumbent body. He looked disappointed the fight was over. He kicked the man, but he didn't move.

Patterson looked at Frankie – who said, 'We can't leave him there.'

Patterson glanced about. 'Well, it ain't a motorway.'

'He ain't movin'. Get him outa sight.'

Patterson grabbed the thin man's legs and waited for Frankie to take his arms. But Frankie just stood. Patterson shrugged and began to drag the man across the ground towards the mill. He was big enough that he could have picked the man up and carried him but Frankie guessed he was trying to make a point. Brits were always trying to prove *something*. Maybe Patterson wanted to show he was bigger than Frankie, as if that wasn't obvious. Maybe he thought he was tougher. But the way he was dragging the man, his head rattling against the ground, was just plain obstinate.

Just as well the man was unconscious, because it sure would hurt.

Patterson kicked open the door and heaved the man inside. Frankie followed. The fetid gloom suggested the place was derelict but there must be some part where the man camped out.

'I'll look upstairs,' said Frankie.

Patterson said he wasn't carrying the thin man up, but Frankie did not reply. He wondered what he'd find. It was an empty place and on his territory. That kind of thing was always interesting.

The wooden stairs creaked and occasionally gave beneath his feet. There were marks in the dust from where someone had walked before. Thinking of which...

Frankie reached around beneath his jacket to where the little Glock was tucked in the waistband of his pants. In the States they'd warned him not to carry a gun in Britain but it was a piece of advice that he ignored. When he'd met the people in London he decided he'd been right. A man needs a light in the dark.

The stairs led onto a landing and another flight of steps. There were bits of stuff about but no sign that this was where the thin man lived. There was a door at the end. Frankie opened it, leading with his gun. A storeroom. Bits and pieces. He went across to the small, square window and peered out. Small and high. He couldn't see the ground, just trees. Not so much a window as an air hole. You could get your head through, but nothing more.

Frankie left the room and paused on the landing. He listened. Nothing. Not even Patterson downstairs. The guy should be up here helping out. About as much use as a stalled motor. Frankie kept hold of the gun and started up the second flight of steps.

He could feel the air, which told him that either the roof was shot or the man who lived here had left a window open – assuming the place had windows that opened. At the top of the steps Frankie found himself in an extended loft. It looked as if the thin man had hauled up the few sticks that constituted his furniture: a sleeping bag, some sacks, several wooden boxes, quite an attractive chair, a primus stove. This must be his studio apartment, his loft conversion. There were a couple of pans, a bucket, and in a corner a rucksack. Frankie ignored it. He didn't need to rifle a vagrant's rucksack.

The man appeared to live alone.

Frankie went back downstairs, the Glock held loosely at his side. No apparent danger. But he didn't like the silence from Dumbo Patterson. On the last flight Frankie called his name.

'I'm still here.'

It occurred to Frankie that Patterson hadn't seen his gun. Don't show what you don't have to – a basic rule of life. He stowed it back in his pants.

Patterson was standing beside the unmoving body. 'I think he's dead.'

Bright sunshine filled the Arcadian glade. The Nibbets and their friends persuaded Tina to give them the whole history again. To them this hidden valley was the finest part of their medieval kingdom. Mrs Nibbet seemed convinced that the village beneath what Tina called the sod was the long-lost heritage of the Nibbet clan. Tina gently explained that the mounds were of a settlement smaller than a village – a farm perhaps – and that only rubble remained.

'And ghosts,' said Myrtle. 'Bet they're still here.'

Walter suggested they lay their picnic.

Myrtle said, 'If we all stand very quiet for five minutes... '

Walter said he was hungry.

From the steep sides of the valley around them came sporadic calls of birds, some of whom had spotted imminent food. Myrtle and her husband had hauled the picnic bags, and were now spreading food on the grass beside the trickling stream.

Mrs Nibbet clasped her hands together. 'In days of old, medieval knights – and lords, like my dear Walter – rode their chargers through the woods and made camp in wooded spots such as where we are. They'd spread a bounteous feast.'

Myrtle interrupted to say she hadn't got cold chicken. 'And this ham's enriched with at least fifty per cent water.'

'Things ain't what they used to be,' said Walter.

His wife said he should pass a law about it.

Tina asked whether they had found the auction exciting.

'Oh, it was fun!'

Mrs Nibbet clasped her hands again – her normal pose for when she told a story. 'Because people were taking part from all over the world, that nice Lord Clive said the only practical way was to hold a telephone auction. I tell you, Tina, the tension was incredible! We'd put in a bid, then a nice girl at the other end would tell us if anyone else had bid, and then we'd bid, and so on till we won. It got desperately close. I really didn't think we'd get there – but we did. Right on the button. It – well, I must confess that this lordship cost even more than we meant to pay but somehow, what with all the excitement and all, and with other bidders creeping in ahead and then dithering, well, we stuck to it until we won! It cost a lot but I tell you, Tina, it's worth every penny. Just fancy, my Walter a real English lord.'

Tina's least favourite lord came storming into the Sickle and Hoe, a pained expression on his face and his nostrils quivering.

'Miss Jane Strachey, please.'

To be forced to enter such a perfidious place! To impart one's business to such a surly person.

Luke said, 'She isn't in.'

'She will be to me.'

'She isn't in to anybody.'

Luke left Delarme while he served a pint of shandy and a traditional Devon ploughman's lunch. He threw away the traditional cellophane wrapper and came back.

'What can I get you?'

'I do not take alcohol.'

'You're in the wrong place.'

Delarme bristled. 'I wish to see Miss Strachey.'

'A popular girl, but she's gone out.'

Luke disappeared along the bar and Delarme shouted, 'Tell her Lord Hexcombe called.'

'Called what?'

Delarme turned on his heel and marched away.

A customer asked Luke wonderingly, 'Is that really Lord Hexo-thing?'

'Oh yes. And I'm the King of Persia. Didn't you know?'

Strachey stepped inside the main door to the Holiday Inn and checked around the lobby for stray lords or their attendants, then cautiously approached Reception and asked if Mrs Gloria Deane had checked in.

'Meesoo?' asked a bored but good-looking girl. Her command of English was in inverse proportion to her looks.

'Mrs Gloria Deane.'

'Chloridene?' mouthed the receptionist, who'd have made many a dentist happy.

'Mr Deane – Mr Lincoln Deane? His wife.'

The receptionist appeared to be counting – but then her face cleared. 'Oh! You are wife of Mr Deane? Yes, I am expecting.'

'You don't look it.'

'He say when *you* come I am calling 'im. I am paging 'im in the bar.'

'Paging' was a good word, a gem in her limited vocabulary. The girl picked up the phone, pressed a button, smiled winningly – then jabbered animatedly in Spanish. Her conversation took an excited turn, full of the Spanish equivalent of 'Oh no, you *don't* say. *Really*? I cannot *believe* it. How can you say such things?'

The girl and her happy smile settled against the counter. For the next half-minute she twittered and purred into the mouthpiece. She gave Strachey an occasional sympathetic smile, while Strachey shifted her feet and coughed meaningfully. The girl stayed on the phone.

Strachey felt a tap upon her shoulder. She spun round.

Lincoln Deane said, 'They just paged me, told me my wife was here.'

Strachey glanced back at the girl, still chattering contentedly on the phone.

'Don't worry,' Lincoln said. 'Spanish is the first language in this hotel, like California. She and the barman, you know, they *go* for each other. Pity. Because she's quite a peach.' He punched Strachey playfully on the shoulder. 'Not as good as you!' He laughed.

'Your wife hasn't arrived yet?'

His face grew serious. 'Jeez. No. Due any minute. Listen, we shouldn't be seen together.' He began to draw Strachey away across the floor. 'Gloria, you know, she gets jealous. If she knew about you and me. Wow.'

She stared at him. He seemed serious. He led Strachey behind an oversize display of plastic flowers and sat her down. Lincoln remained standing up.

She thought he was going to explain the muddled notion he'd got in his head, but he said, 'Hey, I got a better idea. I'm in the bar with a chum of yours – you know, that real-estate shifter, Jeremy what's his name? Why don't you sit in there with him?'

'I'm happy here—'

'He's trying to sell me – what d'you mean you're happy here? Look, Strachey, you mustn't pester me at this moment, you know? I got my wife arriving. I mean, I appreciate—'

'I've come to meet Lord Clive.'

He stared at her. 'Isn't he in America? Clive's staying in this hotel? Why didn't you tell me? Why didn't *he* tell me?'

'He's *coming* here. He's driving down with your wife.'

Lincoln paused. 'They're together?'

Strachey took a breath. 'That's right.'

'That's terrible.'

Strachey shrugged.

He said, 'My wife sees me with you, she'll kill me. He sees me with you, he'll kill *you*. Jealousy? I hate the word. I'm going. We'll pretend we never met.'

As he scuttled across the shining floor he was in time to wave a vague arm to Frankie and Patterson who had just come in. Strachey froze. All these lords in the same stupid hotel. And by the sound of it, they were the only ones here spoke English. How long could the secret be maintained? Damn Clive. How long till he got here?

And could he sort it out?

Strachey should have hidden behind the plastic flowers. Patterson had seen her, and was pointing her out to his boss. She put on a smile. When she fled the pub this morning she had left Frankie scowling at the table. She must be pleasant to him now.

They started walking across. Frankie seemed relaxed. It was Patterson who scowled. He had muddy trousers, as if he had recently been digging in the woods.

Frankie said, 'Whaddya think of this dump? Just like home.'

'A little piece of America.'

'Wouldn't be seen dead in one at home. So. Were you waitin' for me?'

Strachey laughed airily.

He said, 'At least you got rid of that real-estate chump. What did you do with him?'

'Now you're asking,' sneered Patterson, and Frankie snarled, 'You can go. Clean yourself up.'

They watched the big man leave.

Strachey suggested, 'You two don't hit it off?'

'He's the English version of somethin' I thought I'd left behind.'

'Meaning?'

'Meaning you shouldn't trouble your head.' Frankie smiled. 'Why don't I buy us a drink?'

They went into the bar to see Lincoln at the far end, knocking back a swift one.

Frankie said, 'I suppose we gotta join the guy.'

'I'd rather not.'

'What's goin' on between you two?'

'Nothing.'

'He was in the same restaurant as us last night. An' this mornin' I catch him creepin' away from that diner you had breakfast in. It gets me wonderin', you know?'

'Let's take a table over here.'

Frankie studied her. 'I could take care of him, you want?'

'It's OK, Mr di Stefano.'

'Frankie. I could be your friend.'

Strachey steered him towards a table, but he said, 'I got to order the drinks. You want table service here, you wait a week.'

Lincoln had noticed them, Strachey knew. In an attempt to keep him and Lord di Stefano apart, she said, 'I'll get them.'

Frankie frowned. 'Listen, you're with me, I buy the drinks. You want a cocktail?'

'Campari. Tonic.'

She sat down. As Frankie approached the bar she saw Lincoln stand up from his stool. She closed her eyes. But now there were more American accents from her left and when she glanced across she saw the Nibbets come into the lounge. Lincoln had seen them. 'Hey, hey,' he called. 'You still here?'

The Nibbets smiled. 'Why, Mr Deane!'

They had their friends with them. Mrs Nibbet began: 'Well, this is Mr Lincoln Deane. Myrtle, Conrad, Julie, Hunter, I'd like you to meet Mr Deane who we met a couple of weeks back when we were all over here to inspect dear darling little Hexcombe.'

Frankie turned from the bar. Here goes, thought Strachey.

Walter Nibbet added, 'Course, we were rivals then.'

'Lincoln, I'd like you to meet my sister, Myrtle. This is her.'

'It sure ain't me,' Conrad laughed.

'Delighted,' Myrtle said. 'You a friend of Walter's?'

Lincoln chuckled. 'Well, like he said – we've been rivals.'

'For the lordship?'

Strachey saw Frankie watching the exchange. She measured the distance to the door.

Lincoln said, 'I guess we can still be friends?'

'Surely,' said Walter. 'In fact, I'd like to buy you a drink.'

'That's right generous of you. But I guess *I* should be buying these drinks.'

'Oh no,' said Walter. 'I'll buy 'em. You're a sportsman, that's a fact.'

'If you insist,' laughed Lincoln. 'Hell, I guess only one of us could win the lordship.'

Walter laughed back. Strachey got to her feet. Frankie frowned.

Walter said, 'Now, what does an English aristocrat drink?' He turned to his wife. 'What do you think, my dear?'

Myrtle quipped, 'Blue blood?'

Strachey was squeezing between the tables. Lincoln said, 'Well, it's not going to change me – I'm a Tom Collins man.'

Mrs Nibbet prodded her husband. 'Champagne sounds good.'

Walter laughed. 'Oh, I never cared for that. Cheap wine with Seltzer.'

She said, 'You'll get used to it.'

Walter leant forwards. 'Lincoln, I shall join you in a Tom Collins, and I want you to know that I surely do appreciate the way you're taking this.'

'It's not such a tragedy, is it?'

'Certainly not!' Walter clapped him on the arm. 'And you'll join me in a drink to British aristocracy?'

'May it live for ever!'

'That's my man!'

'Why, look!' cried Mrs Nibbet. 'Look who has come in.'

They all turned round. Mrs Nibbet called, 'Lord Clive!'

Lincoln said, 'Gloria!'

Strachey said, 'God.'

Clive and Gloria looked as if they hadn't expected such a loud welcome. Or such a friendly one. As Clive tried to work out the best way to greet his audience, he licked his lips and stalled: 'Lincoln! I've brought Gloria safe and sound. We were on the same flight.'

Gloria had been watching Lincoln's reaction. He looked guilty, if anything – so she swept across to him. 'Linc, darlin'! My honey-child!'

'That's *right*!'

Lincoln wrapped her in his arms. Clive was backing from the bar. 'I'll get the bags.'

But Gloria called back across her shoulder, 'The bellboy will deal with 'em.'

She kissed Lincoln.

Clive caught sight of Strachey, a question in his eye. Strachey moved a finger across her throat. Clive continued backing from the bar.

Mrs Nibbet said roguishly, 'Lord Lane, don't you *dare* to disappear. We've so much to say to you.'

'I'm sure.'

Walter said, 'Well, Clive, I guess we meet on equal terms.'

Clive laughed lightly and continued edging towards the door.

Then came the voice of Frankie di Stefano: 'Goin' somewhere, Clive?'

He froze. Frankie had stayed at the bar and was watching the pantomime before him. Clive said, 'Well, well.'

Lincoln pulled his shining face from Gloria's blonde tresses: 'Another American – what *is* this, the Red Sox playing away?'

Frankie ignored him. 'What's happenin', Clive?'

Mrs Nibbet said, 'What's happening is that Lord Hexcombe is going to buy a magnum of champagne!' She beamed at her husband. 'Isn't that right?'

'Sounds good to me.'

She said, 'And everyone can drink to his good fortune.'

Lincoln laughed. 'Spoken like a true American! A magnum, huh?'

'I think so,' she said reasonably. 'There are eight of us – no, ten, eleven. Why, if we include you, sir–' (This to Frankie.) '— we have twelve! That's a magnum at the very least.'

Frankie snarled, 'Whaddya mean, if you *include* me?' But no one heard him. Walter was reaching for his pocket book, while Lincoln simply called across to the bar: 'A *magnum* of champagne! You hear?' He laughed at Mrs Nibbet. 'Though you've got a *nerve*, some would say.'

'A magnum,' Walter chuckled.

His wife pointed a playful finger at Lincoln Deane. 'I can understand you're being jealous – but you've a wonderful young wife there in your arms.'

'Real consolation,' Walter agreed.

Gloria disentangled herself. 'What am I – a piece of merchandise?'

Conrad muttered, 'I'll say.'

Strachey had reached Clive now. Behind his amiable expression his brain was working fast – but not coming up with an answer.

She whispered, 'I could ring the fire alarm.'

Julie said, 'Now, let me get this straight. Were all you folks over here chasing that same title?'

Walter and Lincoln said, 'That's right.'

Strachey made for the door. But before she could get there she met Jeremy Barrington Downey coming in. 'Ah, here you are,' he said. But he was looking into the bar across her shoulder. 'Good to see you again, my lord.'

The three would-be lords responded less than enthusiastically. Lincoln had had real estate to the teeth, Frankie thought Jeremy was Strachey's boyfriend, and although Walter knew he had seen Jeremy somewhere he had forgotten where. Strachey would grab any straw: 'I'm terribly sorry, Jeremy – Lord Hexcombe's busy right now. But *I* need a private word with you.' She started dragging him from the room.

Frankie said, 'I've had enough of this. What's your game, pal?'

He crossed rapidly to Jeremy, who spluttered, 'I say, do you mind?'

'Get your hands off that girl.'

This was unfair to Jeremy, since Strachey was pulling *him*. With a wave of the hand he tried to indicate this, but Frankie took it as an attempted blow. He parried and came inside. His fist rammed below Jeremy's belt buckle and brought the Englishman to the floor. Frankie kicked him in the chest and grabbed hold of Strachey. 'You all right?'

Startled, she pulled away. 'Let go of me!'

Frankie stood very close. 'Think I'm stupid or something? You got a problem with this guy, I deal with him.'

Strachey tried to reach Jeremy, groaning on the floor. Frankie held her up. Clive tried a 'Steady on, old man,' but Lincoln was more direct – he rushed across the lounge and heaved at Frankie's arm. Frankie spun round and thumped him in the mouth. Lincoln staggered but didn't fall. Like a baldheaded bull he charged the stocky matador. They crashed to the floor.

Strachey mouthed to Clive, 'Let's go.'

Walter Nibbet called, 'Fellers, that's *enough*!'

The barman rang a handbell – the hotel's novelty way of calling time – and the two warriors scrambled to their feet. They weren't finished yet. Jeremy was also trying to stand up.

He clutched at the nearest prop – Frankie's jacket. Frankie smacked his head. Jeremy dropped. Lincoln rushed in again.

Frankie grabbed him in a head lock. He was sufficiently distracted that he didn't see the barman come from behind to smack him across the shoulder with a baseball bat. (Yes, we do have them in England – especially in unruly bars. Around my neighbourhood they're quite common. But then, in my area we have a lot of unruly bars.)

The barman looked disapprovingly around. 'Was that gentleman *with* you?'

The Nibbets assured him he was not. Frankie lay flat out. Jeremy was on hands and knees. Lincoln was rubbing his neck and wondering (one) why he had rushed across the room, (two) who the barman was and (three) whether he had cracked a bone in his nose.

Gloria asked, 'What were you *thinkin'* of, darlin'?'

She glared at Strachey as if she might know what he was thinking and why. Strachey noted Gloria's use of the word 'darling'. An infectious word.

Lincoln smiled manfully at Gloria. He said, 'I was fighting for Strachey's honor.'

'You never fought for mine.'

Jeremy Barrington Downey groaned. He peered around the lounge, trying to decide whether it was safe to get up or not. He saw Frankie out cold and began to rise. Strachey asked if he was hurt.

Jeremy turned to her for sympathy but looked pathetic.

Gloria said – supposedly to the room in general but more specifically to Clive: 'I'm gonna have me a shower.' She glanced around at her largely male audience. 'Just think of that.'

As she stomped away the barman said, 'I assume you no longer require champagne?'

'Yes we do,' said Walter. 'More than ever.'

'Pour the stuff,' Lincoln agreed.

As the barman walked to the bar counter Clive said, 'Perhaps, bearing in mind this – incident – we should take a little break?'

'Or join Gloria in the shower,' said Conrad. 'Sounds good to me.'

Myrtle kicked him.

A champagne cork popped.

Have you noticed that whenever a champagne cork pops, people give a gasp of delight, then relax? It never fails. It didn't then.

Mrs Nibbet cheered politely. Walter clapped. Conrad pulled a face at Myrtle but clapped as well. Hunter took Julie's hand. Frankie grunted from the floor and when he shifted his body, everyone moved a few steps.

The barman poured champagne.

Conrad raised a glass and called, 'Lord Hexcombe!'

Everyone except Walter and Lincoln took a sip. (And except Frankie, for obvious reasons.) Walter and Lincoln stood looking modest, and Mrs Nibbet said, 'Oh, come on, Mr Deane. Drink up. Don't spoil it now.'

He frowned at her.

Clive stepped in before he could speak. 'On behalf of the British aristocracy, may I welcome the new Lord of Hexcombe Manor to his ancestral home? A Lordship of the Manor, as I'm sure you know, is among the oldest titles in this country – indeed, many titles date from before the Norman Conquest to the time of William the Conqueror.' He was trotting out his well-worn patter – anything to keep the lords from opening their mouths. He was also backing towards the door. 'Some rights were originally conferred by Royal Charter and Letters Patent, and some of these may still belong to Hexcombe Manor—'

'Oh Walter,' sighed Mrs Nibbet.

Clive hurried on (and continued backwards): 'In our business affairs a noble title is a priceless asset, but of course that is not the motive of our new incumbent.' Clive bowed to no one in particular. 'Aristocrats don't use their titles for pecuniary gain. Rather than ask, "What can this title do for me?" they ask "What can *I* do for... for my manor?" True aristocrats are reluctant to mention or draw attention to their station in any way,' he continued hopefully. 'They do *not* announce themselves as Lord of Hexcombe Manor, for example, but rely on breeding to reveal their standing. Our new lord, I suspect, will prefer *not* to reveal himself—'

'The hell with that,' said Lincoln. 'You don't pay more than a hundred thousand dollars for something you can't brag about!'

'That's a point,' said Walter.

Clive was looking desperate for a way out. Strachey came up

with one: 'That man's still unconscious on the floor,' she said loudly.

They glanced down at Frankie, who showed signs of coming round. Strachey said, 'Is there a doctor here? He could be more hurt than he looks.'

'I doubt it,' said the barman. 'I've tapped a few like that before and they always get up and walk away.'

Clive took Strachey's cue. Moving swiftly to the recumbent Frankie he felt his pulse. 'We must move this man somewhere more comfortable.'

'Why?' the barman asked. 'He can't feel a thing.'

'Someone take his legs,' said Clive.

After a moment's hesitation Lincoln volunteered. 'I guess it was my fight.'

He and Clive lifted Frankie from the floor. Frankie muttered something. As they began to carry him across the lounge Mrs Nibbet said, 'Lord Walter has a poorly back.'

Lincoln didn't notice – but Gloria did: '*Lord* Walter?'

Strachey tried a diversionary '*Careful* with Mr di Stefano!' but no one had stopped Gloria in ten years. She smiled balefully: 'Hey, Walter – *you* bought a lordship too?'

Walter beamed.

His wife said, 'Why, of course – he's the Lord of Hexcombe Manor.'

Frankie's body hit the floor.

Lincoln said, '*I'm* the Lord of Hexcombe Manor,' and he stared at the Nibbets as if they'd gone mad.

Frankie opened his eyes and said, 'Where am I? What's happening?'

Strachey rushed forwards. 'He's delirious. Fetch an ambulance.'

Lincoln was unmoved. 'What d'you mean – *you're* the Lord of Hexcombe?'

'I bought it,' Walter explained.

'No way. I paid a hundred and twenty thousand for this title.'

Walter's jaw fell. 'I paid a hundred and forty.'

'That means it's ours,' cried Mrs Nibbet.

'I'm dyin',' Frankie wailed.

Lincoln ignored him. He shouted, 'Didn't you just drink my goddamn health? I'm the goddamn Lord of Hexcombe!'

'My husband is, excuse me!'

Walter stiffened his shoulders and agreed: 'I am Lord of Hexcombe Manor.'

'I am!'

'Listen, punks,' roared Frankie, staggering to his feet. 'There's only one new Lord of Hexcombe and you're lookin' at him right now.'

'I told you he was delirious,' called Strachey, halfway to the door.

She halted. Framed in the doorway to the bar, broad as a nightclub bouncer but reluctant to come in, was the black-bearded Edgar Delarme. He glared into the bar. 'Do not take the name of thy Lord in vain!'

He refused to come into the lounge. Since there was no way past him, Strachey circled rapidly but quietly around the room and through the outer door to the patio. A bright sun shone outside, offering no concealment of any kind. Outside was safe. Strachey wove through the patio furniture and vaulted the low wall into the gardens. They were a cropped mix of shrubs and grass, but she ignored the flowers and ran. Somewhere round the other side was her car.

She sprinted along a gravel path beside the hotel. Only once did she glance behind, but there was no one after her. She did not stop running.

To reach the car park she had to run past the front of the hotel and it was as she shot across, head down, arms pounding, that she caught sight of Jeremy Barrington Downey. Friend or foe? He was running towards her, trying to head her off.

Foe.

Though Strachey veered to the left her destination lay straight past him. She tried a dodging run. But Jeremy closed in. She swerved again but couldn't lose him. He panted, 'I'm a rugger blue.'

She slewed to a halt. The indignity. Jeremy loomed in front of her like a prop forward waiting for the fly. He smiled and said, 'I could tackle you to the ground.'

She dodged to her right, tried to slip past, but felt his manful arms embrace her and pull her to his chest.

'Now, now,' he said. 'I could get *terribly* excited about this.'

She shook her golden hair. Be feminine, she thought: 'Jeremy, I simply *can't* go back in there.' She gazed up at him. 'Can you take me off in your car?'

'Tut, tut,' he said. Exploiting the privilege of a captor, he patted Strachey's cheek. 'Who's been a naughty girl, then?'

'I'm sorry.' She fluttered her eyelashes. 'Shall we go?'

'Inside?'

'Away from here. Please, Jeremy.' She hated this.

'Those people would be awfully angry with me.'

'I'll be angry if you take me in.'

'But if I help you get away?'

Christ, she thought, she was practically prostituting herself in the car park. She asked, 'What do I have to do?'

He stared at her sadly. 'Tread softly, because you tread on my dreams.'

'Gosh, Jeremy.'

'I must take you back inside.'

He meant it. His grip was solicitous but firm. As he began to lead her to the hotel she felt a child again, led from the playground to the headmaster.

'You don't have to do this, Jeremy.'

'Now that I've caught you, I do. I live here, Strachey. They know me at this hotel. Even Lord Hexcombe – whichever of those dupes *is* the lord – will know me. Perhaps he might *buy* from me in the future.'

They were at the hotel steps. A commissionaire opened the door. 'Afternoon, Mr Barrington Downey.'

'See what I mean?' said Jeremy as they walked through. 'Mind you, I don't suppose *any* of the Americans have bought a genuine lordship?'

'All of them,' Strachey muttered.

'Poor fools. One of them – the one who looks like a hell and damnation preacher – was announcing the apocalypse as I left.'

'What am I – the Book of Ruth?'

Jeremy sighed. 'Revelations. You owe them an explanation.'

He led her towards the bar.

In the doorway stood Lincoln and Frankie di Stefano. Lincoln glared at her but Frankie grinned. 'Some sweetie you turned out to be.'

Lincoln asked, 'How could you do this, Strachey?'

Frankie said, 'She's English – ain't that enough?'

When Jeremy tried to push past them, Frankie stood right in his way. 'Hold your horses, pal. We got some business out *here* first.' He stared at Strachey. 'You're not denyin' this is a scam?'

She nodded glumly.

'And where do *you* fit in?'

He wanted penitence and humiliation, so she muttered, 'I had to keep you all apart.'

Frankie nodded. 'How many of these lordships did Clive sell?'

A light flared briefly in her eyes. 'I wish to hell I knew. I thought there was only one at first.'

'He suckered you into this?'

Lincoln cut in: 'Watch it, Frankie. She and Lord Clive – they're an item. Remember, back in the States they went around together?'

Frankie shook his head. 'I only met Lord Clive. An' the only pretty thing he had with him was his striped jacket.'

Strachey asked, 'He didn't have a girl with him?'

After a moment, Frankie grinned. 'No, he was on his own – but that was only mid-afternoon.' He chuckled.

Lincoln said, 'They're together, all right.'

Frankie said, 'The thing is, Strachey, we want our money back. I mean, the title, that's gone, I guess, it never existed. But I'm kinda worried about the money. You see, if Clive – he's not a real lord, is he?'

'He is, in fact,' she said. 'He bought his title too.'

Frankie pursed his lips. 'Whaddya know? They're worth somethin'. Anyway, my worry is that *Lord* Clive has taken money from each of us, but I bet he ain't got all of it *now*. I mean, it must've cost somethin' to set this up. So he's still got – what? – half of it, at least, maybe eighty per cent – but as sure as hell he has not got all of it. And what does that tell you?'

To her surprise, Frankie put an arm round Lincoln's shoulder – and continued: 'We are not all of us gonna get our money back. Now, we got three choices. One: we put pressure on little Clive and make him cough up every drop plus interest. I guess that could work *eventually* – but who can wait for ever? Two: we each of us take eighty per cent, maybe only *fifty* per cent, and write the rest off to experience. That ain't my style. Or three: some of us take a hundred per cent, plus legitimate expenses, and we let the rest of 'em sort for themselves. An' I have to tell you, I ain't too impressed with the rest of them guys.'

He removed his arm from Lincoln's shoulder and jabbed him playfully in the ribs. 'I mean, this guy I should hate the *most*. He comes chargin' across the floor at me, we have a fight, an' just as I am thinkin' he is easy meat, he socks a rabbit chop to my neck an' lays me out. The boy has class.'

Strachey flicked a glance at Lincoln. Clearly, no one had told Frankie that it was the barman who had laid him out – with a baseball bat – and Lincoln was not about to disabuse him. Frankie said, 'This guy is not like the other guys. He's a street fighter. So, Lincoln baby, what say you mosey back inside the bar and fetch Clive out for a private pow-wow?'

Lincoln slid away.

Frankie turned his attention to Jeremy. 'I ain't figured you out.'

Jeremy bowed.

Frankie continued: 'My friend Linc thinks Lord Clive has somethin' goin' with the dishy Strachey here. Yet everywhere I go I see *you* and her snugglin' up together. An' here we are again. What's goin' on?'

Jeremy said, 'I brought her back to face the music.'

'Why?'

'She was running away.'

Frankie looked blank. 'So?'

'You didn't want her to escape, did you?'

Frankie shrugged. 'She's small fry. Wait a minute.' He turned to Strachey. 'Here I am thinkin' you're with this real-estate guy, but he chases after you like he's a small-town cop and fetches you back. An' there's Linc thinkin' you're "an item" with Lord Clive but you run out on *him*. So I'm puzzled. What's goin' on?'

Strachey shrugged.

'No,' he said, suddenly serious. 'When I ask a question, I get an answer.'

But Jeremy spoke first: 'I can assure you she's not with *me*. When I saw Strachey slip out of the bar I ran round to cut her off. Now I'm taking her back to face the people that she and "Lord Clive" have defrauded.'

'Like... it's your duty?' Frankie hazarded.

'That sort of thing. So if you'll let me pass.'

'Duty,' Frankie repeated unbelievingly. 'No, baby, you wait here. OK Strachey, what's your version?'

'Can I claim the Fifth Amendment?'

'Not unless you have US citizenship – which would not surprise me. I mean, how much do they sell *that* for nowadays?'

The door opened and Lincoln stumbled through. He looked ashen, pale. Even the top of his bald head was white. He said, 'That wretched man Delarme.'

'The preacher?'

Lincoln said, 'He created such an almighty noise. He... *ranted* at them all... No one noticed.'

Frankie narrowed his eyes. 'Where's that punk Lord Clive?'

'He's disappeared.' Lincoln stared at them blindly. 'He slipped away in all the noise.'

Frankie snarled, 'That bunch of punks.'

Lincoln turned to Strachey. 'And he disappeared with Gloria.'

12

SHE SAW HIM coming – but how could she refuse a man with a tear in his eye, a rueful grin and a manly arm flopping like a bolster round her neck?

'They've left us, Strachey,' Lincoln moaned. Like he cared about it, she thought.

But who knows – perhaps he does. Of *course* he does: his blonde bombshell, ten years younger, five thousand miles from home, suddenly picks up and flees the hotel with a handsome Englishman – handsome? – yes, she thought, that handsome *bastard* Clive, that totally unreliable, irresistible, aristocratic, suave *bastard* Clive, that *Lord* Clive. Lord Clive: that's what clinched it for Gloria. One glimpse of his calm, languid self-assurance and the blonde bimbo melted into her freshly laundered panties. *Damn* Clive. Damn Gloria as well.

'God *damn* it, Strachey.'

'You said it.'

'What are we going to do?'

We, she noticed. He straightened reluctantly from where his bald head had sought consolation in Strachey's far-from-motherly bosom and fixed her with sharp, blue eyes.

'Christ, we're left here together like... the last bottles in a bin.'

'Little orphans of the storm?'

'That's *right*.'

Strachey eased his head away but the rest of his body stayed in close. She asked, 'Did she take her suitcase?'

'Did she bother to bring the thing inside?'

'They flew over together—'

'Drove down in the same car—'

'And I don't think they met by chance at San Fran airport.'

'God *damn* it, Strachey – how could a man behave like that to you?'

He staggered and she stepped away. She looked across the bar to where Frankie and Jeremy were still snarling and Delarme hovered like an eagle. The Nibbets had disappeared to their room. The barman returned to his sink. Frankie started a diatribe on the English race.

Strachey began towards the exit but was unable to shake Lincoln off. One hand on her elbow, he came stumbling after her, spluttering with hurt. She had almost made it when Frankie yelled, 'Stop her! Don't let that goddamn girl get away.'

Strachey measured it: thirty feet between them, a couple of tables in the way. If she ran now she might just make it to the car park. She might *conceivably* get to the car. But she'd run once and anyway, was this what she'd come down to? Strachey had never run from anyone. Till she met Clive.

She stepped back in the bar.

'Hold onto her, Lincoln!' Frankie called.

Lincoln wrapped his arms around her and Strachey smiled. 'Down, Rover.'

She walked out of his embrace towards the party. He followed closely like a dog.

Frankie said, 'You got some explaining to do, Strachey. You're Clive's stooge, right? You work this deal together?'

Patterson guffawed from a corner where he'd been sitting, watching the show. 'Hey, Mr di Stefano – you got to learn to read faster! We passed that point a few minutes back.'

Frankie gave him a look that could have snapped a table leg. 'You still here? Get the hell after him – find where they went.'

'*I* dunno where they went.'

'Find out.'

Patterson began a sneer, then saw the look in Frankie's eye. He got up from the chair, straightened his jacket and strode to the door.

Frankie had already switched to Delarme: 'You're a man of the cloth, so you better let me deal with this.'

'My wrath has not abated.'

'Yeah, great. But this is outside your league.'

'She is touched with sinfulness.'

'Well, none of us are spotless. Look, Strachey ain't gonna speak in front of everyone, so what I say is—'

'I do not shirk—'

'I hear you, Mr Delarme. Tell me – you want a result or you want a showdown? I mean, we can stand here callin' the shots with her, an' maybe we'll get it off our chests – but we won't exactly be makin' progress, right? This girl needs a one to one.'

'She will answer to me.'

'An' if she don't?'

'Then she'll answer to a higher authority.'

'What you gonna do – kill her and pack her up to God?'

'I shall call the police.'

A dazed expression crossed Frankie's face. 'What've *they* got to do with it?'

'She has broken the law.'

'Hm.' It was a novel concept, but too alternative for Frankie. 'You know, the cops, once they get their hands on someone, they do not give that person back. Me, I could get this sorted in a coupla hours. What d'you want out of this?'

'Excuse me?'

'You understand the lordship's gone – you know that? Dead. *Kaput*. It never existed. So it boils down to what you want back. We're in the real world, right?'

'This world of sinfulness—'

'You ain't gonna get *all* your money back. You realize that? Clive has blown. Even if we catch up with him – and I reckon we can if you leave it to me – we're gonna find a good chunk of our money has melted away. It's the nature of things.'

'This wickedness—'

'What're your realistic expectations, Mr Delarme – half your money back? Would you be content with that?'

Frankie was enjoying himself now – carried away with the old game of stringing the mark along – but not so carried away that he didn't spot Lincoln and Strachey sliding to the door. 'Where're *you* goin'?'

At his words Jeremy jerked awake and leaped across to grab Lincoln's arm. Lincoln looked outraged. 'Take your hands off me. Can't you see I'm grieving for my wife?'

'She's dead?'

'She's run away with Strachey's... ' Lincoln turned to her. 'Are you married to Clive or what?'

Frankie snarled, 'She's married to Clive?'

'I don't know – ask her.'

Strachey shrugged as if *she* should know.

Frankie spat, 'Jesus!' and Delarme jumped.

'He's run away with my wife,' wailed Lincoln. 'I've lost more than anybody.'

'Hey.' Frankie was grinning now, a vicious grin, not friendly by any shot. 'D'you smell what I smell? This pile of elephant shit? Here we stand, each of us conned out of a hundred thousand dollars, and just when we should be headin' out to catch a dirty conman he lobs a pineapple to confuse us – he steals Lincoln's wife! Well, that's bullshit.'

'You said elephant shit,' said Jeremy.

'Fuck you an' your fuckin' elephants! This is a *pile* of shit.'

Delarme stamped his foot. 'Good day to you – *gentlemen.*' He stomped away.

Frankie watched him go. 'That's another one we don't have to think about. I don't like the sound of this one little bit.'

Lincoln snuggled closer to Strachey and whispered, 'We'll have to find a way to survive this.'

'What?'

'Our sweethearts have betrayed us. Both of us.'

She shouldn't have asked.

Frankie glanced at Jeremy. 'This has nothin' to do with you, my friend, so you don't hafta stick around.'

Jeremy ignored him and turned to Strachey. 'Do you need a friend?'

'The fuck a friend she needs!' yelled Frankie. 'Get your ass out the door.'

Jeremy blinked twice. His voice box tangled up. But not for nothing had Jeremy Barrington Downey survived ten years of English boarding school: that strangulated English upper class diction stems from the days when little boys, fighting back their tears, face up to bigger boys. They learn to express themselves in measured tones.

He enunciated: 'Would you like me to help you, Strachey?'

'You'd better go.'

His face froze into impassivity. 'Phone me,' he said, and left.

Frankie watched him. 'OK, Strachey, where's Clive?'

'And Gloria?' Lincoln bleated.

'Fuck Gloria – oh yeah, you did.'

Frankie knew it wasn't funny, but he gave a harsh laugh anyway and Strachey saw her chance. With a look of outrage she spun on her heel, saying, 'I'm not listening to that sort of language,' and walked away.

But Frankie caught her halfway to the door. 'Nice try, sweetheart. You're goin' nowhere.'

'You'll tie me to a chair?'

He nodded. 'Probably.'

'I'm leaving.'

He gripped her arm. 'Don't push your luck.'

They stared at each other. He said, 'Here's how it lies. Everybody's gone, leavin' you, me and Lincoln. So I think it's time we cut a deal.'

Her brain was empty. She said, 'I don't know where Clive is.'

'You're his girl, right?'

'I used to be.'

'So he'll get in touch with you.'

'By phone.'

Lincoln said, 'Gloria might phone *me*.'

Frankie glanced at him. 'She done this before?'

'No.' Lincoln stared at the floor. 'But we're married.'

'That makes a difference?'

Lincoln nodded. 'Financially.'

Frankie narrowed his eyes. 'Good thinkin'. I like you, Lincoln. How long might we hafta wait?'

Lincoln grimaced. 'Too long.'

Frankie's grip on Strachey did not relax.

Lincoln said, 'I could report her missing – get the police to help.'

'Jeez. Another guy wants to call the cops. What'll you say – Clive kidnapped her?'

Lincoln seemed to give this serious thought. 'The thing is, Gloria will use her credit cards – *my* credit cards. The police could—'

'Forget it, Lincoln. Christ, we call the cops, we hand the whole thing over to them. Maybe they find 'em, maybe they won't. But I tell you this: we will not see a bent dime of our precious money. Besides... ' He prodded Strachey, hard against his side. 'I guess you're still fond of Clive?'

She shrugged.

'Yes, you are,' he told her. 'Right now you're pissed at him, but *I'm* the one who's really pissed at him. He ripped me off.' He paused. She could feel his fingers sticking in her arm. 'I wanna get my hands on him.'

You could have misconstrued the scene: two men, an attractive blonde, sitting on a bed in a hotel bedroom on a summer afternoon. You would not have thought you were looking at a prison cell.

Frankie was on the telephone. He hadn't said who he was phoning, but he didn't seem to care that they listened in.

'Right,' he said – to whoever it was: 'So you're tellin' me Patterson's all I get?' He scowled at the wall. 'I'm askin' you a favor. Is that gettin' through?' He drummed his fingers. 'If you were over *my* side of the pond an' you wanted help, I'd give you a damn sight more than Patterson. Yeah. No, it's *not* money – it's an honor kinda thing.'

He frowned. They seemed to be telling him something.

'His hire car? What're you sayin' – run a trace? Why should they? He paid for the thing – it's about the only legitimate thing he's done.'

They were speaking again.

'Yeah, that'd be useful. I'll speak to Patterson when he gets back.'

After half an hour the bulky Patterson returned glum-faced, saying he'd found no trace of Clive or Gloria. By the time he'd eased his large body into the room the air smelled stale, as if it had been recycled too often. Strachey and Lincoln sat like grandparents in separate chairs while Frankie lay on the bed. He didn't get up when Patterson came in.

With both chairs taken and Frankie on the bed, there was nowhere for Patterson to sit except the john or the floor, so he decided to sit against a radiator. The metal was cold but he didn't mind that. He'd have enjoyed a cigarette but he was the only one with the habit. People were so prissy nowadays, he thought, that even if he was alone in the room and he lit a cigarette he'd set off a fire alarm. What was wrong with people now? They couldn't stand a whiff of smoke. They were so damn sensitive. The more he brooded the more he found himself longing for a cigarette – but he couldn't leave the room, because they had to sit there waiting for the phone to ring. And he couldn't taint their precious air. He had to sit sucking his thumb.

So he sat like a mangy dog, and every time he moved he released the smell of stale tobacco.

After a hundred years the phone rang. Frankie got off the bed, picked up the phone and gave his name. He looked at Patterson and said, 'They wanna talk to *you*.'

Patterson untangled himself from the floor – his stale tobacco almost *visible* – and held the receiver close to his ear. He answered in monosyllables, revealing nothing to the others in the room. They watched him.

When he had finished he replaced the receiver with elaborate care and paused deliberately. No one said a word. They didn't cough. Since he had to speak at some point, he said, 'The boys have been on to the hire-car company. Your man's turned in the car at Bristol airport.'

13

MRS NIBBET INTERCEPTED Strachey in the lobby: 'Walter wants to talk to you.'

Strachey followed her through the bar, ignored the barman's smile, and floated wearily onto the rear concrete patio. Beneath a rose arbour Walter Nibbet sat at a white plastic table with the full posse of his family: sister-in-law Myrtle, her husband Conrad, stern-faced Hunter, and Julie, his wife. Walter wore a hound's-tooth jacket and open shirt, and sat in the plastic armchair like a chief executive about to close a failing plant. He unpursed his lips and said, 'I'm a reasonable man.'

Strachey nodded. That was a bad start.

'I like to give folks the benefit of the doubt. But we have a situation here.'

Which was a way of putting it.

Mrs Nibbet cut in: 'Would you like a seat, dear? We shouldn't keep you standing.'

Strachey hesitated, then took the nearest chair carefully as if it might have been booby-trapped. But it wrapped around her solidly enough. She crossed her right leg over her left, sat prettily, and felt her shin tremble.

Walter said, 'Correct me if I'm wrong. I bought a title – the Lordship of Hexcombe?'

'Lord of the *Manor* of Hexcombe, yes.'

Julie cleared her throat. 'You don't deny it?'

Strachey kept her gaze on Walter. 'You bought your title from Lord Clive Lane.'

'No, I bought it from the company he works for, Lane Estates – which I believe you own?'

You bastard, Clive, thought Strachey as she smiled back. 'That's correct.'

'And there can be only one Lord of the Manor?'

'Of the Manor of Hexcombe, yes.'

He was like a man completing boxes on an entry form. 'And I bought the title to it?'

'That's my understanding.'

Mrs Nibbet gave a triumphant sigh.

'Now, I'm a simple man, but to me that suggests that I am therefore Lord of the Manor, and I am the only man that is.'

'A fair assumption,' Strachey agreed.

'So how come all these people think *they* bought the title – if it belongs to me?'

'A fair *question*.'

But Strachey didn't know how to answer it. She felt like a kid caught in the orchard with a pocket full of apples, faced by an adult who insists on being so very *reasonable*, ticking off the facts, finger by finger, waiting for the kid to make a full and contrite penance of their own free will.

But what could she say? 'It certainly does seem confusing... '

'*You're* confused? How d'you think I feel?'

Strachey's mind was blank. Any moment the axe would fall. She tried switching tack: 'You do have the relevant papers?'

'Of course. You think I'd hand over a cheque without something in return, relying only on... the word of an English gentleman? No, sir. I have the original parchment.'

Doesn't everyone? Strachey thought.

'Would you like to see it?' Mrs Nibbet asked with a nervous chuckle. 'You weren't there when the sale was closed, and you've only our word that we bought it.'

'I don't doubt you.'

'Very gracious of you, Lady Jane.'

'I'm no lady.'

Mrs Nibbet smiled. 'Oh, I know you don't like to use your title. Are you married to Clive?'

'I'm not.'

'But you *are* a lady?'

Strachey floundered in uncharted waters. 'This has nothing to do with it.'

'So *modest*,' sighed Mrs Nibbet. 'Show her the parchment, Walter.'

He fumbled in his briefcase.

Julie smiled across at Strachey. 'I said you weren't married to that creep. As things turned out I guess it's just as well!'

Strachey smiled enigmatically. She hoped it looked enigmatic and not desperate.

Mrs Nibbet touched her arm. 'I only saw Mrs Deane the once – and I have to tell you, she did not look a nice person.'

'Looked OK to me,' laughed Walter. He had the papers now. Strachey nodded at them. 'Those appear to be correct.'

Mrs Nibbet smacked her hands together. 'I *told* you, Walter! You see, we *have* the papers. That means the title's yours. Now, put on your thinking cap, Lady Jane – how can these other people believe they bought the title, when clear as daylight it belongs to us?'

Strachey shook her head. 'I'm puzzled.'

'You seen those other folks?' Julie asked. 'Frankly, they don't know what *day* it is. You know what I reckon?'

Strachey hung on her words.

'I reckon they got so convinced they were going to win that they won't *allow* themselves to admit they lost. They're in denial. I mean, they flew over a few weeks back, saw the lands and everything, got carried away and *told* themselves they were Lord of Hexcombe even before they'd bought it. Then in the auction they must've gotten themselves confused—'

'It *was* confusing,' Mrs Nibbet agreed.

'Hell, yes,' said Walter. 'Those folks may have thought they'd won it, but I tell you, Strachey, at one point we thought we'd *lost* that auction. Is that not right?'

Mrs Nibbet agreed. Her husband explained: 'We put in our final bid – and then hang me, but some fellow topped it, and Lord Clive asked, didn't we think we could go one tincey wincey step more, and we said no, we couldn't, we'd set our limit and that was the end of it, and he said, well, that would be the end of the sale, and we thought the whole thing was over, and just as we were trying to come to terms with our disappointment Lord Clive came back on the line and told us that this other fellow had messed up his bid and that if we were willing, our bid could stand, since we were the highest underbidders or whatever he called it, and as I say, if we were willing we could have the title, and well, there we were, right up at the highest amount we had intended to pay – a tincey bit over, to tell you the truth – but if we stood firm he said I could be Lord of Hexcombe. And the rest is history because we sealed that bid. Yes, sir.'

'I see,' said Strachey, who saw all too clearly.

Julie snorted. 'No wonder those other folks got confused.'

She laughed derisively and the whole of the Nibbet clan chuckled with her.

Strachey smiled at Walter. 'Here's to you, then,' she said. 'I mean, here's to the Lord of the Manor of Hexcombe.'

Delarme's tenure as Lord of the Manor had been short but telling. The last few days he had been at the gateway to Paradise. He had swaggered around Carmel, had ordered new vestments, had sent printed announcements to key members of his church, and had even toyed with the notion of flying to Britain first class. In those few days he had grown another inch. Now all his hopes were dashed away. Not only would he not be able to establish an evangelical mission in Devon, sweeping aside both Tina and the modern corruptions of her church, but he would have to return to America and admit to his fellow preachers that he had been duped. All is vanity, he thought, and vexation of spirit. He dropped his hired car and stormed – coat flapping, valise swinging – into Bristol airport like a Witch-Finder General on a busy day. But now the frustrations he had already incurred were aggravated by the inevitable frustrations of the little airport: the unmoving check-in queue, the patronising questions: 'Had he packed his luggage himself? Did he have any of the articles on this list? Why did his passport photo not show the beard he wore? Why did the x-ray bleep? Would he mind emptying the contents of his pockets? Could he remove that crucifix because it might set off the bleep?'

He ignored the temptations of duty free and scoured the dismal lounge for a seat where he would not have to brush shoulders with the heathen multitude. He must sit alone, he thought.

Until...

Beneath a sign that thanked the world for not smoking he spied a couple sitting cheek to cheek. They had blond hair. His was straight and streaked, and flopped over his brow in a boyish style unchanged since prep school, while hers was a honeyed whirl of candyfloss.

Delarme stood over them like the angel of retribution. 'You have fled from the wrath to come.'

Clive was discomfited. He stared up like a startled rabbit. Gloria had barely registered Delarme at the hotel, and she glanced at him dully as if he'd come to clear the trash.

Clive said, 'Catching a plane?'

He peered across Delarme's shoulder to see if anyone was with him.

'The wicked flee when no man pursueth.'

'Indeed, but how does it go – let he who is without sin first cast a stone?'

'You paraphrase – he that is without sin among you, let him first cast a stone – at *her*,' added Delarme with surprising vehemence.

'Hey,' cried Gloria. 'What the hell did I do to you?'

'Who can find a virtuous woman?'

'Listen,' she snapped. 'If you're a fuckin' Jehovah's Witness, try someone else.'

Delarme darkened. 'I represent the *true* church—'

'Yeah? Well, we're not buying bibles, thank you.'

Clive raised a hand. 'Are we on the same flight, Delarme?'

'I fear we are – but no, I *welcome* it. Believe me, *Lord* Clive – if you *are* a lord – I shall not let you out of my sight now.'

'Good-oh.'

'Good?'

'Good-*oh*,' said Clive. 'Because you'll recall you owe me something like – what is it now? – a hundred and five thousand dollars?'

'What?'

'He hasn't *paid*?' screeched Gloria.

Clive turned to her (Delarme turned dark red): 'He overstretched himself. You see, at the auction he bid rather more than he could actually lay hands on – and out of the kindness of my heart I gave him a little time to pay.'

'I paid!' roared Delarme.

'A down payment,' Clive purred. 'You said something about going back and asking your church for extra?'

Delarme's eyes bulged from their sockets. 'I want my money back!'

'Hardly. My company requires the full payment due to us.'

'We owe you nothing! You defrauded me.'

In the nearby seats the waiting passengers gave up their own more humdrum conversations to tune in to this.

'*I* defrauded *you*?' repeated Clive. 'You owe a hundred and five thousand dollars. How on earth could I have defrauded *you*?'

Gloria nodded. 'And we're gonna take you for it, brother – you mark my words.'

Clive made a pretence of opening his flight bag. 'I'm sure I have the receipt in here somewhere... twenty-five thousand down payment, one hundred and five grand left to pay.'

Delarme broke his erect stance. 'Make no mistake, *Lord* Clive. We'll sue for every cent of that twenty-five – and we'll win!'

Clive shook his head in assumed amusement. 'Really? Even though the only documentation is your promissory note for a hundred and five thousand? Incidentally, who is this "we" you keep invoking? Only the Queen calls herself "we".'

'My church will eat you alive!'

'That's Christianity,' laughed Gloria.

'We'll sue.'

'Only after you've paid,' responded Clive pleasantly. 'You can't ask for your money back if you haven't paid it.'

'We *have* paid!'

'I have an IOU for a hundred and five grand.'

'I'm getting bored of this,' said Gloria. 'And I'm not sittin' through a ten-hour flight with you two goin' round and round this loop. *Listen.*' She paused to glance round at the several rows of interested eavesdroppers. 'Are you punks *enjoyin'* the show? Get your noses back where they belong.'

A woman with rimless spectacles failed to be cowed. She fixed her steely gaze on Clive and asked, 'Say, excuse me, but are you *really* a lord?'

'Jesus!' snapped Gloria. 'Can't a girl go nowhere without fallin' over goddamn Americans?'

'Well, honey,' responded the woman comfortably. 'This flight *goes* to America.'

Gloria muttered, 'I came over here to get away from Americans.'

'Then you should've taken a flight to Dar es Salaam.'

Gloria stood up and the woman leered at her – she was carrying twice Gloria's weight. But Gloria ignored the woman and grabbed Clive's arm. 'Time we had a coffee.'

'I do not touch stimulants,' declared Delarme, but he trailed behind them to the airport bar.

Delarme wouldn't have a mineral water because he didn't trust the trace elements. Clive had what tasted like recycled espresso and Gloria indulged herself in a paper cup of something pink and fizzy with a corrugated umbrella perched in its rim. All three were standing now – but they kept their voices down.

Gloria said, 'You guys wanna stop acting so macho? It gets us nowhere. The thing is – the way I see it – all that matters is this.' She gazed wide-eyed at Delarme to let him see that she was an impartial, honest broker – though to him she looked like the whore of Babylon. 'D'you want the title or do you want your money back?'

'The title is worthless, a trinket of no further consequence.'

'Worthless?' She seemed astounded.

Delarme turned to Clive: 'You sold the same one several times over.'

'Not exactly,' said Clive, wondering what *exactly* he should say. But he needn't have worried: Gloria was on the ball. She smacked her forehead as if struck by a sudden thought.

'Wait a minute – you do want the title, don't you, Mr Delarme – I mean, you would if you could rely on it being yours for sure?'

'Well,' said Delarme weakly.

'All you have to do,' she said brightly, 'is be the first to pay – the first to come up with the full askin' price.'

He frowned at her. She explained, on a wing: 'I mean, you made part payment, right? But you didn't come across with the full caboodle. Well, no problem, honey – nor did no one else. I mean, no one's gonna pay full whack first time they're asked. An' you're no fool – you were being sensible, weren't you?'

'Ye – es... '

'So get in first. You got an advantage here.'

'I have?'

'Sure, you're standin' here with me and Clivey. You got the man by the elbow. He's the *man*, man. You got an edge – so don't let any other mother get in before you.'

'Do I follow you correctly?'

She laughed a gloriously dirty laugh. 'Oh honey, I bet you're way ahead of me.' She nudged him. 'You crafty rascal. So what do you owe now – a hundred and five thousand? Chicken shit. How long does it take to get your hands on that?'

Delarme looked wary. 'I'm not so sure—'

'Of course, you may not want the title as much as some people.' She shrugged. 'But I guess you're going back to the States for the money, right?'

'Actually I was merely flying home.'

'OK, that's cool. You can go. We'll let one of the other guys have it.'

Gloria sipped daintily from her pink concoction.

Clive coughed, taking over: 'Well, somebody has to have the title, and I *had* rather looked forward to it's being you. This is an important title, Delarme. We need a man of quality. However... '

He smiled engagingly.

Delarme thought about it. But even as he stood poised to bite, they heard an unwanted message from the tannoy: 'Would Lord Clive Lane – that's Lord Clive Lane – please come to the Virgin sales desk? We have an urgent telephone call for Lord Clive Lane.'

Clive stiffened. He felt like Sylvester the cat in that freeze-frame moment just after he has stepped off the cliff. He can see dry land ahead of him, far out of reach – and a long drop below. Sylvester turns to the camera, grins inanely, and begins peddling his legs to stay in the air. Then he falls. Clive did not want to answer the phone. He especially did not want to respond to a public tannoy blaring his name into a building crammed with anonymous people. Nobody knew he was at the airport – yet someone had paged him. And if someone knew he was here – someone who *wanted* him – that person might be here in the airport, waiting. A telephone call, was it? Maybe.

Delarme prompted: 'Wasn't that call for you?'

'Was it?'

'I'm sure it was. The Virgin sales desk. Perhaps there's a problem with your ticket.'

Clive was turning a pale shade of green. He knew he couldn't hang around any longer, pretending that he hadn't heard. Besides, it was only a phone call. It couldn't hurt him.

'The Virgin desk?'

'We could come with you,' said Delarme. 'In case there is a problem.'

'You stay with Gloria – Mrs Deane,' said Clive hastily. 'This won't take long.'

It *was* a phone call. He was handed the receiver by a brunette whose badge claimed she was a Virgin. Clive stood with his back to the sales desk, feeling as conspicuous as a moth at a lighted window. He kept his eyes on the crowd. Delarme and Gloria watched from across the hall.

'Hi, Clive, it's me – Strachey.'

'Darling!'

'No, Clive – It's Strachey. "Darling" is Gloria.'

He groaned, still studying the aimless passengers in the concourse. 'How did you know I was at the airport?'

'*Everyone* knows you're there, Clive. Ray Patterson traced you through the hire-car company.'

'Who's Patterson?'

'Someone you'll meet,' she answered ominously. 'I tried your mobile but... '

'Flat battery. Haven't had a chance to recharge the thing.'

'It's so hard to keep up with housework when you're on the run.'

'Strachey, Strachey, don't give me grief.'

'You're with Gloria, of course. Well, her husband knows where you are. And you remember Frankie di Stefano – the one you said must be a hood? He is a hood. He knows where you are too.'

'And this... Patterson?'

'Works for di Stefano. What time's your flight?'

'Well... '

'I can look it *up*, Clive. What I'm saying is that you may have an hour and a half before Patterson and di Stefano get there.'

'An hour and a half... Yes, that should be enough. Thanks, Strachey.'

'Get yourself through Passports into the departure lounge, where you'll be safe.'

'I'm already there. I do *love* you, Strachey, you know.'

'And Lincoln loves Gloria.'

'Oh.' Clive sounded contrite. 'Yes, it must seem pretty shitty. Listen, Strachey, this whole deal has gone rather pear-shaped—'

'For God's sake, Clive! At least *talk* like a lord.'

'Yes, yes, point taken. Everyone knows I'm at the airport? And they've realised about the scam?'

'That's why you ran, isn't it?'

'Look after your*self* then, darling. Get out while you can. I'll sort things out with you later.'

'What's left to sort?'

'The money. Look, don't get upset about Gloria – she... isn't important. Concentrate on the cash. And if there's anything you can do to delay this Mr di Stefano—'

'He's on his way. Seriously, Clive, d'you think you can run away from him for ever – or disappear?'

'I don't intend to hang around and have a chat with him!'

'You might be wiser to pay him off. He is not a pleasant man.'

'He'd want well over a hundred thousand dollars – and that's just *his* money. What about the others? We made *several* hundred thousand, Strachey – you and I.'

'You and I? Great. Well, we couldn't live for ever on it.'

'It'd last several years. Look, the important thing is to get away. Where are you phoning from?'

'The Holiday Inn.'

'Get in your car and drive out of there. I'm concerned for you.'

'Sure. Give my regards to Gloria.'

'Oh, Strachey, I didn't mean to hurt you. I'm sorry. Truly. Look, you really can't stay around those people.'

'I noticed.'

'Once they find that they can't catch me they're going to switch all their guns onto *you*. Technically, you own the company. Before long they're going to realise that I'm not responsible anyway. You are.'

It was a stunned Strachey who put down the phone. She walked like an automaton across the hotel lobby. Through the glass doors she could see the sun shining, there was garden greenery, there were gleaming cars. Clive was a bastard, but was right about one thing: she had to get out of this hotel.

She didn't make it to the door. The way he took her arm, Frankie di Stefano could have been a store detective, and Patterson the janitor.

She said, 'You're still here, Mr di Stefano? I thought you'd gone after Clive.'

Frankie wasn't smiling. His face held an intensity she hadn't been subjected to before. 'That's where *you* were goin', right?'

They were beside the exit door. A lad outside in livery glanced at them through the glass. Strachey thought of signalling to him but Frankie kept his grip on her arm and led her away towards the Holiday Inn easy-clean settees. Patterson trailed behind. Strachey paused beside an armchair but Frankie pulled her a few steps further. He pushed her onto a settee and sat close beside her.

He said, 'Clive may have duped you as well. I wouldn't know. What I do know is you ain't leavin'. You're staying here.'

'I'm not coming up to your room.'

'You're goin' where I tell you, babe. My friend Patterson will look after you.'

Patterson jumped slightly, as if he'd been dreaming on his feet. He put an intelligent smile on his face to show he'd been listening to every word.

Frankie said, 'This shouldn't take long. I phoned the airport, see?'

She frowned. '*You've* spoken to Clive as well?'

'What's the point in that? I phoned some friends of mine – well, friends of Patterson's boss.'

Patterson beamed again. He was keeping up.

'What sort of friends?' asked Strachey. Frankie grinned.

It was that rare smile that Mrs Nibbet noticed as she spied them across the lobby – snuggled up together on the settee and holding hands. That's why he's in England, she thought. Mr di Stefano is courting Lady Jane.

Well, fancy that.

In the safety of the boarding lounge Clive was strangely silent. The room had filled with passengers looking forward to – or dreading – their trip to the States, and Clive's pallor suggested that he was nervous about the flight. He kept consulting his watch, regardless of the large clock on the wall above the desk. He glared at the two flight attendants lounging behind the desk beside the exit door and stabbing disinterestedly at the computer terminal. They were in no hurry. Four people wandered towards the desk and begin a tentative queue but the attendants shooed them off again. They peered at their terminal as if it didn't work.

Delarme had attached himself to Clive and Gloria and they sat as a threesome in the soulless lounge. Clive sighed impatiently. The flight was due to leave in twenty minutes but there was no sign yet of their being asked to board. He squinted at the information screen: 'Flight boarding'. But it wasn't. The girl at the boarding desk answered her phone, picked up the mike:

'Would Mr Clive Lane please make himself known to the flight desk? Mr Clive Lane to the flight desk. Thank you.'

His throat felt dry.

Delarme gave a thin smile. '*Lord* Clive, surely – or is it plain Mr now?'

Gloria took his hand. 'Another phone call?'

'It won't be anything.'

'Perhaps they're giving us an upgrade – you being a lord.'

'They called him Mr,' Delarme put in smugly. 'Aren't you going to answer it?'

'I can't be bothered with silliness at this stage. The flight's about to board.'

'You wouldn't be hiding something from us?'

Gloria squeezed his hand. 'It'll be all right, darlin'.'

Clive stood up, wiped his hands quickly on his trousers and walked as casually as he could towards the boarding desk. The girl glanced up at him. 'Mr Lane?'

He nodded. He didn't insist on his title.

'You're wanted urgently.'

The word 'wanted' rang through Clive's brain. She looked at her screen. Was it his imagination or did her expression change?

'One moment, sir. We'll be with you soon.'

He smiled feebly. 'You're with me now.'

'Someone's coming for you.'

Though the girl smiled as she said the words she might as well have torn up his ticket before his face. He stood trembling as she studied her screen. She picked up her mike: 'Attention please. This flight will shortly begin boarding. Will those passengers in Economy Class holding tickets for rows one through to twenty-four please now come forward?'

She repeated this message at dictation speed as Clive stood there. He was quickly joined by early boarders who formed a queue behind him. A woman jostled at his elbow. He felt flustered, hemmed in by anxious passengers. Neither girl behind the desk took any further notice of him – one moved to the door while the other keyed instructions into her machine. The woman immediately behind him in the queue pressed against his back. Her breath smelt.

Clive leant across the desk. 'What am I supposed to do now?'

'Be right with you, sir. Boarding any moment.'

She had forgotten all about him.

Could he just get on board and ignore the message? Clive turned round and saw a red-coated woman striding across the lounge. A gold badge bounced brightly on her breast, proclaiming her to be a Virgin too. He hesitated. She noticed.

'Ah. Mr Lane? Come this way, please.'

'But we're boarding.'

She was already leading him away. 'Yes, don't worry, sir. This way please.'

Gloria and Delarme were on their feet. 'What's happening, Clive?'

Clive shrugged theatrically. The woman strode ahead. Delarme grabbed his arm. 'Is this a trick?'

'Of course not.'

'Are you running away again?'

'Don't be ridiculous.'

Gloria said, 'We'll miss our plane!'

He lingered. 'You get on, darling. Save me a seat. I'll be with you—'

'This way, sir. Please.'

Gloria said, 'But I'll never see you again! Jesus, Clive, what have you done?'

'Nothing,' he said helplessly.

The woman yanked his elbow and led him to a side door that he hadn't noticed. As he went through he turned back to see Delarme and Gloria staring after him. One last glance, he thought – the last they saw of him: Delarme angry and suspicious; Gloria – bless her, dear sweet blonde *darling* Gloria – desperately anxious. Caring. Reaching out to him...

But the door had closed. There was another man in the room – a man Clive hadn't seen before. He approached Clive, saying something he didn't hear. Clive looked quickly around the room. The man and the woman were right beside him. The woman touched his arm.

'Would you like to sit down, sir, please?'

'I don't want to sit down.'

'I think you should, sir.'

A silence fell. Clive glanced from one to the other. They were watching him. She was a Virgin. The man was a Virgin – he was not a policeman: wrong uniform. Someone from the airport. Clive sat down.

The woman said, 'There's been an accident, I'm afraid.'

'Accident?'

She placed her hand lightly on his shoulder. 'I'm afraid your mother's dead.'

'My *mother*?'

'Yes, sir. Dead, sir. I'm terribly sorry.'

'I haven't got a mother.'

They stared down at him. He stared back.

The man said, 'Everyone has a mother, sir. It's how people get made.'

Clive exhaled sharply. 'My mother's dead.'

'I know, sir. We're very sorry.'

'She died five years ago.'

The man looked at the woman. She said, 'I realise it can be a shock—'

'It's not a shock! She died five years ago. How can it be a shock?'

She licked her lips. 'We received a telephone call—'

'But my mother's dead! Already dead.'

They gazed at each other like three poker players, each concealing their hand. The man stared at him: 'You are Mr Lane? Mr Clive Lane?'

'Yes, I—'

Clive was tempted to say he was no mere *Mr* Lane, he was *Lord* Lane, Lord of the Manor of Lower Marsh, but thought better of it. No point making things more complicated.

'You were going to say, sir?'

'What?'

'I asked if you were Mr Lane and you said "Yes, I". Yes, I what, sir?'

Clive shook his head. 'This is ridiculous. I haven't got a mother. It's a hoax.'

'Why would that be, sir?'

'To stop me catching the plane!'

The man squinted at him. He held the pause.

'Why would anyone want to stop you catching the plane?'

Clive's mouth worked but nothing came out. Perhaps his mouth *didn't* work. He tried again. 'I don't know.'

'The caller was most insistent your mother had died. They're sending a car for you.'

'What?'

'They're coming to fetch you, sir.'

Despite her objections, they took Strachey to Frankie's bedroom after all. She could have protested. She could have shouted for assistance from the hotel staff – but as Frankie said, she could insist on having the *police* brought in if she really wanted to. She was the only representative of the company that had defrauded him, so by all means *call* the cops. Frankie would get the front desk to call them for her – was that what she wanted? Come to think of it, he said – if she hung around this lobby much longer one of the other cheated buyers might decide they should call the cops themselves. Where would she prefer to be – a police cell or a nice hotel bedroom? Four star, minibar and shower, he pointed out.

It wasn't an easy choice. Frankie's motives were clear, but she had noticed what Frankie perhaps had not: an unusually contemplative look in Patterson's eye. Patterson did not seem the best of company for a pretty girl trapped in a Holiday Inn bedroom, she thought – and when they did get there she sat alone in an upright chair.

It was Frankie's turn now to behave disquietingly. All he did was discuss his options on the telephone as if Strachey wasn't in the room – as if it didn't matter what she heard because she wouldn't get an opportunity to tell anyone. She began to think it might have been wiser to let him call the police.

But by this time she realised that Frankie di Stefano wouldn't have let her make the call. No way. Calling the police wasn't in his repertoire. He discussed his options further with the lumbering Patterson, using the man for what he was best at – as a solid sounding board, off which ideas could be bounced but from which no new ideas would come. He called a man in London and badgered him down the phone, insisting he think up some decent ideas of his own. He called the airport and broke the sad but urgent news of Mrs Lane's death. Then he phoned London again and badgered some more.

When he had run out of phone numbers he sat on the bed and glared at Strachey.

He asked, 'D'ya think the "Mummy's dead" routine will work?'

She shrugged.

'No, nor me,' he said. 'But it'll hold him up for a while. What time's the flight?' He stared at his watch, puffed out his cheeks and exhaled noisily. 'You guys got a nerve, fuckin' around with me.'

Patterson chuckled. 'Don't like to be conned, I bet.'

Frankie ignored him. 'So who's got the money – you or Clive?'

'Well, *I* haven't,' she said.

'An' when I get my hands on Clive and ask him, what d'you think *he* will say?'

'You seem convinced that you will catch him.'

The telephone rang. Frankie took it himself, nodding and grunting approvingly. When he put it down he looked at Strachey and said, 'Yeah, we'll catch him. You can count on that.'

He wore a shark-like grin now, and he went to the window and stared outside – almost as if he wanted to hide his grin from her. He was thinking, she knew. She and Patterson waited to hear his verdict. It didn't take long.

Frankie turned round and clapped his hands.

'A coupla hours, and I should have both of you. We'll finish it then. Yeah. You ready to leave, Strachey? Oh, of course, you are – you ain't even stayin' at this hotel. Oh, well.' He stared at her. 'You're going for a drive with Patterson.'

She tried to stay calm. 'Where to?'

'He knows.'

It seemed to take hours but in reality it was only a few minutes before Clive convinced the suspicious airline staff they had been hoaxed. Then, to make up for the inconvenience and embarrassment – and to ensure he caught the flight – they whisked him through on FastTrack to the waiting plane. It was impressive, in a dingy sort of way: they ran him along a corridor and through a single door, out around a luggage trolley and a van, onto the open airstrip. The fresh air in his face felt good. Weak English sun bounced off the dirty tarmac. They were half running, half walking, and the airline woman skittered slightly on medium-height heels. The man said, 'Don't worry, sir. We should have just enough time to make the plane.'

Clive could see it, throbbing ahead of him on the runway. He could hear the huge continuous roar of the powerful engines. He could smell the fuel. With a surge of relief he saw that the side door was open and the ladder still in place. Someone was waiting for him at the top. She came out into the daylight.

But it was Gloria. That was odd, he thought. A stewardess was holding her arm. When she saw Clive, Gloria started running towards him down the steps.

'It's all right,' he called. 'Get inside! I'm coming on.'

But his voice was lost in the din of the engines. She continued down the steps. When she reached the bottom she ignored the stewardess behind and ran across to him. She looked distraught and clutched at his arm.

'Clive,' she shouted. 'What's going on?'

'Why aren't you in the plane?' he shouted back. 'Think I wouldn't make it?'

She shook her head. 'Haven't you heard? They've impounded our goddamn luggage.'

Back in the room that he had hoped he'd never see again, Clive stood dumbly beside a windswept Gloria. The room was gradually filling with officials, but he took no notice of them. Whatever happened now didn't alter the fact that their flight had gone. Another three officials came in but they seemed more interested in talking to the others than to Clive and Gloria, so he led her to a metal-frame chair and made her sit down. He couldn't sit himself. He stood behind her and gripped her chair. It was as if an instinct for flight kept his body tensed. A flight instinct, Clive thought ruefully – that was rich.

Finally, a man detached himself and approached.

'We're bringing your luggage,' he said.

'At least you haven't sent it to New York.'

'We wouldn't do that, sir.'

He stared Clive in the eye – but Clive was adept at that himself. He put on a baleful aristocratic stare and forced the other man to give way. A small, Pyrrhic victory.

The door opened again and their suitcases were wheeled in.

Gloria started from the chair but Clive restrained her. They watched as the cases were wheeled across the room and laid before them for inspection. There was something faintly ludicrous, Clive thought, about two suitcases being the focus of attention of all the people in the room. He waited for someone else to speak.

'Did you pack these bags yourselves?'

He stared at them. 'Is this a terrorism thing?' They stared back. 'I packed mine, and I'm sure Mrs Deane will have packed her own.'

'And what is *in* your bag, sir?'

'Do you want an inventory?'

'Why not?'

Clive narrowed his eyes. 'You don't imagine I *stole* the bag?'

'No, sir, I shouldn't think so. An inventory, you said?'

'Oh, for goodness' sake! Just the usual things – a suit, couple of jackets, a spare pair of slacks. A pullover.'

'A pullover!' exclaimed Gloria. 'How sweet.'

'Anything else, sir?'

'Papers. Toiletries. A book, perhaps.'

'Papers, sir?'

'Is this the Spanish Inquisition?'

'Was there anything valuable in your suitcase?'

'What d'you mean by valuable – how valuable?'

They were both being cagey now.

'That's for you to say, sir.'

Clive paused. 'Has something happened to my luggage?'

'What sort of thing might have happened to it, sir?'

'I'm growing tired of this,' said Clive. 'Shall I unpack the case – or have you already done so?'

'There was nothing to unpack, sir,' said the man – as with a theatrical flourish he flicked the lid of the unlocked case. It was totally empty.

Clive sighed. 'What have you done with my things?'

'What things?'

Clive closed his eyes. The man continued: 'Our baggage handlers became suspicious because your cases seemed so light. We always check in... suspicious cases. Excuse the pun. Normally we're looking for something that shouldn't be there. But this time we found nothing at all.'

'Nothing?' shrieked Gloria.

'And because of that you turned us off the plane?'

The man frowned. 'It's hardly normal behaviour, sir. Did you intend to fly to America with empty suitcases?'

Clive knew that he'd been set up. First the fake call about his mother's death – now this. He could try explaining it to the officials – letting them see that someone was playing tricks to keep him off the plane – but what was the point? It would simply take more time. And whoever was playing these tricks would want to delay him for as long as possible.

He said, 'All right, yes, we chose to fly with empty suitcases. We intend to do a lot of shopping when we land. Now, since we haven't broken any law – and since we've missed the wretched airplane – can we go home?'

'But Clive,' squeaked Gloria. 'I didn't have an empty suitcase! God, there was a Betty Jackson in there! And a Dollargrand handbag.'

The man gleamed at Clive. 'How about that, sir?'

Gloria was on her feet. 'You tellin' me some scumbag stole my things? I'll sue!'

'This is getting interesting,' declared the man.

But they were interrupted by the phone. Everyone sensed that a drama was being played out before them. They stood silent while the call was answered.

'Mrs Deane?' said a woman holding out the phone. 'This is for you.'

The Inquisitor leant back in his chair. The woman held out the phone. Gloria hesitated – and she was not the kind of girl to hesitate.

'But nobody knows I'm here.'

The woman pointed the phone like a sword. 'I think you should take it.'

'One moment!' The Inquisitor leant forward. He opened a drawer and produced a tangle of telephone flex. 'Who used this last?' he grumbled as he slipped the jack into the phone.

He nodded to Gloria. 'Away you go.'

'This is a private call,' she snapped indignantly.

'I'm counting on it.'

'I don't have to speak to no one if I don't want to.'

The man's eyes glinted. 'Wouldn't *that* look suspicious, madam?'

She glared back at him but accepted the phone. She and the official placed their headsets to their ears. Everyone else leant closer, hoping to hear what would be said.

Gloria gave a cautious hello.

The answering voice sounded bright and cheerful. The official didn't recognise it – but neither did Gloria. She had expected Lincoln but it was Frankie di Stefano, putting on an assumed voice. It was a rotten effort but what did that matter?

'I hear you missed your plane, Gloria baby. Now, ain't that too bad. Just to let you know that when you land in JFK my boys will be waitin' – whichever flight you're on. Tell Clive for me, will ya? By the way – "Red Haddock" is the password.'

Frankie put down the phone. He had said all he needed. Gloria glared at the lifeless handset. 'The hell was that about?' she asked.

'You tell me.'

The official laid his handset down more carefully. Clive stepped forward. 'It must be abundantly clear by now that we are the victims of a nasty hoax. Someone is determined to make us miss the plane.'

'It didn't sound like a hoax, sir,' replied the man, without a trace of sympathy. 'Somebody's "boys" will be waiting for you at the airport. And whoever "somebody" is, he asked specifically that *you* should be told. Well, I've passed on the message, sir. Now perhaps you'd tell me exactly what is going on.'

14

PATTERSON STOPPED THE car beside the derelict old mill in the valley. Strachey in the back, confined by no more than child locks on the doors, wondered what connection this grim place had with di Stefano. Of all places in the area, this was where she had been attacked on her first day in Devon by a man who came out of the mill – someone who claimed that he lived there. Could he, in some bizarre way, have been associated with di Stefano? Could he work for him?

Strachey didn't know that the man's unmarked grave lay nearby. She didn't know that Patterson had killed him – and *he* didn't intend to tell her. He only said, 'Inside.'

She paused at the heavy wooden door. It would need a hard push to open it. Out here in the daylight the valley was in shade, yet fresh air had never smelt so sweet. Patterson towered over her. This, she thought, is my last chance to escape.

He pushed the door open. Strachey ducked beneath his arm and made a dash – but he caught her at the second pace. He hardly had to move for her. He just reached out his arm.

'There's nowhere to run.'

Patterson pushed her through the door and followed her inside. With his foot he closed the door. The semi-darkness smelt fetid.

'Up the stairs.'

The first flight led to a landing littered with bits of rubbish. She could make out a small door at one end and another flight of stairs, which Patterson motioned her to take. At the head of the second flight they reached a large loft area, in which someone seemed to have been living: she saw a sleeping bag, some sacks and wooden boxes, a primus stove and a chair. Against the wall stood cooking pans and a bucket.

'You can have the chair,' said Patterson. 'I'm such a nice man.'

She eyed it warily. It could be full of fleas. 'I'll stand.'

'You don't have a choice.'

She didn't want to provoke him, so she sat down.

Patterson walked across to a broken window and peered out. It was very quiet. Light from the shady valley seeped into the darkened room but instead of illuminating it, the light seemed confined to the rectangle where it fell. The edges of the floor were lost in gloom. Balls of fluff and small debris lay scattered like waiting rats.

He lit a cigarette.

Patterson stood at the window, blowing smoke into the open. He wasn't being considerate. He just preferred the view.

And she preferred him to look outside.

After a while he turned to stare at her in the chair. His cigarette was nearly finished, and he drew on it to extract the juice. Then he threw the stub on the wooden floor, spat a scrap of tobacco, and ground the glowing end with his foot. Strachey kept her eyes cast in her lap.

He smiled. It worried her. 'Comfortable?' he asked.

She clutched her handbag. 'You need a chair.'

'And I should leave you here and look for one?' He stared at her. 'You shouldn't have tangled with di Stefano.'

'Will we be here long?'

'Depends.' She waited. 'On how soon Clivey boy turns up.'

'Then what?'

He shrugged again. 'Lonely here, isn't it?'

It was little more than fifteen minutes, though to Strachey it felt two hours. During that time they stayed where they were, saying little – he at the window, she in the chair – until eventually they heard a car pick its way down the narrow lane on the other side of the valley. They heard splashes as it crossed the ford. Patterson glanced out to check it was the right car but didn't go down to it. He lounged instead against the wall.

They heard the wooden door creak open and shut. Footsteps on the stairs. Frankie's head appeared through the trap and when the rest of him came through she saw that he had a pistol in his fist. He scowled at Patterson. 'You should've said hello or somethin'. You could've got shot.'

Patterson sniffed.

Frankie kept an eye on him as he stuffed the pistol out of sight. Then he glanced at Strachey. 'Havin' fun?' She shrugged. 'Like a fuckin' morgue. Well lady, looks like you'll have to stay here a bit longer. Whaddya think of that?'

'I'll learn to live with it.'

'You hope.' He looked around the room. 'So, this is it – the baronial hall? It goes with the useless title your boyfriend sold me.' He stamped the floor and raised some dust. There was a faint sound of falling grit. 'Enjoyin' the joke?' He glared at her. 'Your man slipped away at the airport. Managed to convince those Virgin idiots it was a hoax. I should've put a bomb in his bag.'

She held his gaze and tried a wild card: 'Yes, you should have blown him up. Made us both feel better.'

He paused now, watching her. 'Meanin' you'd like him dead?'

'I'd like him damaged.' She blinked angrily. 'Maybe not dead.'

'So you're sayin'... ?'

She tried to look like a slighted woman. 'How would *you* feel? He left me for that blonde girl – Lincoln's wife. I'd like to get my hands on both of them.'

He nodded, still watching her. 'You gonna tell me where they've gone?'

She threw her hands wide (overacting, if truth be told – but who's talking about the truth?). 'I wish I knew. They left the airport?' He grunted. 'But you don't know where they went?'

'If I did, I wouldn't be talkin' to *you*. Look, skip the 'wounded' shit. Clive's cut out – where would he go?'

'Somewhere he can keep his head down.'

'With Little Miss Goldylocks, is that right?'

'Well.' The bitter taste in her mouth wasn't entirely counterfeit. 'I expect he'd take a hotel room. He only needs a bed.'

Frankie studied her. 'You're jealous, huh?'

'I could ask around the airport hotels for you. There won't be many.'

He grinned. 'Nice try, Strachey, but I don't think I'll send *you*. We'll catch him, you can count on that. Meanwhile you stay here.'

She looked round the room. 'Here?'

'Oh.' His face was blank. 'Nothin' so grand as this.' He turned to Patterson. 'You oil that lock?'

'It works now.'

They led Strachey down the first flight of stairs to the

mezzanine landing, then along to the small door at the end. It glided open: Patterson had oiled the hinges as well as the lock. It was little more than a store room. There was a small, high window – a cell window, too small to squeeze through – and there were remains of broken old furniture. Patterson kicked a rusty bucket and said, 'Every mod con.'

'How long will I be in here?'

Frankie said, 'As long as it takes.'

They stared at each other through the gloom. Patterson had a thought: 'When's the next flight – you know, America?'

'I guess, same time tomorrow. Think he'll be on it?'

'Could be.'

Frankie glanced again at Strachey. 'Well, you could be here a day.'

'What's the point of this?'

'What's the point of livin'? Answer me that.'

Frankie gestured to Patterson and they left the room. She heard the key turn. The room was dark, but not so dark she couldn't see. She sat on a box, exhaled, and listened to the sound of her breath in the gloomy room.

For a while she sat limp as a rag doll, letting the tension drain away. She let her mind empty. Though she made no effort to listen, she could hear their voices downstairs, but she couldn't make out the words. She heard what sounded like the heavy front door – a scrape followed by a thump. She heard a car start and move away. Then she heard the other car do the same. Both cars. Both gaolers gone.

A silence fell.

Strachey stood up and stared at the little window. Too high. She went across and tried the door. Locked tight. Then she circled the cluttered room. The exterior wall was stone but the interior ones were wood. She banged her fist against them, to no avail. Maybe if she had something sharp...

When she looked around the floor, the only things were wood or cardboard. There was no nail she could prise between the planks...

That kind of thing only works in stories.

Strachey sat on the box and listened for a noise outside. Silence. Not even birdsong. She was trapped. Presumably Frankie and Patterson would leave her for an hour or so while they sorted out what to do next. So she might have an hour to break free – if she were Supergirl. But she wasn't Supergirl, she was Strachey, so she took the other option. She reached in her purse for her cell phone – no, she reached in her handbag for her mobile. Typical men, she thought – didn't dream of looking in my bag. She dialled a number and waited, the little phone snug at her ear. After three rings she heard him answer.

It was his voice: 'Mickey Starr.'

15

LINCOLN DEANE SAT alone at the bar, a romantic figure, he felt. He remembered that Frank Sinatra song: The Wee Small Hours of the Morning. He'd been a man, Sinatra. He'd lived a life. Lincoln clutched his glass and stared deep into it in the way he remembered Sinatra had in that film – which was it? – The Joker Runs Wild. Was that it? The one where he's a top singer and gets his throat slashed but by the end of the movie he comes back to sing again. Well... it seemed believable at the time. Sinatra magic. There was a scene in that film where he sat all alone at the bar, nursing a glass, his cheekbones highlighted and his face slightly haunted. No one could stare in a glass like Sinatra.

Lincoln sighed and drained his highball. Where was Gloria now? How long had she played him for a sap? He ran his finger around the rim of his glass. It was possible, but surely not likely, that she and Lord Clive had been up to their tricks in the States before he left. Clive had stayed at the hacienda overnight. But Gloria couldn't have slipped out of the marital bedroom and joined Clive beneath guest sheets. Though she didn't have to, he remembered. Twice he had left her behind while he came to England, and on both occasions Clive had remained in the States. How many times, lord, how many times?

Lincoln had Sinatra songs going round his brain – like: if she walked in the door and said the right words he'd have her back. Wouldn't he? Wouldn't he be hers, if only she would call?

Yes, he thought, humming beneath his breath, his lonely heart had learned its lesson.

'Why, Mr Deane, I *am* ashamed of you!'

He turned on the bar stool to find Mrs Nibbet. 'At this time of day!'

Lincoln grinned ruefully. 'Night-time is the right time,' he announced.

'Are you drunk?'

'No,' he said – and he wasn't. 'I'm just trying to put my life together.'

She touched his arm. 'I hope you're not too cross with us?'

'Cross?'

'Oh, come on, I understand, I truly *do*. You invested a lot of your hopes in that title—'

'More than hopes—'

'But it was a fair auction and... well, you know, in life there can only be one winner.'

Lincoln frowned. He didn't think he agreed with that.

She said, 'I guess you'll be staying on for a little holiday. And I... well, I was rather hoping that while you're here, you might find time to speak to Walter and wish him well.'

'I wish him well. Sure I do.'

'But it would mean a lot to him if you congratulated him on his title. Do you know that *nobody* has congratulated him at all? Nobody, that is, except his family. Why!' She laughed a little and prodded him. 'Anyone would think you were all so jealous that you couldn't even bring yourselves to speak to him! And I am *sure* that isn't true.'

She glittered like Eleanor Roosevelt on campaign.

Lincoln suddenly realised that neither Mrs Nibbet – nor presumably the rest of the Nibbets – believed Clive had tricked them. But they had been there in the bar...

He mumbled, 'You know, Lord Clive hasn't played exactly fair—'

She smacked his arm playfully. 'Oh, I know you're mad at him because he flirted with your wife – but you have to realise he's a lord and everything.'

'What's that to do with it?'

'Well, he's a lord. Lords are entitled – you know, *droit de seigneur*?'

Lincoln gaped at her.

She said, 'Exactly. Now you remember, Mr Deane, a word to Lord Walter would not come amiss. I just *know* I can rely on you.'

Mrs Nibbet sparkled again.

He shook his head. Yes, he ought to have a word with Walter – to see if he shared the same delusion as his wife. But if he did – what did it matter? What did it matter if *all* the Nibbets thought their Walter was Lord of Hexcombe? What did it matter to Lincoln Deane? He'd lost his wife.

'That's right' he said, talking as much to himself as to Mrs Nibbet. 'But has Strachey really lost Clive?'

'Lady Jane? What do you mean?'

'She's vanished too. Oh, I don't know.' He picked up his glass but found it empty. 'First I thought Clive had walked out on her. But now she's disappeared and I'm beginning to think, Mrs Nibbet, I'm beginning to wonder if she isn't in on the trick after all.'

'What trick?'

He thumped the table. 'Perhaps the whole damn thing's a conspiracy! I don't know whether you've noticed, but that strange Mr Delarme and that Mr Highly Suspicious Frankie di Stefano have vanished too. Something's wrong with this.'

'Not at all,' she said. 'It's just you've been drinking too early in the day. Mr di Stefano hasn't disappeared. Why, my sister was in the lobby not half an hour ago when she heard Mr di Stefano go to the desk and confirm that he'll be staying on a few more nights. And I am pleased about that – with any luck I can persuade Mr di Stefano to congratulate Walter too. So, don't you forget now, Mr Deane – I am counting on you to do the decent thing. And I *know* I can count on you,' she said, slipping away, 'because you're American, and we Americans know what's right.'

She had practically left the bar when he thought to ask her, 'Where's Mr di Stefano now?'

He was, in fact, barely sixty feet away, almost directly above, about ten degrees from the vertical that rose from Lincoln's head – but separated by two hotel floors. And he was stamping around his room in an increasingly foul mood. When he phoned the London mob he found that they expected congratulations on their airport baggage manipulation and were surprised to hear he wanted more. How the hell, they asked him, were they expected to help him find Lord Clive? They had gone beyond the call of duty already – hadn't they? – in finding tame baggage handlers to doctor the luggage *and* they'd delayed the couple enough to bump them off the plane. But, they continued, it was time to make one thing absolutely clear: up till now they had been helpful, *very* helpful, one businessman to another, but at some stage enough was enough. If Frankie had crossed a local conman it was his affair. Unless perhaps this was a deal he wanted to cut them into? Some deal he hadn't told them about? Some deal that he, an American guest in their fine country, was running on his own? Some deal that maybe, under these circumstances, he *ought* to tell them about?

By then Frankie was at the snarling stage, and he told them there was no damn deal to cut them into. In which case, the voice responded, what is your beef? The call ended on less than friendly terms.

From this conversation Frankie had cooled barely half a degree when Patterson, in a masterpiece of mistiming, wandered in. Frankie gave him a rundown on the English psyche.

'You don't want to upset those people,' Patterson advised him. 'They're my employers. You get up their nose they'll give me stick.'

'That should worry me?'

Patterson pulled a well-yes-maybe-it-should-do kind of face.

Frankie said, 'I'm gonna hafta squeeze it outa Strachey. She's well locked in?'

'Well, the room's locked. And the front door.'

'You tied her up?'

Patterson gazed at him.

'Jesus Christ,' sighed Frankie. 'We better get back there.'

'I haven't eaten nothing since breakfast.'

'So?'

'Are we eating at the hotel?'

'Get outa here!'

'Are we eating *any* place?'

'Grab a take-out on the way.'

'A take-out – in Devon? This is the countryside, Mr di Stefano. You've seen the kind of place this is.'

'People live here, don't they? Don't every English village sell fish'n'chips?'

16

AS A DOG returneth to his vomit, Delarme thought smugly, so a fool returneth to his folly. Neither Clive nor Gloria had rejoined the flight, and their disappearance confirmed how right he had been to pull out himself. Clearly, the wicked pair had pretended they'd take the flight purely so that he too would go back to America. Or perhaps they *had* intended to take the flight until he discovered them at the airport. Either way, they'd abandoned their trip. Where would they go?

Back to their vomit.

He searched, in neon-lit darkness, up and down the Holiday Inn car park. In that watery electric light the bright colours of the various cars were flattened and dulled – but he knew what he was looking for. That car was Strachey's; that Lincoln Deane's. And scattered around the car park were several other hire cars, any one of which could have brought Clive and Mrs Deane back from Bristol to their Devon lair. So there was every chance the sinful couple was already here. Perhaps even now they were sitting in the hotel bar, laughing with their partners.

This was a trick to deceive him. But he was cleverer than they knew.

Whatever confusion Clive tried to draw round the lordship there were only two facts that really mattered: first, as both Clive and Mrs Deane had admitted at the airport, no one had made the full payment – so the title was still available to the first person to pay in full; and second, a fax in Delarme's coat pocket confirmed that his church in America were willing to subscribe the full hundred and five thousand dollars *provided* they could be convinced (and that meant provided *he*, Delarme, could be convinced) that this time the title – and the transfer of that title – was both genuine and beyond reproach.

The fax confirmed the money was in his bank account. Armed with that fax he could write Clive a cheque *now*, tonight, and seal the deal. Of course, the wily Englishman might be inside the hotel this very moment trying to persuade another bidder to settle a higher bid, but he, Delarme, had money ready. He,

Delarme, would close the deal. The Lordship of Hexcombe Manor was meant for him.

Delarme bounded through the hotel entrance. He must be wary. He must make sure no competitor had stolen ahead. And he must make absolutely sure this time that the title transfer was watertight.

Strachey, alone and unattended in the small, dark storeroom, could smell pungent vinegar and fish'n'chips. She could hear the two men talking, but still couldn't make out the words. The only thing she *could* make out was the mouth-watering smell. She swallowed hard. She hadn't realised she was starving till the smell of that greasy food wafted through the crack around the door and permeated every scrap of stale, dark air. It hung around her and tantalised like a droning fly in the dead of night.

She heard feet on stairs. They paused at the door. A key turned in what sounded a very rusty lock and the door creaked open. She caught the flash of white light – it swung towards her – and she was blinded by the beam. As she turned her head to shield her eyes she felt like an imprisoned maiden in the tower. They kept the flashlight on her. One of them said something.

Strachey said, 'What?'

'You change your mind yet?' That would be di Stefano. 'Where's Clive?'

'I told you, I've no idea.'

That damned light. She had to keep her head bowed.

'That's what you said a coupla hours ago. You still not seein' sense?'

'Can you turn that light away?'

'I like watchin' you, Strachey. See what you're thinkin' – know what I mean?'

It didn't flicker. It was like a spotlight. She said, 'He ran out on both of us.'

'You're wastin' your time protecting him. He took Lincoln's wife – you know that? Left you in the lurch.'

She shrugged.

He said, 'Well, I can leave you here till I find him. An' while you're cooped up in this lousy room your boyfriend is screwin' the blonde girl. What d'ya think of that?'

'He's not my boyfriend.'

'Not now he's not.'

She was used to the light now, but she couldn't look at him. He remained a voice coming from the dark. He changed his tone: 'You oughta help me, Strachey.'

'Stuck in here?'

He chuckled. 'You can come out anytime. Just say the word.'

She shrugged again and Frankie said, 'Oh, well.'

While he kept the light on her, Patterson belched. Frankie snapped, 'D'you mind?'

'Sorry. Fish makes me burp.'

'Hey, Strachey – you hungry or what?'

'Fairly.'

'You're gonna get hungrier unless you talk.'

The two men went outside and stood at the edge of the shallow river. In the darkness it was hard to see how deep it was. Moonlight caught the ripples, and the sound of water flowing across smooth stones was surprisingly loud. The night air had cooled and it held a leafy smell from nearby trees. Patterson lit a cigarette.

Frankie kept his voice low. 'So what's *your* idea?'

'Me? I do what I'm told.'

Frankie glanced at him and shook his head. 'Maybe she knows and maybe she don't. But she's all I got.'

'There's Lincoln Deane. He could've heard from his wife by now.'

'Oh, *very* likely. Usin' a bedside phone.'

'Now, there's a picture,' said Patterson, chuckling. 'I can imagine *her* in bed.'

'Imagining is all you'll ever do.'

Patterson was still chuckling. 'Well, a man can dream. That's some woman, isn't it?'

'Forget Mrs Deane. What about *this* one?'

'Her indoors?' Patterson chuckled again.

'What's *in* that fuckin' cigarette – whacky baccy? Look: Strachey, what about *her*?'

'Yeah, she's some woman too.'

Frankie exhaled. 'I mean, d'you think she knows what's goin' down?'

'I bet she knows about going down. I bet she knows a lot of things.'

'Jesus,' Frankie muttered. 'Why'd I come to this country? OK, forget it – *I'll* do the thinkin'. We can either sit here waitin' for Strachey or we can go back to the hotel and see what Lincoln knows.'

'The hotel's more comfortable.'

'That's your recommendation – we leave Strachey up there in the storeroom, the whole night through? That don't sound sensible. Give her a few hours up there, anythin' could happen. Maybe I should go back to the hotel and leave you to keep an eye on her.'

Patterson stubbed his cigarette eagerly. 'Yeah, I'll look after her!'

'Will you leave that out?'

Patterson shrugged. 'Just thought we could get *something* out of it. I mean, let's face it, you fancy the bird yourself.' He looked at Frankie meaningfully. 'It's gonna be a long night, in the middle of nowhere. Let's face it, we already *killed* one guy out here.'

Patterson glanced between the trees to where his grave lay.

'He was a drifter,' Frankie muttered. 'No one knew he existed.'

'And what's she? I mean, if she vanished, who'd be surprised?'

'Enough of that.'

Patterson stretched his neck and peered up at the stars. He was taller than Frankie. 'Well, you asked my opinion. What's *your* idea? We wait forever and see if she cracks or we give her some pressure and she cracks tonight? I mean, *you're* the boss, Mr di Stefano, but I think the longer we wait, the further Clive gets away.'

Frankie scowled in the darkness.

'Let's go in.'

She shouldn't have missed him: in the hard lighting of the hotel lobby, Delarme stood as dark and dominant as John the Baptist in the sun-baked desert – but the reverend Tina had stepped too far into the lobby before she saw him, and from across the glittering floor his eyes fixed on her like a hawk on a vole. The fact that she emerged from the hotel bar was not in her favour. Neither was the grin on her face. Nor the way it froze.

Still, she thought, he didn't matter any more. When Mrs Nibbet had phoned the vicarage, Tina wouldn't initially let herself believe her, but now that she had come to the hotel and talked to the entire Nibbet clan in the Holiday Inn bar, she was reasonably convinced that the Nibbets had secured the title. Mrs Nibbet alone might not have persuaded her, but supported by an increasingly stately Walter – not to mention Myrtle and Conrad, and Julie and Hunter, and 'just another little top-up' of tinkling Champagne – even the most hardened cynic would be convinced. The vicar of Hexcombe was hardly a cynic. She *wanted* to believe very much. To learn that her parish was to be blessed with the wonderful Nibbets instead of the thundering Delarme was bliss indeed.

But here in her path stood the vanquished contender. The vicar took a deep breath – to clear the smell of Champagne – turned her cheek towards him and approached with a smile. 'Well,' she said. 'It was a hard-fought battle but in the end there could only be one winner, I suppose.'

She tried to keep her beaming smile sympathetic.

He nodded. 'It was close indeed. Though I would have preferred a tidier contest.'

'Are you flying back tomorrow?'

'Not for several days.'

'Sightseeing?'

'I shan't have time for that.'

'Oh. Well. What are you going to do?'

'There is some remaining paperwork. Nothing important,' he hurriedly assured her.

'Paperwork?'

He shook his head. 'Of no consequence at all.'

Her smile had developed rigor mortis. 'But... you're staying in the area?'

'Yes. I don't think I shall be able to fit you in tomorrow, Miss Gum – but I know where to find you.'

'Ah,' she fluttered faintly. 'Might you want to?'

He gazed upon her face. 'Be in no doubt.'

She swallowed carefully. 'Would that be a social call?' she tried bravely.

'We have things to discuss. Things to amend.'

She tried to keep a flippant tone. 'There'll be some changes made?'

'Certainly.'

'And your role in this?'

'Well, as the new Lord of the Manor of Hexcombe—'

She shuddered. He licked his lips carefully. 'I take a keen interest in the spiritual wellbeing of my people.'

'The new lord... '

She couldn't bring herself to complete the sentence – a *sentence* upon the entire parish of Hexcombe. She said, 'But I've been talking to the Nibbets—'

'Are they still here?'

'In there.' She gestured vaguely towards the bar.

Delarme shrugged. 'They're of no consequence now.'

'You're the new lord?'

She had to ask it. She had to hear the sentence confirmed.

'I am,' he declared – and because he couldn't resist it: 'I am the Lord.'

Here's a curious thing: when Patterson was excited he felt no need for a cigarette. Old army training, he supposed: once the action starts you use no naked lights, you make no smells. Anyway, once the adrenaline began to flow, the last thing he needed was a sedative. He followed Strachey and Frankie up the darkened wooden stairs to the upper loft floor. Frankie led the way. Patterson hung back, watching Strachey's rear in the gloom. He had only to reach out and he could rub both hands on her hips.

They made the top floor. Either the gloom was lighter here or they were growing used to the dark. Even as Frankie cast his flashlight around, they could make out shapes in the darkness outside the beam. There was a window space – any glass had long disappeared – and a grubby moonlight stole through and wilted on the floor. Parts of the roof had fallen in. Arranged against the wooden walls were murky shapes that could have been either boxes or some kind of furniture. Frankie's light rested on the wooden armchair.

'That's got my name on it,' he declared. He sat down, the flashlight resting in his lap and shining across the room. 'Where are ya?' The beam swung round and fixed on Strachey. She had to turn her head away to shield her eyes from the glare.

'Third degree,' he said. 'Only this time I'm the cop.'

He was probably grinning at her, but all she could see was the light. Something moved to her right: Patterson settling himself on the floor.

Frankie spoke again, his voice harder. So he wasn't grinning.

'OK Strachey, it's late and I've run outa patience. Where the fuck is Clive?'

'I'm supposed to guess?'

He roared at her: 'Answer the question!'

She kept her eyes shielded and stared at the floor. She said, 'My *guess* is that he's further away than when you asked me last time.'

'One more crack,' said Frankie softly, 'and I'm gonna come and smack you in the face. I'm probably gonna hafta do that anyway.'

'I don't know where he is.'

'Oh well,' came his voice from the darkness. 'Looks like we're gonna have to beat it outa you.'

She heard his chair creak. He asked, 'Is that how you want it?' He was standing now, and the flashlight wavered. 'I'll give you one last chance,' he said flatly. 'We're tired and alone here. This is no place for heroes.'

'I can't help you. I don't know where he is.'

Di Stefano sighed. 'I quite like you, Strachey. You know that? Are you gonna make me do this?'

'You don't have to,' she told him. 'Unless it's the kind of thing you like to do.'

She raised her blonde head and stared into the glare. She had to show she wasn't afraid – though if they thought she wasn't afraid it could make them surer she was lying.

Patterson's voice from her right: 'She thinks we don't like beating women up.'

Frankie: 'It never bothered me.'

'No, you hit 'em, they throw up or they faint or something and get hysterical. I reckon there's better ways.'

'You do?'

'Yeah. I reckon it's better to humiliate 'em. You wouldn't like that, Strachey, would you? I mean, you're alone with two men... '

Frankie jerked the flashlight in disgust. 'You wanna rape her – is that it? Keep your dick in your pocket. I'm lookin' for information here.'

'I didn't say nothing about rape.' Patterson's voice was measured and calm. Maybe it was the darkness gave him confidence. Maybe he knew what he wanted. 'She just takes her clothes off—'

'Shut up.'

'It's an old trick – you know, strip the prisoner. Remove their protection. Give 'em nowhere to hide.'

'I'm not listening to this.'

But the seed had been planted, Strachey was sure. The flashlight quivered.

Patterson said, 'Well, *she's* listening. Look at her.'

She stood frozen in light like an actress in close-up, every expression on her face exposed. She tried to stay impassive while the two men held the silence. It was easy for them: they were out of the light. They could keep quiet and watch. The longer she stood, the more ridiculous she felt. The light beamed remorselessly and all she could do was stand in it like a statue. And the longer she stood, the longer she *had* to stand, because anything she said now, anything she *did* now, would seem loaded with significance. She blinked once, and blinked again. She wanted to keep on blinking – she wanted to screw her eyes tight and shut out the light. But she mustn't do that. She felt her eyes water.

'Last chance, Strachey,' Frankie said.

She shrugged helplessly. 'I can't do anything. I don't know anything.'

'You shouldn't have started playin' with the big boys.'

There was a pause. She was dazzled by light. They were out there, comfortable in the darkness, while she was trapped in the glare.

Patterson broke the silence. 'We gonna do this or what?'

'I think we have to.'

'OK. *I'll* take her clothes off.'

Strachey said, 'No.' She couldn't let that big oaf undress her. Once he got his hands on her body, the next step was all too predictable. She mustn't let him touch her.

'I'll do it myself.'

Could she take them off unexcitingly? Could she behave as if she were in a private room at a motel? Nothing sexy – just take the clothes off, fold them on the floor. An everyday, functional act – an ugly one, almost, as she pulled off her tights. Maybe they'd let her stay in her undies.

Maybe not.

She heard Patterson: 'OK, *you* do it. Sounds good to me.' Anticipation in his voice.

Frankie's voice was flat. 'Get on with it.'

He wasn't happy with this, she could tell. When he'd said he liked her, it was the truth – not that he'd let that stand in his

way. But she knew he'd prefer not to humiliate her. What
Frankie would like – and she knew it – was for her to tell him
where Clive was, and for them to have a drink together
afterwards and agree 'no harm done'.

She kept her face expressionless as she slipped out of her
warm jacket. She folded it quickly and laid it on the floor. She
stood up, paused, then undid the buttons on the cuffs of her
shirt. She must not excite these men. For a moment there was
silence, then Patterson laughed and 'la-la'ed the opening line to
The Stripper. He laughed again. He was enjoying this.

Frankie said, 'Shut up.'

He was right. In those few seconds before Patterson opened
his mouth the silence had grown intense. Patterson had broken
the spell. Never underestimate the power of silence. When it was
silent all they had to do was concentrate on Strachey. And her
body.

She paused and asked, 'Have you ever heard of the *Arabian
Nights*?'

Someone grunted. It struck a chord somewhere but sounded
intellectual.

She said, 'The Sultan wanted the girl to sleep with him but
every night she told him a story instead. After a while they found
they preferred the stories.'

Frankie was guarded: 'You wanna tell us stories?'

She had to disarm the silence. 'Well, not instead. *She* got
away with that but... well, I guess you're a whole lot smarter
than the Sultan.'

'What're you sayin'?'

'She told stories *instead* of going to bed with him. I could tell
you stories as *well* as taking off my clothes.'

'The point of this?'

'I tell a story, and at the end of each one I take something
off. It makes it more interesting.'

Patterson chuckled. 'I'll go with that.'

But Frankie wouldn't. 'You think I'm stupid? You're buyin'
time. Just save us the embarrassment, Strachey – tell me where
Clive is.'

'Where he is or might be – is that my story?'

'To hell with stories! Tell us where he is or get your kit off.'

She was feeling chilly without her jacket. 'Did you hear the
one about the city slicker who went out bear hunting?'

'Stop it!' The light wavered angrily. 'One more crack an' I smack your puss.'

She smiled reasonably. She must not stop talking. 'Think back a minute. Did you notice when Clive turned up he had Mrs Deane perched on his arm? Was he showing her off to us?'

'The hell I should care.'

'No, for you it wasn't important, Frankie. But for me... I wondered whether he was sending me a message.'

'Like what?'

'Like... look at who I've brought in with me – take a *good* look, because this could be important.'

'You're buyin' time again, Strachey. Take off your clothes.'

She pulled her blouse out from her skirt and let it hang untidily. She bent down and kicked off her shoes. It was cold in here.

Don't let silence return. 'Strange, isn't it, that Clive flies all the way from America with her, drives to the hotel, *parades* her in front of her husband – then disappears?'

They didn't reply. Frankie had read her script and Patterson was happy to view.

Now they were using silence on *her*.

With an unsexy grimace she reached up beneath her skirt, grabbed the top of her tights and yanked them down. She left them ruckled at her ankles as she said, 'There could be more to Mrs Deane than meets the eye.'

No reply again. They could have been an audience in a theatre listening to an actress recite her lines. She had to make them speak. 'She must be ten years younger than Lincoln, wouldn't you say?'

Silence.

'Is he actually married to her?'

Patterson started to reply but Frankie said, 'Shut up.'

She assumed it was addressed to Patterson. Keep talking, she thought. Say anything.

'If they came to the hotel together—' She unzipped her skirt. 'And walked in, hand in hand—'

'Just get on with it,' Frankie said. 'An' they didn't walk in hand in hand.'

'Very nearly,' she said – nodding in the direction of the flashlight as if this was an everyday conversation – but then dragging the skirt down and kicking her legs free of it unprettily.

She kept her panties on. 'They didn't make much attempt to hide the fact that they were together. Are you *sure* they weren't hand in hand?'

'She went straight across an' kissed her husband. So much for *that* idea.'

Strachey was down to just three more items – blouse, bra and panties. The blouse hung below her hips and made her look as if she was wearing nothing else. From here on it was going to be a lot harder to distract these men.

'Who else was in the room?' she asked.

'What room?'

'The bar, when they walked in?'

'What *is* this – Armchair Theatre? Just take your kit off. I'm gettin' bored of this.'

'I'm not,' said Patterson.

She fumbled glumly with the buttons to her blouse. Don't give up talking now. 'I don't remember that religious freak – *what's* his name?'

'Delarme.'

Got you, she thought – don't clam up on me: not for this embarrassing and dangerous next half-minute. Strachey shivered in the torch-lit night air. She had undone every button now, but she paused with the shirt hanging open, a thoughtful expression on her face. For those who were looking at her face.

'Maybe that religious business is all an act. Do we know anything about this man – really?'

'Search me,' said Frankie, knocking *that* discussion on the head.

She continued with it. 'What would a religious freak want with a lordship?'

She pulled the blouse off now. The cold night air pricked against her skin. She hadn't expected the talk to *prevent* her reaching this point – it was just that now she was standing in the harsh light, wearing nothing but bra and panties, she had to give the men something else to think about. She was freezing here, while they'd be getting hotter by the second.

Strachey tried to look as businesslike as an attractive woman in bra and panties could. 'Well, that's it,' she said. 'I'm stripped. I'm freezing. But I still haven't the faintest idea where Clive is.'

It didn't work, of course – as Patterson immediately demonstrated: 'You ain't stripped. You've hardly started.'

She gazed scornfully into the dark. 'Oh, is that what you want?'

'You bet.'

'Frankie? You're running this show.'

'Get the rest off.' He sounded tired. It was the voice of a man who had disassociated himself from whatever happened next.

The least sexy way, she thought, was to lose the panties first. Men can never resist a woman's breasts. In the cold unblinking light she stooped and pulled the panties down her legs and stepped out of them. Careful, she thought. She squatted, knees together, her body turned slightly away from them as she scooped the crumpled panties up and tossed them on the small pile of her clothes. Strachey felt colder. She felt dead inside.

When she stood up she was wearing only the bra – one of her prettier ones, lace-edged, chosen specially because Clive was coming back to her. What a long time ago *that* had been.

She could hear it again, unwelcome in the room: silence, brooding menace creeping from the dark. No, not completely silent. She could hear them breathing – or might it be the wind outside? There was a kind of shushing noise: wind in the leaves of trees heard through the empty window frame. In those few seconds that she let the quiet hang, the never-silent outdoor noises rattled in her consciousness: wind and leaves, wind rattling branches. She was listening. The men were watching. She knew she had to speak again.

'While we hang around here playing games, where do you think Clive and Mrs Deane will be? I'll tell you. They're laughing at you, Frankie – at you, and everyone of you.'

'Shut up,' he snarled.

'Every minute you waste is another minute that helps them get away.'

'Get on with it.'

'Yeah!' laughed Patterson hoarsely. 'We wanna see your tits.'

He coarsened the word, killing any sexiness in her actions, but showing the brutality of his mood. This striptease act wasn't to make her *talk*. And if she had ever thought it was she knew better now.

With her hands behind her back to unhook her bra, Strachey forced herself to keep talking. She was shivering constantly now, but what she mustn't do was show she was cold. She knew what Patterson would say to that: he'd warm her up.

She said, 'Clive used to have a flat in London.'

'He still got it?'

She hesitated – a tiny moment, but just too long. Frankie said, 'You're stallin'.'

She said, 'In West Kensington.'

Her hands were still behind her back but it was a pose she couldn't hold. Patterson said, 'Get your bra off.'

She looked above the flashlight to where Frankie's face should be. Patterson said, 'Then we'll see if you're telling the truth.'

Not a word from Frankie. He wouldn't save her now. She unhooked the bra and as she let it fall she leant forward to lay it on the floor, letting her arm half shield her breasts, making the action as unerotic as she could manage. She stood up, shoulders slumped, one leg crooked, trying to make her magnificent body look ordinary.

Patterson sniggered. He said, 'That's better. We can see what's what.'

Frankie said, 'So he's got this flat in West Kensington?'

She nodded.

Patterson said, 'We can't *hear* you.' He laughed again.

A gust of wind stirred the trees outside. She knew that now, more than ever, she had to keep talking, to tell them anything – one of those stories from the *Arabian Nights*. 'It's not much of a place, but convenient. It's at the back of a house, overlooking the railway tracks. Second floor. I suppose... I could take you there?'

Frankie didn't answer. He would be studying her, she knew, to see whether in her nakedness she told the truth. Patterson would be watching for other reasons. He said, 'Stand straighter. Let's get a look at you.'

Well, she thought, this can't last much longer. It's end game now.

She stood straighter.

From the darkness she heard Frankie's intake of breath. Patterson muttered, 'What d'you think then, Frankie?'

'Mr di Stefano to you.' It was a warning. Would Patterson take it?

Apparently. 'OK. Mr di *Stefano*. What d'you think? She's telling the truth?'

'Who knows?'

'I reckon it's time we put some pressure on her – you know, *probed* a little?'

Patterson chuckled. From his voice alone it was clear that *he* had reached endgame – or the *start* of the game. He'd got her naked. She'd started talking. They were miles from anywhere. The night was young.

He moved. For the first time, he came into the light. Out of the darkness beyond the flashlight he lumbered towards her, across the wooden floor. His face was in shadow but she didn't need to see it.

She glanced in the direction of di Stefano. 'Do you want him to do this, Frankie? Do you want to watch?'

But he didn't answer. He knew the power of silence.

Strachey stepped backwards. This was it, she knew. If she started running, where could she go? She took another step. Somewhere behind him, beyond the blaze of harsh light, lay the wooden stairs. But she couldn't reach them. He was in the way. And though he'd paused to hear Frankie's answer, he was moving now. He had paused that moment, that final moment, to allow Frankie the chance to speak. He had given one tiny pause, the faithful retainer, but had not been checked. So he continued forward. Strachey backed away. He reached out. She jerked away from him, but was against the wall. When he took the last step he blocked out the light.

His hands moved suddenly, grabbing her arms, wrenching them, pulling her naked body against the roughness of his clothes. She felt his big hand squeeze her arm. He released her other arm, restraining her by one hand alone. His free hand groped for her unprotected breast.

As she struggled she heard a cry from Frankie – and she sensed, more than registered, that the beam of light jolted and swung crazily through the air. A moment of darkness. Then half-light. But she was busy with Patterson. He was hugging her to him and forcing her against the wall. He was too strong for her. Neither of them realised what had happened.

Frankie had reluctantly kept the beam on them till he heard a thump on the floor behind. He had spun round and for one brief moment his flashlight showed a man crouching on the floor. Who was this? The man must have come in through the window. He was leaping through the air. Frankie's arms went up. Too late. He felt the crack on the jaw – but before he felt it his world went black.

The flashlight tumbled to the floor and blazed like a searchlight at the rafters. At the dim, far wall Strachey was blocked by the overwhelming Patterson, forcing himself on her with the blind determination of a Rottweiler on heat. The fist that crashed into his cheek sent him staggering to the side. He reeled to face his attacker, but the man seemed to have bricks in his fists. Patterson fell to the wooden floor but found no respite. The man grabbed him by the collar and head-butted him in the face. It was like an axe had smashed his nose. More blows thundered in. The pain was more than he could stand. Patterson's last thought as he lost consciousness was that the world was so unfair.

It continued to be. The man jumped up, stood over him, and kicked him viciously in the side. Patterson's body gave a grunt but he barely moved. The man didn't even glance at the naked Strachey.

'Get dressed,' he said as he hurried back across the room. He gave the recumbent Frankie a kick to see if he would move.

He picked up the flashlight. When he shone it around the room he kept the light away from Strachey, and he kept his back to her as she picked up her clothes.

'Did I get here too late?' he asked.

'Almost,' she said. 'But not quite.'

'And there's just the two of them?'

'Yes. I need a hug, Mickey.'

He turned to look at her now, the flashlight turned away. Mickey Starr. In the half light she faced him, the clothes held lightly in front of her, belly high. She wore her nakedness naturally, head up, eyes fixed on his, her breasts two unblinking eyes. Her lips parted but she said nothing. She dropped the clothes and stretched out her arms to him. In that curious amber light she looked like a nymph in a Victorian painting: Lost And Found Again.

He lumbered towards her, the heavy flashlight clumping against his thigh. He looked down at it as if it were an extra limb, grown there by accident. Then he placed it on the floor and took her in his arms. She melted into him, her soft blonde hair a tangle against his chest, her eyes closed as she breathed him in. He stared at the wall beyond her. Anyone watching would have thought *he* was the one who had been tortured.

They didn't kiss. She remained pressed against him, her arms tight around his trunk like a drowning swimmer clinging to the bulwark that stopped her floating away.

'Mickey, what have I been doing?'

He couldn't answer. He had framed a wisecrack but he couldn't trust his throat with it. He dropped his arms and stepped aside. She lurched towards him as if still joined. But he said, 'You have to get dressed now, Strachey,' and he stepped over the fallen lamp and prodded Patterson with his boot.

Strachey pulled her clothes on. She watched Mickey cross to the sleeping Frankie and prod again. It had been several months now and she had forgotten how well-built Mickey was. Tall, she knew – but solid. Shoulders like a boxer. He wore a sweater, nothing under it, and tight blue jeans. His hair could have used a comb. He looked as if he had leapt straight out of bed and grabbed the first clothes that came to hand.

He probably had.

She was dressed now, and he seemed to sense it. He glanced round and asked, 'What are we going to do with these two babies?'

'How soon will they wake up?'

He shrugged – his familiar gesture. 'A few minutes. Maybe less.'

He was staring at her. Memories flooded back – but she said, 'Forget them, Mickey. Let's get out of here.'

'You know what they were going to do to you.'

If Mickey had a knife, she knew he'd fillet them. 'It's over. Let's get away.'

'I'll tie them up.'

'There isn't time.'

'If I tie them up, we'll have all the time we want.'

She peered from the window into the night. 'I didn't hear your car.'

'You weren't meant to. It's parked half a mile away up the hill.'

In the moonlight she could see tiny waves gleaming on the small river. But across the ford the hill was an invisible wall of dark. He said, 'I ran down from the top of it. Got my feet wet at the bottom.'

She smiled. 'I'll buy you a new pair of shoes.'

He switched off the flashlight. 'Any rope around?'

'God knows.'

'I should've brought some. We can't just leave 'em here.'

'We'll have to.'

Patterson groaned. Mickey went swiftly across to him. She cried, 'Mickey – no!' But he had already stooped and in the same movement thumped him on the jaw. He returned to Frankie at her feet. She said, 'No.'

'They're friends of yours?'

'No, but—'

Mickey was crouching over Frankie. He said, 'When I was a kid and our dog got old, my dad had to get rid of it, you know? Well, the day he killed the dog he sent me off to my uncle's house. I knew what Dad was going to do but I didn't have to stick around and watch him do it. You better go downstairs.'

'You can't.'

Mickey's face in the darkness was a mask. 'The alternative?'

'No, Mickey, we just need a rope to tie them up. You can't kill them.'

'Why not?'

'We can't.'

After a moment he stood up. 'If I'd got here two minutes later I'd have *had* to kill them.'

'You're not like them, Mickey.'

He looked at her. 'Not quite.'

She placed her hand on his arm and she felt him tremble. 'Not in any way, Mickey.'

He couldn't tear his eyes away. But all he said was, 'It's half a mile uphill.'

They arrived at the Sickle and Hoe at two in the morning and all the lights had been turned out. When Mickey switched off the car and they stepped out into the darkness, they could have had velvet across their eyes.

Mickey said, 'I'd forgotten what the country is like.'

He flicked on a little flashlight and they made their way to the pub front door. Mickey held the pencil light while she fumbled in her handbag for the key. The door opened noisily.

He said, 'How do we turn the lights on?'

'This one here.'

She switched on a side light. 'It's for late-comers.'

Mickey glanced around the pub. 'Quaint. This is where you're living now?'

'It *was*. I enjoyed it here.'

He shrugged again. 'Those guys know you live here?'

She sighed. 'Yes. D'you want to wait down here while I pop up and pack?'

'And get arrested for drinking after hours? I don't think so. You'll have to trust me in your bedroom.'

She gave a half smile and took him upstairs.

While she was throwing things in her suitcase she said, 'The room seems smaller with you in it.'

'Sorry.'

'The whole world seems smaller.'

'Don't, Strachey.'

She caught his gaze. 'I'm sorry.'

'For what?'

'Everything.'

He glanced away, around her little room. 'So,' he said carefully. 'You're sleeping single again.'

She grunted vaguely.

'What happened to Clive?'

'He's still around.'

Mickey nodded. 'He came back with you from America?'

'He has now.'

'Oh.'

'But when I was in trouble I phoned for *you*.'

Mickey looked away. 'Is that it – just the suitcase?'

'I travel light.'

She had two coats over her arm. Automatically, she handed him her suitcase.

He said, 'What's that?'

'My suitcase.'

'I heard something.'

She paused. 'We're not the only ones in the pub.'

'Outside. Could've been a car.'

They listened. Silence. 'You're not nervous, Mickey?'

'You make me nervous.'

He made *her* nervous. But she didn't say so: 'You said you'd forgotten what the country's like.'

Halfway down the stairs he stopped again. 'What was that?'

'A door, I think. Come on.'

They continued creeping down the stairs. But as they reached the bottom a voice called from above them: 'Who's that down there?' A light came on. 'What's going on?'

A man appeared on the stairs – the barman. He wore a quickly tied dressing gown.

'Strachey?'

Luke stared at Mickey Starr.

She said, 'Sorry. I have to leave now.'

The man looked at his wrist but wasn't wearing a watch. She asked, 'Did I wake you?'

'Who's he?'

Mickey kept his mouth shut. She said, 'A friend.'

'Another? Which one's this – the Lord of Darkness?'

It took a moment before she smiled. 'They're not all lords, you know. No, this one's unique.'

'Lucky him.'

The barman came down some stairs. She said, 'I'm not really doing a moonlight flit.'

'Because there isn't a moon tonight? Well, you paid in advance, so it's not a moonlight flit.' He was still watching Mickey. 'Can I ask what's in that bag?'

Strachey said, 'It's just my suitcase. Did you think we were burglars?'

'I don't know. Strange man wandering around, dead of night, carrying a large and heavy suitcase. Why should I think he's a burglar?'

She said, 'Open the bag, Mickey.'

He hesitated but then did so. He placed it on a nearby table, flipped open the lid and revealed the contents. Luke came closer to get a better look. 'Thank you, *Mickey*.'

He stood on the far side of the table from Mickey. Luke was big but not that big. And he wasn't stupid. He asked, 'Can I?' and began turning over her clothes.

Mickey glanced at Strachey, who said, 'Of course you can.'

Luke could see she hadn't run off with the family silver. 'Not even a bottle of Scotch. Well, I had to check.'

'I know this looks suspicious.'

'What, *this* – middle of night, and all? No, no. Though if you're hoping for the early bus it won't come till Thursday.'

'Something urgent cropped up.'

'I guessed that.'

'Well.' She shrugged helplessly. 'We must be off now.'

'It looks that way. Well, Strachey, you've been an entertaining guest – but won't you leave a forwarding address?

No, I didn't think so – not even for the Lord of Hexcombe?' He stared at her. '*Any* Lord Hexcombe?'

She smiled. 'There's only one.'

He sang softly, 'There's only one Lord of Hexcombe.'

'Great meeting you,' Mickey growled. 'And a great voice. But don't call us – we'll call you.'

As he drove out of the dark car park, Mickey said, 'Sounds like you've got a story to tell me.'

'It's complicated.'

'Surprise me.'

The lane was overhung with high-banked hedges and in the light from the headlamps they were dirty yellow. A rabbit ran across the road.

She said, 'You never met Clive, did you?'

'Oh, your new boyfriend's behind this?'

'He's running a scam. He bought one of those redundant manorial lordships, you know? Then tricked a dozen Americans into buying it at an inflated price.'

'I love your taste in men.'

She ignored that. 'Actually, it's not illegal.'

'Just a scam.'

'You can buy these defunct titles at auction once or twice a year. Clive bought two, and he uses one himself – he's Lord Clive of Lower Marsh now. He took the other to America and hyped it up as something precious.'

'The hat-in-the-window trick.'

'What's that?'

Mickey's eyes stayed on the road because the lane was narrow and enclosed. 'A shopkeeper had a job lot of hats and he piled them in the window marked "Hat Bargains – £5 each". But they didn't sell. So he cleared the whole window and left a clean empty space and displayed just one hat on a pedestal, marked "Exclusive – £49.95". He sold the lot.'

She smiled. 'That's roughly what Clive did. These titles *can* cost over a hundred thousand pounds, but cheap ones cost a few thousand. America's a long way away – people wouldn't know that. Anyone who did realise would never buy from Clive.'

'One born every minute.'

Mickey chewed his lip. It seemed to Strachey that he had stopped making eye contact. She said, 'Pretty shabby, eh?'

He paused before answering. 'You certainly get yourself into things.'

She sighed. 'I get bored. You know, life goes on, the sun shines, every day seems the same – I have to break the pattern and find some way to add excitement. It's a weakness – but what else is life about?'

'I remember when the sun shone.' He glared out into the night. 'I guess it was exciting when "Lord Clive" came courting you?'

'It takes more than a title to impress me, Mickey.'

'So what *did* impress you? No, stupid question, forget I asked. Where is he now?'

'God knows.'

He glanced at her. 'That was short.'

She touched his hand on the wheel. 'He ran out on me – ran off with a blonde. But the worst thing is that he left me holding the baby.'

His head shot round. 'Baby?'

'I mean the business baby.' Her hand was still on his. 'Technically I own the company that sold the title. I thought we were only selling one title – bought for five grand, sold for a hundred thousand – nice little profit. I didn't know he'd sold it over and over again. I was waiting in Hexcombe to welcome the new lord and... I didn't know there'd be a whole plane-load.'

'Seems an obvious trick.'

'Everything's obvious with hindsight. Clive suckered them, and he suckered me. But even he didn't realise they'd *all* come over – not straight away. He assumed that because it was a vanity purchase, they'd sit and gloat over the title document for a while and then drift across one by one.'

'And he's a judge of human nature?'

'You're prejudiced, Mickey.' Of course Mickey was prejudiced. She squeezed his hand. 'Anyway, four have flown over and that won't be all of them. Clive may have sold four *dozen* for all I know. They may *all* come drifting across.'

'But you won't be here to welcome them?'

'God, no.'

He paused. 'Where *will* you be?'

She removed her hand. 'I don't know, Mickey. Somewhere far from anywhere, where I can lick my wounds.'

'Meanwhile, where are we going *now*?'

She sighed. 'I don't have a home to go to any more. All I have is that suitcase.'

'Then we'd better find Clive.'

'I've no idea *where* he is. He has probably flown to America with Gloria. Oh, I don't care, I just want to get away. I want to forget this ever happened.'

'I think we should find him.'

'He can rot in hell. I'm getting out.'

'You can stay at my place,' he said tentatively. 'While you get yourself together.'

'It won't take long.' She closed her eyes a moment, then turned to him in the car. 'Do you hate me, Mickey – I'm such a cheat?'

'Hate you?' He chuckled bitterly. 'I should've stayed in bed.'

She leant towards him, her arm around his shoulder. 'I'm sorry. I really am – are you wearing a new aftershave?'

'Shave?' He rubbed his cheek. 'I haven't shaved for – what is it? – twenty hours. No, this is the real me you're smelling.'

'Wrong, asshole, she's smellin' me.'

The new voice was so unexpected it nearly shot the car into the bank. It came from behind, in the tiny space between their heads. Mickey took one glance across his shoulder but Strachey spun round to face Frankie di Stefano and his gun.

'Like you said, mister, you shoulda stayed in bed.'

He laid the gun barrel against Mickey's jaw. 'Just keep drivin'. Don't try no tricks.'

Strachey reached casually for his gun but Frankie flicked it round so she and the gun were mouth to mouth. 'Goes for both of you,' he said.

Strachey stared him down. 'I'm bulletproof – if you want to find Clive.'

'I been listening, and you just told me you don't know shit.'

'That's all right, then. Can we drop you off somewhere?'

'Turn your pretty face to the front.'

She hesitated, but did so. Frankie said, 'In case you're wondering, I sent my buddy off to Casualty. He's got my car.'

Strachey said, 'I was so worried about him. Might he live?'

Frankie chuckled. 'Yeah, to fight another day.' He tapped Mickey's cheek. 'You better look forward to that, 'cos I think you broke his nose. Take this car to the Holiday Inn.'

'Where's that?' asked Mickey.

'Tell him, Strachey.'

She widened her eyes. 'How on earth do I know? Mickey's driving. I don't know where we are.'

'Stop the car,' said Frankie.

Mickey pulled to the side.

Frankie said, 'OK, big boy – get out.'

Mickey held his gaze. 'So you can shoot me?'

'Get out.'

'Do it in the car. Then *you* can clean up the mess.'

'A nation of fuckin' comedians,' snarled Frankie. 'Listen, I've had a bad night. I am really pissed. Get out.'

Mickey frowned at him. Strachey guessed his next line: she'd heard Mickey use it once before. He leant forward and said, 'OK. But answer me one question.'

Mickey was looking genuinely puzzled. He had his big hands on the seat back. Before Frankie could reply, Mickey's hand shot forward and grabbed the gun. Both men had hold of it, and as Mickey tried to wrench it free Frankie pulled the trigger. Boom! It was as if he'd tossed a hand grenade in the car. The detonation seemed to buckle the walls. But before the echo faded Mickey had the pistol in his fist.

'You all right, Strachey?'

'Yes.' She sounded shaky. 'But there's a hole right through the roof.'

Frankie's eyes blazed with fury. 'I'll kill you for that.'

'A little late, my son. Now it's your turn. Get out and walk.'

Frankie stared at him. 'You're dead,' he said.

'I'm holding the gun.'

'Next time.'

'Oh, there's going to be a next time?'

Strachey interrupted: 'Will you two stop acting like a pair of schoolboys? No one's going to kill anyone. It's only money, Frankie.'

'It's pride,' he said.

He glared at Mickey. But Mickey nodded. 'I can go with that. But the man you want is this Lord Clive character.'

'An' you two don't know where he is. I heard that much, squashed behind your seat. But you two are all I got.'

'You haven't got us. You're getting out.'

Frankie settled back in his seat. 'You wanna clean the car?'

Strachey said, 'I hate to say it, Mickey, but I'm in so deep I can't run away.'

'From this guy? I don't have to kill him, Strachey. I leave him here at the side of the road. By the time he gets home you're a hundred miles away. Take a plane, you're a *thousand* miles away.'

'He's only one of the buyers.'

'And they're *all* villains?'

'My company owes each one about a hundred thousand. I don't know how many buyers there are, but even ten buyers means I owe a million dollars. I can't just fly off to a sandy beach and bury my head in it.'

Frankie sat back while they talked it through.

Mickey said, 'You have no choice, Strachey. You don't have that kind of money. Stay around and you'll get slapped in jail.'

'Which helps no one,' she said. She turned to Frankie: 'Does it?'

Frankie stirred. 'Oh, I'm way ahead of you. What you're sayin' is that we both got the same objective.'

'We've *all* got the same objective.'

'All? What – the other buyers? What the hell could those jerks do for us? Listen, when we find this goddamn Clive it is as sure as hell that he won't still have all the money. But he'll have a lot of it. He'll have my hundred thousand dollars, for instance.'

'Which is what you want?'

Frankie stared at them balefully. 'I want every penny that he's got. An' then I want his gizzard. How about you, Strachey – which part of him do *you* want?'

17

ONE OF THE many American virtues is an appreciation of personal hygiene. At the Holiday Inn, Frankie took it for granted that Mickey and Strachey would want to use his room – one at a time, of course (he wasn't *that* understanding) to take a shower. He subtly established himself as gang leader by insisting that he sat downstairs with Mickey while Strachey bathed, then with her while Mickey took his turn. But Frankie didn't risk leaving them alone so he could take a shower. Trust didn't come easily to him. He went with them to the Creamery for breakfast, where they took the fresh-fruit option and drank a vat of coffee.

By the time Lincoln wandered in, conversation had petered out and the effects of a lost night's sleep were beginning to tell. They waved to Lincoln in case he'd thought he could slink to a table on his own, but he was in no mood to avoid them. He ambled across, fresh as a peeled grape, another American who wouldn't start the day without a shower. He gave Frankie a grave 'Good morning', twinkled hopefully at Strachey and squinted at Mickey.

'Shall I join you?'

She moved the chair. 'Meet Mickey Starr.'

'Lincoln Deane. Pleased to meet you, Mickey.'

'Sorry to hear about your wife.'

Lincoln raised his eyebrows. 'Is it in the papers?' He laughed nervously. 'Well, I guess we live in a global village.'

Strachey said, 'Mickey had to be told. He's my personal advisor.'

Lincoln poured some muesli. 'Professional?'

Frankie said, 'I'll say.'

Strachey leant forward. 'Unfortunately, Frankie has to leave us.'

It was news to him but Strachey kicked him gently beneath the table and smiled in Frankie's face: 'We'll stay with you, Lincoln, for a little chat.'

Frankie didn't budge so she added, 'Perhaps we can compare notes.'

'Oh, right,' said Frankie grudgingly. 'You comin', Mr Starr?'

'I'm her advisor. I have to stay.'

Frankie exhaled angrily and stood up. 'I'll be in the lobby.'

'That's good to know.'

Lincoln watched him leave. 'Unhappy man.'

Strachey gave a sympathetic smile. 'How are you feeling, Lincoln, after a good night's sleep?'

'Worse than I look!' He laughed shortly. 'Did you sleep well?'

'Couldn't sleep a wink.'

Lincoln glanced at Mickey as if that might have been *his* fault. 'When did you get here?'

'An hour and a half ago.'

That answer seemed to pacify Lincoln. 'You've eaten, right?'

They nodded. He took a spoonful of muesli. 'I gotta say this,' he munched, 'I'm glad to see you here, Strachey. I mean, after last night I thought we'd never see you again.'

'Everyone thinks I'll do a moonlight flit.'

Lincoln shrugged. 'What's your role, Mickey?'

While he thought of an answer Mickey smiled and placed his coffee cup back in its saucer. 'Friend and confidant.'

Lincoln considered that, then laughed. 'What d'you make of di Stefano? Is he on the level?'

Strachey asked who *was*.

Lincoln gave a straight reply: '*I* am. That's my trouble – I've been on the level all my life. Too goddamn honest!' He laughed, caught her eye, then busied himself with his bowl of muesli.

She probed: 'Never cheated on Gloria?'

'I'd never do that.'

She held his gaze and smiled. 'Have you heard from her yet?'

His gaze dropped. 'Hell, no. I doubt she's out of bed yet,' he added bitterly.

'Think she'll get in touch?'

He shrugged. 'Who knows? This is new territory for me.'

'Because wherever Gloria is, Clive may be too.'

Muesli stuck in his tooth. 'Great,' he said. 'That really cheers me up.'

'We have to be realistic.' She leaned towards him. 'We have to help each other.'

'Like how?'

'If Gloria gets in touch, will you let me know? Better still, find out where she is.'

'Like she'd tell me.'

Mickey said, 'Put a trace on the call.'

Lincoln studied him. 'Then you'd go visit her – is that your role, Mickey?'

Mickey gave a noncommittal shrug.

Lincoln said suddenly, 'Oh, Jeez. That's *it*. That goddamn prick.' He looked agonised, as if muesli had stuck in his windpipe.

Strachey smiled. 'Whose prick?'

'That prick who's come through the door. That self-righteous prick.'

They turned to see Edgar Delarme striding across the restaurant. He swooped on their table. 'Consorting with the enemy?'

'Who's that today?' asked Lincoln.

'You break bread with the woman who defrauded you of your fortune.'

'Only a hundred thousand, give or take,' replied Lincoln. 'Which may be a fortune to *you*.'

'To you it's insignificant?' Delarme sneered.

'I can hack it.'

Delarme almost smiled. 'I bumped into Lord Clive,' he announced casually.

He got the reaction he wanted. They almost leapt from their chairs. 'Where?'

'At the airport. He and... They were waiting for a plane.'

'Figures,' said Mickey.

'But they didn't catch it. There was a fracas.'

Strachey said, 'Clive gave you the slip?'

'Not at all. He and I and... ' He looked at Lincoln and coughed. 'And another person were in the boarding lounge when *Mr* Lane was called away.'

'Called away?' snapped Lincoln. 'Was he with my wife?'

'Yes, and she went with him.'

'They didn't come back?'

Delarme pursed his lips. 'I didn't think they would. So I didn't take the flight.'

Lincoln couldn't help a 'Jesus Christ! Where'd they go?'

Delarme ignored the blasphemy. 'You should have been at the airport.'

'Je – ee – eosophat!' cried Lincoln. 'You followed them?'

'I had no need.'

'Why not?'

'I have already concluded my business with Mr Lane.'

He said no more, and wasn't going to. Like a poker player with four aces, he knew he'd won – all bar the shouting. He had simply to give Lord Clive the cheque. There was an outside possibility that one of the rivals might also be able to pay in full, but as long as they didn't know where Clive was, it didn't matter. He beamed thinly upon the breakfasters.

'I must go now,' he said. 'I can't say I have enjoyed our intercourse.'

Lincoln stood up. Delarme gazed at Strachey. 'You are a deceitful woman, fallen from grace. Sin no more.'

He swept away.

Mickey said, 'What did I say about your choice in men?'

Strachey ignored him. She said, 'Delarme *concluded* his business with Clive. What does that mean?'

'And why did he call him *Mr* Clive – no, Mr *Lane,* he said, not Lord Lane – what's the significance of that?' asked Lincoln.

'For Delarme there's only one higher authority,' suggested Strachey. 'But I think they cut a deal there at the airport. And according to him, Clive and Gloria did not fly out. They're still here. All we have to do is catch up with them.'

18

FRANKIE WAS WAITING for them in the lobby. Waiting was
the word – he'd placed himself in a large square armchair, face-
on to the Creamery exit, so he wouldn't miss them when they
came out. He bounced from the chair.

'Up to my room.'

Mickey smiled at him. 'Think we'd slip away?'

'You might try it, if you're stupid.'

Mickey towered over him. 'We could walk out now.'

'You'd be a dead man.'

Mickey stepped closer, Frankie's head against his throat, and
when Frankie tried to step away he found Mickey's hand behind
his head. Mickey hugged him to his chest and smiled pleasantly
round the lobby. He said, 'You're a stranger here,' He patted
Frankie's cheek. 'You don't know the customs of our country.'

'Where's Lincoln?'

'Dining in style.'

Frankie's fingers twitched like a gunfighter's before a duel.

Mickey let him go, saying, 'Now, are we on the same side or
what?'

Frankie grunted.

'Was that a yes?'

Strachey interrupted: 'If Clive could see you two he'd know
that he was safe. Come on, we'll go to Frankie's room – but
Frankie, you be good.'

She could have been their mother. 'Follow me.'

As Frankie stood aside to let them in he grinned. Once they were
in the room he shut the door and leant his body against it.

'It's only us, mother,' he called sarcastically.

The bathroom door swung open and Patterson stepped out.
He had a splint across his nose, fastened with sticking plaster to
his cheeks. His eyes defied anyone to make a crack about it.

No one did.

Frankie said, 'OK, let's talk. I don't suppose Lincoln heard
*any*thing?'

Strachey confirmed: 'Not a word.'

She glared at Patterson, then looked away.

Frankie asked, 'Deane's gonna stick around in case his wife phones?'

Patterson sneered. 'He's lost without his baby.' He sounded like a man with a heavy cold.

Strachey took an unconscious step closer to Mickey Starr.

Frankie scowled. 'What else we got?'

She said, 'Delarme came.'

'I saw that. He know anything?'

'Would he tell?'

Frankie sniffed. 'Shame he ain't Catholic – I could extract a confession.'

'I expect you've heard a few.'

She said it to mollify him, and it seemed to work. He strutted over to the mini-bar. 'You been in here yet, Patterson?'

'I just arrived.'

'An' you didn't even put the kettle on.'

Frankie rumbled through the contents. 'Dinky little bottles, ain't they? Nothin' we could share.'

Strachey smiled bravely. 'There must be Champagne.'

'This?' He produced a half bottle and squinted at the label. 'When was the sell-by? No one drinks this stuff.'

'We don't even have champagne flutes.'

'*Flutes?*' He hooted, and Strachey smiled. She was trying to lighten the atmosphere. Frankie put on an affected English accent: '*Oh*! I say. We *hevn't* any *shempen* flutes! Drink from the bottle, girl, like us.'

He struggled with the cork a moment – until it popped, feebly. A spurt of fizz foamed from the mouth.

'Ladies first,' said Strachey, reaching out her hand.

He grinned at her. 'Don't wanna catch anythin'?' He handed it across.

She took a swig. When she took her moist lips from the neck she saw all three of the men watching to see who'd get it next. She handed the wet bottle to Mickey Starr.

Frankie said, 'You were sayin' about Delarme.'

'Apparently he bumped into Clive and Gloria at Bristol airport.'

'Delarme went there too?'

It surprised her. 'You *knew* Clive was at the airport?'

'Sure. But he never caught the plane, right?'

Strachey sat on the dressing-table chair. 'Why don't *you* tell us what happened, Frankie? You know more than I do.'

He shrugged, as if it were common knowledge. 'I pulled a stroke an' got 'em yanked off the goddamn plane. But before we could get to 'em they disappeared.'

'Where did they go?'

'Why d'you think I'm askin' *you*? I didn't know Delarme was up there with 'em.'

'He didn't say he was *with* them—'

'He was at the goddamn airport! He was catchin' the same plane. An' when they didn't catch it, lo and behold – as *he* would say – he drops out too? You reckon he wasn't with 'em – I think he was. Then I think they ran out on him.'

'They did better than that,' said Mickey.

Patterson glared across his nose-splint as if Mickey had spoken out of turn. Frankie asked, 'Whaddya mean?'

Mickey handed him the champagne bottle. 'They sold him that title you want so much.'

'Sold him? He already bought it. We *all* of us bought the thing.'

'Well, he looked like a cat who'd finally got the cream.'

Strachey agreed. 'That's right. He said he'd *concluded* his business with Clive. And he said he knew where Clive had gone.'

'Where, for Chrissake? *Concluded* his business with him?'

'He got a refund?' Mickey suggested.

'A refund – of a *hundred grand*? That goddamn Clive wouldn't give a refund on this *bottle*.' Frankie waved it to emphasise his point. 'No, "concluded"… You think he bought the title a second time? Could he be that stupid?'

'Delarme could,' said Strachey.

'Either way, he thinks he got something,' Frankie mused. 'Either a cheque or somethin' to guarantee the title. But whatever Clive passed off on him, Delarme wouldn't let him disappear.' He thumped the bottle down on a writing table. 'Of *course* he knows where Clive is. Goddamn Delarme holds the key. Where the hell is the guy – which room's he in?'

Strachey said, 'He isn't staying at this hotel.'

'The Holiday Inn's not good enough? Where is he – a goddamn monastery?'

'I wish.'

'You must have his address, Strachey – you sold him the title.'

'I don't have his address – I don't even have his *American* address. Clive handled the business side.'

'Why do I think I shoulda realised that? Clive kept you in the dark?'

She nodded. 'Afraid so.'

Patterson joined in: 'So you don't know nothing. You're a waste of space.'

They all three looked at him. They worked out what 'you dohn doh duffing' was supposed to mean while Patterson ploughed on: 'An' 'cos you dohn doh duffing you fink we oughta jud det you go?'

She ignored him. The only sound came from the air conditioner.

Frankie said, 'Time to find Delarme.'

After Strachey and Mickey had gone, Patterson sat on the bed and stared glumly at the mini-bar. From time to time he raised a finger to the side of his nose as if to check it was still there. The *pain* was there – his nose felt like a candle stub of burning molten wax – but was his nose splint holding up? He glanced at Frankie staring out the window. 'You think we'll see *any* of them bastards again?'

'Why not?'

Patterson stared at his back. 'Why should we?'

'Delarme: because he ain't got no reason to run an' hide – I mean, he waltzed in here to show off at breakfast – and Strachey: because she is in the deepest doo-doo. She has a line of angry customers, each one thinkin' she owes 'em a hundred grand.'

'Which is why she *won't* come back.'

'She's gonna run forever?'

'She could go to jail forever.'

'She was hoodwinked like the rest of us. Can you see her standin' up in court – big eyes appealin' to the judge? No, all she wants to do is get her pretty hands on Clive – have that big boyfriend of hers teach the man a lesson. Like she says, we're on the same side.'

Patterson kept his tone light – as light as a man could, when honking like a sea-lion: 'Does she really owe you a hundred grand?'

Frankie stiffened. 'Yeah. Someone does, anyway.'

'Clive will have stashed it.'

'He'll have to unstash it, won't he? An' I want more than a hundred grand.'

'How much?'

'Depends what he's got.' He turned round. 'What would *you* want?'

Patterson shrugged. 'His kidneys on a plate. And his girlfriend for afters.'

'You're a *dirty* bastard, Patterson.'

'It's a dirty world. She owes us something.'

'Keep your mind on Clivey boy.' Frankie stared at him from the window. 'Wherever he's stashed it, he must have several hundred thousand dollars. He's got the title deed too.'

'Unless Delarme bought it.'

Frankie rubbed his jaw. 'I don't think so.'

'Maybe he *thinks* he has.'

'We all *thought* we had.'

'There is a real one, though?'

'I believe.'

'If there *is* a title and there can only be one real lord, he's got to be the one who gets the deeds and a bill of sale from Clive. But, if you want *my* opinion, this title ain't worth a tuppeny fart.'

'That's your considered opinion?'

'Yep.'

'You know somethin' about this, do ya?'

Patterson sensed the annoyance in Frankie's tone. It would have been difficult *not* to sense it, but Ray was feeling sore himself.

'I wouldn't buy a title from Clive if it was signed in the Queen of England's blood.'

'We had the deed checked in New York. It's genuine.'

'Who checked it – one of Lord Clive's friends?'

Frankie didn't like being put on the spot – but was determined to ram it home to Patterson. 'Everyone round here *knows* it's real. I spoke to the local vicar, *an'* some poncey real-estate agent, *an'* the guys who run this hotel – even the goddamn *barman* in a country pub. Of course it's genuine. It's just that Clive don't want to sell it.'

'There was a guy once sold Big Ben.'

'Meanin'?'

Patterson shrugged. 'Why do *you* want a sodding title? You're American.'

'What the hell has *that* got to do with anythin'? Ain't I good enough – is that your point? I'm good enough, brother, you better believe it.'

'If a title makes you feel good—'

'A title makes people know who they are dealin' with. Back in the States, Patterson, where *you'd* find it hard to earn a goddamn livin', this title could be very useful in some deals I'm puttin' together at City Hall. So does that make *you* feel good?'

Patterson knew he could go no further. 'Oh, I'm feeling good. Yeah, sure.' He touched his aching nose.

'An' I'll tell you what I'm learnin' about the English? Especially *you*, Patterson. Whatever *you* think must be wrong.'

As she got into Delarme's car, Strachey could see Mickey watching her from the hotel entrance. He would have preferred to keep her in sight but to track both Delarme and Lincoln Deane they had to separate. If Strachey had to be alone Mickey would prefer it to be away from Frankie and Patterson – and indeed, from Lincoln in his own sad way – which meant somewhere outside the hotel. Delarme was a religious man; she'd be safe with him.

Delarme said, 'I wanted to get you on your own.'

He looked both ways along the road. As he eased out into non-existent traffic he said, 'You have sinned in the past but I sense contrition. Am I right?'

'You judge me well.'

She lowered her eyes like a nun.

He said, 'Confession would bring peace.'

'I have done wrong.'

There was a pause. Each waited for the other to make an opening.

'You abetted Lord Clive,' he prompted.

'I bedded him as well.'

The car swerved momentarily from its course. She wondered if Delarme had ever knowingly had a fallen woman in his car before. Well, not *had*, but...

In a surprisingly gentle tone he said, 'Perhaps you allowed your feelings for him to persuade you into wrongdoing?'

'I was led, Father, yes.'

'I am not your Father.'

She mustn't lay it on too thick. Even so: 'You are like a Father – a religious father. I feel I can trust you.'

'I'm glad.'

'And I hope I can... earn your trust in me.'

He glanced at her.

'Why should I trust you?'

She opened her eyes and gazed at him. 'I have been made grubby by this. I need to find someone who'll trust me again.' She was beginning to flounder. She must get to the point. 'If there is any way I can help in the search for Clive I'll happily do it.'

Delarme smiled knowingly. 'Ah, you want to find him. Everyone does – either to wrest the lordship from him or to regain their money.'

'And you?'

'I met him yesterday.'

'At the airport.'

'Lord Clive explained that no one has yet paid the full amount. It was, of course, a huge sum of money. But I am now in a position to pay it all – which is why he'll want to see me.'

Delarme's eyes actually twinkled.

'How true,' she said. 'While the others will try to get their deposits back from me.'

'Do you have their money?'

'No.'

Delarme seemed in surprising good humour. Perhaps he liked having a pretty woman beside him in the car. 'You were never paid your wages of sin?'

'I'm afraid not.'

'That's important, don't you see? You're less tainted. Legally you are, I believe, owner of Lane Estates?'

'Technically.'

'The law is ruled by technicalities. As owner of the company, you are its decision maker.' He shot her a sharp look in contrast with his gentle tone. 'You may actually be in a more powerful position than the missing Lord Clive.'

She frowned, and he explained. 'You may be able to lay the fraudulent sales at Clive's door. In fact, I'm sure you can,' he added, a little too smoothly. 'Doing that might get you off the hook. Meanwhile, as legal owner of the company, you are perhaps the only person who can ratify Clive's sale. You,

Strachey, can make one of the duped buyers the unassailable winner.' His friendly smile was becoming smoother by the second. 'Lord Clive has already confirmed that I have the soundest case by far.' He smiled with all his teeth. 'And I have the money – ready in full.'

She smiled back. 'That's why you wanted to talk to me?'

Marvellous, she thought, how Clive could talk his way out of a jam. Not only had he talked his way around Delarme but he had sold him another slice. 'You have the money?'

'Every cent. One hundred and five thousand.'

'Pounds?'

'Dollars.'

'A hundred and five thousand.' She rolled the numbers around her tongue. They tasted fine.

He risked a long look at her. She kept her eyes on the road ahead. He said, 'A hundred and five thousand is a lot of money. I imagine one of you is on commission, while the other takes the bulk.'

'The title owner takes the bulk.'

'Lord Clive's cousin?'

She nodded. Delarme seemed determined to believe that tale.

He rapped his fingers against the wheel. 'But Clive has the title documents. Come now, you surely know where he is?'

'None of us knows where he is. But if we work as a team – Mr Deane tracking down his wife, you and I following after Clive, and Mr di Stefano...'

She faltered. There seemed no way Frankie could fit the plan.

Delarme said, 'We are rivals, not a team. But you and I – *we* could be a team.'

'Mm,' she said enigmatically.

'I believe we can reach Clive first – as a *team*.' He stressed the last word. 'If we are both motivated.'

'Oh, I'm motivated.'

'Perhaps I could motivate you a little further?'

She glanced at him in surprise. But he explained: 'Another ten thousand – for you alone?'

'Ah, money.'

'It's indelicate, I agree – but I think I know where Lord Clive is.'

His eyes glinted in triumph. Strachey said, 'You mentioned that before.'

'I know his approximate destination. Perhaps if I told you the general area you could pinpoint more exactly?'

It was tempting. What *did* Delarme know? 'Let's try,' she said.

His face tightened. 'But can I trust you?'

'Of course.'

'You've given me little reason thus far.'

'Forgive the sinner. Where is this "general area"?'

He pursed his lips. 'Perhaps I *don't* need you. Perhaps he'll contact me anyway.'

'Why?'

'He knows I've got the money.'

'Good thinking. So where – approximately – has he gone?'

Delarme stared through the windscreen for inspiration. 'No, I can't trust you. Forget I mentioned it.'

'I can't *forget* it! I thought we were a team?'

'We might become one.'

Strachey shifted uneasily in her seat. With any other man she might have thought Delarme was coming on to her. But he was a religious man – like Brutus, an honourable man. She asked cautiously, 'We might become one when?'

'Tomorrow.'

'Tomorrow!' She laughed. 'What'll we do with ourselves today – drive around the countryside?'

'Clive may contact me. But if he doesn't, I'll come back to you.'

'You know how to make a girl feel valued, don't you?'

'I'll drive you back to the hotel.'

She gave him another look – but there didn't seem to be a hidden motive. He was staring as resolutely ahead as if glaring from his pulpit. Maybe he was repressing manly desires.

'Fine,' she said. 'I'll talk to the rival buyers.'

'I forbid that.'

'Mr di Stefano asked me—'

'You should not consort with a man like that.'

Well no, she thought. But she said, 'That poor Mr Deane—'

'Doesn't want the title. He wants only to find his wife.'

She raised her eyebrows but that let it drop. 'Then there's the Nibbets—'

'They're irrelevant.'

She paused, then said sarcastically, 'It seems to leave only you.'

'Precisely.'

The Nibbets didn't consider themselves irrelevant. Frankie di Stefano had just disentangled himself from the whole clan in the hotel bar – where he discovered to his amazement that they still believed they'd won. Walter had been enthroned on a chrome-plated bar stool from which he beamed down upon his entourage as if the title had run in his family for generations. The rest of the clan preened like a gaggle of courtiers.

Frankie strode across the lobby, shaking his head. What was going on? He knew England was stuffed to its pinstriped collar with freaks and weirdos, but the goddamn Nibbets were American! They'd surely realized Clive was a conman: they couldn't believe *anyone* had bought the lordship – let alone themselves? Though of course, they'd paid their money and, like customers everywhere, once they'd paid they'd convince themselves they'd chosen right.

He stood by the elevator and thumped the button again. Didn't nothin' work? He stared at the panel, alone in a world of dumbos.

There was a well-oiled groan, the door opened and he stepped inside. He was staring back through the closing shutters when he saw Strachey enter the hotel through the revolving glass from outdoors. He stuck his foot out. The doors closed on it, shuddered as if they didn't like the taste, then recoiled back the way they'd come. He called across to her.

She said, 'Just the man I wanted to see.'

'Get in the elevator. We're goin' upstairs.'

The atmosphere in his bedroom was like a weigh-in before a fight. Frankie and Strachey might be make-weights but Mickey and Patterson exuded enough testosterone to create a fog. Mickey was prancing, the cocky contender, while the injured Patterson breathed noisily and looked as menacing as he could while wearing a splint across his nose. Frankie paced the room, the referee.

'So what you're tellin' me,' he said, 'is that no one knows nothin'. I pump the Nibbets who talk and talk but live in cloud-cuckoo-land. Strachey goes on a scenic tour with the preacher man, who seems to be bluffin' about knowing where Clive is. And Mickey chats to goddamn Lincoln who's up to his eyes in gloom and misery about his cheatin' wife.' He turned to Patterson. 'An' I told you to get on to the London mob to get some help.'

Patterson shrugged. 'They said they already helped. Call Pinkertons, they said.'

Frankie pointed his finger at him. 'You make that up? Because I don't like funny guys.'

'He makes *me* laugh,' said Mickey.

'That's enough from you.'

Mickey studied him. 'I haven't started.'

'Boys, boys,' said Strachey.

Frankie glared at her. 'I reckon you know where he is. You're still soft on him.'

Mickey pointed at Patterson: 'Order *him* about. Me and Strachey are leaving now.'

'You're goin' nowhere.'

Mickey glanced at Strachey. 'Grab your bag.'

Frankie said, 'Listen, punk. There must be a dozen guys who'll sue her for a hundred thousan' dollars. The only way she shakes off this kinda crap is if she feeds 'em little Lord Clive – an' even then she's in a mess. You being around don't make a squat of difference. So why don't you grab *your* bag an' sit down yourself?'

Mickey and Strachey strolled through lifeless hotel gardens among dusty shrubs that looked as if they'd given up hope of life outside a tub.

'No one will sue you,' said Mickey. 'You've no money to sue for.'

'Clive will make sure he has none. He can't be sued. That's why I own the company. Stupid, wasn't I?'

'You've never been stupid, Strachey.'

'I've a stupid taste in men.'

She slipped her arm through his. It was good to be with him again. She said, 'I've got to find him.'

'So they sue. You can only go bankrupt.'

'Frankie won't sue. He wants his money back. If I run away, he'll find me again.'

'We'll have to find your boyfriend.'

She squeezed his arm. 'My ex-boyfriend.'

'It's over, is it?'

'What do *you* think, Mickey? Of course it's over.'

Mrs Nibbet phoned her cousin at the American embassy.

'A *lordship*, Gretchen – you understand what that means?'

'Sure, honey, it's a pretty title—'

'We get a family crest, a coat of arms, some ancient papers – and there are several square miles of old England that *belong* to Walter, like a kind of fiefdom.'

'It sounds to me, honey—'

'The Nibbets *arrive*! Can you imagine what they'll say back home?'

'Yes, it might play better there.'

'I don't know why you're so unimpressed, Gretchen. Just because you work at our embassy – how many of you folks have titles there?'

'Titles, schmitles.'

'Let me tell you, we had to *fight* for this.'

'What, a tournament – Walter *jousted*?'

'No, but we had to fight off half a dozen buyers – really important people, all American. I guess the Brits can't afford the price. We're talking over a hundred thousand here.'

'A hundred *grand*?'

'Sure. That was the kind of money all the leading players were prepared to pay. But you know Walter – he went that extra mile.'

'Yes, I know Walter. How many players were in it?'

'Who knows? We had a telephone auction.'

'Ah.'

'No, no – they're genuine players. Five came over with us when we viewed the property – well, that's five *including* us – and four of us are here for the final showdown. But we *won* it, Gretchen! Walter Nibbet is Lord of Hexcombe Manor.'

'What kind of people, for goodness' sake?'

'*Lord* Walter – oh, Gretchen! I am so excited! What *kind* of people? Why, there's a famous wine maker from California, Mr Lincoln Deane—'

'Never heard of him.'

'Well, you're teetotal, Gretchen – you wouldn't. There's a religious man, Mr Edgar Delarme—'

'Never heard of him.'

'There's a New York businessman, Mr Francis di Stefano—'

'Frankie di *Stefano*?'

Gretchen fell off her chair.

19

MICKEY SAT AT the bar of the Sickle while Strachey used the phone. The barman asked, 'What will you have, my *lord*?' and he found this quip so droll that he put Mickey's pint down with a 'Here you are, my *lord*,' and retired sharply to the far end of the dark wood counter where he smirked and polished the glasses. Mickey decided folks didn't get much fun in the country.

Strachey returned. He said, 'I didn't get you a drink yet,' but she picked up his glass and sipped it. 'This will do.'

He took the glass from her and cupped it in his hands.

She said, 'I think Delarme was bluffing. He told me he knew the "general area" where Clive was heading, but now I press him on it he's strangely coy.'

'Maybe he just likes talking to you.'

'He thinks I'm a fallen woman.'

'All the better. He'd like to wash away your sins.'

'Whatever. He was with Clive at the airport so he knows *something*. Could Clive have caught another plane?'

Mickey snorted. 'Is he collecting air miles?'

'Delarme said he knew the "general direction". If they caught a plane maybe Delarme knows which one he caught.'

'Perhaps he *did* catch the New York flight.'

'Frankie said he didn't.'

'Was Frankie there?'

'Delarme was.'

'Maybe Delarme got off, then Clive got on?'

She pulled a wry face as the barman appeared. 'Excuse me, my lord.' Mickey ignored him. 'A couple of messages for you, Jane, while you've been away.'

'Jane?' mouthed Mickey.

She asked who from.

'Mr Jeremy Barrington Downey. Very keen for you to get in touch.'

'Who's he?' asked Mickey.

The barman smiled. 'Another admirer.'

'He can wait,' said Strachey. 'Come on, Mickey, we've work to do.'

Lincoln knew it was a bad sign – hanging around his hotel room, no energy to go out. He didn't want to meet people, face questions, dredge up a smile. He used to do this as a kid and his mother would get at him, warning that no good would come of it, he'd grow up stunted. He'd sit behind his locked bedroom door and let her hammer from outside. Every minute she'd expect the worst.

When the phone rang he could hardly raise his hand to answer it. Hotel phones ring so timidly, so decorously quiet, they just beg to be ignored. It kept chirping though, so he answered it.

He was glad he did.

'Gloria! The hell are you?'

'Don't swear at me, darlin'. You OK?'

'I'm worrying myself sick.'

'D'you miss me? I miss you.'

'You're coming back?'

'It's complicated.'

'Don't tell me. Come back to me, Gloria. I'll forgive you. We can make everything all right.'

'I can't afford the air fare.'

'Where *are* you, for Chrissake – back home?'

'Not that far.'

'Come back here.'

'I can't. You put a stop on the credit cards.'

'They're my cards, hon.'

'*Your* cards? Suddenly they're your cards? I'm your wife – what about that "for richer, for poorer" kinda stuff?'

'Yeah, me being the poorer.'

'"With all my worldly goods I thee endow" – remember?'

'Oh, is that why you're phoning – to put a handle on my goods?'

'I only want what's mine.'

'So do I. You're mine, you're my wife.'

'Oh, Linc darlin', don't let's fight.'

'Not till the divorce courts, is that what you mean? Till then an uninterrupted line of credit?'

'You're so mean to me.'

'Mean? Christ, I'm stuck here in a lonely hotel room, pining for you, and you're out gallivanting with some two-timing English lord. Ask Clive for some money.'

'He hasn't got none.'

'What d'you mean? He's got a hundred thousand of *my* dollars – let alone what he rooked from the other guys.'

'It's all tied up.'

'Take a knife to it, Gloria – slice the knot.'

'Couldn't you take the stop off a credit card – just one? I only need a little.'

'You *serious*? You want me to shower cash on you – while you jump in and out of that shyster's bed? You're still with him, I take it?'

'Oh.' She hesitated just a fraction too long. 'I want *you*, darlin', but I can't afford to fly home.'

'Home? I'm not home, Gloria, I'm in Devon, England. Where the hell are you?'

'I mean I can't afford to fly *back* – back to *you*, Linc, back to dear old Hexcombe, Devon, England.'

'Are you in England?'

'Well... '

'Christ, either you are or you ain't.' His mind was racing. 'You gonna tell me where you are?'

'I can't do that.'

'Why the hell not – I mean, if you're so anxious to come back?'

'You'd come up here.'

Up here, Lincoln noticed. Where exactly was 'up'?

'You want some money?'

'You *are* a darlin'.'

'I'll bring it to you.'

'No, don't.'

'Why not? I can't release the cards, honey – once the companies put a stop on they stay stopped. They're going to mail me some fresh ones. Should be here inside a week.'

'A *week*?'

Got her, he thought, the phone removed from his ear. 'Oh, a week would be too long?'

'I'll say.'

'I'll *bring* the money.'

'No, no.'

'Then we're kinda stuck.'

If she wants it, he thought, she either tells me where she is or she comes back here to fetch it.

He waited. She said, 'Just one measly little credit card?'

'Oh, I would, honey, but it can't be done.' He waited again, then added, 'I could mail you, I guess. What's your address?'

'If I tell you, you'll come up.'

'No, no.'

'You will, darlin', I know you.' She chuckled, cosier with him now. 'Hey, I been married to you for long enough, Linc. I know what a *devil* you can be.'

'OK, honey, I don't like to see you in a jam. But how can I help if you won't tell me where you are?'

'Can't you use some kinda messenger service?'

'They'd want an address.'

'I could send someone to *you*.'

'Send Clive.'

'Lincoln!'

'What? Some stranger turns up and asks for a thousand bucks in cash? I don't think so, Gloria.'

'A thousand? Couldn't you make it three?'

He smiled – that was his Gloria. 'OK, you win. That's how you are, Gloria, you wrap me round your finger. We'll play it your way. I'll mail it – but not to your address, since you don't *trust* me, honey – I'll mail it *poste restante*.'

'The hell is that?'

'You know, Collect. I send it to your local post office. You just turn up with some proof of identity.'

'And you're waiting behind the door?'

'Honey-*child*. This is safe for you, anonymous. You don't even have to collect the cash yourself. Just send someone you trust.' He grinned to himself: who would she trust with three thousand dollars? 'If you collect the cash yourself, you even choose the time. You don't have to tell anyone. You just turn up when you feel like it. That's pretty damn safe.' He paused. 'Isn't it?'

'I guess so,' she said reluctantly.

'Where's your local post office?'

'No, darlin', not so fast. I'm out in the boonies here. Send it to… ' She hesitated. 'Send it to Glasgow Central. They must have a central post office, right?'

'Bound to.' Glasgow, he thought, where the hell is that?

Scotland – what's she doing there? *Up* there. Glasgow. 'Consider it done. You get the money, then you'll buy a ticket and fly back to me – is that the plan?'

'Sure.'

Oh yes, for sure.

Glasgow Central, he thought. Well, Gloria could whistle for her money. The only question was whether he should hop on the first plane alone, or to tell Strachey where Clive was now. Maybe she would like to come along.

Strachey had also been to the bank, leaving Mickey parked on a yellow line. She came round the car and climbed inside.

He said, 'I didn't think they had traffic like this outside London.'

'It's a market town. People drive in from all around.'

He pulled away. 'They give you a hard time in there?'

'I've been a sucker, haven't I?'

They were at the traffic lights.

She said, 'As soon as the auction bids were cleared, Clive drew an enormous cheque – not for everything, but most. It turns out he'd warned the bank beforehand, putting the money on deposit, he said – overnighting it – the kind of term they like. He's the kind of *man* they like, sensible with money.'

Mickey nodded, keeping his eyes on the busy High Street, letting her blow off steam. She said, 'Obviously, he's got another account somewhere – but they won't tell me where.'

'You ask?'

'And arouse their suspicion? They thought I knew all about the transfer. I had to stay poker-faced.'

'So Clive cleaned you out?'

'Most of it. Yesterday he drew another cheque for cash. Living expenses, I guess.'

'Nice guy.'

'He drew the cheque in Kirkintilloch – you heard of it?'

'Sound Scottish.'

'I'll check the map.'

She checked the index, and flicked the pages. 'It's a small town near Glasgow.'

'It'll take all day to drive there.'

'We can fly from Bristol.' She snapped the book shut. 'Remember Delarme said he knew the "general direction"? I bet

Clive never left the airport – he just jumped on a flight to Glasgow.'

'Perhaps he's bought the lordship of Kirkintilloch.'

'You never know.'

They were driving at normal speed now, in the outskirts of Tavistock. 'It's a small town, you say?'

'That's how it looks like on the map. Ever been there?'

'Scotland?' He shivered. 'This'll be my first. We'd better try this small town he draws his money in.'

'Biggest cheque they've cashed in months.'

'Which makes Clive a big fish in a little pool. He should be easy to spot.'

He wasn't difficult to spot that morning. Glasgow airport sported tartan advertisements and garish plaid boutiques, but its passengers dressed down. Even the businessmen looked dull – faces shone but suits were drab. As for the rest... anyone under twenty wore a teeshirt, the under-forties dressed in jeans, while over-forties dressed in clothes they ought never be forgiven for.

Lord Clive Lane was dressed in a particularly striking pale biscuit tweed. His blond hair gleamed with conditioner and his skin tingled with the scent of lime. He had a thistle tucked discreetly in his buttonhole, and a citron handkerchief peeping from the breast pocket of his tweed jacket. His shoes were brown – but he could be excused that, being out of town.

He had come alone to meet a fresh party of English buyers. Having flown up from Heathrow they'd have preferred a Scottish welcome but Clive wasn't up to that. The best compromise was that he be at his most aristocratic. He was, after all, Lord of the Manor of Lower Marsh. Outside the airport the day was moist – as Scots euphemistically describe their weather – and Clive's greeting would be as warming as a glass of malt.

He had to sell at least one of these visitors a manorial seat.

20

MICKEY DROPPED STRACHEY at the hotel entrance and went back to park the car. By the time he reached the lobby he found that Strachey had attached herself to yet another attentive male. This was a languidly elegant public-school type – the kind whose public-school education ensured he never felt out of place. The kind who put Mickey's back up.

He slouched to join them in the lobby. Strachey said, 'This is Mickey Starr. Mickey, this is Jeremy Barrington Downey.'

A name like that did not raise him in Mickey's estimation. 'You left messages.'

'I did indeed,' said Barrington Downey. 'Visiting Devon?'

'Passing through.'

Their eyes clashed like antlers.

Jeremy said, 'Perhaps we could join you for a coffee, Mickey? After I've had a private word with Strachey.'

Strachey said, 'Mickey and I have no secrets.'

'About Lane Investments,' Jeremy purred.

'He knows.'

Jeremy shrugged and carried on. 'I hadn't realised you were the chief executive of that company.'

'I hadn't fully realised myself.'

Jeremy glanced again at Mickey, then continued: 'I've been asked about the bona fides of Lane Investments. I was telephoned yesterday by a colleague – another estate agent, actually – in Scotland.'

'Hoots,' said Mickey, but no one laughed.

'My Scottish contact had a party of rich potential buyers recommended to him by Lane Investments.'

'Not by me,' she said.

'Then I think we can guess by whom. Especially since they want to view a decrepit old manor house that my colleague has had on his books up there for years. Hardly anyone looks at it.'

'And the only person who has looked recently…?' she hazarded.

'My friend didn't tell me that. No reason he should, of course.'

'Do you have the address of this decrepit manor?'

He stroked his cheek. 'I have more than the address – I have full particulars.' He produced a folded fax from his jacket pocket and handed it to her. 'There you are, Strachey, I've told you everything I know about this business. Now, what do *you* know?'

She grinned at him. 'Where the action is.'

She and Mickey sat at a table in the Creamery waiting for Frankie to come downstairs. Buying him coffee avoided meeting him in private. Strachey could afford it: 'While I was in the bank I drew the last couple of thousand for myself. Sauce for the goose.'

'At least Clive left you something. I guess he took out a damn sight more than that?'

She shrugged. 'It's his money, really. It's his scam.'

'But your company. Your head on the line.'

'Enjoy the money while we can.'

She sipped orange juice. He drank tea.

She said, 'We could blow three hundred on a lunchtime plane to Glasgow. But we have to tell Frankie we're going, or he'll assume I've done a bunk.'

'Here comes the man himself.'

Frankie grinned malevolently as he walked across. 'Can't get enough of me, huh?'

Strachey said, 'Clive's in Scotland.'

'Well, whaddya know?'

'We're going up to find him.'

He sat down and grinned again. 'That's my girl – when you got a weak hand, you play it strong. What makes you think I'll let you go to Scotland?'

Mickey stirred in his seat. He wasn't happy that Frankie thought he could stop them, but he let it ride.

Strachey said, 'Clive may have meant to go to Scotland all the time. The New York flight from Bristol is *via* Glasgow, it's not direct. Quite a lot of people get off there.'

'Well, well,' mused Frankie. 'Scotland – small country, huh?'

'It looks small on the map.'

His face brightened. 'Hey, I noticed that. Over here, you look at a map an' see some place a coupla hundred miles away an' you think, fine, it should take three hours or so. That's the most it would take in America. Over here, for some reason, the cars go faster an' it takes twice as long.'

She assumed a TV narrator's voice: 'In this mysterious, fog-ridden island you enter a different time zone, a new dimension.'

'It's foggy, all right.'

'There's a flight at lunchtime,' she said casually. 'We'll take that.'

He grinned at her. 'You slip 'em in real smooth, Strachey. OK, you go to Scotland – but this feller stays here.'

He nodded at Mickey, who said, 'Get stuffed.'

Strachey intervened: 'Boys, boys! I need him with me, Frankie.'

'Why?'

'To put a hold on Clive.'

Frankie chewed his lip a moment – and from the look on his face his lip did not taste good. 'Maybe I'll stay around in case Clive comes back. And who knows? Maybe Gloria will show. Could happen. OK, you two fly up to Glasgow – but take Patterson with you.'

Lincoln had not shifted from his bedroom. He sent the maid away, ordered brunch on Room Service, but when it came he did not eat. He didn't even break the cellophane. He lay on his bed and stared at the ceiling. He gazed at two pictures on the wall – some kind of lilies in a vase, and a lakeland scene. Wishy-washy. He wondered what the hotel paid for them. They obviously bought these things in bulk – just as they did in the Happy Hacienda chain back home. He should talk to the Hacienda people about it. He bet he could supply pictures cheaper than they were paying now – more colorful too. These things were muted pastel, thinly printed – while the ones in the Hacienda tended to be mountains and golden plains. (Christ, there was even a buzzard in one of them. You want a buzzard in your restaurant?) No, he could give the Hacienda something decent, something bright – lots of reds and strong vibrant Mexican dames, dancing the whatever-it-was that those dames danced. The one where they twirled their skirts a lot and showed their thighs. The kind of thing you wanted in a restaurant.

The phone warbled. He was so lost in reverie that for a moment he thought it might be the Hacienda, but it was Gloria. He was almost disappointed. She was so predictable.

'Linc, darlin', I been down the post office.'

'Uh-huh.'

'Is there a problem, Linc?'

'Well... funny you should ask. I got this nagging pain in my gut.'

'I mean is there a problem with the money?'

'You're not interested I'm in agony?'

'No, that's terrible, Linc, I'm really sorry. Did you wire the money like you said?'

'It's great to hear your voice.'

'*Did* you?'

'I forgot to say good morning, didn't I? Good morning, Gloria.'

'For Chrissake, Lincoln, you *promised* you'd send the money! What's going on?'

'Well, not a lot – it's quiet here—'

'*Lincoln!*'

'They hadn't got your money at the post office?'

'No.'

'The *Central* post office?'

'*No.*'

'Edinburgh?'

'*Glasgow!*'

He chuckled. 'Oh, Glasgow, yeah, that's right.'

'Where did you send the money, Lincoln?'

'You only call me Lincoln when you're mad at me.'

'You didn't send it, did you?'

'Don't this guy Clive spend *anything* on you? He must be worth a fortune.'

She sighed.

He added, 'A *small* fortune anyway. Is he as rich as me?'

She sighed a second time, then snapped: 'What are you asking, Lincoln – is he as *rich* as me? Is his dick as *big* as mine – is that what you want to know?'

'No, no, everyone knows English dicks are smaller than American. It's like beds, you know – we have king size, they have queens.'

'He is *not* a queen.'

'Did I say he was? Oh honey, if I'd realised you were *sensitive* about his sexuality... I thought he was a normal man, you know?'

'He *is*, for Chrissake! Where's my money?'

'A normal man sends you begging from your husband?'

'Lincoln, I need some spending money of my own. It's a cash-flow thing.'

'You have *been* down to the post office?'

'Yes, but Glasgow – not Edinburgh, Linc.'

'I was kidding, hon. You must have gone down there too soon. This is Britain. You got to get used to the slower pace of life.'

'There's nothing slow about Glasgow. Compared to Fresno it's New York.'

'Is that right? Maybe I've been in Devon too long – I'm going native, slowing down. Maybe I should come up to Glasgow, start speeding up?'

'No way!'

'You don't want me, my little precious?'

He reached across to the bedside table as she backtracked: 'Darlin', I understand what you're going through, I really do. I'm so *sorry*, you know? But you coming up to Glasgow is not going to help us learn how to deal with this.'

He picked up a packet from the bedside table. 'Look, the money's on its way, so why don't you spend today in town and collect the cash tomorrow?'

'Tomorrow? Christ.'

'Tomorrow morning, first thing.'

He looked at the air ticket in his hand and smiled peacefully. Bristol-Glasgow return, teatime today.

Mid-afternoon Glasgow, the morning mists had rolled away, and the sky glittered like polished pewter. Mickey and Patterson stood side by side in the arrivals lounge, and the two men looked grimmer than the weather. Patterson was irritated that they wouldn't tell him where they were headed, and now that Strachey had slipped away to the toilet he stuck close to Mickey in case he also tried to slip away. Mickey remarked that he thought Strachey had female trouble and that she would probably be some time. Patterson stood as close to him as was respectable. Strachey took her time.

The two men waited.

Eventually Patterson broke. 'They queuing for it or what?'

Mickey shrugged. 'Women's lavatories.'

'Why do women always take so long?'

'Plumbing.'

'No, their plumbing's easier than men's. They just pull their knickers down.'

'Lavatory plumbing: each woman needs her own cubicle.'

Patterson thought about it. 'Why does it take longer in a cubicle?'

'There aren't *enough*.'

'How many do they need?'

'One each.'

'I *know* that—'

'Think about it. A man needs a length of wall. Against that wall you stand six men – but in that same stretch of wall you can only fit three cubicles. That's why men get through quicker.'

Patterson nodded. 'That's logical. Then there's make-up, of course.'

'You wear make-up?'

'Women have to do their make-up.'

'That's why Strachey takes so long.'

Patterson glanced at Mickey along his nose splint. 'You tryin' something on?'

Mickey smiled. 'Why would we bother? If we wanted to ditch you I'd just pop you on the nose.'

Patterson scowled. They stood in silence till Strachey reappeared. 'We need a taxi,' she said.

They went outside into grey steel Scottish light. Strachey told Patterson he could choose any cab he liked. But he was city-wise: 'We have to take the front one.'

'We're going to need the cab all day. Shouldn't you negotiate a rate?'

'All *day*?'

'A couple of hours, at least. See what's the best deal for *half* a day. It's your boss's money.'

Patterson cursed and approached a taxi. He thrust his head in and, being city-wise, bargained aggressively. But Glaswegians know aggression: they'd say they wrote the book. The taxi driver leaned back in his seat, eyed the unpleasant Sassenach, then spat out a figure in dialect. Patterson flinched, which he had intended to do whatever the quote, and said, 'Twenty quid an hour.'

The driver laughed.

Patterson said, 'No more than twenty-five quid.'

'Listen, Jimmy,' the driver began.

By the time they'd reached agreement Patterson regretted he'd ever tried to save Frankie money. He gave in reluctantly and turned around. But Mickey and Strachey had gone.

By teatime Lincoln felt sanguine. Having rejected perfectly acceptable food in the Holiday Inn, he drove to Bristol airport and bought coffee and a Danish. It was a mistake. Because the English didn't know how to make them he'd deliberately avoided a sandwich, but he'd assumed a Danish would be a Danish. It wasn't. It was a muffin – a different shape but just as soft. As little flavor as an English sandwich.

He sat in the boarding lounge and licked his fingers – which tasted better than the Danish – then glanced around to locate the washroom. Might as well freshen up before the flight. He stood up, was halfway across the lounge, when Frankie di Stefano hurried in. They stared at each other.

Frankie came across. 'You goin' to Scotland?'

'No, I'm going to the john.'

'I take the high road an' you take the low – right?' Frankie grinned savagely. 'Well, here's a coincidence – not!'

Lincoln raised sugar-coated fingers. 'I need to wash my hands.'

Frankie walked beside him. 'You avoidin' me, Lincoln?'

'Come if you want to.'

'Sticky fingers, right?' They pushed through the door. 'You're a dark horse, Lincoln, I always knew. What else has stuck to your sticky fingers?'

Lincoln marched to the nearest basin. 'You can watch me wash my hands.'

'Why're you headin' for Scotland?'

Lincoln rinsed. 'I'm looking for my wife. Why are *you* going?'

'Come on, Lincoln, don't fool around.'

Lincoln went to the hot air drier. 'I guess you're chasing after Clive.'

'And you're chasin' after Gloria. Maybe we can economize on cab fares.'

21

SINCE SHE HAD hired the car, Strachey drove. She and Mickey headed north along roads that quickly became emptier and more exposed. Kirkintilloch, she told him, was simply a convenient stop off the motorway, while the address Jeremy had given was high in the Campsie Fells, far from anywhere, let alone a bank.

'Clachan Castle,' Mickey said. 'Falling down?'

'Jeremy's description was decrepit but not derelict.'

'Estate agents put a gloss on things. Still, it is a castle.'

'Two a penny up here. Plenty of fine manor houses call themselves castles.'

'Fine manor house, then.'

'You've seen the fax.'

He skimmed through it again. 'Hm. "Benefiting from an enviable elevated location" – means it's up a hill. "Set amidst 6 acres of mature woodland" – a tangled forest or overgrown garden. "Dates from 1791 and built in the Scottish Baronial style of architecture with round tower and craw stepped gables". 1791 is late for castles, isn't it?'

'Not up here,' she said.

'Nothing else to do, I guess. 'The entry porch was added in 1859 and the late Victorian west wing in 1896'. So it's a Victorian makeover of an older house. Still... "Adam fire and door surrounds'. That sounds good."

'Every decent house then was in the Adam style. The Conran of his day.'

'"Seven bedrooms, three *further* bedrooms..." Don't knock it, Strachey.'

'It's been on the agent's books for years. What does that tell you?'

'Oh, well.' Mickey looked out at the gorse-strewn hillside. 'Makes a nice day out.'

'Shame Patterson couldn't make it,' Strachey said.

'Before we lost him at the airport he gave me a detailed picture of why you were taking so long in the loo.'

'He's a disgusting man.'

'We certainly strung him by the *nose*.'

'Maybe we should have brought him with us – to *sniff* Clive out.'

'I'll keep *my* nose in the map,' Mickey said. 'We're not far away.'

Clive was not easily perturbed. He spotted them shortly after they had parked their car, as they were walking towards the house, some way behind the small party he was leading around the exterior walls. He waved a casual hand as he continued his sales spiel, acknowledging them verbally with 'Two more interested buyers'. Two of the five men with him turned round. The other three kept their eyes on Clive.

'This is Scottish granite, of course – will last another thousand years. It warms the heart to imagine one's family living here through the centuries. You'll have noticed that the gardens need a little maintenance but those enormous weeds simply show the fertility of the manorial soil. This estate can be back in top form in no time at all.'

He smiled anxiously at Strachey as he took his party on.

'Down there – under what now seems little more than an unkempt lawn – was a rococo garden. Imagine the view from here, across the restored rococo gardens and on across the fells toward Loch Lomond.'

'Is that far from here?' somebody asked – English, Mickey noticed, not American.

'Fifteen miles,' Clive said. 'Nothing at all.'

'About an hour's hard drive,' Strachey muttered. 'If ours was anything to go by.'

Clive said, 'Take a moment to admire the view. Imagine it when the morning sun shines on the fell! Excuse me a moment.'

Clive had added plus fours to his biscuit-coloured tweed. He approached the newcomers with a hearty smile. 'Welcome to Clachan Castle!' He threw his arms wide, and used the gesture to shepherd them away. In a quieter – though still chirpy voice – he continued: 'Wonderful to see you, darling – and who's this gentleman?'

'A friend.'

Clive chuckled happily. 'That's a relief. For a moment I thought he was a policeman! He's big enough.'

He squeezed Mickey's arm. Mickey removed his hand, saying, 'You got some explaining to do.'

'Surely, my friend, no problem at all – but not at this moment, eh? Let's keep the punters happy first.'

'I'm not your friend.'

'Sorry. You were introduced as Strachey's friend – and any friend of hers—'

'My name's Mickey Starr.'

'Delighted.' Clive glanced at Strachey for amplification. 'Let's not rock the boat just now, all right? You stand to make a lot of money out of this, Strachey.'

She snorted. 'How does that work out?'

'Didn't I explain?'

'Explaining is not your style.'

Clive laughed a little too loudly and turned to check briefly on the rest of his party. He quickly muttered, 'Don't blow it – you could earn a hundred thousand,' then, with a wave of his tweed arm, he scuttled back to his quarry.

'Come and see the stables,' he cried. 'Or where they used to be!'

The five men trailed behind him round the corner of the house.

'That's my Clive,' said Strachey. 'Leading 'em up the garden path.'

She and Mickey paused before following on. 'D'you know what he's up to?' Mickey asked.

'Selling houses, but don't ask me why.'

'He doesn't own this?'

'Nor did the man who sold London Bridge.'

'This so-called castle is falling apart,' Mickey said. 'God knows what it's like inside.'

'A little maintenance, he'll tell them – sympathetic restoration.'

Mickey poked at a rotting window pane. 'It'd be cheaper to knock it down and start again.'

'There's always the land,' she suggested.

'Six acres of moorland?'

'Come on,' she said, moving down the path. 'This isn't why we're here.'

The interior was not as desperate as they had thought. Shabby, but by no means derelict. Clive dwelt upon such period features

as there were – the several walls of panelling, the Adam
fireplaces and door surrounds, the mock Jacobean staircase – but
he hurried them through the dingy hallways and less well-
preserved rooms. Someone – it could only be Clive – had
disguised the smell of dampness by burning incense sticks all
around the house. Several huge vases of flowers had been
strategically placed, as if *they* produced the pungent smell.

Listening to Clive's patter they realised that even in this tiny
group he was aiming at two audiences – those who might
actually choose to live here and those who might develop the site
into a conference centre or discreet hotel.

'Why would they want it?' Strachey whispered.

'Maybe he's sold the lordship of Kirkintilloch.'

'No, no,' she laughed – the laugh quickly dying. Had he?

They tagged along with the small party. Clive seemed thrown
by Strachey's showing up and uneasy about the big man by her
side. As they moved from room to room he snatched an
occasional muttered word. His story – in muttered outline – was
that if he pulled off the property deal, all payments would be
made to Lane Investments – which Strachey owned. So it wasn't
in her interest to stop him now.

Alone with her again, Mickey said, 'Don't believe a word of it.'

'Part of it's true,' she said. 'I do own the company.'

'But Clive can write cheques from it.'

'I could stop that – couldn't I?'

Mickey looked at her. 'So you'll support him whatever the
scam – as long as it makes money?'

She wouldn't look at him. 'Since when were you so pure and
holy?'

'That man's got you wrapped around his finger.'

Frankie and Lincoln came through the arrivals barrier like
captains of opposing football teams. They smiled at the
indifferent crowd but seemed to be bustling each other aside.
Frankie was met by Patterson. Lincoln emerged alone.

Frankie spurned his waiting henchman: 'You're a useless pile
of shit, you know that?'

Patterson snorted through his splint.

Frankie turned away. 'Hey, Linc, you've met Rob Roy here?'

Lincoln nodded. 'We seen each other at the hotel.'

'Word of advice: don't give him anythin' to look after, 'cos he'll lose it.' He glanced around. 'So, Linc, where are you meetin' Gloria?'

'We've nothing planned. See you, Frankie.'

'Hey! Hey! You walkin' out on me? We're supposed to be a team.'

'I changed my mind.'

'What you gonna do – walk around Scotland till you find her? Get real. I'm not an idiot, Linc.'

Lincoln shrugged.

Frankie said, 'We work together, we nail that guy. But if we don't work together, we work *against* each other. An' you're not workin' against me, are you, Linc?'

'No.'

'Then don't walk away from me.'

Frankie hung his head over, stuck his arm out. 'Come on.' It was a buddy-buddy thing.

Lincoln stepped towards him. 'I'm not doing anything this evening.'

'You're doin' somethin' now.' Frankie turned to Patterson. 'OK, where's the car?'

'What car?'

'You haven't hired a *car*?'

Clive drove his prospects to the town of Balloch on Loch Lomond. The fifteen-mile trip took forty minutes but the journey was a scenic one, across the Scottish moorland in evening light, then down to a turbid Loch Lomond in the gloaming. Clive used the word 'gloaming' several times.

Mickey and Strachey followed in their car and waited close at hand as Clive dropped his party at the Station Hotel. It was starting to rain. The five English prospects hurried inside but Clive stayed outdoors.

'Great country,' he said. 'Shame about the weather.'

Strachey nodded to the hotel behind him. 'Is this where you're holed up?'

'Good lord, no! Never get too close to your customers.'

'You should have thought of that in Fresno,' Strachey snapped. 'Where *are* you staying?'

Clive evaded that with practised ease. 'I thought we'd eat at a lochside restaurant tonight. I've telephoned Gloria. She'll meet us there.'

He smiled bravely at Strachey and looked away.

She said, 'Why should I want to meet Gloria?'

Clive gave a sympathetic shrug. 'These things are never easy but... ' He made an attempt to look resolute. 'We have to face life as it is. Running away is never the answer.'

'You're such a bastard, Clive.'

'True, true.' He shrugged. 'I assume you two are an item?'

'Me and Mickey?'

Clive raised an eyebrow. Mickey didn't react. She said, 'We're not an item, Clive.'

He glanced from one to the other. 'We'll get soaking wet out here. You can follow me to the restaurant. It's called the Robert L Stevenson Inn.'

Gloria Deane was dressed to kill. She knew nothing about the geography of the British Isles but she did know Loch Lomond was romantic. Having had the afternoon to herself she'd spent a large part of it laying the foundation for a romantic meal. First came the dress, bought in a boutique off Glasgow's Sauchiehall Street. Then a not-bad-all-things-considered Scottish haircut. Then a long, toning bath in jacaranda salts. Then the make-up. Over the years (and it wasn't so many years) Gloria had spent an extraordinary amount of time on make-up.

The onset of Scottish drizzle was a disappointment, but she assumed the restaurant would be beside a covered section of loch and lit up like that place in Storyland – and there would be a canopy out to the cab, so the evening shouldn't be too bad, even if Clive had damn near ruined everything by inviting his ex-girlfriend and her new beau to make a foursome.

When she arrived at the restaurant there was no canopy out to the cab.

And it wasn't what she'd call a cab. She damn near told the driver. But she remembered Lincoln had once told her that Scotland was a second-world country so she had better make allowances. Poor old Lincoln. She ought to keep him sweet.

And here she was, at the restaurant early! Gloria Deane did not like to come early. (She didn't like to *arrive* early either, she thought with a dirty laugh.) She asked for the nearest payphone, which was in a lobby. With no view of the loch.

She checked the Holiday Inn but they confirmed what they'd

said earlier when she rang: Mr Deane was away for twenty-four hours but was coming back. They were holding his room.

So she rang his cell phone.

Frankie made Patterson drive, and he sat beside him in the front seat while Lincoln rode the rear. Patterson drove with his head high because he couldn't see properly round his splint. Frankie shrunk into his seat and passed much of the journey with his eyes shut, while Lincoln peered out into the fading light. An entertaining journey.

But it was a surprise to everybody when Lincoln's phone rang.

'Gloria?' He gulped on the word. It was not a conversation he wanted to share.

Frankie and Patterson pricked up their ears.

He said, 'Well, I'm not in the hotel. I'm somewhere else.'

He crouched over the handset.

'Doesn't matter where I am. No. Doesn't *matter*. Does it *sound* like a car? Well, you know – where the hell are *you*?'

He took a deep breath.

'OK, *be* like that. I *mean*. What? Yeah, I told you, go down tomorrow.'

'She'll go down tonight,' sniggered Patterson.

Lincoln snarled, 'Will you guys shut up?' He returned to the phone: 'Yeah, sure, there's people here. So what, I'm supposed to live life on my own? No, it's none of your business, Gloria. What d'you expect – I sit around like a monk?'

He had to listen to an earful. 'It's nothing to do with you whether I'm in my hotel room or not. I'm... I'm out somewhere. No. *No*. We've been through that – it'll be there in the morning. But will *you*? I'm just asking. *You're* the one wants the money, Gloria, you're the one phoned *me*. I'm just telling you that if you're in such a damn hurry for it, you better hotfoot down there first thing. Yeah, Central Post Office. What? Listen, I'm doing you a favor here, aren't I?'

He took the handset from his ear and stared at it. 'Well, what d'you think of that?'

Frankie said, 'She hung up on you.'

'Yeah.'

'Dames do. What's this money you're givin' her?'

'Oh, nothing. My business.'

'You're holdin' out on me, Lincoln.'

'This is private business. Me and her.'

'You an' me are private business. That's money too.'

'Yeah, but we're trying to get our money *back*, not give it away.'

'You're givin' money to your wife?'

'Yeah.'

'Who has run off with this other guy?'

Lincoln grunted.

Frankie pressed him: 'An' this other guy is the same guy who took our money?'

'Yeah, yeah.' Lincoln stared out of the window.

'That don't add up.'

Lincoln hesitated, then said, 'Well, I won't be giving her the money, will I?'

'I thought you just said—'

'It's a trick.'

'Tell me about it.'

Lincoln ground his teeth. 'I told her it'd be at Central Post Office in the morning.'

'So?'

'So she'll go collect it. And I'll be there.'

Patterson snorted. 'That's good. It's like *cherchez la femme*.'

Frankie glared at him. 'I didn't see that movie.'

'No, it's like... follow the woman. You want to catch the guy, you follow the woman he's with.'

'That's the size of it,' said Lincoln.

'Tomorrow morning,' said Frankie. 'Where's she tonight?'

'Who knows?'

'She just rang you. Ain't you got dial-back on that phone?'

Lincoln stared at him. 'Oh yeah, right.'

He stabbed numbers in and listened. 'Oh, excuse me,' he said into it. 'Where was that again? Ah. Listen, I know this sounds stupid, miss – but can you tell me where exactly *is* the Orbital Stevenson Inn?'

The restaurant was part of a small chain that included the Pavilion On The Links and Ballantrae. The loch beside it wasn't lit up as Gloria had hoped but it did have a few small lamps bobbing on its surface. The water looked black, and sitting at a window looking out at it made the diners feel chilly. But they warmed up with Virginibus Cocktails and took refuge behind large menu cards from where they could peep around the corners at each other. Sitting between Mickey and Clive – and opposite Gloria, whom she ignored – Strachey found she had no appetite at all. Clive seemed blithely untroubled and Gloria – whom Strachey ignored – sparkled and twinkled like a Christmas angel. She chatted to Mickey and Clive, turning from one to the other like a queen to her courtiers. Indeed, Gloria – whom Strachey ignored – seemed determined to make the evening swing. She turned in her chair to point out across the dark loch – a graceful, artless movement, allowing the others to see that she'd shaved her blonde armpit and that when her arm raised, her breast lifted like a living animal.

'We got a lake like that in Fresno,' she said. 'You know, Millerton – you heard of it? I mean, it's famous, it lights up at night.' She turned to Mickey. 'You can hire a boat, you know, five dollars – take it out at night. Can you imagine, alone with your girlfriend in the dark? Bobbing up and down on the water.' She nudged him.

'Five dollars,' he said.

'Well, I think so,' she chuckled. 'I don't normally pay for my ticket.'

'You sneak on free?'

'No!' She prodded him playfully. 'A lady never pays.'

Strachey muttered, 'It only costs a man five dollars.'

The waiter appeared. They ordered two Silverado steaks, Chicken Vailima and, for Gloria, a Child's Garden of Herbs. With the menu cards removed, they faced each other across the cloth. Clive asked Mickey if he'd known Strachey long.

'We're old friends.'

Clive smiled calmly. 'She never mentioned you.'

Strachey said, 'Because he's someone I trust.'

Clive bowed his head. Gloria – whom Strachey ignored – asked Mickey if he were Scottish, and suggested he'd look good in a kilt. 'Tell the truth,' she said, 'I'm disappointed. We been here two days and I've seen pretty well no guy in a kilt.'

'Have you been looking?' Clive asked.

She laughed and touched his arm. 'Hell no, Clive darlin', you know I only have eyes for you!' She glanced back at Mickey. 'A friend of mine came over last year and wanted to find out the Scotsman's secret – you know, whether they wear anything under their kilt? She sees this guy in a kilt and asks him about it. But he says, "Stick your hand up, honey, and find out." She sticks her hand right up underneath his kilt and screams, "Oh, that's gruesome!" The guy goes, "Stick your hand up again, honey – you'll find it's grew some more!" You get it?'

She hooted at her joke. Mickey smiled politely.

'Lincoln used to keep me in check,' she said, with a wry smile. 'But not in tartan!'

Strachey said, 'Frankie di Stefano wants his money back.'

Gloria was on a roll. 'And Lincoln will, you bet. You can pay Lincoln's share to me!'

'Di Stefano won't go away.'

Clive put his glass down. 'A tough character, Strachey, I grant you that. But we don't get rich by refunding people's money.'

'He's not people.'

Clive studied her. 'What would you like me to do?'

'Refund him.'

Gloria held her hand out. 'And Lincoln, please.' She laughed and drank some wine.

Strachey said, 'You left me to carry the can for you, Clive.'

He smiled urbanely. 'What's your role in this, Mickey?'

'To get Strachey out of a jam.'

Strachey said, 'I'm *in* a jam – I own the company, supposedly.'

Clive said, 'Let Lane Investments go bankrupt, if necessary. Bankrupts don't go to jail.'

'Why should *I* go bankrupt?'

He glanced at Mickey again. 'Is... Mickey fully aware of what you've been doing?'

'What *we've* been doing – yes.'

Clive concentrated on him: 'So you know that Strachey is not a naive innocent whom I've wickedly led astray? You know she was a fully participating partner?'

Mickey sniffed. 'She ain't participating in the profits, because you cleared the bank account.'

'Of course, Mickey – because if Lane Investments is to go bankrupt, it mustn't have money in its bank account. So I moved it out of harm's way. Common sense.'

Strachey checked: 'It is still accessible?'

'Of course.'

They stared at each other. Gloria broke the pause with a laugh. 'Well, that's a relief!'

Strachey said, 'Where's my share?'

'Invested and earning interest for you. Strachey, if a

bankruptcy investigation does arise, you don't want cash that can be in any way associated with you. You'd lose the lot. I've arranged things so you'll not lose a penny – even if the worst should arise.'

'My money's safe? Where is it?'

Clive shook his head. 'It's better you don't know.'

'Don't give me that!'

'No, if there *is* an investigation and you genuinely don't know, you can't tell them – whatever they do. This is the safest way.'

'They're not going to torture me for the information.'

Clive looked hurt. 'I'm sorry you don't feel you can trust me—'

'Trust you?' Strachey waved an angry arm at Gloria. 'You dumped me for this – for one of your customer's wives—'

Clive chuckled. 'I didn't dump you, Strachey—'

'Well, what's she doing here?'

Clive coughed delicately. 'We're not a married couple, Strachey. Ours was a business relationship. We're in a different phase now.'

'Ours was a *business* relationship?'

Gloria said, 'I understand how you're feelin', honey—'

'Stay out of this.'

'I'm tryin' to help you here.'

'Don't bother. You used me, Clive.'

'I've made you rich.'

'What!'

'It's your company—'

'You kept the books.'

Gloria chipped in: 'I'd *love* to know how much it was. Come on, Clive darlin', you been hidin' somethin' from those who love you – and that's not *honorable*, is it?'

Clive raised his hands, clean as a bishop: 'You're an interested party, Gloria—'

Strachey snapped, 'Another *business* relationship.'

'We have to trust each other.'

'Trust!'

The waiter coughed. 'Could I ask ye to keep your voices down? There's been a complaint.'

'A *complaint*!'

'Darlin', that accent is *adorable*. You Scottish? D'ya wear a kilt?'

'I have to ask youse if ye'll no mind keeping your voices down. Now, who's the one for the Silverado Steak?'

With the night black outside the window, their reflections merged with lamps bobbing in the water like a double image in a film. Clive kept pouring wine and though he himself drank lightly, he became more voluble as they ate. He beamed as benevolently as a visiting uncle and when night blanked off outside, their dining table seemed to shrink and bring the little party closer.

Clive said, 'Clachan Castle is magnificent in its way: a magnificent folly perhaps, but a *folie de grandeur* – and such things are beyond price. Our customers are successful city men – but outside the metropolis they are lost souls in search of guidance. We shall guide them, darlings. We shall guide men who live in well appointed apartments or houses with sixty-foot gardens and we shall show them a *castle* in six *acres* of its own land.'

His inclusive use of 'we', rather than I, was to draw his listeners in. He was a master storyteller and the time had come to reveal the Secret of Campsie Fells.

'A castle with ten bedrooms – all right, seven bedrooms and three attic rooms that once accommodated starving servants. A castle within spitting distance of Loch Lomond – rather a long spit, I'll grant you, but we're sitting at the lochside now, aren't we? We are eating our dinner at the side of the most romantic loch in Scotland, and it's just a short drive home across Campsie Fells till we reach our own castle in the wilderness. Being in the wilderness, we shall not live in this castle permanently – we'll treat our Scottish castle as the royal family treats Balmoral. It will become, if you like, our own Balmoral.'

Clive broke off briefly, and smiled.

'But you don't want to hear the sales spiel. You want to hear what's in it for me – for us. *We* have bought this manorial castle and we are offering it for sale to the highest bidder. Now, you and I, we know it's been for sale for ages but it hasn't been properly *placed*, properly *presented*. So we will stress to the city-based businessman that, among its many benefits, this is a manorial castle – oh yes, it is. Manorial – that mythic word! Here on the fells lies a defunct title, the Lairdship of Dymquhosh. It's a Scottish Feudal Barony – much the same thing as an English lordship, though even more impressive, don't you think? To be honest, the Lairdship has absolutely nothing to do with Clachan Castle, which we'll rename Dymquhosh Castle, but once we have sold them the castle we *must* be able to sell them the title later. After all, if you owned Dymquhosh Castle, what wouldn't the Lairdship of Dymquhosh be worth to you?'

'I like the sound of this,' declared Gloria. 'I mean, even knowing it's a scam I could be tempted myself—'

'It's not a scam,' demurred Clive.

'Gee, if I was still with Lincoln I might just persuade him to buy the thing – I mean, I *like* it: a *lairdship*, a feudin' barony?'

Clive gave her a shrewd look. He was wondering whether she *ought* to stay with Lincoln. She chattered on: 'Clive, darlin', you could keep the title yourself. Just think of it, you and me here – what would I be, Lairdess?'

'A baroness.'

'A *baroness*!' she shrieked. 'Me? Clive, *keep* the place!'

It was a pleasure for Strachey to watch Clive squirm.

Mickey asked, 'How much will it cost to do the place up?'

'A fortune,' confessed Clive. 'Which is why it hasn't sold. Anyway, once we've sold the lairdship, I thought we might sell them a quick ennobling ceremony. These are the sort of people who'd pay thirty thousand for a *wedding*.'

Strachey cut in to ask how he'd paid for the castle.

'Paid?'

'You said you owned it.'

'Ah yes... '

Clive refilled his glass, then offered the bottle all round. They waited for his answer.

'I haven't actually paid for it—'

'*Ah*!'

'But I put down a gesture of good intent.'

'How good?'

Clive raised his glass but didn't drink from it. 'That's why there's so little money left to bail out our creditors.' He shrugged calmly. 'Now our punters will be asked to do the same – put down a standard ten per cent holding deposit, while the – er – paperwork comes through.'

'Punters?' queried Strachey. 'How many deposits have you taken?'

'I'm in the process... '

'This is like the lordship scam, isn't it? You're selling the same property to each of them, taking ten per cent off each.'

Clive nodded and sipped his wine.

Mickey asked, 'Why stop at ten per cent?'

Clive smiled encouragingly, pleased to have drawn Mickey in. 'Each ten per cent deposit brings us thirty thousand. Perhaps I can rope in half a dozen. That could be a hundred and eighty thousand.'

'But the full price is three hundred grand?'

'Thereabouts.'

Mickey nodded. 'And how many punters are you hoping will pay the full price?'

'Hang on,' said Strachey, rapping her glass on the table. 'This isn't going to work.'

Clive smiled broadly.

She said, 'In Scotland these property contracts are binding. It's not like England: once you've accepted someone's offer you have to close the deal. You can't take several deposits and then not go ahead.'

Clive's tone was reasonable: 'Under any law I must only sell once.'

'So how are you... ' She petered out.

Clive continued. 'As it happens, I haven't signed a Scottish contract with my buyers. They're Englishmen, you see – they're more comfortable with English law.'

'In their shoes I'd be less comfortable,' argued Strachey. 'Under English law they have to put up a deposit with no guarantee of an eventual sale – whereas under Scottish law they know they're safe.'

'Precisely why I chose English law. Of course, I've allowed them to protect themselves.'

'How?'

Clive's grin was too broad. 'I had a private chat with each of them – and pointed out the problem of rival bidders sneaking in ahead. You can guess how they responded. Each made private deals with me to freeze out the others.' He raised his glass. 'Chin, chin.'

When they left the restaurant it was a shock to find it raining outside – lochside rain, softer, wetter than rain elsewhere. They ran to their cars through a soaking mist. It was as if a cloud had sunk under its own weight like a collapsed bladder inside the glen. They could barely see their cars. They ran towards them – Strachey with Mickey, Gloria with Clive – and as they fumbled in the rain for keys they ignored the voice. Till Frankie shouted louder: 'Don't nobody move!'

Clive rattled the car door.

'Stand still!' Frankie yelled.

They couldn't see him. Frankie had no choice. He fired. The gunshot beside the lochside was barely louder than a car's backfire – but it was a damn sight more mesmeric. They stood like statues in the downpour. They heard Lincoln cry, 'Hey! Careful, Frankie.

'Linc darlin'!' wailed Gloria.

'You all right, honey?'

'I'm *soaking*!'

'No one's hurt,' called Frankie, emerging into view. 'But they will be next time.'

Lincoln appeared with Frankie. Where Lincoln had his jacket over his head, Frankie stood unconcerned, as if the gun in his hand would keep him dry. He said, 'OK, Clive, come over here.'

Clive stood uncertainly, rattling his keys.

'Move!' Frankie snarled.

Clive tossed the car keys to Gloria.

Frankie fired in the air. 'No tricks, smart ass. Get over here!'

Clive edged towards him. He walked stooped, as if the rain pressed him down.

Gloria put the key in the car door.

'Get back, Gloria! I shoot women same as men.'

This time Frankie's gun wasn't pointed in the air. It was straight at her cleavage. 'Drop the key.'

She pointed. 'It's stuck in the door.'

'Pull the goddamn thing out!'

'I'm soaking!'

'Pull it *out*!'

She reached for it and twisted. The door opened. She ducked.

When the gun fired, the bullet disappeared in the dark – not because Frankie had aimed to miss. He had been knocked sideways by Mickey Starr. At Frankie's earlier warning shot, Mickey had stooped below the height of the cars and come round the back. The two men hit the wet concrete with Mickey on top. No contest. The gun skidded across the ground.

Lincoln rushed forward. But when he tried to help his wife she screamed, 'What you doin' here, you bastard? Get your filthy hands offa me!'

'But honey—' cried Lincoln as she ran past.

Frankie was scrambling up when Gloria got to him. Her foot caught him in the face. 'Get in the cars!' she shouted. She fell on Frankie and began pounding his head. In a straight fight, Frankie was no slouch. He'd have no trouble with a woman – even a hellcat like Gloria. Except Mickey Starr grabbed his collar and pulled him away.

'Thanks, feller,' spluttered Gloria – then: 'You with this bastard, Linc?'

'No way!'

'Then get the hell outa here while you can.'

A car engine roared. Its lights flared. Lincoln dithered and ran towards it. Apart from those lights they could see nothing across the car park. The rain was so solid it seemed to have overflowed from the loch. Gloria turned to see if Mickey needed help. Which he wouldn't have – except: 'Behind you!' she screamed.

He half turned as Patterson thumped a wrench down at his head. Half a turn was enough. In the beam of the car Mickey and Patterson were highlighted. The wrench had caught Mickey's upper arm, dropping it dead at his side, but his right fist drove into Patterson's gut. The big man stumbled. As he tried to swing the wrench again Mickey punched a second time, following through with his body to push Patterson down. The wrench clanged onto the ground. As the two men scrambled for it, Frankie was left free. He darted toward the fallen gun. But Gloria was closer. She dived but couldn't grab it. He landed on top of her, and they writhed as one body in the slithery wet. As they neared the shining gun she reached out and knocked it away. Frankie tried to scramble after it but she grabbed him in the place that stops every man. He yelled out and lashed back.

The gun fired.

A bullet ricocheted off the concrete and banged against a car. Frankie and Gloria peered up from the ground. Above them stood Strachey, the gun pointed at Frankie's head. She was as soaked as they were.

'Hands behind your head,' she shouted. 'Turn round. Lie down.'

Frankie glared at her. 'I ain't lying in that.'

'I'll count to three. Starting one,' she snapped. 'Two.'

Frankie crawled round and lay face down.

'I said hands behind your head.'

'Jesus Christ.'

'No use calling for Jesus. It's his night off.'

Mickey Starr appeared by her. 'Where's Lincoln?'

'In the car. Patterson?'

'On the ground.'

'OK, Frankie,' she said. 'I want you to crawl around that car to your left, then go and lie on the ground by Patterson.'

'What *is* this?'

He tried scrambling up. She cocked the gun.

Frankie set off to join Patterson.

They followed him. Strachey saw Patterson lying motionless and glanced across at Mickey. 'Maybe you should knock Frankie out. It would save *tying* him up.'

'Yeah, get in the car. I'll deal with them.'

She narrowed her eyes. 'Meaning?'

'Fetch Lincoln.'

'I'm here,' he said, grimly triumphant. He was holding Clive by the arm. Clive's elegant blond hair was plastered across his face, but Lincoln's bald pate looked no different in the rain. A little shinier, maybe.

'D'you want Clive down there with those two?'

Mickey said, 'I want *you* with those two. Clive stays with us.'

Lincoln's mouth fell open – but before he could speak, Gloria said, 'Linc isn't with them, Mickey.'

'He *came* with them.'

Strachey said, 'We can't leave him with these crooks. He's on *our* side.'

'*They* were on our side.'

'There are ten different sides, Mickey, but Lincoln is straight. Keep an eye on those two while we sort ourselves out.'

Mickey shrugged angrily and kicked Frankie instead. 'You want trouble?'

Strachey led Lincoln and Gloria away, saying, 'Take Frankie's car.'

'No way,' snorted Gloria. 'Much as I love you, Linc darlin', I ain't driving home alone with you.'

He gleamed like a cherub in a fountain. 'Aw, come on, Gloria, give me a break.'

'I know what you're gonna say, Linc, *and* how long it will take. Get Frankie's car. I'm staying with Clive.'

Strachey said, 'I'm taking Clive. You and your husband can travel how you like.'

'Oh, miaow! What do I do – catch a bus?'

'Mickey can bring you. Sorry, Lincoln, you'd better go.'

'Where to?'

'Back to the airport, I don't know. But keep away from di Stefano.'

He blinked at the women, implacable in the rain, then turned and trudged away.

Mickey appeared. Strachey said, 'Lincoln's taking *their* car, so if we take the others, we can leave these two to lie here and drown.'

'Where'll we meet?'

'I'm not saying in front of them – assuming they're conscious?'

'One is.'

Strachey nodded at Gloria. '*Their* place. Come on, Clive, you can show me the way.'

He squelched towards her. Gloria said, 'I've got the keys, Mickey. I suppose you trust me to bring the car over?'

'Why not?'

'Just checking.'

She splashed away. Mickey was left with two sodden bodies on the ground. He said, 'You'll have to swim home, I guess.'

Frankie said, 'I'll get you next time. No mistake.'

'Don't tempt me.'

One of the cars came squelching across the car park. They heard another start up and edge their way. Frankie scrambled to his knees. Mickey pointed the gun at him. 'Lie flat – now!'

Frankie stared for a second, not moving, waiting to see what might happen. Mickey shrugged. 'OK,' he said. The gun quivered – but Frankie said, 'No,' and eased himself down in the puddle.

Gloria had brought the car across. Mickey opened the door. He gave Frankie a final 'Welcome to Scotland' kick, then leapt inside.

The car heater changed the temperature of their wet clothes but didn't dry them, not one little bit. Any water that *had* come out settled on the windows, leaving a sheen of mist they had to keep wiping with their sleeves. The rain outside reduced main-beam visibility below ten yards. Outside that beam was darkness. They had passed two isolated houses – pale lights glimmering in the dark – and were now grinding along the rainswept road beside the loch. They couldn't see the loch. They couldn't see anything.

Mickey asked, 'How far is it?'

Gloria squinted across the steering wheel. 'Don't know yet.'

'You as wet as me?'

'Sodden. This was a good dress, too. Bought it today. How's your arm where that guy hit you with the wrench?'

'Feels like rheumatism.'

'I like the way you handled yourself back there.'

'You did OK yourself.'

She could only glance at him for a moment, then she had to concentrate on the road. 'Excuse me asking', but are you with Strachey or what?'

'We've been through that.'

'In the restaurant? We weren't exactly frank and open there, were we?'

'No?'

She chuckled. 'You play poker? Bunch of friends sittin' round a table, drinkin' and jokin'. Behind the smilin' faces, they watch each other like hawks.'

'Is that what was happening?'

'Come on. You were watching Clive 'cos he's the bad guy. She was watching me 'cos I took her man. You know he was her man, Mickey?'

'Used to be.'

Gloria leant forward to peer through the screen. 'An' you're just a friend?'

'Uh huh.'

She didn't say anything. He asked, 'Why?'

'I thought you might be carryin' a torch for her.'

He wasn't going to answer that. 'How long till we get to your hotel?'

'Can't see anything I recognise.'

'Great. We *are* on the right road?'

'I'm wondering that myself. You know, Clive was driving. When you're passenger you don't take nothin' in.'

'Does any of this look familiar?'

'I can't *see* nothin' except tarmac.'

'What's the name of the place?'

'I don't know.'

'Gloria!'

'You sound just like Clive. Must be the accent.' She dropped her hand onto his knee. 'Except your voice is deeper.'

'It's gonna get angrier if you don't watch out. Have you no idea where we're going?'

She parodied an English accent: 'Have you no sense of adventure?'

'I've *had* adventure. I just want to dry out and get to bed.'

'I'll go with that.'

'Keep both hands on the wheel.'

She lifted her hand. 'No sense of adventure.'

He peered through the window. At nothing. 'I reckon this road's going to John o'Groats.'

'Do they have a motel there?'

He exhaled. 'I guess Clive knows where the hotel is.' He reached in his pocket. 'I'll ring Strachey.'

'She's probably half a mile ahead of us.'

He keyed her number. 'Or twenty miles the other way.'

But his own phone rang. 'What the—' He put it to his ear. 'Hello?'

It kept ringing. He took it from his ear and stared at it. Then he reached in his pocket and took out another phone – the one that was ringing.

'Oh hell, I've got Strachey's phone.'

Gloria giggled. 'Did you get dressed in a hurry?'

He cursed and cut the call. 'Great. I've just rung myself.'

'Well, she's got your number. She's got both of them.'

'But no phone.'

'You don't have pay phones here?'

'Yeah, in cities. We're in the middle of nowhere – there won't be a phone box.'

'She can phone from the hotel.'

'Jesus.'

'Oh, such a sulky little bunny.' She touched his leg again, well above the knee. 'Oops, sorry, not allowed.'

'We better turn the car round.'

'Why? Like I say, they could be half a mile ahead of us.'

'I bet.'

'If we go back, the first place we'll reach is that restaurant.

We could ask Frankie where they've gone. Give him a lift.'

'It isn't funny.'

'*He* won't think so, that's for sure. Lights ahead.' She slowed the car. 'This place does not look familiar.'

'Amaze me.'

She stopped. 'Gimme a chance, I guess I could.'

Now they had stopped they could hear soft rain on the metal roof. It made a shushing sound, like a feather coverlet on a bed.

She said, 'Well, it's not the first time I've been out at night with a guy in a car and it mysteriously breaks down. Only I'm not usually driving.'

'We haven't broken down.'

'We could pretend.'

'Listen, what are we gonna do – keep on driving, hoping you'll see some place you recognise?'

'Till eventually we go right round the loch? Whoopee. I'm soaking. Doesn't that sign say 'Bed and Breakfast'?'

'What's the name of the hotel Clive's staying at?'

'Well, it isn't this place.'

'I know that.'

'Don't get shirty, darlin'. We could go in here and dry off.'

His phone rang. It could only be Strachey. She could only ask, 'Where are you?'

'God knows. Which way did you turn from the car park?'

'Left.'

'Great.'

'You turned right?'

'How'd you guess?'

'I wondered why I didn't see your lights in my mirror. How's the weather up there?'

'Scottish.'

'Are you still in the same clothes?'

'Well, I'm not swapping with Gloria.'

Strachey laughed. 'How far have you gone – I mean, how far have you driven?'

'Not that far. We're creeping through the rain like a duck with a hangover.'

'But you've been driving all this while? If you haul back to the restaurant and then come right out here, you'll be driving another hour.'

'At least.'

'Are your clothes drying?'

'You're joking.'

'Oh Mickey, I'm sorry. It's teeming down here.'

'Wonderful. How are *your* clothes?'

'Oh, I'm… ' She hesitated. 'I'm OK. I borrowed something of Gloria's.'

She didn't tell him it was a bathrobe. And Gloria's bathrobe was not a homely wrap designed for cold Scottish corridors. It was a pale pink double-layer chiffon, with an abundance of flounces and frills. It was not to Strachey's taste.

But Clive said, 'You look fantastic.'

He was in a manly burgundy thing. She couldn't help saying, 'You don't look bad yourself.'

He smiled the full dazzler. 'How could I ever have let you go, Strachey?'

Her smile faded. 'Too damn easily. You didn't just let me go – you dropped me in a tank of Devon sludge.'

'I'm sorry.'

'No, you're not. You abandoned me.'

'My love!' He glided forward solicitously. 'I *am* a bastard but I did not abandon you. We're still a team – in all that matters.'

'A team!'

He was close enough to take her in his arms. 'You're the only one.'

She resisted more feebly than she had resisted anything before. The more of a bastard he was, the more helpless she became. She should not have let him get alone with her. She should not have come to his room. She should not have had a bath, and should not on any account have worn Gloria's sexy gown. She knew all of that. But she melted against his chest.

She said, 'Get away from me,' but he acted as if they were the most enticing words he'd heard.

His fingers in her hair. His lips against her eyelid. His breath against her cheek.

She said, 'You bastard, Clive.'

His fingers against her chin. His lips on her throat. His breath at her shoulder.

She lifted his face and kissed him on the mouth.

He opened her layers of soft chiffon and dropped them to the floor.

In the Bide-Away guesthouse the landlady was appalled at their wet clothes.

'What *have* you been doing?' she asked. 'Swimming in the loch?'

It was awful late, she remonstrated, but on such a terrible night she couldn't turn them away. She had a nice, warm bedroom ready and because she was a Christian soul and outside was raw, she'd gladly make them a wee cup of soup with a chunk of nourishing brown bread – which came with butter, not margarine – and there was a hot radiator in the bedroom, though she must ask them not to drape those soaking clothes across it because it would stain the wallpaper – but then, if they were to hang them anywhere except the *en suite* they'd make the carpet damp, so perhaps it might be best after all if the poor tired couple were to let her take all the clothes in a bundle, which she could put through the tumble drier for a small fee. And had they not brought any luggage? It was nae bother, not at all – though they'd understand that in *that* case she'd need the bill settled in advance?

Clive lay in near darkness and stared at the ceiling. Despite the foul weather, a murky orange light crept through the curtains from a street lamp below. Scattered around the hotel room were little glowing spots of red – the standby on the TV, the kettle switch, a wall plug, the digital clock, the smoke alarm on the ceiling by the door. There was a gentle noise like falling rain, but it was only air conditioning. Outside was locked away.

Strachey slept beside him in the bed, her arm thrown across his chest and her hair brushing his face. It tickled and made his nose itch. He tried to move her head and then began, very slowly, to slide from beneath her. She stirred, mumbled something, and he had to hold his position for several seconds till she settled down. He eased himself away again. She grunted. With extraordinary gentleness he lifted her head, softly kissed her, and placed her head on the pillow.

Her hand rested on his chest, and her fingers tightened now on a small fold of flesh as if she didn't want to let him go. He put his hand beneath hers and carefully untangled her fingers. Then he eased himself sideways and placed her hand on the warm sheet where he had lain.

He was free now. He listened as Strachey's breathing became regular. Clive Lane enjoyed solitude. He enjoyed standing outside

the rushing world like a heron at the riverside, watching the
current swirl dumbly by, waiting for the moment to dip in and
catch a fish. Recently he had had too much company. For three
months in America he had returned from darting fishing trips to
the small, rented room where Strachey would be waiting. She
was a lovely girl and he liked her very much, but he needed his
own space. It wasn't Strachey's fault. It wasn't anybody's fault.
It hadn't been Gloria's fault either, once Strachey had gone. He
had hoped Gloria would leap into bed as he, the heron, dived
into a pool; and that after one sparkling moment she, like him,
would quit the pool and fly back to her own nest. But she had
clung to him. Everybody clung.

He lay in the cooler part of the bed, untouched by anyone.
Strachey slept while he lay awake. Somewhere north along the
loch, he thought, Gloria and Mickey Starr were almost certainly
in the same bed, either asleep or – who knows? – one of them
might be doing what he was doing right now, lying silently
beside the other and staring thoughtfully at the ceiling.

Wondering what to do next.

22

WHEN STRACHEY WALKED into the dining room for breakfast she saw Clive at a window table. He flashed a formal, business smile. In his mind he had left the hotel, she thought: but had he left her too?

She told him she'd phoned Mickey.

While he continued cutting rind from his bacon, his face was as bland and unreadable as a director's at a shareholder's meeting.

She said, 'They're having breakfast.'

She hadn't told Clive she would phone, although he must have realised that she would, but she had wanted to speak to Mickey before Clive could put a spin on what she'd say.

'I'd avoid the eggs,' Clive murmured.

'I'll just have toast.'

They didn't sound like lovers who had got back together, Strachey thought.

'Weather's picked up.'

Behind him, through the window, she saw morning sunlight drying the exterior stonework. She asked the question she had avoided in the bedroom: 'What will you tell Gloria?'

'Why should I tell her anything? Here comes the waitress.'

Their conversation – such as it was – went on hold while the waitress took her order. Strachey dragged it back. 'Gloria will assume she can move back in.'

Clive sucked on a tooth. 'Did you tell them to come here? That's a pity.'

'What else could I do?'

'We could have met at the airport. Neutral ground – no personal questions.'

'I think Gloria asks personal questions any place she wants. Why the airport?'

'We're finished here.'

'There's a lot *un*finished.'

'Oh, we can sort that out.'

'How?'

Clive laid his knife and fork down and took her hands. 'Trust me.'

When Mickey and Gloria arrived, Clive ushered them to a table in the hotel lobby, a *neutral* area, where he ordered coffee before disappearing to make a phone call. Strachey was left to 'sort things out'. She had the impression that no one else was in a rush to sort *anything* out. No one referred to last night's sleeping arrangements. No one discussed repaying money. Lincoln was only mentioned in passing, when they wondered how Frankie and Patterson had got home.

In one of the hotel's public call boxes, Clive was through to the local estate agent.

'My goodness,' the man exclaimed. 'I've been in the office five minutes and the phone has not stopped. Two separate gentlemen have been asking how to get hold of you. That's a – let me see – that's a Mr di Stefano and a Mr Lincoln Deane. I hope it was all right for me to give them your hotel address?'

23

In two cars they drove onto Scottish moorland. Clive had wanted them out of the hotel fast and he claimed that out there, a million miles from anywhere, they could talk in peace. The others were not convinced until he told them that Frankie di Stefano was closing in. On the lonely moorland they drove across barren land and finally stopped in a copse of trees. Mickey said they should get their cars off the road.

'Nothing to worry about,' said Clive.

Mickey looked unhappy. 'Except that di Stefano likes guns.'

Strachey nodded in agreement. 'This could be the site of another Scottish massacre.'

'Nonsense,' cried Clive. 'Safe as houses here.'

'Now I'm really worried.'

Gloria clapped her hands. 'This won't be a long meeting, for Chrissake. Too cold.'

Clive smiled. 'Isn't it beautiful after yesterday's weather? Look how the rain has washed everything clean—'

'For God's sake, Clive,' snapped Strachey. 'You're not selling the Highlands.'

'I wouldn't bank on it,' he laughed. 'But these aren't the Highlands. We're in central Scotland.'

'Gloria's right,' Mickey said. 'Get it done.'

Gloria glanced from one man to the other as if trying to decide which one to choose.

'This is ridiculous,' said Strachey. 'We're hiding in the fells as if afraid for our lives.' She glanced back along the road. 'If anyone does come by they're going to wonder what on earth we are doing.'

Clive said, 'A bunch of scaredicats—'

Mickey cut him short. 'You realise what's happening, Clive? You tried this "joke" of yours on a man who carries a gun and likes to use it. You owe him a hundred thousand dollars.'

Gloria added cheerfully, 'You owe Lincoln more than that. Plus the other guys.'

Clive seemed unconcerned. 'But we also have several businessmen prepared to invest huge sums in Scottish property.'

Strachey stared bleakly across the moorland. 'Look Clive, you may get away with this latest scam – though I have to tell you it looks thin to me – but you're up to your neck in the other one.'

'The one you ran away from,' Mickey said.

'Oh, I'd hardly say I ran—'

Gloria intervened. 'Clive darlin', even you must realize that this di Stefano is a guy you don't cross. You're gonna have to repay his money – plus some.'

Clive laughed. 'There's always a di Stefano.'

'Come *on*,' snapped Gloria.

'I'll make a settlement with him.'

He beamed, as if that solved everything. Mickey pressed again: 'You'll meet him face to face?'

'If necessary.'

Mickey peered at him. 'Are you from planet Earth?'

Gloria supported Mickey. 'You and whose army, Clive?'

He threw his hands wide. 'Isn't that what you all want?'

Gloria said, 'If you pay Frankie, you pay Lincoln. You can give *me* the money – save embarrassment.'

Clive laughed. 'You see where this is leading? In very exceptional circumstances I might consider one repayment – but I can't repay everybody. I can't repay the whole million, can I?'

Gloria raised her eyebrows. 'A million, huh?'

Clive blinked. 'I used a large chunk of the money for the deposit on Clachan Castle.'

Strachey said, 'Hang on. You said the deposit was thirty thousand.'

Clive shrugged. 'A little more than that.'

She said, 'But you're sitting on a million? Thirty thousand is chicken feed.'

'Some chicken,' he said.

'You can easily pay di Stefano. Why don't you?'

'Pay Lincoln too,' said Gloria.

He stared at her. 'Gloria my love, aren't we together?' He didn't wait for an answer. 'All right,' he said. 'You win. It's getting cold. Let's pop into town and I'll write out a couple of cheques.'

Frankie di Stefano had a stare like a dentist's drill. The girl behind the hotel desk took it head-on. 'Yes, sir,' she said nervously. 'Lord Lane was staying here but he checked out this morning. And yes, sir,' she said, 'his wife – if that was his wife – checked out with him. There's absolutely no doubt about that.'

Frankie stomped off with Patterson.

They went out to the hotel car park in time to see Lincoln locking his car. Lincoln almost climbed back inside.

'Where'd they go?' Frankie asked him.

Lincoln looked miserable. 'Has Gloria gone?' Then, as if Frankie might have denied it: 'I guess she slept with that goddamn Lord Clive again.'

Frankie clapped a hand on his shoulder. 'No dame's worth it. How'd you know they'd be at this hotel?'

'The real-estate guy—'

'Me too.' He stared at Lincoln some more. 'Last night in the car park, Lincoln, whose side were you on?'

Patterson snorted. 'He weren't on no one's side. He didn't fight.'

'I was on Gloria's side.'

Frankie renewed his dentist stare. Then he switched it off. 'You're gonna have to get over that dame.'

'She's my wife.'

'That's important? Well, if you want to find 'em you had better come with us. First stop, the real-estate office. See what they know.'

Mickey returned with three cups of airport coffee on a tray. As he stooped over the two women he had the feeling someone was watching him. When he glanced up he realised that in the chairs around, plenty of waiting passengers were peeping furtively – not at *him* but at the girls: Strachey was an aristocratic good-looker – he'd known her so long that he'd forgotten, almost – and Gloria was a stunner too. Sprawled in the airport settee, legs akimbo, hair tumbling in eye-catching chaos, open coat thrown back, she looked every inch a film star. Put the two women together – at an airport – and you couldn't blame people for thinking they'd spotted someone famous. Especially when they had a tame giant in tow.

He sat down.

'What time's the flight?'

'They should call it soon.'

'Think Clive will make it?'

The two women chorused, 'No.'

Mickey put down his coffee. 'When did you reach that decision?'

Strachey said, 'When you asked.'

Gloria said, 'Our Clive sure is a smooth talker, isn't he?'

It was aimed at Strachey, who didn't reply. Gloria grinned. 'So we'll have to share *you*, Mickey. Who gets which part?'

They continued to wait for Lord Clive. He had left them after Check-in so he could phone two buyers about their deposit cheques. It had seemed right that he should tidy that piece of business – after all, he had said, each buyer meant another thirty thousand in immediate cash. He told them he'd send the buyers on a sightseeing tour of Loch Lomond to keep them occupied another day.

It had sounded reasonable.

Strachey felt depressed. In the hotel last night Clive had been loving and tender: everything had gone back to how it had been before. Clive had returned to her. They had walked through Check-in hand in hand.

He had kissed her cheek, then slipped away.

She felt unwell. She stood up shakily, gave a muttered excuse and made for the ladies room. Some waiting passengers watched her. Then they glanced at Gloria to see if the starlets might have quarrelled.

Gloria leant towards Mickey. 'How're you feelin', big boy?'

'We shouldn't have let Clive disappear.'

'We've got his bag.'

Mickey did not look convinced. Gloria said, 'I thought maybe you were makin' your mind up between me an' Strachey.'

'Oh?'

'That's right – *oh*. You're fond of her, aren't you?'

'We're old friends.'

'She knows we slept together.'

'You told her?'

'She can tell. Be honest, darlin' – am I muscling in between you an' her?'

'No.'

'I mean, last night was great but I'll understand if it was a one-off.'

She looked into his face but Mickey could not be read. He seemed troubled. 'On the other hand,' she said, 'if you want to drop Strachey and hang out with me, that's cool too. I mean, I'm willin' if you are.'

'I'm not with Strachey,' he muttered.

'I've seen how close you are.'

Mickey stared at the floor. 'This is the wrong time.'

Gloria patted his knee. 'Well, the offer's open. And don't worry about Clive – even assumin' he turns up again, which I doubt. He'll be upset if I drop him, but life's a bitch, ain't that right?'

'What do women see in a guy like that?'

Gloria leant back in her chair and grinned. 'Oh, he's a rascal,' she said. 'But hey!'

She'd seen the man himself approaching their table, accompanied by a smiling Strachey. Clive was glancing at his watch. 'Close,' he said. 'Beginning to think I wouldn't make it.' He and Strachey beamed for different reasons. 'A very satisfactory spot of business. And I'm delighted to announce that we're a little better off!' Strachey chuckled on his arm.

'So it's off to jolly Bristol,' he said. 'Where – between you and me – another punter is waiting to confirm his investment. So do play along, my dears – we all stand to gain.'

In the plane they skipped lightly over any awkwardness and seated themselves according to their previous alignment: Mickey with Strachey, Gloria with Clive. They settled into their seats and flicked through the rumpled pages of in-flight magazines while late arrivals and standbys climbed aboard. The flight wasn't full and they would be less than one hour in the air – barely enough time to skim the magazines. It was one of those flights where they had waited at the airport longer than they'd be in the air, and where they now sat in the plane, engine rumbling, stewards scurrying, with no immediate sign of leaving the ground.

Among the last standby passengers were a Mr Patterson, a Mr Deane and a Signor di Stefano. As the stewardess shepherded these latecomers towards the rear, they nodded to Strachey and paused beside a suddenly ashen Lord Clive Lane.

Frankie prodded the stewardess. 'No one gets off now, right?'

'Not now, sir, it's too late.'

He patted Clive's shoulder and grinned at the stewardess. 'Lead on, MacDuff.'

He laughed as he followed her along the narrow aisle – but Lincoln paused to lean over his glamorous wife: 'Hold onto your hairstyle, honey. It's gonna be a bumpy ride.'

She raised a ramrod finger.

Frankie di Stefano called along the aisle: 'Oh, the ride will be easy. But the landing could be hard.'

24

MOST COUPLES WOULD have sat out the flight in resentful silence, but Gloria was not famed for silence: 'You slept with Strachey?'

'My dear Gloria—'

'Kiss and make up? All better now?'

It was Gloria's normal volume – good and loud. Clive glanced about. 'Why on earth should you think that?'

'You dropped me in the middle of nowhere and scooted off with the nearest blonde.'

'*You're* the nearest blonde,' he quipped uneasily.

'At least I'm a real one.'

'So is she.'

'You should know, Clive. So what about *me* – I'm yesterday's news?'

He tried a counter: 'You and Mickey Starr—'

'What're you sayin'?'

'You did spend the night together—'

'You *dumped* us by the lake, Clive. Don't change the subject.'

'This *is* the subject—'

'You spent the night in Strachey's bed.'

Several passengers glanced round. Clive said the wrong thing: 'Darling, please try to keep your voice down.'

Lincoln sat three abreast with Frankie and Patterson – Lincoln in the middle where he couldn't get out and Patterson with a leg across the gangway. The stewardess had twice asked to come past him, but he had grinned at her as if his big leg might turn her on. It stood more chance with her than did his nose splint.

Lincoln asked Frankie: 'Who's the big guy next to Strachey?'

'You know who he is. He's a friend of hers.'

'But where does he fit in?'

'The hell do I know, Lincoln? A bodyguard, I guess.'

'She needs a bodyguard?'

'She takes a lotta risks.'

Lincoln frowned at the seat back in front of him. Patterson chuckled. 'I'll guard her body any day. Special rate.'

Frankie said, 'Way she's actin', she won't need a bodyguard, she'll need a body bag.'

Above the Anglo-Scottish border, Gloria eased off on Clive and spoke more quietly. She stroked his knee – which soothed most men, she had found.

'You hurt me, darlin', let's face it. First chance you got, you ran back to your old girlfriend.'

'A mere accident. In the confusion after the rough and tumble—'

'Oh, was my poor little boy confused?' Her hand inched higher along his leg – which softened her remark, but nothing else. 'And in the rough and tumble did your old sweetheart set things straight for you?'

'It's you I love, darling – you know that.'

'But Clive, you abandoned me.'

'We're together again now. And you can't be jealous of Strachey – she's with Mickey.' He glanced slyly at her. 'Assuming nobody has turned Mickey's affections?'

She rode over that. 'They're a team, are they? Do they have somethin' on you, Clive?'

'Such as?'

'They keep saying they want you to repay all the money. Do you go along with that?'

'Well, I wouldn't like to see Strachey in a jam.'

'Don't give me that malarkey. You made over a million dollars, didn't you?'

'Pounds – but that's a detail.'

'And you're gonna pay off this di Stefano?'

'It looks as if I have no choice.'

'And Lincoln?'

Clive hesitated. 'He's on the plane too.'

'An' then you'll pay all the other suckers?'

Clive chuckled delicately. 'A gentleman always pays his debts.'

'Except you're no gentleman, Clive. How much exactly did you make?'

He shrugged evasively. 'It's too early to know the final figure.'

'This Scottish castle – how much from that?'

'The deal isn't settled.'

'But you're sittin' pretty, aren't you, darlin'?'

He coughed. 'I hope so.'

'Because I like successful men – a successful *man*, I mean.'

'One at a time?'

'Yeah.' She chuckled. 'How long's this flight?'

'Another half hour.'

'D'you think there's time for you an' me to renew our membership of the Mile-High Club before we land?'

Lincoln decided he couldn't spend the whole flight, even a short one, squashed in between Frankie and the bulky Patterson while his wife – or the girl who was supposed to be his wife – was sitting a few rows in front of him *with the guy she'd started sleeping with!* He had to do something. When he struggled to his feet he found that no one tried to stop him. But then, it wasn't as if he could *go* anywhere.

Lincoln straightened his shoulders and walked down to Gloria.

'Remember me?' he said stupidly.

'Could I forget?'

He pointed a finger. 'It's make-your-mind-up time.'

'I hate it when you push me, darlin'.'

'It's me or him.'

'Then one of you is gonna be awful disappointed.'

Lincoln couldn't meet her eye.

She said, 'The seat-belt light has come on.'

'Huh?'

A message came over the speakers, confirming her words: would all passengers kindly resume their seats?

He said, 'Well, I mean it, Gloria. Make your mind up before we land.'

She gave him a loving smile. Her eyes widened like two pools. 'I'm still awful fond of you, Linc. You do know that, don't you, darlin'?'

He gulped and stared down at her. Then he trudged back to his seat.

Clive said, 'Awful fond? Well, well. Sounds as if you might be going back to him.'

'It don't cost nothing to be kind.'

Their eyes met. 'Ah,' he said. 'I see. An each-way bet.'

'After the way you dumped me last night,' Gloria said sweetly, 'I don't know if I can trust you, do I?'

'How can you ask?'

She gave her limpid-pools look. 'We've got to talk, Clive.'

He panicked slightly. 'I think the plane's about to land.'

'You men are so romantic. I guess we both know you have to return this money—'

'*All* of it?' he asked gently.

'Some of it – be reasonable. But what I want to check, darlin', is that if you return the money, they got to give you the lordships back. Is that right?'

'Not exactly.' Clive glanced out of a small window. 'We're coming in to land.'

'You got a thing about landing, haven't you? Now, let me get my head round this – as the lap dancer whispered—'

'A lordship is a *concept*.'

'That doesn't help. What about your own lordship – is that a concept too?'

'The Lordship of Lower Marsh is very real.'

'You haven't sold it anyone?'

'Good Lord, no.'

'You bought the thing legitimately?'

'Yes.'

'So whatever happens, you're still a lord – they can't expel you or nothin'?'

'I'm still a lord.'

She smiled contentedly. 'A real English lord. That's fine. And let me say this before we land, because this is the answer to somethin' you once asked me, Clive. It's yes, I am willin' to marry you, darlin', since you're so—'

'I asked you?'

'Sure, darlin'. Don't you remember?'

He laughed desperately. 'You're married already.'

She sniffed. 'Like marriage is for life?'

Clive looked as flustered as he had ever allowed himself to look. 'Gosh, we're practically on the ground – maybe we should save this for another time. Although to be honest, I find the idea of marriage so incredible that perhaps it's best discussed in an unreal setting, such as in a plane twenty thousand feet up in the air.' He smiled.

'That's your idea of being honest, Clive?'

He was prattling and he knew it. 'You'd only be marrying me for my title.'

'And your money.'

Lord Clive laughed. 'I've less money than you.'

The plane touched down. 'Gloria darling,' he continued anxiously. 'Suppose I do make a million out of this – a huge supposition – I'd still not be as rich as *you*. Would I?'

Being American, she answered directly. 'I could go for half of Lincoln's estate, and even with a bum deal I'd get a third of it, so that makes me worth... hell, I don't know, somethin' over four or five million dollars. That's leavin' his business out of it – which I'm not *inclined* to do.'

Lord Clive blinked. 'Four or five million?'

People around them were stirring, ready to leap up and clog the aisles.

Upwards of four million dollars: he gave her an appraising look. 'The idea of marriage does have some appeal, Gloria, I must admit. I have been a little naughty in the past, but I dare say I could repay some of my victims—'

'Pay 'em back? No way.' People were beginning to stand up. 'Get real, Clive. Listen, the only problem so far is that you've been sellin' these titles more than once?'

Clive glanced about nervously. 'I think we should be getting ready to leave now.'

'Hell, they won't open the doors for ages. Listen, *someone* won the auction, right? Someone coughed up the big one? Let that guy keep the prize.'

'While I keep the money?'

'*His* money, that's legitimate. Refund the others – or most of 'em. How much would you have to give back at worst – a million dollars?'

Clive tried to keep a straight face. Oh yes, he thought, just like that – hand back a million dollars. A *million dollars* – against a possible five million of Gloria's dollars, which would be near impossible to prize from her soft, feminine hands. Oh yes, he thought, I'd do that. Some chance.

Gloria said, 'You got to keep *some* money, Clive. We'll need somethin' to tide us over these next few months.'

25

FOR BRITISH PASSENGERS, coming off an internal flight is an anticlimax – no passports, no customs, no shuffling delay. And Bristol is a small airport, from which one steps almost immediately into the bustle and freedom of the everyday world.

In theory.

In the arrivals area (you can't call it a lounge) Clive was not allowed to slip away. Frankie and Patterson fenced him in so close they could have been handcuffed to him. Lincoln bobbed about, threatening to take a poke at him and demanding an answer from his wife. She asked Mickey to quieten him down. Strachey said they had better *all* quieten down if they didn't want to be arrested.

Clive said, 'This has gone on long enough.' (Always start with a statement that everyone can agree with.) 'I've taken Gloria's advice.' (A less impressive statement.) 'I must give the money back.'

No one argued – but they did not look satisfied. It seemed too easy.

He said, 'I assume you'll all take cheques.'

Lincoln spluttered.

Clive said, 'What else can I do? I don't have a hundred thousand in *cash*.'

Frankie snarled, 'You owe me more than a hundred grand, Clive. Plus expenses.'

Clive raised a hand. 'We have a teeny problem here.'

'*You* have a problem,' Patterson said.

Clive continued quickly: 'The cash is in the bank.'

'So get it *out* of the bank.'

'No bank will give me two hundred thousand in cash.'

'It's your money.'

'Well, no.' Clive laughed. 'It's *your* money.'

No one laughed with him. He said, 'You'll have to decide on your priority – to get revenge on me, or to get your money back.'

'Both,' Frankie and Lincoln said together.

'But which first?' He watched them confidently. 'If you take revenge too soon you'll never get your investment back. No, what you want is money back, plus compensation, then we'll call it quits.'

'Quits!' echoed Lincoln.

Clive said, 'But unfortunately, it may take a little time. In the meantime you'll want some surety.'

Frankie said, 'Your surety is your life. Which is why you ain't goin' nowhere till we get our money.'

Lincoln said, 'Twice our money back.'

'Plus compensation,' added Patterson.

Clive said, 'I'd better pop down to the bank.'

Frankie prodded him. 'We *all* go to the bank, get things started, then *you* come along with us. I know just the place you can hole up.'

'The Holiday Inn?'

'Almost. A place nearby. It's called the Old Mill Hotel.' Frankie laughed harshly.

'Never heard of it, I'm afraid.'

'Afraid? You should be. Strachey can tell you all about it.'

Frankie laughed again – but his laugh faded when a familiar voice boomed, 'Lord Clive, I'm sorry if I'm late.'

They turned to see the unexpected, black coated Edgar Delarme.

They gaped at him. But the evangelist ignored everyone except Clive. 'I'm sure we can find somewhere on our own.'

'Certainly,' said Clive.

'No way!' said Frankie. 'What the hell is goin' on?'

'Lord Clive and I have private business. Kindly step aside.'

'Get your ass outa here, mister.'

'Your threats don't trouble me.'

Passers-by glanced at the squabbling Americans. Gloria asked, 'What *is* this private business?'

Delarme's icy gaze flicked in her direction. 'The Lord may forgive you, woman, but I cannot.' He turned away. 'Lord Clive?'

'Ready if you are.'

Frankie shouted, 'No one moves a goddamn muscle!'

They were beginning to attract attention. Frankie's voice dropped: 'Private business?'

'It's no concern of yours.'

'It's every damn concern of mine! What's goin' on?'

Delarme sighed. 'I suppose you think you can still acquire the Lordship of Hexcombe? But I'm afraid it's sold.'

Frankie was ready to wipe the grin from off his face. 'An' *you* bought it, right?'

'I did.'

'You bought it, all right. You don't know the half of it.' Frankie punched the air.

'We were rivals once,' said Delarme calmly. 'But I have secured extra money from my church – and Lord Clive and I are now ready to complete the bargain.' He leered triumphantly. 'I realize this may be a disappointment to the rest of you.'

'I've had enough of this,' snapped Frankie. He glared at Delarme, but he didn't notice the uniformed airport attendants closing in.

Clive did. He saw his chance. 'These men are threatening me!'

Patterson grabbed him. Two officials grabbed Patterson. More uniforms closed in, and fists began to fly. In the midst of the melee stood Delarme, with his arms aloft like a painting of Moses when he divided the Red Sea. He boomed for obedience.

When a uniform grabbed Frankie he immediately lashed out. A stocky security man – balding, approaching retirement – took a tentative hold of Mickey, who calmly smiled down at him and asked, 'Who are these American people?'

Strachey followed his cue. With an anxious look she interposed herself between Mickey and the official. 'Darling,' she cried. 'What's happening? Who are these ruffians?'

Lincoln had been seized and was arguing vociferously. Gloria stood like Old Liberty in the harbour, insisting that any man who touched *her* would be sued for assault. Frankie was restrained, Patterson had a nose-bleed. Delarme and Clive scurried away.

Clive had a well-practised way of strolling at great speed, and despite his greater height Delarme found that he had to lengthen his own stride to keep up. They were quickly outside the arrivals concourse.

Delarme asked, 'What did that madman think he was doing?'

'He's only jealous. You have a car?'

'Over there.'

'Thank Heaven for small airports,' laughed Clive. 'Everything's close at hand.'

'Includin' me,' came from behind.

They spun round to find Gloria – slightly out of breath, a fur wrap across her shoulders, her small case in her hand. 'You nearly lost me, darlin'. Now we're together again.'

Delarme snapped, 'I will not be party to wickedness.'

Gloria smiled sweetly – like an angel, she hoped, though the only kind of angel she looked like was honky-tonk. 'They're searching for us inside. You wanna hang around and wait?'

It was a rhetorical question. Through a clutter of taxis, buses and idling cars they darted across to the short-term car park. Delarme produced a key. 'I assume you have not struck a deal with one of the others?'

'Certainly not,' said Clive blithely – but he added, 'Di Stefano made a better offer. I suppose that's why he seemed so angry.'

'Better than mine?'

Clive gave a deprecatory shrug. 'A mere trifle. I think Mr di Stefano thought that if he could beat your offer by even a little, I'd be morally obliged to accept.'

Delarme paused by his car. 'And were you?'

Clive glanced towards the terminal. 'Shall we talk about it in the car?'

26

INSIDE THE TERMINAL it took twenty minutes for the fracas to be sorted out. Frankie and Lincoln were cautioned, Patterson was placed on a first-aid trolley six inches too short, Mickey and Strachey were dismissed as passers-by. They were let out of the interview room ahead of the others but waited by the exit.

'No point running,' Strachey said. 'We're back at square one now that we've lost Clive.'

Mickey shuffled his feet. 'Why hang around?'

'I'm responsible for the money. Legally.'

'That's nonsense. The rest of those punks will catch Clive eventually, and you don't want to be around when they do.'

She looked grave. 'I can't run out and leave him.'

Mickey shook his head. 'Why'd you get yourself mixed up with this guy?'

'You have some dodgy friends yourself.'

'I don't sleep with them.'

She placed her head against his shoulder. 'I'm just unlucky with men.'

He didn't say anything.

They looked out across the traffic. She said, 'I suppose I fall for men like Clive because they're different to all those safe, comfortable, *boring* men I was brought up with. He doesn't obey the rules, he doesn't *believe* in them.'

Mickey's voice was tight. 'He's a crook.'

'No—'

'I was brought up with crooks, Strachey. I've spent half my life trying to get away from them.'

'Clive's not a crook, he's... oh, a confidence trickster, I suppose – but that's fun!'

'You call this fun?'

She thought a moment. 'It's exciting.'

They looked across to the crowded car park.

'You could've done anything,' he muttered.

'You can't buy excitement. Oh, you can buy artificial excitement, Mickey, all the things you'd hate – skiing, water sports, that sort of stuff – but I need the real thing.' She wouldn't look at him. 'Clive gives me that.'

'He'll leave you.'

'They all do. And if they didn't, I'd leave them.'

Frankie said, 'This time it'll be easier. We ain't lookin' for Clive in the middle of nowhere, we're lookin' for Clive, Gloria and the preacher. They'd stick out at a freak's convention – I'm sorry, Linc – an' the three of 'em are prancin' around a piece of countryside where folks are so private they notice any schmuck they're not *related* to. What's more, there ain't many places these schmucks can go. First choice, the Holiday Inn – Mickey and Strachey, you take that; second choice, the country house hotel where Delarme stays – me and Linc are gonna take that. And after that we all meet up at the office of that stuck-up-real estate merchant who has got the hots for you, Strachey, and we make any extra plans from there. Are we ready? Good. Now, Patterson – I suppose you wanna know what happened to him? He's on his back inside the terminal, bleedin' like a kosher chicken. Some guys will do anythin' to take time out.'

It confirmed what Delarme had long suspected about women priests: they interfered, could not be trusted, and were disloyal. Among men of cloth there was a kind of freemasonry, a closed society in which members put aside their differences to unite against the secular world outside. All professions had their guilds, their secret practices – but women did not have the discipline to observe the guidelines. They did not bond.

Tina Gum had hidden her knowledge from him. All this time, while Lord Clive had been reselling the lordship of Hexcombe and passing off worthless papers on gullible buyers, she – the high priestess of the Hexcombe flock – had retained possession of the genuine deeds. Clive might defend the woman, claiming she never knew he was passing off copies as the real thing. He might claim she was no party to his perfidy, but Delarme knew that women were created sinful. And now Clive had told him to drive to Tina's vicarage, where the genuine documents would be produced and the deceitful woman would guarantee the deal.

Delarme drove in wrathful silence. In the back seat, Clive and Gloria were silent too. When Lord Clive had revealed the truth Delarme heard Clive's painted harlot mount an objection –

claiming it wasn't fair to let Delarme have the title and that her abandoned husband should be given another bid – but Delarme wasn't fooled by that pretence. Women were ever deceivers. They were subservient to man, placed on earth to be man's helpmeet. He noted with satisfaction how Lord Clive had quietened her by declaring that it was for *him* to decide the title's future, that he was tired of all the fuss it had caused, and that the business should be concluded that very day.

Lord Clive understood a woman's place. How Clive had become associated with her was beyond Delarme's comprehension, but women had their artifices; they infected sensible men with a kind of opiate that drugged them, that deadened their senses and led them ultimately to unmanly acts. Clive appeared not to have reached that sad conclusion – so there might yet be hope for him. Perhaps after this business was done, Delarme could help him cast out the female's influence. The Lord of Hexcombe could bring solace to the Lord of Lower Marsh.

Strachey wasn't surprised to find that Clive was not at the Holiday Inn. She would have quit the hotel immediately but Mickey intervened. He smiled at the girls behind Reception, produced a ten-pound note, and had them promise that if Clive or Gloria did appear the girls would immediately ring him on his mobile. One of the girls looked as if she might ring Mickey anyway.

As he and Strachey left the desk she heard her name. Almost instantly the lobby filled with teeming Nibbets. The whole party was there, laden with luggage. They seemed cheerful enough, and Strachey quickly realised that as far as the Nibbets were concerned there was no cloud over the lordship. Walter Nibbet was ushered forth to shake her hand and to be introduced to the man the Nibbets assumed to be her chauffeur. Mr Nibbet was cheery, delighted at his good fortune, and unreasonably grateful to Lady Jane.

'I'm not a lady,' Strachey insisted yet again.

'Oh, come!' said Mrs Nibbet. 'You're not ordinary, that's for sure.'

Walter invited them into the hotel bar for a champagne cocktail.

'My lordly command!' he said, his blue eyes twinkling. 'A farewell drink. We're flying home today.'

'You're leaving?' Strachey tried not to show relief. 'I hope you enjoyed your holiday?'

'One of many visits!'

His wife agreed. 'Now that Walter is Lord of the Manor we'll be popping over several times a year. But come and have this drink with us.'

Strachey glanced at Mickey, who shrugged: why not? So Strachey allowed the Nibbets to lead them into the low-lit hotel bar, empty as ever, where as a shoal of goldfish they floated to the bar. Walter Nibbet was such a benign old lord that no entourage could resent him. Mrs Nibbet fussed around him as if he'd invented a cure for old age, while her sister Myrtle and husband Conrad felt touched with nobility by association. Even Julie's husband Hunter welcomed another drink – and the barman was happy: there were times he could stand half an hour waiting for trade, and it was his delight to serve champagne cocktails.

When the cork popped, Julie said, 'This is the happy ending to a fairy tale!'

Strachey looked momentarily sad. 'I feel terrible about this,' she whispered to Mickey. 'I'll have to break the news to them.'

'Not now,' he said. 'You can't.'

Mrs Nibbet cried, 'What are you two whispering about?' She eyed them saucily. 'You're a well-built young man,' she laughed.

Glasses were handed round.

Julie said, 'I hate to say anything against a fellow American—'

'That's not stopped you before!' cried Mrs Nibbet.

'But it's such a relief to have those other guys *out* of here.'

Walter said, 'Mr Deane was not so bad. He knew a thing or two about wine. But I tell you, although young Lincoln could hold his drink, he couldn't hold his women!'

Mrs Nibbet hooted. 'You are awful. There's no stopping you now. But Miss Strachey, I feel I really must warn you about Mr di Stefano.'

'Oh, he's a character,' she agreed.

'Worse than that! I have a cousin at the embassy—'

'Top you up?' called Walter, bottle in hand.

'My cousin says—'

'I'll have a little one,' said Julie.

'And I'll have a big one!' Hunter boomed.

'My cousin at the American embassy—'

'Who else is for a drink?'

'My cousin says—'

'Miss Strachey, can you manage a little one?'

'Mr di Stefano is very well known, she says, in New York—'

'And how about you, sir?'

'I'm driving.'

'And apparently he's a gangster!'

'And you, sugar, a little drop more?'

'Walter, I'm talking!'

'I'm your lord, my dear!'

'I'm your wife and that takes precedence. Do you hear what I'm saying, Miss Strachey? My cousin says Mr di Stefano is a well-known criminal. It is even said that he has killed people.'

'Ah,' said Walter, empty bottle in hand. 'It's also said that he's trying to get into politics. He should go far!'

They laughed.

'The further the better!' said Julie. And they laughed again.

Frankie and Lincoln had struck it lucky – if you count learning that Delarme was still registered at the country house hotel as lucky, when some people might think downing champagne cocktails more agreeable. Frankie stormed back to the car, Lincoln in tow.

'I ain't waitin' round here all day till that schmuck gets back.'

'Elegant place, though,' said Lincoln hopefully. 'We could stay for lunch. He might show up.'

'We'll try all the other places he might go.'

A vicarage should be open to all comers, but Tina Gum's bungalow hadn't housed such an unlikely collection for quite a time. Delarme, at least, should have been at home in a vicarage – though perhaps only if it were Gothic, with a haunted crypt and chapel – while Gloria was the type of girl most vicars warned against, and Clive had betrayed Tina's trust.

She stared at him fixedly, unsure he meant what he'd just said. 'You really want the original title deeds – for the Manor of Hexcombe? The actual documents?'

'That's the packet,' he replied.

Tina was trying not to look at Delarme. How could Clive inflict this ogre on her? Only yesterday she'd been told that their new lord was Walter Nibbet but now here was Clive himself to confirm that the lordship would be awarded to Delarme, who at this very moment was prowling around her small living room as if measuring it for a make-over.

'So we'll present the deeds,' she continued hollowly, 'to Mr Delarme?'

'The deeds *belong* to the Lord of the Manor of Hexcombe.'

Delarme smiled like a hungry tiger circling an unattended goat. 'Upon this rock I will build my church, and the gates of hell shall not prevail against it.'

'Yes, yes, I can do bible quotes as well – but I get enough of that at work.'

'You lack commitment. Are you equipped for holy office?'

'You mean, have I got the balls for it?'

His eyes blazed. 'He that is not with me is against me.'

'Oh, *yawn*,' said Tina crossly. 'I could give you "Beware of false prophets, which come to you in sheep's clothing, but inwardly are ravening wolves"—but honestly, where does all this quotesmanship get us?'

'I rather like it,' gushed Gloria. 'I love Shakespeare, I really do.'

Tina sighed. Clive studied the ceiling. Tina said, 'I'll fetch the documents.'

Delarme raised a hand and in a small voice asked, 'I wonder if you could show me... the little boy's room.' He picked his case up from the floor.

Tina said, 'It's unisex – across the hall.'

She went to the door and opened it. As Delarme strode out she stepped back inside.

'You betrayed me, Clive.'

Gloria looked startled, but Tina continued: 'You've saddled Hexcombe with the worst possible choice.'

'He's not so bad—'

'He's insane. He'll infuriate the locals so much that there'll probably be another Peasant's Revolt. He'll plague the bishop with attempts to have me unfrocked.'

Gloria said, 'Don't let him touch you, darlin'.'

'Can't we have someone else?'

Clive shrugged. 'He won the auction. You wouldn't ask me to cheat?'

'Would it be the first time? The whole thing's a scam, Clive.'

Gloria jumped. 'What does this woman *know*?'

'A scam?' laughed Clive. 'Come, come. Mr Delarme bought an ancient document giving him a genuine, if meaningless, title with no tangible rights. He'll be a nuisance for a week or two, then he'll go away.'

'And what does Hexcombe get out of it?'

Clive couldn't reply. He tried his charming but empty smile.

Tina persisted. 'I agreed to hold the documents and oversee the handover but I never expected it to be to someone so eminently unsuitable. Not Delarme – please!'

'It's too late,' he whispered. He looked uncomfortable – but with Clive, how he looked and how he felt were seldom the same.

She said, 'All those other lovely Americans – rich, generous buyers.'

'Not all of 'em were generous,' Gloria cautioned.

'Can't one be persuaded to increase his bid?'

Clive looked helpless, which was how Tina felt. She shook her head, went to the bookcase and pulled out a large and particularly dingy volume. When she opened it they saw that the pages had been hollowed to form a home-made deposit box, in which sat a clean manila envelope. She replaced the book and walked towards Clive, tapping the envelope against her palm. He watched it carefully.

They were interrupted by Delarme coming through the door.

Perhaps they should have expected it – after all, he did leave the room clutching his case. Delarme was now arrayed in full regalia, as made for him by his US tailor. Across his right shoulder, fastened with five gold buttons, he wore a deep purple robe with a barred helm garnished with gold. Perched on his head was a cap of maintenance, edged with white fur. He carried a pair of white gloves and some sort of metallic device that appeared to be a collapsible orb.

'Very Versace,' Gloria sneered.

Tina snapped, 'I can't have this. We'll be a joke.'

Delarme reached out his hand. 'Are those my title deeds?'

'They belong to Clive,' said Tina, handing them to the embarrassed Englishman. 'As far as I'm concerned, he's still the owner.'

Clive took the envelope and said, 'I haven't actually cleared your cheque yet, old boy.'

Delarme's face began to match his robe. 'More trickery?'

Tina intervened: '*I'm* supposed to be honest broker – so I'll hold on to the documents till the cheque has been cleared. *Has* it been cleared, Clive? Please tell me not.'

'Any day now,' declared Clive.

'Any *day*?' Delarme wailed.

'Any *hour*. I expressed it. Perhaps it *has* been cleared.'

'Perfidious Englishman!'

'I'll phone the bank,' Clive said. 'Believe me, Delarme, I want this done. The whole thing has dragged on far too long. Where's the telephone?'

'Out in the hall,' said Tina.

Delarme scowled at her. 'I never thought I'd see the day—'

'Me neither – it's a nightmare.'

As Clive left, Delarme raged: 'You are an insult to your profession! You are partner to this evil man.'

'She better not be,' called Gloria. She followed Clive.

'Women plot and scheme. It is my belief that you actively worked against my ennoblement. You never wanted me here.'

'That's true,' said Tina. 'I admit it – cheerfully. The thought of you gallumping around my patch wearing that ridiculous garb, disturbing my parishioners with your fundamentalist mumbo-jumbo—'

'Mumbo-*what*! You are an Antichrist!'

Tina exhaled. 'I don't know why I put up with this. You're a bad joke, Delarme.'

'Is there no end to your depravity? Do you realise who I am?'

'A nobody. A nobody who'd like to become a somebody.'

'Avaunt!'

'A nobody who thinks he can *buy* himself an identity – with other people's money.'

'Give me my lordship.'

'I wouldn't give you your daily bread.'

'I demand my documents.'

'Get out of my house.'

'This is *God's* house.'

'Oh, you think you're God now?'

There was a moment's silence. She said, 'Oh, take it up with Clive. Pay your stupid money – how much *did* you pay?'

'Give me my documents.'

'Clive's got them. He's on the phone.'

They looked at each other. They looked at the door.

They heard the hire car roar away.

27

DOWN THE DEVON lanes Mickey took the car at the fast but comfortable speed that comes too easily after champagne cocktails. He had his window open and the breeze wafted through the car, air-drying their hair. The sun shone from a bright blue sky.

In a shady high-banked section they slowed for an approaching car. As they eased past they realised it was Frankie di Stefano and Lincoln Deane. Frankie hooted. Mickey would have driven on but Strachey said, 'He wants to talk to us.'

'He wants a driving lesson. See how close he came?'

'Americans drive on the right.'

'No excuse.'

Mickey stopped. Everyone got out. Mickey looked at his watch. 'We're blocking the lane. Any minute now we'll get the armoured bank van come down with a load of bullion.'

Frankie fell for it. 'You serious?'

'Or maybe a farmer with a load of bulls.'

Frankie's face hardened. But Mickey was high on champagne cocktails: 'Stand in the sunshine, Frankie – it could thaw you out.'

'Hilarious. Was Clive at the hotel?'

Strachey shook her head. 'No sign of him – nor Gloria, I'm afraid.'

'So they're still together,' said Lincoln bitterly. 'Well, that's just fine. This is the first time a woman dumped me in front of all my friends.'

'You have friends?' asked Mickey.

Strachey touched his arm. 'I think I'd better do the driving. Yes, of course you have friends here, Lincoln. *I'm* your friend. I'm really sorry how things turned out.'

Lincoln grinned at her hopefully. 'Well, in that case, looking on the bright side – I'm unattached now.'

Frankie snapped, 'What is this – marriage guidance? We're lookin' for a guy owes each of us a hundred grand. You forgettin' that?'

'A virtuous woman is worth more than rubies,' Mickey Starr declared.

'How many did you have?' asked Strachey.

'I've got a weakness for champagne.'

Frankie said, 'You'll get a weakness in your balls, you don't shut up. Now, Clive ain't in neither of the hotels – an' we already phoned that Barrington guy, who ain't seen him neither. So who's comin' up with the next bright idea?'

'Rules me out,' said Mickey.

Strachey said, 'How about the Reverend Tina Gum?'

By this time Clive and Gloria were at the airport. Clive put the car in Short Term and marched inside like a man who *owned* the place, rather than one who earlier in the day had run away from it. A word with an official, and he and Gloria were striding up the stairs, heading for the small suite of meeting rooms available for hire. Gloria was impressed with this, not realising there could be anyone who chose to meet at airports – but as Clive explained to her, busy businessmen did it all the time. 'Lincoln don't,' she mused. 'I guess he just ain't busy enough.'

'It's for career businessmen,' Clive said. 'They reach a peak in their hectic lives where they spend more time travelling than sitting in their offices. The easiest way to get them all together is to choose an airport in the middle of where they are and converge on that.'

Gloria sniffed. 'Some guys should get a life.'

On the bare landing outside the business suite, Clive paused. He'd had second thoughts. 'Let me put this tactfully,' he said. 'I'd better go in there on my own.'

'Hey!'

'We don't want them to know that you're American.'

It was the best line he could think of, but it didn't stop her: 'I could give 'em my Scottish brogue.'

'Pop downstairs for a coffee and I'll meet you there.'

'You runnin' out on me?'

'So soon?' He smiled at her. 'No, this is just a little spot of extra business. It won't take a minute.'

She glanced at the closed door. 'You got a hooker in there?'

'I'm not insatiable. Gloria, darling, we need a little more money.'

'You made a million already on this deal.'

'Before expenses – and not as much as a million, nothing like. The way these deals run, all the money flows in at once. You have to squeeze out every drop while you can, so you can be prepared for the long, dry period that may come afterwards.'

'Like in the San Benito desert? I was out there once—'

He was shepherding her away. 'That's a great analogy. Pop downstairs for a—'

'Who says I got an allergy?'

'Ten minutes, darling. That's all I need.'

Clive wafted into the meeting room like the leading actor in weekly rep.

'Sorry I'm late,' he breezed. 'Had a problem with one of the horses.'

'You rode here?'

'Back in the stables at the estate.'

The two men stared at him, none the wiser. 'In our country place,' said Clive. 'Oh, forget it. These things happen to the aristocracy!' He was acutely aware that each of his lines so far had bombed. He was more nervous than he had realised, so he abandoned levity. 'Well, gentlemen, a pleasant flight?'

'It was on time at least.' This was the American lawyer.

Clive turned to his real target – the New York businessman, Mr Cantabulet. 'I believe congratulations are in order?'

Cantabulet looked tired. 'Lord Clive, we're on a crowded schedule here.' He wore an expensive dark blue suit, barely crumpled, and a loosened tie that drew attention to the faintly soiled collar of his white cotton shirt. He shot his cuffs – the last throw of a weary player. 'I guess you've cleared my check?'

Clive nodded. If the marks weren't in the mood for patter, then he'd play silent – pleasantly silent, with a pleasant smile. One may smile and smile, yet be a villain.

The lawyer's manicured hand was on a small sheaf of legal pages. 'Your people had no problem with this?'

'None at all,' said Clive, who had skimmed the papers days ago before tossing them aside.

The lawyer said, 'You don't have someone with you?'

'A lawyer? Here in England we take a gentleman's word.' Clive smiled regally. 'In a few moments Mr Cantabulet will become Lord of the Manor of Hexcombe – which will make him a gentleman of the very first rank. I hardly think I have cause to doubt him.'

Cantabulet licked his lips – more from dehydration than from enthusiasm. 'My company thinks this a worthwhile investment. It'll give us pedigree in England, and should even carry some weight stateside. But I don't want this lordship to satisfy any *personal* ambition. I'm a modest man, Lord Clive.'

'With so much to be modest about. Now, the people of Hexcombe are most eager to meet their new lord. When might they expect that pleasure?'

Cantabulet glanced at his Rolex. 'I can't make today, but I may have a window in a couple of weeks.'

His lawyer seemed in a hurry too: 'You have the papers with you, Lord Clive?'

'Of course.' He patted his jacket pocket.

The lawyer looked as if he'd expected them to be handed over in a jewelled casket. 'Well, if you're happy with our contract, we need your signature right here.'

He offered Clive his Mont Blanc, but Clive reached inside his jacket to produce a Waterman fountain pen from the 1920s, bought from a garage sale last year. Leaning over the document, Clive signed a florid signature and beside the lawyer's finger.

The man said, 'We've already signed your copy.'

'I noticed.'

The man drummed his fingers. Clive enjoyed the pause. While they waited for him to hand over the packet of title deeds he closed his pen and slipped it inside his jacket. His hand brushed the envelope which Tina Gum had given him. This was the first time he had closed a sale of the lordship with the genuine documents on his person. Having them gave added gravitas. He glanced down his aristocratic nose at the two men in the meeting room and wondered whether to give them the genuine packet or a fake. He had one of each. He could go either way. This particular scam had run its natural term – and indeed, he thought, it had become such a headache it should now be ended. It really should. The game was over.

Clive reached in his pocket and pulled out the fake.

As with any decision, once it has been taken one immediately senses whether it is right or wrong. Clive felt right with this. His natural savvy had persuaded him to keep the original documents – and his dislike for the jaded businessman encouraged him to cheat on the final card. He didn't care about the legal papers he'd signed: it wasn't *his* signature anyway. He could take the money and disappear. They wouldn't pursue him for long. Once they realised how ridiculously they had been duped, they'd lick their corporate wounds in private. Injured pride shuns publicity.

He said, 'Gentlemen, I'm sorry you have to rush to catch your plane – but it has been a real pleasure to do business with you. Lord Hexcombe, may I be the first to welcome you to the British aristocracy? I do so heartily. Indeed I do. But now I must bid you both farewell.'

It was a delicate moment, but they were not aware of it. The two businessmen sat at the table tidying papers while Clive wrapped his fingers around the door handle. There was no window in the door. At these delicate moments, Clive preferred to see what lay ahead – or in this case, what lay outside the door. A job was never over till the cheque was banked. They had the papers; he had their cheque. If they were going to try anything, this would be the moment. But why should they? They were only dupes. They knew nothing – yet. And no one knew that Clive was at the airport. No one would be waiting outside the door. He was free to go. He opened the door and stepped outside.

As he skipped lightly down the stairs Clive wondered whether to join Gloria in the coffee lounge. She was a gorgeous girl but the world was full of them – though if she divorced Lincoln she would have a lot of money. Eventually. Did that make Gloria a worthwhile investment? Clive chuckled to himself. Business and pleasure should be kept apart.

Hardly aware of the milling people, Clive began to cross the airport concourse, still unsure whether to join Gloria or not. That he could ask this question made the answer obvious. Then he heard his name called, and felt a hand thump on his chest.

'Lord Clive! Hold *on* a minute.'

He was surrounded by half a dozen Nibbets. But it was immediately obvious that they were pleased to see him. As they babbled greetings, jokes and transatlantic flight details, Clive realised they had not yet realised he had cheated them. 'Lord Walter' pumped him by the hand, 'Lady Hexcombe' clutched his arm, and the exuberant Myrtle fired off her camera. The camera! What might those snaps reveal?

Did it matter?

The warmth of their greeting was irresistible. He smiled, then laughed with the jubilant party. People turned to stare but unlike the last time Clive had attracted attention on this same concourse, the passers-by just smiled. The Nibbets were such good people, so natural and disingenuous, that their goodness seemed to make Clive clean. On an inevitable impulse he reached into his pocket, took out the genuine title deeds and pressed them upon the surprised Lord Walter.

'So glad I caught you,' Clive assured him blithely. 'I've been meaning to give you the proper documents.'

Mrs Nibbet began, 'But we've already—'

'Those were only *pro tem*, pending completion. You know how these legal eagles are! But now, my dear Lord Walter, if anyone questions your right to the lordship – won't happen, of course! – you can show them these authentic documents. Reverend Gum can verify them. She'd love to, I'm quite sure. But don't let me keep you from your flight. Must fly. Bye, bye!'

'Must *fly*!' laughed Myrtle.

Walter grabbed Clive's arm. 'Thanks, Clive. You came all this way for us?'

'Consider yourself welcome, my *lord*!'

Clive bowed, rushed out, and disappeared in sunshine.

It is said that Christ liked to welcome sinners into his household – although there's some doubt about that, since it isn't too clear from the gospels that Christ actually had a household. From what it says in the book, he spent most of his time trekking from place to place, taking shelter where he found it, in the tradition of holy men throughout the ages. But although it doesn't do to take the bible too literally – that kind of thing has caused enough trouble already – Tina was prepared to welcome sinners into her household any day.

She even welcomed Frankie di Stefano.

She offered him a cup of tea. (She always offered sinners a cup of tea.)

Being a sinner, Frankie insisted on coffee – as if her vicarage bungalow was a church drop-in centre – and he stamped about her small living room cursing the British, their aristocracy, the weather, Strachey and any other damn thing that he could think of. Lincoln rested his arm around Strachey's shoulders: he foresaw himself free of his wife, and was unaware that at that very moment Gloria was sitting over a stone-cold cup of airport coffee, repeatedly glancing at her watch and trying to deny that Lord Clive had disappeared.

Lincoln declared, 'No, no, Strachey's not to blame.' He saw Mickey watching him, so he gave Strachey one more squeeze and removed his arm 'But whatever. The time comes when you have to cut your losses. We could spend months chasing Clive around the world. What would we get out of it? Life's too short.'

'He owes me a hundred grand,' snarled Frankie.

'Actually,' said Strachey, 'Clive owes more than seven hundred grand. I managed to freeze the bank account, but it doesn't have anywhere near as much as seven hundred grand.'

'Which is what you owe us,' Frankie said.

'Sue me.'

'I got better ways, believe me.'

Tina sighed. 'Do you really owe seven hundred thousand pounds?'

'Pounds, dollars, I don't know. I'd pay it if I could, but ... ' Strachey shrugged.

Tina touched her arm. Frankie said, 'You can pay me first. To hell with the others.'

Tina flared up. 'You're as selfish as Clive. We're fighting each other instead of working as a team.'

Frankie sneered. 'That's easy for you to say.'

'Not so easy, if you want to know. I'll have to put up with Delarme – who thinks he is now my legitimate lord.'

'Delarme! Legitimate?'

'Clive finalised the sale to him in this very room.'

The others stared at her, hollow-eyed. Tina frowned, then continued: 'Then he ran off with the deeds.'

'Delarme?'

'Clive.'

'Then it doesn't count,' said Lincoln. 'It was just another scam.'

Tina brightened. 'Delarme won't be lord? Then it's not such bad news, is it?'

'For you maybe,' Frankie sniffed.

Tina said, 'You know, prayers can sometimes be answered in unexpected ways.'

A phone rang. Strachey reached in her bag for her mobile. 'This is Strachey.'

She walked to the window.

'Is that Miss Jane Strachey? Chief Executive of Lane Estates?'
The Chief Executive closed her sad green eyes. 'I'm afraid so.'
'McGillirankin here.'
She hummed warily. Who was he?
'McGillirankin of McGillirankin and Ross.' His accent was resolutely Scottish, as if his name were not Scottish enough. He had a voice like liquid haggis. 'You and I have not yet spoken.'
'I'd remember it.'
'Up to now, you see, I've always dealt with your Lord Clive.'
'I'm hoping to catch up with him soon myself.'
'I'm delighted to get through to you at last, Miss Strachey – the Chief Executive and, I believe, proprietor, of Lane Estates?' His rolling accent made 'proprietor' sound awfully grand. 'You may be aware, Miss Strachey, that your sales director, Lord Lane, recently showed some businessmen around Clachan Castle in the Campsie Fells? Well, I am pleased to say that one of those businessmen – representing Bowman Developments, no less – has come up with a firm offer for the place – at a price which between you, me and your Lord Clive, is extraordinarily good.'
Strachey flushed. She shivered.
The voice continued: 'Aye, it's extraordinarily good. Most remarkable. You are Chief Executive, so I'll confess to you what I told Lord Clive: the price he was asking was absurdly inflated. The place has been on the market for two years. Two years! But your man does have the gift of the gab. Oh aye, indeed.'
'He has, oh aye.' Strachey turned away from the others and huddled into Tina's window recess. 'I didn't realise he could sell the house so soon?'
'Well, strictly speaking, it's a touch unethical – but after all, you do own the place.'
'Own it?'
'Certainly. Your company paid the ten per cent deposit, did you not? And, as you know, up here in Scotland a firm offer is legally binding. So you own the castle, and therefore technically it is yours to sell. Admittedly, Lane Estates has yet to pay the original ninety per cent purchase price ... '
He seemed to pause delicately, so Strachey muttered lightly, 'Of course.'
McGillirankin continued: 'But as the price you'd be *selling* at is so much higher, and as—' The Scotsman coughed delicately.

'As all moneys will come through McGillirankin and Ross, there'll be no problem there.'

'I see,' said Strachey, hoping that she did.

'I assume, of course, that Lane Estates still wants to sell the property? As I recall, that was always your intention?'

'Oh yes, certainly,' Strachey murmured. 'Remind me of the numbers.'

A silence fell behind her. She could sense the others listening, and she pressed the phone close to her ear.

'Lord Clive bought it for three hundred thousand – of which two hundred and seventy thousand remains unpaid, I must remind ye – but the present offer is for – ahem – eleven hundred and fifty thousand pounds. This would leave you with a profit, as I see it, of eight hundred and eighty thousand pounds. Before commission, of course.'

Strachey faced the others in the crowded room.

Through the vicarage window a sudden shaft of sunlight blazed down from above, so bright that everyone had to avert their eyes. Strachey was silhouetted against a golden fire. She heard a disembodied voice inside her tiny phone: 'Just say the word, Miss Strachey – do we have a bargain?'

She could only manage one word. That word was 'Done.'

Also by RUSSELL JAMES, published by THE DO-NOT PRESS

Oh No, Not My Baby

ISBN 1 899344 53 5 paperback   (UK £7.00)

Oh No, Not My Baby is a dark noir mystery set amid the blood and gristle of the meat-processing industry. Musician Nick Chance does an old flame a favour and finds himself sucked into a dangerous world of corporate gangsterism, animal rights terrorism and sudden, brutal death. Oh No, Not My Baby is Russell James at his very best.

'A British crime poet of lost souls and grey streets. Relish the darkness.'
Time Out

'This guy is good! James makes it all come starkly alive, dangerous and fascinating.'
Hardboiled magazine

'Something of a cult – He goes looking for trouble where more circumspect writers would back off.'
Chris Petit, *The Times*

Also by RUSSELL JAMES, published by THE DO-NOT PRESS

Painting in the Dark

An *Independent on Sunday* Book of the Year – 2000

ISBN 1 899344 62 4 paperback (UK £7.50)

London, today: An unscrupulous art dealer, the gargantuan Gottfleish, believes that 85-year-old Sidonie Keene is hiding a small hoard of her notorious sister Naomi's valuable paintings. Naomi was a British Nazi in the 1930s, a friend of Goering and Hitler, she spent her war years in Germany. Denounced as a traitor after the Allied victory, she died a forgotten artist. But in death Naomi's intimate portraits of Hitler and his inner circle became collectors' items, rarely on the market, and commanding astronomical prices.

Gottfleish and his unprincipled assistant, Ticky, set out to steal the paintings from the old lady, little realising that there is more to Sidonie than meets the eye.

> Painting in the Dark is his masterpiece to date, eclipsing much of contemporary British mystery writing with its compassion, meticulous plotting, historical relevance and chilling subject matter.
>
> *The Guardian*

> James cleverly interweaves the past and the present to unfold a sophisticated, chilling story of deceit and betrayal. A thoroughly gripping, multilayered novel from an acknowledged British master of hard-edged crime.
>
> *Mail on Sunday*

Also published by THE DO-NOT PRESS

First of the True Believers
by Paul Charles
'The Autobiography of Theodore Hennessy'

ISBN 1899344 78 0 paperback (£7.50)
ISBN 1899344 79 9 hardcover (£15.00)

THE BEATLES formed in 1959 and became the biggest group in the world. Among other less celebrated Merseybeat groups of the time were The Nighttime Passengers, led by Theo Hennessy, who almost replaced Pete Best as drummer of the 'Fab Four'.

First of The True Believers tells of a decade in the life of Theodore Hennessy, intertwined with the story of The Beatles. It begins in 1959 with his first meeting with the beautiful and elusive Marianne Burgess and follows their subsequent on-off love affair and his rise as a musician.

The Beatles provided the definitive soundtrack to the '60s, and here novelist and musicologist Paul Charles combines their phenomenal story with a tender-hearted tale of sex, love and rock 'n' roll in '60s Liverpool.

Also published by THE DO-NOT PRESS

Mr Romance
by Miles Gibson

The new novel: an epic tale of love, lust, jealousy, pain and purple prose

ISBN 1899344 89 6   paperback (£6.99)
ISBN 1899344 90 X   hardcover (£15.00)

'Miles Gibson is a natural born poet'
Ray Bradbury

Skipper shares his parents' boarding house with their lodgers: lovely Janet the bijou beauty and Senor Franklin, the volcanic literary genius. Life is sweet, until one night the lugubrious Mr Marvel seeks shelter with them.

Who is the mysterious fugitive and what dark secret haunts him? Skipper sets out to solve the riddle. But then the astonishing Dorothy Clark arrives and his life is thrown into turmoil. Skipper falls hopelessly in love and plans a grand seduction. He'll stop at nothing. But Dorothy is saving herself for Jesus...

The Do-Not Press
Fiercely   Independent   Publishing

Keep in touch with what's happening at the cutting edge of independent British publishing.

Simply send your name and address to:
The Do-Not Press (Dept. PAT)
16 The Woodlands, London SE13 6TY (UK)

or email us: pat@thedonotpress.co.uk

There is no obligation to purchase
(although we'd certainly like you to!)
and no salesman will call.

Visit our regularly-updated web site:
http://www.thedonotpress.co.uk

Mail Order
All our titles are available from good bookshops, or (in case of difficulty) direct from The Do-Not Press at the address above. There is no charge for post and packing for orders to the UK and EU.

(NB: A post-person may call.)